As Time Unfolds

AS TIME UNFOLDS

a novel

BARBARA ZERFOSS

NEW YORK

LONDON • NASHVILLE • MELBOURNE • VANCOUVER

AS TIME UNFOLDS

a novel

Published in New York, New York, by Morgan James Publishing. Morgan James is a trademark of Morgan James, LLC. www.MorganJamesPublishing.com

Proudly distributed by Ingram Publisher Services.

Morgan James BOGO™

A **FREE** ebook edition is available for you or a friend with the purchase of this print book.

CLEARLY SIGN YOUR NAME ABOVE

Instructions to claim your free ebook edition:
1. Visit MorganJamesBOGO.com
2. Sign your name CLEARLY in the space above
3. Complete the form and submit a photo of this entire page
4. You or your friend can download the ebook to your preferred device

ISBN 9781631957420 paperback
ISBN 9781631957437 ebook
Library of Congress Control Number:
2021945308

Cover Design by:
Megan Dillon
megan@creativeninjadesigns.com

Interior Design by:
Chris Treccani
www.3dogcreative.net

Author Photo by:
Kayla Ashcraft

Morgan James is a proud partner of Habitat for Humanity Peninsula and Greater Williamsburg. Partners in building since 2006.

Get involved today! Visit MorganJamesPublishing.com/giving-back

To Mom and Rosie in Heaven.
Keep the light on.

PROLOGUE

Marguerite stroked the journal's embossed cover. Spanning three centuries, the years had softened its well-read pages, but the leather remained strong. Generations of first daughters each penned one entry to their first daughter, sharing nuggets of wisdom in this guide, a how-to for the next generation to use their God-given wings to fly.

The significance of scribing a single note taxed Marguerite's cancer-ridden body. But like with all the others, a stronger hand guided hers. What message should she leave for the child she never got to raise? As a writer, she knew words, but she did not know her daughter. The other contributors raised their young, but she watched hers secretly from afar, unnoticed and invisible. On that tearful day thirty-eight years ago, she had given up her newborn with the only piece of her she could share, a family heirloom—her birthright. And now with death near, she would soon leave her daughter something more.

Marguerite sat by the hearth in the historic home as a small fire burned. The hand-carved mantel above her revealed lilies expertly chiseled in its center. The firelight danced with a mesmerizing rhythm. The wood popped. Filled with inspiration, she wrote to her daughter, Bethany, who was on her own race against time. Always fluttering about to accomplish more, ambition fueled her quest to make every second count.

If her daughter only knew about the lilies. How, in due season, their beauty appeared, and, without toiling or spinning, their fragrance filled the air.

Marguerite dreamed of seeing her flowers bloom once again, but the clock's chimes signaled the late hour. Her first message to her daughter would be her last. If only she had more time . . .

CHAPTER 1

Eyes project words the mouth dares not speak.
Memories captured in the moment
remain as silent images
until thrust up from the deep.

L ike a child straying from her preoccupied parents, Bethany Miller
left her film crew and wandered unaccompanied. Her insatiable
desire to exceed her advertising client's expectations propelled her
to look for more. Turning the metal knob on the heavy steel door, she
entered the adjoining Costa Rican factory building. It stood in stark contrast to the brightly lit one she emerged from, where lights illuminated
every corner. Here, the darkness nearly succeeded in obscuring the workers. But amidst the shadows, Bethany's eyes saw the women. And when
she got closer, she realized they weren't women at all. They appeared too
young for factory work.

The air was cooler and fresher next door where the video shoot was
happening, but upon entering this space, Bethany's nose winced at the
smell of sweat. Her mouth pleaded for water, though moisture hung in
the air and stuck to her sleeveless white blouse. There was nothing of
marketing value to film here, but something pulled her into this darkness.

With red-painted toes protruding from high-heeled shoes, she
maneuvered the dirty floors and stepped deeper into this place, which
appeared time forgot. A sharp noise intruded her thoughts. Bethany's
footsteps stopped. A girl wheeling a squeaking plastic bin missed Bethany's exposed toes by inches.

Did factory personnel have the right of way? she wondered.

The gray uniform the girl wore gave off a false air of maturity because upon closer inspection, she appeared to be a teenager—sixteen, seventeen at the most.

Continuing deeper into the building and pulled by a feeling she didn't understand, Bethany came upon workers enclosing eye pencils into narrow boxes. Most were high-school age or early college at best, and they were all female. It wasn't just their ages or lack of smiles that captured Bethany's attention. It was their eyes. Their gazes revealed a dullness, a deadness inside.

Lured by a shiny object in the distance, she walked toward the back wall where a row of metal tables formed a barrier. At the far end, a brunette with model-like facial features sat alone, repeating a task with lifelessness and a look of defeat.

Snap, click. In the bin. *Snap, click.* In the bin.

Despite Bethany's approach, the girl continued her work. The mirrored object in her hands beamed like a signal from a deserted island and drew Bethany closer. When she was within a few feet, the girl's deep-brown eyes locked on her target and seared into Bethany like a branding iron burning flesh. The sudden jolt of heat flipped an internal circuit in Bethany, cutting off air to her lungs. Those eyes shot a message, and the silent transference left Bethany numb.

From behind, a hand yanked her limp arm. "Nothing to see here, *senorita.* We film over there."

Breathing again but still stunned from the encounter, an unsteady Bethany let the plant manager pull her back toward the door she'd entered alone. As her brain rebooted, it replayed the girl's penetrating eyes. Like a laser, they had beamed a message to her without words. *A warning? A cry for help?* With her feet shuffling forward, she turned her head to look at the girl, but the workstation was empty. The girl was gone.

"Where did she go?"

"Shift change," the plant manager answered.

But as Bethany passed through the building, she noticed all the other girls still at their same stations.

Bethany rejoined her film crew next door in the state-of-the-art facility with freshly painted floors. *Such a contrast,* she thought, still trying to reconcile what she'd seen moments earlier.

Her client, Baxter Buchanan, had sent them to Costa Rica to showcase his new production facility. The crew filmed rows of automated machinery in the well-lit space, where machines mixed the precise ingredients of makeup formula, designed to make women beautiful. This modern building, with its clean floors, high-tech equipment, and bright lights, contrasted sharply with the hot, dark, and oppressive one right next door. One step in there and Bethany's spirit had been dulled.

As the entrepreneurial CEO of B.R. Miller Advertising, Bethany Miller forged her own destiny. Her inquisitiveness and relentless passion created marketing breakthroughs, but today, these traits led her into a world she knew nothing about and did not ask permission to enter.

After finishing their last shot, the film crew packed up their equipment and followed Bethany outside to their rental cars. Standing beside her car, an eight-year-old boy held the hand of a barefoot four-year-old girl whose dark curls covered the sides of her dirt-smeared face. *"Por favor, senorita,"* the boy said as he put out his hand, hoping for spare change.

Bethany's eyes lowered to the girl's dusty, shoeless feet. Without answering the boy, she unzipped her wallet filled with Costa Rican colón bills and handed them all to him.

"Guys." She waved to her crew, who was busy loading the van with cameras. Each took direction from their boss and opened their wallets.

Clutching the wad of bills too big for his small grip, the boy said, *"Gracias,"* and with two hands, stuffed the money into his ripped pockets.

Bethany squatted on the dirt parking lot and looked at the little girl. Recalling her Spanish, she said, *"Que linda tu eres,"* then reached her hand to touch the little girl's cheek. Her small eyes looked up at Bethany, giving her a shy smile.

Unclasping the chain on her arm, Bethany fastened the oversized bracelet on the girl's tiny wrist. And, as if each stroke soothed her, the girl touched the silver heart in the center.

"*Fuera de aqui!*" the plant manager yelled, storming toward them with both hands in the air as he shooed the kids away. The boy grabbed the little girl's hand and ran.

"Very sorry about the beggars, *senorita*. Big *problema* here. Sometimes, the workers' families beg outside."

"It's okay. They're sweet, actually," Bethany said, watching the kids run away and feeling her heartache. As the little girl struggled to keep up, the boy tugged at her arm while she protected the bracelet hanging from her undersized wrist. At the edge of the woods, they stopped and turned around.

A bell rang loudly, and moments later, the older workers, with exhaustion showing on their faces, exited the main factory followed by the girls. But the one Bethany encountered was not with them. The little boy and girl remained at their post, looking at the door with anticipation.

The hour-and-a-half drive to the restaurant near the airport drained energy from Bethany. While the crew chatted at the table about the tasty dorado fish, outside the window pelicans glided above waves in search of food.

Nature provides for the birds. But some people have it tough, she thought.

Here at the table filled with plenty, Bethany remembered the young factory girl's eyes. The temperature rose in her body, and she instinctively reached for her chilled bottled water.

"*Satisfecho?*" The waiter checked on the table, and Bethany let him whisk away her still-full plate.

Her lack of interest in the table conversation sent her focus inward, where she began feeling an internal nudge. Seeing no one was paying attention to her disconnectedness, she reached for her phone to text her assistant and ended the communication with, "I'm confident you will make it happen."

The delayed flight home from Costa Rica afforded Bethany only four hours of sleep, not enough for what lay ahead of her. Her puffy eyes broadcasted her lack of rest from the red-eye that was not supposed to be.

This stormy day in Alexandria, Virginia, started like all other days. In her townhouse bathroom, she applied her "war paint," preparing both for corporate battle and the battle inside herself.

A loud crack jolted the mascara brush in her hand as lightning hit its target nearby. Though the bathroom lights flickered, the power remained on, and she wiped away the unintended black mark on her cheek.

Studying her facial canvas in the mirror, it reflected the best of her talents acquired from professional training, a fringe benefit from her cosmetics company client. But despite her efforts, tiredness still showed. Eyes were impossible to disguise. They always spoke truths from deep within the soul.

With her focus broken, her mind wandered. She thought not of her own eyes but those of the Costa Rican girl. *What was she trying to tell me?* Now that she had time to reflect, she thought the girl had warned of impending doom. But for whom? The girl or Bethany?

"Focus, Bethany. Focus," she said aloud to herself. She needed to forget the haunting eyes of the girl—for now. It was time to prepare for what she did best: work.

With her black coffee in one hand and briefcase in the other, she headed out to confront the rain. Trying to keep up with the downpour, her car's windshield wipers beat in rhythm with her throbbing head. The caffeine she sipped failed to provide the energy needed to combat the weather fighting against her. She hated rain, had hated it ever since that night when she was eleven. Now at age thirty-eight, rain not only proved an inconvenience, it slowed time a little and allowed memories to catch up.

Despite her need for speed, traffic crawled. Blue lights from a police car approached an accident twenty cars up on the left. Her eyes scanned for a way out and quickly saw a side road to the right. The detour worked but cost her more precious time.

Traffic in Alexandria further slowed her pace until she eventually reached the reserved parking spot at B.R. Miller Advertising. Most others took the metro, but Bethany preferred having her car at the ready. Reaching into the empty back seat, she realized she'd forgotten an umbrella.

With the sky unleashing its wrath, she dashed into the building. Water she squeezed from her long, dark hair fell onto the mat in the lobby. Irritated to be starting the day wet, she felt even more on edge when she reached the elevator and read the sign posted on the doors: OUT OF ORDER. MAINTENANCE CALLED.

"Not again," Bethany said, raising her hand to check her watch. It showed she had fifteen minutes before her important client meeting, so she darted toward the stairwell.

Counting her four-inch heels, her five-foot, ten-inch, lean frame climbed without effort. Behind her, a high ponytail bobbed like a thoroughbred's tail. At the top, she bolted out of the third-floor metal door.

"Good morning," Bethany said to her assistant as she hurried past her desk.

The corner executive office windows gave view to nearby historic Old Town, comprised of eighteenth-century townhouses. In contrast to that scene, Bethany's office had all the modern-day trimmings. Advertising awards lined the walls and sat atop the contemporary credenza behind her desk, proving she was one of the best advertising executives out there. She was at home here, in control and confident.

Her assistant, Holly, a vogueish thirty-year-old, sprang from her chair and caught up to her boss. "Sorry about the flight," she said to Bethany. "Hope you got a few hours of sleep."

"Enough. Baxter here?" Bethany answered without looking up from her folders.

"No, but Scott's in the conference room putting up slides," Holly said, leaning her head until her shoulder-length black hair fell across her face. But her attempt at making eye contact with her engrossed boss failed.

"I need to talk to Scott before Baxter gets here." And with that, Bethany sprinted out of her office and down the hall to the conference room.

❖

By the end of the meeting, Baxter Buchanan, CEO of BXB2 Cosmetics, approved the brand plan for his soon-to-be acquired company.

"This will get me from six hundred thousand to my first billion," Baxter gloated to Bethany and Scott Franklin, who served as vice president of B.R. Miller Advertising. "My dad will be proud," Baxter said. His confident white smile suited his sand-colored hair, lightened even more by recent time spent with customers on his boat in the Caribbean.

As Baxter strived to enlarge his kingdom to catch up to his mega-billionaire father, Bethany envisioned her own fortune, albeit a much smaller one, increasing as well. Baxter's rise meant Bethany's, too, because her company did all of Baxter's multimillion-dollar advertising. Inseparable since they were freshmen at the University of Southern California, Bethany and Baxter were like siblings; therefore, Scott excused himself to let Bethany talk alone with her client and close friend.

"How did the factory shoot go?" Baxter asked.

She waited for Scott to depart before responding. "We got a lot of good video for the website. You were right. That new factory shines."

"Once this deal goes through, I'm moving additional lines down there. There's plenty of room to expand." Baxter smiled broadly, but she had none to return to him.

"I saw your extra space in the old building next door."

"What were you doing over there? I told the plant manager I wanted you to film in the main building."

"We did film the main building," she reassured him. "The guy tried to keep an eye out, but you know me. I wandered off to be certain there wasn't something better." She forced a smile as she told Baxter half the truth, unsure about sharing the intuitive force she had felt draw her to that dark building.

"There's nothing good over there, Bethany. You wasted your time."

"The workers in that other building looked young. What are the child labor laws in Costa Rica?"

"Well . . . it's a poor town. Many don't finish school. They work to feed their families."

The non-answer did not assuage her. "What's the minimum working age?" she said with the voice of a mother cornering her son.

"Sixteen-year-olds can work thirty-six hours a week with a signed parental note."

"Don't you think that's too young? It's sad to see teenagers working in a factory."

"Bethany, we are doing good. Without my company giving them jobs, they are worse off. We are one of the few employers for miles. We are helping them, Bethany," he said, reaching across the table and touching her hand in a familiar friendliness.

"Always spinning everything to a positive. That's your secret to success." She gave his hand a gentle squeeze before letting go.

Baxter's salesmanship and optimism topped most others except for Bethany's. Her advertising creativity sold products to people who didn't realize they even needed them.

Despite his reassurance to the contrary, Baxter's altruistic answer did not quiet the lingering uneasiness inside her. The Costa Rican factory girl's eyes had radiated heat into Bethany. Keen instincts refused to let her forget those eyes. Something wasn't right in that building next door. *How should I tell Baxter about that girl?*

"Got to go. I'm preparing for a board meeting," he said and came around to her side of the table. "Oh, Amy's stopping by to see you."

With her high heels making her close in height to Baxter, she stood and said goodbye with a brushing of cheeks. Usually, she also returned his light embrace, but this time, Bethany's arms remained at her sides.

Returning to her office, she couldn't miss all the doors and cubicles covered with printouts of hearts. In the center of each was a photograph of a child from a different nation. Having not seen them earlier, she stopped at Holly's desk and inquired.

"Remember?" Holly said as she stood up and folded the creases in her dress. "You texted from Costa Rica and asked for an employee project that connected with our company's purpose—bringing beauty to the world. To save time, we went with an idea I was already working on. We're working with a charity and sponsoring children in each country where our clients' products are sold. Made it happen like you asked.

"Everybody on board with it?"

"We did have a bit of a debate about it at first. Some felt there's so much need, our efforts won't really matter. Well . . ." Holly said as she pointed to a little boy's photo taped next to her computer screen. "It will matter to this one."

"You never cease to amaze me, Holly," Bethany said, smiling with pleasure.

Picking up a spreadsheet to put in front of Bethany, Holly said, "We are sponsoring ninety-seven kids, one for each of our ninety-seven associates, from forty-four different countries. We know we can't help all the kids in the world, but we can at least pour our hearts into ninety-seven of them."

"Love it. You all are the best."

"We're going to get letters from each of the children," Holly added, but Bethany was already headed to her office. Her boss watched the clock and afforded little time for chitchat.

"Oh, I forgot! Holly shouted to her. "You got a call from a real estate lady who asked if you wanted to sell your Jameson, Virginia property."

Bethany stopped and turned her head toward Holly. "You know I don't own any property in Jamestown, Virginia. She's got the wrong person."

"She said *Jameson*, Virginia, not Jamestown. Asked specifically for Bethany *Rose* Miller."

"Well, I'm not *that* Bethany Rose Miller. There's some mistake."

"How did they know your middle name? You never use it," Holly said, shooting Bethany an ominous glance. "What if it's identity theft?"

"You watch too many true-crime movies." Bethany swatted her hand in the air to dismiss Holly's notion and approached her office. Taped to her door, in the middle of a heart, the smile of nine-year-old Carmen from Honduras confronted business-faced Bethany. After all, the boss was one of the ninety-seven associates, and the team included her in this company-wide project.

Work had piled up while she was away, and Bethany aimed to catch up—until Holly disrupted her flow. "Sorry, but you need to see this," Holly said as she put a certified letter in front of her. "It's from that real estate agent. She's inquiring about your property on Knowles Lane in Jameson, Virginia."

This is serious. "I'll check into it." Feeling frustrated and concerned, Bethany called her attorney, Michael Alexander.

"You did the right thing to call me," Michael said. "Scan a copy and email me. I'll have answers in the morning. Can you stop by my office on your way in tomorrow? I also want to review my monthly retainer with you."

Bethany agreed and ended the call but forgot to ask Michael something. She picked up the phone to call and tell him what she saw in Costa Rica. She was concerned for Baxter and his reputation. Baxter relied on others to look out for him, like his head of manufacturing and the Costa Rican plant manager, who had yanked her away from the other building. Too many young women worked in that adjacent building. It was overcrowded, dirty, and who knew what else! Michael would understand her concern. He was aware of her close relationship with Baxter, and he worked with Baxter's attorney on many contracts. They were all business friends.

Before she could reconnect the phone call, Baxter's wife, Amy Buchanan, popped into Bethany's office. "Am I interrupting?"

"Just got off," Bethany said, motioning for Amy to take a seat in the leather chair across from her. She had work to do, but Amy had been one of her closest friends since they became college roommates. After she played matchmaker to Amy and Baxter, the three of them formed a unique "hybrid" family.

"Did my absentminded husband remember to tell you I was coming?" Amy asked, taking a seat and pulling her straight, blonde hair behind one ear.

"Got to give him credit this time." Bethany laughed at Baxter's social forgetfulness. He was all business and little pleasure, pushing her to a close second place in the workaholism category.

"I saw this in a shop, and it just screamed Bethany. Open it," Amy said, excitedly pushing a gift bag across the desk.

Bethany untied the yellow ribbon and pulled out a six-by-six-inch framed print of a hummingbird sitting on a red flower. Below the image it said, *Be Still and Know.*

"So sweet. You're always thinking of others," Bethany said as she moved around the desk to hug her friend.

"You always fly at the speed of a hummingbird." Amy's fingers fluttered in the air. "There's no stopping you."

Ha. Bethany got her point. Amy was right.

"Better let you get back to work. Don't forget the bag of clothes for my foundation. Tomorrow's the last day to collect items for the rummage sale."

"Good thing you reminded me. I'll do it tonight." Bethany half smiled as she waved goodbye. *One more thing on my to-do list.*

As she did every night when she got home, Bethany put on her silk pajamas—light pink ones tonight—and washed the makeup off her face. Needing something to eat, she went to the kitchen where the like-new, shiny white cabinets, Italian marble countertops, and white tile backsplash gave the impression no one lived there. The stainless-steel range sat unused since installed a year ago. Because she lived alone and worked late, Bethany often got takeout. Tonight, for a change, she munched on olives, cheese, and crackers and poured a glass of red wine. An internet radio station played songs in the background with enough sound to cut the stillness. Unless her mind focused on work, Bethany hated silence. It reminded her of being alone, something "single Bethany" had years of experience with.

Walking into the den off of the kitchen, she passed the carefully selected blue accessories that accented the white and beige contemporary décor. A monochrome pallet provided a peaceful rest for her eyes. She worked all day in the outskirts of historic Old Town Alexandria and preferred an entirely modern space for home. Yet despite the setting change, she took work with her wherever she went.

After a long day and a near-sleepless night before, Bethany pushed the button to recline her leather chair. She video called Mitzi, her best friend since third grade.

Mitzi's face appeared on the screen as she chewed a bite of hamburger. Empty wrappers sat on the hotel room table. Working temporarily in Denver, Colorado, her room looked well-lived-in with clothes thrown across a chair and files strewn on the bed. "How was Costa Rica?" Mitzi asked.

The question shifted Bethany's forward-thinking mind backward. *Something wasn't right in that other building.* Warning bells went off inside her. *Child labor law issues brought down many a great company.* She didn't trust the plant manager to look out for Baxter's best interest. The manager had watched over her and the film crew like a guard securing a prison.

"Bethany?" Mitzi said, but Bethany didn't hear her. She was lost in her thoughts about what was going on.

Serving as Baxter's public relations firm as well as his advertising agency, her heightened concern made sense. Baxter's life spun even faster than hers. And more than being her largest client, he was like a brother and a father figure to her; he gave advice and pointed the way while also being a good friend to spend time with.

"Bethany? . . . Earth to Bethany," Mitzi spoke in a teacher-like tone to regain her friend's attention and waved her hand at the screen.

It worked. Bethany's mind returned to the conversation, and Mitzi shot her the *what the heck* look only a best friend could get away with. She decided not to mention the factory girl to Mitzi, or anything else she saw. Foremost, it was Baxter's business, and she needed to gather more facts. Instead, she chose to share the other head-scratcher.

"Something weird happened at work today," Bethany said. "I got a certified letter asking if I wanted to sell my property in Jameson, Virginia."

"When did you buy property?"

"Didn't. Holly freaked out and guessed identity theft. I called Michael to look into it."

Mitzi gulped the food in her mouth and put the phone closer to her face. "What if it's connected to your biological family? Maybe a long-lost aunt left you a fortune."

"Leave the creative thinking to me, Mitzi. They got the wrong Bethany Miller."

Leaping from her chair, Mitzi asked, "Did you ever send in that DNA kit I gave you?"

"No . . . and your constant asking me about it won't get me to do it," Bethany said, tiring of the question.

Mitzi's professional sales training honed her second effort. "Come on, Bethany. Find your biological family now that yours is all gone. You need family."

"Done fine by myself this far."

"Maybe there's family out there looking for you. Did you ever consider that?"

The uncomfortable subject caused Bethany to hold her breath. She looked at the time on her phone. It was eight o'clock. "I promised Amy clothes for her charity sale." Jumping from the recliner, she swished her red wine against the top edge of her glass but rebalanced it in time to prevent a spill. Inside the kitchen pantry, she pulled out two garbage bags and headed toward her bedroom.

Mitzi stayed on the video call and talked as Bethany walked. "How about going through some of your mom's things? It's been two years."

"Too many memories."

"Use that DNA kit to find your biological family and start making new ones," Mitzi said.

"Don't need anyone, and I'm not sure I want to meet strangers." Standing in front of her bedroom closet, Bethany flipped the light switch. She shook the empty garbage bags for Mitzi to get the hint she had things to do, but it didn't work.

"You need to know your history for medical purposes. Look how many women get breast cancer. Promise me you'll send that DNA kit in," Mitzi pleaded.

"What if they're ax murderers?" Bethany's flair for drama aimed to cut the tension only her best friend could cause without making her mad.

"Now *you* sound like Holly." Mitzi laughed as the two women said their goodbyes.

Seldom-worn business suits filled Bethany's back closet wall. She needed to keep only a few and added four to the bag. Inside, she also put shirts and sweaters with tags still hanging on them. *Clothes often looked better on a mannequin,* she thought. Within half an hour, she had filled one garbage bag and a half of another one.

A bit of hanger space opened up, but brown moving boxes filled the upper shelves. One marked BEDROOM DRESSER contained her adoptive mother's items.

Reaching to turn off the light, an internal nudge persuaded her to go through the box. *Get it done. Maybe there are things inside for Amy's charity sale.* She stood on her toes and pushed the box sideways to shimmy it off the edge. The un-taped box top opened, and scarves toppled on her head.

Bethany didn't wear scarves; they weren't her thing. She called her style "artsy business casual." Jeans, a pricey silk blouse, expensive handmade jewelry, and four-inch heeled sandals or knee-high boots completed her standard attire.

Looking through her mother's scarves one by one, she held memories in her hands. She brought the scarves to her face and breathed in a hint of her mother's scent. Setting aside one to keep, she put the rest in the charity bag.

She reached her hand back in and pulled out a small, sterling silver box. Tarnished from lack of polish, it still looked special, with a *K* engraved on top. Cradled inside on bright-blue velvet, a small, carved wooden butterfly pendant sat attached to a thin strip of leather. Holding the handmade necklace, she admired the workmanship then noticed a small folded piece of paper sat underneath the necklace. She lifted it off the regal blue velvet, unfolded it, and read.

"PLEASE GIVE THIS TO MY BABY DAUGHTER. IT IS A TREASURED FAMILY HEIRLOOM—MKM."

"Why didn't they give this to me?" Sitting on the closet floor, her hand flew up in the air. Confused words spilled out of her. "Were my parents afraid I would find my birth family?"

This carved butterfly, the note, and the certified letter she received at work spun a mystery inside Bethany's creative head. If just for medical reasons, she decided to do as Mitzi instructed her.

Rummaging through dresser drawers, she found the DNA kit, and after she spit in the tube up to the designated line, she sealed the package. "Enough for one day."

Still tired from the Costa Rica trip, she brushed her teeth and crawled into bed, where the soft mattress and protective covers soothed her tired body. Reaching for the bedside light, her eyes fixed on the silver box. The note and carved butterfly inside called her to discover their significance to her past. But her worn-out mind beckoned her to sleep so she could speed her way into tomorrow.

In Costa Rica, a young factory girl with piercing eyes disappeared.

CHAPTER 2

lick, click, click, click. The sound of Bethany's heels and swift feet on the shiny marble-tiled floors echoed into the law office's lobby. Michael Alexander, a fifty-one-year-old attorney, escorted her to his office and closed the door.

"Got information for you about that letter." Michael's voice held a professional tone. "Only one property on Knowles Lane. Records show Marguerite Knowles Marchand owns it."

Bethany leaned forward. "Say the name again."

"Marguerite Knowles Marchand. I searched the name and found a will recorded in Lancaster County, Virginia, just last week. Marguerite passed away."

Bethany slouched in her chair, and her breath left her like pinched fingers releasing an untied balloon. The paneled wall behind Michael trapped her mind inside this unwanted conversation.

"The will is a public document, so I read it. Bethany Rose Miller is listed as the sole heir." Michael paused. "You alright, Bethany?"

Her lips parted, and her eyes tried to see something that wasn't there. After a moment, she nodded.

He proceeded. "Amongst other things, a home in Jameson, Virginia was left to you."

Bethany sat in silence and shook her head in disbelief. She did not know a Marguerite Knowles Marchand. She hesitated to tell Michael she was adopted. It was not something she shared with business associates, even ones as close as him.

"Bethany?"

"Yes, I'm listening," Bethany answered in a low voice.

"I'm sure you will hear from the estate attorney soon." She watched Michael speak as the small but noticeable scar he had received from a motorcycle accident when he was twenty moved up and down with his lips. "The attorney's name is Peter Jameson III. He's in Jameson, Virginia. Would you like me to call him for you?"

Her mind fought back control from a rolling wave of shock and fear. Marguerite Knowles Marchand—MKM—those same initials on the note in that silver box. She decided to call the estate attorney herself and left Michael without giving him a chance to talk to her about his monthly retainer.

Back at her office, she stopped at Holly's desk.

"I need to free up time," she said with no explanation and a look of bad news on her face. "Reschedule my project update meeting," Bethany said midturn. Her heels clicked on B.R. Miller's wooden floors as she walked down the hall to the conference room. She knew sounds traveled, and though she shared most everything with Holly, she didn't want even her to hear what she had found out. She needed to be alone with the news first, to let it sink in.

Checking the time, she looked at the Swiss watch she had given herself eight years ago on her thirtieth birthday. A second hand marked the seconds, and the engraving on the back noted her often-used expression: *Every Second Counts.* Time was a scarce commodity in Bethany's world, and she made the most of it by using every drop of energy in a twenty-four-hour day.

It was 9:05 a.m. She pulled the phone in the center of the conference table toward her and typed the estate attorney's number. Peter Jameson answered on the second ring.

"Hello, my name is Bethany Miller. I own the B.R. Miller Advertising Agency in Alexandria, Virginia. Yesterday, I received a call from a real estate agent, and afterward, I received a certified letter asking if I wanted to sell a home I own in Jameson, Virginia. My assistant thought it might be identity theft, so I called my corporate attorney to check into it." She took a breath.

"I'm sor—" Peter Jameson started to speak, but Bethany cut him off and continued her story.

"He found only one home on Knowles Lane, and Marguerite Knowles Marchand owns it. My attorney read the will with your name listed as the estate attorney." She stopped for another breath, and this time he waited before venturing to speak.

Peter Jameson handled the incoming rapid-fire monologue like a true pro. Once it appeared Bethany had finished, he said with a steady voice, "Miss Miller, I'm very sorry you found out about this from someone other than me. Legal matters take time. Paperwork needed to be in order before I reached out to you. Don't know what happened. I handled this discrete matter myself."

"What is this about?" Bethany's heart pounded inside her ears.

"It involves an inheritance. You're included in my client's will."

"Are you sure I'm the right Bethany Miller?"

"I have confirmation. I'd like to tell you more in person. Are you free at your office, let's see . . . tomorrow afternoon?"

Tomorrow? Tomorrow? She reached for her cell phone and spilled a cup of B.R. Miller Advertising pens across the conference table. Her calendar showed an opening at three o'clock until the end of the day, and Peter took the appointment time.

Sitting motionless, she stared out the window, her mind blurring the city scene below. She looked at the clock on the wall. *It's seven fifteen in the morning, Denver time,* she thought. Mitzi was still out of town, covering for a fired salesman. *I need to talk this through with Mitzi.*

"Oh, Bethany. I'm so sorry, girlfriend." Mitzi held out her arms in an airy embrace on the phone's screen.

"The estate attorney is coming to my office tomorrow," Bethany said.

"I can't believe this is happening. I want to jump through the phone and hug you," Mitzi said, looking at the time on her phone. "Ugh. I'm heading out to a breakfast appointment and can't be late. Call me right after your meeting tomorrow."

Bethany twisted a pen in her hand.

"At least it's an answer," Mitzi said. "I wish I were there right now. Dang this good-for-nothing Colorado salesman." She picked up her purse from the hotel room chair. "I should be in town for you."

"I'll be alright. Let's see what I find out tomorrow."

News of a will interrupted Bethany's well-planned life. She liked being the director of her fate and wondered where she had lost command. The past was far behind her and was meant to be kept buried. She hadn't sought it out. The past had found *her*.

In Bethany's world, time moved forward as fast as she did. Now, time threatened to rewind and drag her back into a world she never wanted to know.

Peter Jameson would arrive tomorrow at three o'clock with answers. Answers she had half-hoped would stay hidden inside a silver box.

CHAPTER 3

To not go stir-crazy by watching the clock, Bethany kept an extra-busy schedule prior to Peter Jameson's visit. She met with the head of marketing for a hand lotion brand, and he committed to make B.R. Miller Advertising their agency of record. She put another "win" in her column.

"Good to get that big one," Scott said, high-fiving her in her office. "It'll help balance all the business we have with Baxter."

Bethany and Scott had worked hard the last eighteen months to gain new clients. Her Vistage CEO advisory board members warned that B.R. Miller Advertising relied too much on one customer's business. It put the company in a vulnerable financial position and would even more so once they worked on Baxter's new company's brand. She took their advice and, although she and Scott acquired new clients, Baxter's cosmetic brands still represented nearly fifty percent of her total revenue.

After Scott left her office, Bethany shouted out so Holly could hear her. "Can you pick up coffees for both of us? My treat."

"You bet!" Holly called out and went to retrieve their afternoon booster.

The sustenance Bethany gained from eating half of a salad during her lunch meeting had worn off. So she pulled out a square of dark chocolate from her desk drawer and ate it while her coffee cooled with the top off. She replaced the lid and took a sip, then she felt black coffee drip onto her light-pink blouse. The dark mess soaked through to her camisole beneath. Feeling the seeping heat, she hit her knee on the desk as she lurched for a napkin. Seeing the stain, she wished she had one of those scarves to cover it up.

Peter Jameson arrived right on time at three o'clock, and Holly showed him into Bethany's office. With her face turned away from Peter, Holly's eyes opened wide as they shifted in unison toward him. Four inches taller than Bethany, he was handsome, and his starched white shirt under his suit accented his well-groomed, dark-brown hair. He looked to be in his mid- to late thirties.

"Sorry about my appearance." Bethany's blushed face said it all. She felt like an idiot and looked down at the visible stain on her blouse.

"Don't feel bad. Happens to the best of us," Peter said, looking at her face instead of the stain on her shirt.

"Thank you for coming to me. Can't say I have much time for personal things right now. Well, never actually."

They took a seat at her round conference table, and Holly closed the door behind her. Putting his brown leather briefcase on the floor beside him, Peter waited for Bethany to speak. She didn't, so he opened the conversation.

"I'm sorry for not being the first to reach out to you. I'm checking into how this happened."

Bethany sat up straight in her chair with her hands folded on the table. She often took the lead in conversations, but not today. She let Peter Jameson do all the talking.

"I would like to ask you one thing first," Peter suggested, then paused and looked at Bethany, who remained in quiet control as if in the middle of a negotiation. "First one who speaks loses" was her view about negotiations. This was not that situation; regardless, though, she intended to hold her thoughts and emotions inside.

"Did you know . . . you were adopted?" Peter asked.

"Yes, my parents told me when I was six years old."

Relief filled Peter's face. "Good," he said as penned-up air released through his lips. He reached into his briefcase and handed Bethany the signed legal adoption paperwork. "A private adoption, handled by an attorney in San Diego, California."

Caressing the signatures on the page, she said, "I always called California home even though I moved to Alexandria when I was two years old."

21

"I'm sorry to tell you," Peter said, hesitating a moment before continuing, "but your biological mother recently passed away."

Bethany had never met this woman, but the words "biological mother" and "passed away" hit her like rocks out of nowhere shattering a windshield.

"I'm sorry to deliver this news."

She squeezed her lower lip between her teeth. "It's okay. Made me think of my mom and dad," she said, explaining her rising emotional state. "My mom passed a couple of years ago, and my dad when I was eleven."'

"So young," he said.

She stared out the window. "Car accident—my dad, that is. We were super close. Never had enough time with him." She remembered the rainy night she received news of death, and now word of death found her again. Ironically, it was brought to her by another stranger.

"My dad did most everything with me. He called me his shining star. He would have loved to see me own this business."

Scanning her wall plaques and crystal awards, he said, "I'm sure he knows your success."

"Lost my idol."

"And your adoptive mother?" Peter asked.

Bethany brushed under one eye. "I had to grow up fast. She had rheumatoid arthritis and a congenital heart condition. After my dad passed, she relied on me to help clean and cook until I went away to college."

She uncharacteristically let her steel guard down. The emotional mood in the room needed to be rectified, so she added, "I still can't cook. Have a stove and oven I've never used." Bethany smiled with her lips closed. She brought her hands from her lap and folded them back on top of the table. "I'm sorry. I interrupted you telling me about my biological mother. Was her name Marguerite Knowles Marchand?"

"Yes," Peter said with his countenance changing from one of empathy to back on business. "She lived in Jameson, Virginia, in her family's historic home. It was built in 1858 and sits on 167 acres outside of town. She made a will, and you are the sole beneficiary."

"How did she find me?" Bethany leaned across the table.

"Mm . . . She always knew . . . how to find you." Peter said the words slowly and with care, but they landed like a blow onto Bethany. She sat back and clutched the chair arms.

Before she could verbally emote, Peter continued, "Your adoption was private. Marguerite would only agree to it if she knew who the adoptive parents were in advance. Per her wishes, she remained anonymous."

"Did my parents know this? That my biological mother knew who they were?" Her voice cracked at the end.

"The attorney had to have informed them before your adoptive parents agreed to the adoption."

Bethany's body sat across from Peter, but her mind traveled to her bedroom and that tarnished silver box with the note inside. *Did my mother worry for years that my biological parents would show up? Is that why she never gave it to me?*

Her eyes winced. "If my birth mother knew where to find me, why didn't she reach out to me before she passed?"

"She didn't want to interfere in your life. She hoped you would try to find *her*."

Bethany never had an interest in finding her biological family, and after her adoptive mother died, she focused even more on her business. It was the one thing left she cared most about. Her business was her life.

Peter rubbed his thumbs across his clasped hands. "Your biological mother suffered from a brain tumor and met with me several months before she passed. She told me about the adoption when we were making up her will."

"This is all so much to take in." Bethany's eyes fixated on the signatures on the adoption papers. For thirty-eight years, she knew those names as her parents, and it made no matter to them she wasn't their biological child. She was always loved, and now another mother was thrust into her well-ordered world. Did she, too, once love her? Bethany touched her adoptive parents' signatures.

"I can't imagine," Peter said.

She did her best to hold the emotion inside, but watery eyes smudged her mascara beneath one eye.

"We need to finalize paperwork and can do that from afar, but it's best if you came to Jameson to see the home and property."

Bethany shook her head. "I run a business. There is never an extra moment. Ninety-seven people depend on me, plus all my clients. There's no way I can take off to someplace called Jameson."

"It's a beautiful town in the Northern Neck area of Virginia. You might know the Northern Neck is famous for being the birthplace of three presidents: Washington, Madison, Monroe, and also of General Robert E. Lee," Peter informed.

"Never heard of it. Where exactly is Jameson?"

"It's about two and a half hours from here, near where the Rappahannock River and the Chesapeake Bay meet. The historic downtown is close to the water. It boasts stunning sunsets and sunrises too."

Bethany's mind thought of more important things than scenery. Calculating what this news meant for her, she needed time to think and looked at her watch.

Peter got the hint. "I know, I've hit you with a lot of information all at once. Let me know when you can visit. In the meantime, I'm managing things for now."

"I'm sorry. Thank you. I have a lot on my mind already." Looking at his briefcase on the floor, she again signaled it was time to end the meeting.

As he rose from his seat, Peter reached for his briefcase. "The adoption papers are a copy I made for you. You can keep them."

She walked Peter to the door and grabbed the knob. "Wait," she said, turning around toward him. "What about my father?"

"I'm sorry. Your mother didn't tell me his name."

She caught a split-second flash across Peter's face. Bethany had learned about micro-expressions and was certain she saw fear. *If he doesn't know who my father is, why does his face show fear?*

When Bethany opened the door, Holly discerned the nod from her boss and jumped up. She smoothed her cotton dress wrinkles and came around her desk to escort Peter to the elevator. Bethany caught her stare at Peter's bare ring finger and no doubt would hear from Holly that she liked him and approved. With keen intuition, Holly was a quick judge of

24

character. The only one Bethany could not convince Holly about otherwise was Baxter. Holly got along with Baxter but felt he didn't deserve all he had. She didn't like that he looked at his sweet wife, Amy, as a prize he won but did not earn.

With Peter gone, Bethany closed herself inside her office and video called Mitzi.

"We need to find out more," Mitzi said, sitting in her rental car as she sipped a drive-through cola. "Did you do that DNA test yet?"

Bethany checked her watch. It was four o'clock in Alexandria. The mailman usually came at two. "I put it in the mail this morning."

"Good girl." Mitzi raised her cup as a toast.

"The attorney wants me to go to Jameson, but I can't get away from work. We're about to start new projects for Baxter, bigger ones than ever before."

Bethany couldn't tell Mitzi about Baxter's new company until the deal became public. B.R. Miller Advertising's business was about to double, thanks to Baxter.

"Go down there. Get away," Mitzi instructed. "It's Bethany time now. You either go like a racehorse or only stop when you're dead asleep. You allow for nothing in between." Mitzi started her car's engine.

"There's no way I can leave work. This personal stuff has to wait."

"Talk to Scott about it. I wish I could get on a plane right now and help you. I'm stuck here for at least another few weeks. This area is a mess. I'm even staying the weekend to interview candidates to take over the territory."

"I'll handle it. You know I always find a way." Bethany sat at her desk, shaking her head at the adoption papers in front of her. The past had caught up with her, and this time she could not run away.

Inheriting a historic property from a mother she never knew made owning a business feel a lot easier than dealing with personal issues. At thirty-eight, Bethany was still single for a reason.

Arriving home late, she turned on the TV to disrupt the silence. She watched but didn't hear a word. Sitting in the recliner, she thought of two mothers. One who gave her up and knew where to find her. The other in physical and also mental agony concerned about a possible knock on the door. Wrapping her hands inside her arms, she comforted herself. She'd had enough of this day and wanted to be in another, so she turned off the TV and went into the bedroom.

The silver box on the nightstand held a note and gift from her biological mother. MKM was Marguerite Knowles Marchand. Her birth mother gave her up with that silver box and carved butterfly inside. *How could someone who so treasured a family heirloom give up their newborn child?*

Pulling the covers over her head, guttural cries emerged from deep inside. "Why didn't you keep me?" she yelled, though no one could hear her cry.

CHAPTER 4

Arriving before most of her associates, Bethany walked past offices and cubicles decorated with the children's photos inside the ninety-seven hearts. Seeing their faces reminded her of that small Costa Rican town far removed from fancy hotels and beaches filled with vacationers. She thought of the young women she saw in that other building. Baxter said his company offered help in way of jobs, but that simple explanation didn't feel right. The girls in that dark, sweaty place looked too young for factory work.

Though this inheritance required her immediate attention, Bethany never let loose of something that bothered her. That girl's silent but jarring communication had locked itself into Bethany's mind, and she shuddered, remembering the way she screamed at her without words. *Was it anger? Fear?*

Her phone buzzed in the purse over her shoulder. "Running late," the text from Scott said. Similar to her in age and having worked for her since the year after she opened the agency, he knew the business as well as she did. The one thing missing was his last name. Scott's name wasn't Miller. The company belonged to Bethany.

She met with a shampoo client for two hours, then afterward, asked Holly about Scott.

"He came looking for you twice," Holly said. "Baxter called, too, and said he needed to speak with you about an important matter. I told him I couldn't interrupt your client meeting. So he asked me to transfer him to Scott."

"Call and tell Scott I'm available."

"Any news you want to share? You were still closed up in your office when I left last night," Holly blurted out before she punched in Scott's extension.

Because sound traveled throughout the open office space, Bethany kept her voice low and leaned in toward Holly. "I found out who is . . . was . . . my biological mother." Bethany was flustered but continued with details. "Her name was Marguerite Knowles Marchand. She willed me a historic family home in Jameson."

"Wow. That's great," Holly said before her mind caught up with the sad part of the news. "I'm sorry, Bethany," she added, but Bethany had already turned to walk to her office.

"Personal business came up, and I need to figure out a way to handle it," Bethany said to Scott, who sat across from her desk. "My biological mother, whom I never met, passed away and left me a historic home in Jameson, Virginia." Bethany stopped to look at Scott as if he held an answer.

"I'm sorry to hear." Scott shifted uncomfortably in his chair. "Anything I can do to help?"

"I've got to hire someone to check it out and handle it. These new projects for Baxter are a dream come true for us. I already envision industry articles being written about us." Bethany didn't show it on the outside, but the personal news affected her. Her eyes always gave her away, and although she tried to conceal them, they were puffy and showed she lacked sleep.

Scott scooted to the edge of his chair. "Bethany, the timing is all meant to be. Baxter called this morning and said the new company purchase is delayed. Our contracts for the advertising projects won't happen for two months. Go to Jameson yourself. Learn about your family and check out the house. Maybe you'll want to keep it."

"Keep an old house? I don't think so. Besides, we have other business to look after." Bethany pointed to the major brands and global company names on the awards across her wall.

Putting his arms on her desk with palms upward, he said, "You know I've been asking you to let me handle more. This is the perfect opportunity. Take time off to handle this, and I'll manage the business while you are away."

Bethany shook her head.

"People work from anywhere nowadays," Scott said. "We can video chat as often as you want, and I'll update you every day. Trust me. Trust all of us. We'll take care of your baby." Scott cringed at the unintended pun, and Bethany jumped in to end the awkwardness.

"Let me bring Holly into this," she said, opening the door and motioning her to come in. Though an executive assistant by day, Bethany wondered if Holly moonlighted as a therapist or life coach—she was that good at advising her on personal as well as professional matters.

Sitting in the chair next to Scott, Holly looked straight at her and said, "You need to go to Jameson, Bethany."

With Mitzi, Scott, and Holly all in agreement, it was three against one, but Bethany was stronger than all three. "No way I can leave town, even if the new projects are pushed back. I've got to call Baxter. Leave me to it." She motioned for them to depart.

Because half of her business came from Baxter, to leave town for any length of time required his blessing. Baxter understood business even better than her, and he would agree she should stay in Alexandria and handle this personal interruption from afar. Getting no answer, she hung up; after another minute, she phoned him again.

"Better be important," he said. "I just left two US senators waiting on me for lunch." After hearing her news, he said, "You'd be crazy not to do this, Bethany. You haven't had an adventure since college. Go find your roots. Check out that house. Maybe you can make it into a great getaway that Amy and I can use too."

Bethany had counted on Baxter to tell her to push aside the personal and focus on business. That's what *he* would do. She took the phone from her ear and looked at it. Who was she was talking to? Baxter's advice surprised her.

"The Northern Neck is a short drive from Alexandria, far enough away but close enough to get right back, if needed," Baxter said. "I boated on the Chesapeake Bay near there on my father's yacht. Scott has what it takes. Let him manage things while you are away. We'll keep in touch. But I want you to go find out about your family."

Bethany's number-one client ruled her business day, every day. And right now, she was smart enough to let him guide her personal life, too, as long as he represented fifty percent of her revenue.

Taking his advice, she crafted a four-week plan to give her ample time to take care of matters at the house and research her family. The DNA kit said it would take six weeks for results—too long for Bethany. She knew how to find quick answers, and she already had one clue. It sat inside a silver box from thirty-eight years ago.

*In Costa Rica, another young
factory girl disappeared.*

CHAPTER 5

Meetings with her managers ended with each of them wishing her well, but she didn't feel *well*. She felt like they were sending her off to cross an uncharted ocean, an ocean she never desired to explore.

It was June sixth, and if all went on schedule, Bethany planned to return to Alexandria by the fourth of July, at the latest. So much had happened in the last week. Her world had reshuffled, and she felt she must regain control. Life in Alexandria needed her, and she needed it. Mitzi told her to discover her family. Scott told her to let him handle things. Holly told her to enjoy "being Bethany," but Bethany forgot who she was long ago. Baxter said she never cut loose anymore, but Bethany couldn't *feel* fun. Work and the company she built meant everything to her. Fun was something others spent scarce time on.

The GPS showed the more direct route via Highway 210, and the series of roads, including State Route 3, was the same time as taking I-95 South through Fredericksburg. She scheduled to meet Peter Jameson at the house tomorrow morning and, thus, had no set time to arrive this evening. Regardless, she took the direct route, which happened to be the more scenic one. Peter told her along the way, she could divert slightly and visit Stratford Hall, a National Historic Landmark, and the home of Robert E. Lee. But Bethany didn't have sightseeing on her mind. For her, she saw this trip as work, albeit it personal. And so, she planned to drive straight to it.

As she left Alexandria and drove toward Jameson, she lost her bearings. Bethany's compass had always aimed for the future. Now, she was heading to the past to discover a family she never knew at a house she had never called home.

Once she crossed the Woodrow Wilson Bridge across the Potomac River, the cityscape she was accustomed to changed. There were smaller buildings on this other side. And after an hour's drive from the city, the world she knew transformed into a foreign land. The road had fewer cars and took her past places she didn't know existed. People lived out here, away from the city. Why did she never know this other side existed? Had she never crossed the bridge? Getting closer to the southern end of the Northern Neck, towns became even smaller. She was less than a hundred miles from home, but this serene landscape made her uneasy. Unlike other people, peace was not a state where she felt comfortable. To her, it meant something bad was about to happen.

A restaurant named Yesterday Family Café caught her attention. *How appropriate*, she thought. But she didn't know yesterday. She only knew tomorrow.

In her thoughts, she spent a lot of time projecting positive outcomes for her business. She planned for all scenarios and knew her role well. But her personal life? She didn't do much future thinking there. Her biological past was unknown, and she wished to keep it that way. But circumstances and coincidences were now pushing her backward to confront memories she never got to make.

"Welcome to the Jameson Inn." The woman's thick Southern accent greeted Bethany before her words caught up to her drawl. Bethany was still in Virginia, but the accent differed here. Bethany asked Holly to book her at The Tides Inn, a resort and spa, but it was booked with June weddings.

The Jameson Inn was an early twentieth-century home, and at Bethany's insistence, Holly ensured her the room had a private bathroom. After signing the registration for three nights, she informed the desk clerk, "I might leave sooner . . . or later. Not sure how my business here will go." It all depended on what she found at the house. She did not know what condition it was in and if she could sleep there or even wanted to stay more than a day in this town.

"Any recommendation on where to eat?" Bethany asked the desk clerk.

"Moonlight Café is the next best thing to home cooking," she answered, pointing out the window to the left.

"Take any seat," the waitress said as Bethany walked in the door. She chose a booth by the window, next to a table with a thirtysomething woman with dark hair, dressed in skinny jeans, wearing a flowy blouse and a long, beaded necklace with a large stone on the end. *Good sense of style*, Bethany thought. *Love that outfit.* The woman sat alone as she looked through a Black woman's magazine, and Bethany recognized it. It was *Onyx Beauty and Fashion*.

"Great magazine. My company placed several ads there for our client's products," Bethany said.

The woman looked up and smiled. "Been reading *Onyx Beauty and Fashion* for years. I love fashion. Do you work in the industry?"

"Advertising. Mostly beauty products—makeup, shampoo, perfume, lotions . . . things like that," Bethany said.

The waitress delivered her a menu, and Bethany searched for something to eat. Seeing her take a while to decide, the cheerful woman said, "The meatloaf is my favorite. Comes with mashed potatoes and green beans. Can't go wrong."

"Sounds good and tempting, but I usually eat healthy," she said, searching the menu.

"Lots of people like the Cobb salad," the woman added.

"Sold." Bethany folded the laminated menu and motioned to the waitress.

Turning sideways in her chair to face Bethany, the woman asked, "Are you just passing through?"

"I'm here for personal business. Not sure how many days it will take," Bethany said.

"It's a great little town. There's a concert at the gazebo tonight. You might want to check it out. I'm heading over." She got up from her table, and the chunky emblem that hung from her long necklace clinked against the chair as she pushed it back into the table. "Enjoy your stay."

"Thank you. I hope to get lots done." *People are friendly here*, she thought as she watched the woman walk down the sidewalk and place her fashion magazine inside a satchel.

A sit-down dinner after driving two and a half hours stiffened Bethany's muscles. She decided she could use a walk and headed out the door toward the sound of a band that was playing '60s music. People in lawn chairs sat in front of the gazebo, and a few couples danced on the grass. *Big weeknight out in Jameson?*

In her high-heeled sandals, Bethany walked past a mix of single- and two-story buildings that looked to have been built between eighteen hundred and nineteen hundred, not as old as some of the buildings in Old Town Alexandria, but still old. Constructed of brick and a few covered in stucco, the buildings looked well preserved. Streetlights with banners announced the summer evening concert series. A clock on top of the town hall stood at the far end of town in the direction of the Rappahannock River. *Peter was right. Jameson is a quaint little town.*

The clock showed 6:30 p.m. *Early for a concert and a weekday too. Small towns are sure different.* The band was good, but it was not her kind of music, and she didn't have a chair. Since the stores were closed, she decided to browse and stopped to look in a jewelry shop window.

"Nice evening," a man's voice said behind her.

Bethany turned around. A partly bald gentleman, who looked to be in his late seventies or early eighties, sat on a bench.

"Yes, it is," she replied.

"You new to town or just passing through?"

This is the second person who asked. Do they know every person who lives here? "I'm in town to handle some legal . . . err, real estate business."

"Peter Jameson. Best there is. Well-heeled. From a noble family, that young man is."

Bethany's eyes opened wide, and her head tilted to the side. *This stranger guessed right.*

Remaining on the bench, he said, "I'm Oliver Bridgewell. Pleasure to make your acquaintance."

"Pleased to meet you. I'm Bethany."

"The Knowles Marchand girl," he stated confidently.

It took Bethany a moment to answer. "Ah . . . yes." It was the first time someone referred to her by that name, her biological mother's name. She started to ask how he knew, but he spoke before she could ask.

"Sorry about your mother. Brilliant woman. Didn't get to see her much after she went off to school. Traveled for work until the last few years. Mighty fine people, your grandparents too." Oliver sat on the bench with his eyes fixed on Bethany.

Only an hour in town, and I found someone who knew my mother and grandparents? I might get back sooner than even I thought. Bethany's internal clock was moving fast as always. "Thank you," she said.

"The Knowles home is one of the oldest around. Survived the Civil War. The Timekeeper is still standing too."

"The Timekeeper?" she asked, with curiosity building.

Oliver's eyes danced as he spoke. "The home's grandfather clock. Quite a beauty, that one is. Exquisite craftsmanship and detail. Lost art." Oliver put his head down toward his lap. When he raised it, his eyes dimmed.

The music stopped and the crowd clapped. Oliver reached into his pocket and pulled out a gold pocket watch with a protective hunter case and checked the hour. "Time to head home. I hope your dealings go well. In the meantime, enjoy yourself in our special little town." He closed the cover on the watch, returned it to his pocket, and used two hands to push himself up from the bench. Walking down the sidewalk in the opposite direction of the café and inn, he headed toward the water.

Townspeople carried folding chairs and walked past Bethany on the way to their cars. The town hall's lights illuminated the clockface as dusk approached. Bethany yawned. She needed rest before meeting Peter at the house in the morning and making decisions about what to do. One person already expressed interest in buying the home, and she brought the real estate lady's letter with her.

It was 9:30 in the evening when she finished unpacking and checking emails. She felt a pang of stress picturing Scott in charge. *He'll do okay*, she told herself, but just in case, she planned to keep a close watch on him from afar.

As Bethany slept at the Jameson Inn, only four miles outside of town discoveries about the past awaited her. Inside the historic home, the Timekeeper stood like a sentinel guarding palatial jewels. The clock's lower cabinet, last opened by a tearful and weak Marguerite Knowles Marchand, hid messages penned by six of the family's first daughters.

Standing through three centuries, the grandfather clock remained in this very spot as births were celebrated, heartaches comforted, and wounded souls were set free. Marking the hours since 1859, this evening its melody harmonized with the stillness.

Soon the house would be empty no more, and the Timekeeper's guarded contents would reveal secrets from the past.

. . . and the Timekeeper chimed one.

CHAPTER 6

Through the open spaces between the plantation shutters, the morning light entered Bethany's room. At 7:15 a.m., she texted Peter Jameson to reconfirm their 8:30 meeting time and place.

The Jameson Inn served coffee and muffins for guests in the living room filled with antiques. The dark wallpaper added to the room's minimal light. A middle-aged couple sat on the couch, reading the newspaper and talking about today's weather report. Skipping the complimentary muffins, Bethany reached for a to-go cup for her black coffee, then sealed the lid tight.

The directions to the house would take her away from the Rappahannock River and east of town, but before she headed out, she wanted to see the water. She drove down Main Street and turned on Harbor Street to see the marina.

The expansive river, over two miles wide, drifted south toward the Chesapeake Bay. An osprey circled above while it looked for prey. She recalled a long-ago school report she wrote. *Ah, yes. Ospreys can sight their underwater prey from up to one hundred thirty feet above.* Swooping down from the sky, it landed feet first into the water. It missed and flew upward to try again.

She turned the car around in the marina parking lot and let the GPS reorient her toward Knowles Lane. Looking ahead, she saw one turn between town and the house, making it almost a straight shot.

Within a minute outside of town, houses spread out with acreage between them. The oldest historic homes were barely visible, hidden behind trees and off the road. From what she could see, there were many older farmhouses and new ones designed to fit in with the old. *Nice try.* To

Bethany, the new homes stuck out as artful imposters next to the old and disrupted the realms of time.

The expansive landscapes unsettled the woman accustomed to the security of concrete buildings. A mix of oaks, maples, and pines grew along mostly flat terrain. Only three cars passed her on the road. The speed limit through town was twenty-five, and although it increased here, temptation urged her to let her car's sport engine reach her destination even faster. Thinking she might as well get this over with, her hands gripped the wheel, but she relinquished the desire for speed and obeyed the posted limit. She was about to encounter her family's legacy. A family she never met and wasn't sure she wanted to get to know.

Knowing her tightly pulled, high ponytail would keep her hair in place, she pushed her window button and let the warm summer air blow past her. Two minutes from her destination, she crossed a metal bridge over a wide creek. Full from recent rain, small boulders lined both sides.

"You are at your destination," her GPS informed her. Bethany's mind got distracted with the creek, and by the time the GPS spoke, she breezed past the house. She saw no cars and made a U-turn in the middle of the empty country road.

At the Knowles Lane sign, she turned right onto a gravel road, traveled two hundred feet, and navigated around a bend. The house she saw only in online tax photo records now appeared before her. Greek Revival in style, the white two-story was distinctive with its four columns and expansive front porch, the kind seen in movies where characters sit in rocking chairs while drinking iced tea. But there was no furniture on this porch and no one drinking tea. The historic house was very old. Tax records stated it was built in 1858.

Despite the unkempt yard and tall grass, the house's setting nodded to a time of grandeur. Flanked by tall, hundred-year-old oak trees, it looked as if someone chose its rightful place on the highest point of the land. Dense woods surrounded the property, which she was told was over one hundred acres. The overgrown grass area looked to be at least two acres.

Elongated windows on the first and second floors sat symmetrically atop one another, long and narrow, fitting the era when the home was built. Deep-green shutters hung beside each. *Pretty good shape. Must have been painted not long ago.* Unlike the home's well-kept appearance, the weeds in the yard reached as high as the second step on the porch. Bethany's face winced as she thought about what might be hiding amongst the tall grass. Hanging from black metal poles, two empty bird feeders stood in the middle of a landscape bed long neglected.

Bethany stepped out of her car to survey the house and property. She created for a living and constantly visualized what could be. With one foot upon the soil, she envisioned the possibility of a return to grandeur.

The front walkway and steps, made from a concrete-like substance with oyster shells mixed in, provided a solid welcome. The wide and deep-gray painted porch boards were firm beneath her feet, and the high porch ceiling made the space feel even larger. *Enough room to host a cocktail party for thirty. This should please Baxter. He'd love for me to host his customers here.*

Bethany cupped her hands and leaned to peer into a front window. She shrieked. A man's reflection appeared in the glass.

"Sorry to frighten you," Peter Jameson said. "Parked in back to turn on the well and get water to the house." Bethany's face still held the look of surprise. "Let me unlock the door for us," he said.

Peter took an antique metal key from his pocket and turned it in the front door's lock. As he pushed open the three-inch-thick oak door, he waited for her to enter. *Hmm . . . modern man practices this old-school gentleman thing,* she thought.

After following Bethany inside, Peter flipped the light switch. The antique hall chandelier offered limited illumination, but the sunny day and tall windows filled the space with rays of light. Bethany sniffed the stale air.

"Sorry about the musty smell. Been closed up for a couple months now," Peter said. Bethany put her hand to her face and hoped the smell was not permanent.

"It's a grand place," Peter said, twisting the metal key in his hand. "Been in your family since 1858."

The wide heart pine floors welcomed them in the foyer along with a grand staircase with a hand-carved finial at the base. Bethany's eyes focused on the worn stair treads where footsteps walked during three different centuries. "Original staircase is of the finest craftsmanship," Peter said, sounding like a real estate agent trying to convince a buyer.

A living room was to the left and a dining room to the right. "Never been in such an old home. I always lived in newer houses," she said.

Holding out his arm to the left, Peter suggested they take a tour. The living room had a fireplace with a hand-carved wooden mantel. Bethany stroked the flowered carving with her hand. Tall, narrow windows framed the left front and far side of the room. *This ceiling must be twelve or more feet high,* she guessed.

"Pretty room," she declared as she turned around in a half-circle to take it all in. "Lots of light." The near floor-to-ceiling windows had no curtains.

To the left of the fireplace, a door with an iron knob opened into a spare bedroom. "Hmm. That's unusual," she told Peter as she walked inside. The singular entrance to the downstairs bedroom was through the living room. Plenty of light filled this room as well, and it looked out to the backyard with even taller oak trees than in the front. Empty of contents, a closet door hung slightly open. Bethany turned the doorknob, and hinges creaked as she looked inside the small space. "That's right. People back then owned fewer clothes and less of everything than we do nowadays," she said, thinking of how big her closet was in her townhome. It was filled with more items than she had the opportunity to wear.

Across the hall from the living room, the dining room also featured a fireplace and two long, tall windows that looked out onto the front porch and yard. It connected to a butler's pantry and the kitchen. "Smaller kitchen than I would have thought for such a big house," she observed. Its last update looked like it occurred in the 1980s. Light-yellow wallpaper covered every wall. A painting of a garden scene graced one wall, and three framed prints of flowers hung side by side on another. Two windows looked out to the backyard, and a door led to the yard and woods behind. Behind the home to the right about fifty feet, Peter's white SUV was parked.

Finishing her tour of the kitchen, she walked into the entry hall. Against the wall it sat, the grandfather clock Oliver Bridgewell told her about. "The Timekeeper," she said as her eyes took in the seven-foot-tall antique.

"How did you know its name?" Peter said with surprise.

"A man in town last night. Oliver Bridgewell. He guessed I was part of the Knowles family. Said the Timekeeper's been here since before the Civil War."

Peter shook his head at the floorboards. "Nothing gets past Oliver in this town. He's one of the largest property owners. Owns half the buildings downtown."

"Incredible craftsmanship," she said as her hands smoothed over sections of the wood. Carvings on its black walnut cabinet bore the mark of a skilled hand. The windowed main compartment showcased the brass pendulum and weights, and above the clock face was a painted floral garden.

"I've done as Marguerite requested and kept Walter Fitzsimmons stopping by the house every week to wind it. She wanted to make sure it stayed in good working order and on time until you came. He specializes in antique grandfather clocks. Quite a few in this area . . . and in Richmond too. Loves to keep them going. He's quite the tinkerer, not to mention a general tradesman who did work here for Marguerite," he said looking down the hall. "Old homes take constant upkeep and care. I told Walter you were coming to town, and he'll be stopping by soon to meet you."

She didn't acknowledge Peter's last comment. Inside the glass case, the swinging pendulum held her attention.

They walked to a half bathroom just beyond the clock. As they reached the stairs, Bethany placed her hand on the thick wood railing. It was lower than she was accustomed to.

Peter chimed in to explain. "People were shorter in the 1850s. You might want to raise it." Bethany touched the carved finial at the base before going upstairs to find two more bedrooms and two full baths needing updates. One featured blue tile and had a small walk-in shower. The other was decked out in pink tile and a 1960s tub with a handheld shower encased by a plastic curtain. A bedroom at each end had a fireplace and a custom-crafted mantle.

Remembering she saw a teapot on the stove, she felt it time to have her second cup of coffee.

"Do you think there might be coffee here?" she asked Peter.

There was no coffee, but Peter found a box of teabags, and Bethany quickly boiled water. Peter added sugar to his, but she kept hers straight.

They took their tea to the living room, and Bethany hoped they could now get down to business. She looked at her watch.

Besides the warmth from the tea, the temperature rose in the closed-off house, prompting Bethany to fan herself with her hands. "The home has central air, but since it's been closed up for so long, let's open windows to get fresh air inside. Alright with you?" Peter stood up and walked toward the front windows. The windows stuck, but they opened enough to get air into the room.

"Ah, that's better," she said as she placed her teacup on the coffee table.

Bethany sat on the floral upholstered, wine-colored couch, and Peter took a seat across from her in a high-back burgundy upholstered chair by the fireplace.

"How long since Marguerite was here?"

"Couple of months." Peter cleared his throat and looked out to the front yard before turning back to her. "Sorry about the grass. When she left the house and went into hospice, she asked me to just keep an eye on the house itself."

Bethany planned to get right to business about the inheritance paperwork she came to handle. After the mention of her birth mother dying and seeing the distressed look on Peter's face, she paused. She reached for a fringed pillow to put behind her back and sat into the couch. "Can you tell me about her?"

"Did some projects for her when she first arrived in town, and then, of course, I handled the will." Peter picked up his cup from the small table beside his chair and took a sip of tea. "Marguerite went to college at Northwestern in Chicago. After college, she traveled the world and wrote for travel and news magazines. A few years after inheriting the home, she came to live here. She enjoyed two good years before she got really sick all alone in this big house." Peter put his head down toward the teacup in his lap. "I'm sorry, Bethany. That was insensitive of me. I apologize."

Bethany saw Peter's regret as soon as the words left his mouth. She didn't know her mother; therefore, she couldn't be here to take care of her.

With closed lips, Bethany smiled as she nodded. Looking around the room, she thought about Marguerite, who must have sat on the same couch as she was right now.

"Does she have any brothers or sisters?"

"She had a brother who died years ago. Never married."

With her mother being only fifty-eight, Bethany half-hoped someone else in the family still lived. An emptiness began to permeate her mind. She needed to rid the discomfort by changing the subject, but Peter beat her to it.

"What about you? Do you have any brothers or sisters?" he asked.

"No. It was always just me and my parents." She played with the tassels on another pillow beside her.

"Was it lonely growing up?" Peter asked.

"Didn't know anything different. My best friend, Mitzi, is the best 'sister' I could imagine. Known each other since we were eight." The thought of Mitzi put a smile on Bethany's face.

"It's good to have someone you can count on," he said.

Bethany soaked in the handsome view in front of her. "I checked you out on your website before I called you. What is a Georgetown Law School graduate doing in this small town?"

"Ha." Peter smiled in acknowledgment and leaned forward to put his empty cup on the coffee table. "Like yours, my family has a long history in Jameson. Out of law school, I worked for a firm in Baltimore. My dad always wanted me to come home and keep the family business going. And so, after he died, it seemed the right thing to do."

Peter's mood changed to a somber one when he mentioned his father's passing. She knew that feeling of loss of a father and this time jumped in to help *him*. "Do you have a brother, sister, uh . . . other family here?"

"I'm the only one in Jameson. My sister, her husband, and their two kids live in Indianapolis."

Single. Just like Holly said. "Do you get bored here?" Bethany asked.

Peter gave a short laugh. "I know why you ask. I lived in the DC area during undergraduate and law school and lived another eight years in Baltimore. It's a few hours away but worlds away from the pace of life in Jameson."

"Do you miss the pulse of the city?"

"There's always something to do. If you want more action, Richmond is a little over an hour away. Jameson's a small town for sure, but it's a perfect getaway for folks looking to escape the busyness of the city. We live a laid-back life here with no need to impress anyone. Retirees love Jameson, as do couples with young families."

"Do you have kids?" Bethany asked.

"No, I'm divorced."

The Timekeeper broke into their conversation. It was the first time Bethany heard the clock's sound, and she didn't want to talk over it. After the Timekeeper finished its melody, it began its chiming.

"That's beautiful," Bethany said after the ninth chime.

"It chimes the number of each hour and once on every half hour."

Bethany liked the sound at first but wondered if it might drive her nuts. Her eyes already watched time as she counted every second. Now her ears would hear time, too, reminding her that hours were slipping through her hands.

"How long do you plan to be in town?"

"I've blocked off four weeks but want to be here less, if possible. Never been away longer than a week. My friends and associates ganged up on me to take time away to handle this."

Peter nodded as his client opened up. He remained quiet and let her explain.

"I built the business a couple of years out of college. I've never taken much of a real vacation. I enjoy working, and I'm afraid I'm addicted to it. Don't be surprised if I start jonesing." By the blank expression on Peter's face, she was not sure he understood the slang term and so she elaborated. "You know when addicts need a fix, they start shaking like this." She laughed as she held up both hands and shook them nervously.

44

Peter threw his head back and laughed with her. "There's plenty to keep you busy here so you won't get those shakes. Do you think you might keep the house?"

"My friends told me it would be a great getaway just a few hours from Alexandria."

"Several D.C.-area families own second homes here. It's a quiet place to unwind," Peter said. "I lived both places and know what this town brings to people's lives."

"We'll see . . ." Bethany said as her voice trailed off.

Peter looked at his watch. "Time for me to get back to the office to finish paperwork I need you to sign. Better cover the critical items with you before I go." He took out a paper with handwritten notes. "The house operates on a well, and you can put the electric in your name in the next few days, no rush. Marguerite canceled the satellite and internet service, so you'll need to get those both turned on if you want. Anything I can do for you before I leave?" he asked, handing her his notes.

"I'll head back to town and get the internet turned on. I have to stay connected to work and might as well take care of the electric while I'm there too."

Peter locked the front door and held the antique piece of metal in front of her. Wrapping her fingers around the key to her family's history, she looked up at Peter gazing into her eyes.

"The home is yours now. I know Marguerite is smiling," he said. "She wanted this to happen." Peter stood close with his good-looking brown eyes catching hers.

Bethany shifted her eyes away and took a step to the side. *No romance. Too much work to do.* She turned toward the stairs. "You said you had papers for me to sign. I'd like to get moving. Can I come by your office this afternoon after lunch?"

He held his hand out for Bethany as she descended the stairs in her high-heeled sandals. Two hours south from Alexandria, but Virginian chivalry reigned much more here. She politely shook off the gesture and maneuvered her heels among the cracked oyster shells protruding from the concrete.

Walking to her car, Bethany thought Holly was right. Peter's good looks made him hard not to consider. And although people always tried to fix her up, her last date took place eight months ago. Depending on who played matchmaker, she sometimes agreed to lunch because she had to stop a few minutes every now and again to eat. And meeting someone in the middle of the workday gave her an excuse to end things quickly if needed. But Bethany wasn't here to find love. She was here to do business, albeit personal.

Peter needed to focus on the road, but with her car in front of him, his thoughts remained on Bethany. There weren't many women like her in this small town. The closest he could find to someone like her was in Richmond, but the distance made dating inconvenient. He was attracted to Bethany, no doubt about it. She was smart and quick and a business owner like him. But despite his business demeanor while with her, he couldn't help but wonder how her long legs might look in a skirt.

Putting his mind back on the business Marguerite hired him to do, Peter struggled with when to tell Bethany what more he knew. He planned to tell her at the house this morning, but the timing didn't feel right, and he didn't want to scare her away. Best to let her settle in first and wait a few days before the revelation. No one but Marguerite knew Bethany existed, and besides handling legal matters, he was paid to tell her why her mother had to keep her birth hidden.

CHAPTER 7

"The Knowles place," the woman at the electric company responded when Bethany told her the address. "Pretty spot. We'll make this effective tomorrow."

The quick action pleased Bethany, but her luck at the satellite company with a new young worker was not as good. The earliest appointment available was a week from today. "I at least need internet service," she said to the girl. "I can wait on TV. Can you check again, please?" An older gentleman at a desk behind the front counter heard the plea and found an opening tomorrow afternoon.

She walked out triumphantly from the satellite company's office. The time on the town hall clock showed 11:15 a.m. Close enough to lunch, and she didn't want to waste time until she met with Peter.

Looking out the café window, she watched passersby. Jameson moved at a slower pace than she was accustomed to. People chatted with each other as they strolled and stopped to look in a store window or said hello to someone they knew. Supervised by their mothers, children played in the green space near the gazebo where the band had played the night before.

After her lunch and a stop at the Jameson Inn, she still didn't need to move her car from the electric company's parking lot. Peter's office was only one block away. She had a few minutes and could squeeze in a bit of exercise, so she crossed the street and walked past a beauty salon named Monarchy. Inside, she recognized the woman who was cutting hair. She had met her at the café last night.

The shop's logo on the window included a butterfly. *How fitting*, she thought. A new hairstyle meant transformation. Because her high ponytail was quick and easy, Bethany's hairstyle had remained the same for years. She knew other women changed their styles more often, including girls in the office who came in looking different after a divorce or breakup. Next door to the beauty shop was Molly's, a boutique clothing store for women. She finished her loop by passing by the town hall.

Peter greeted Bethany in the law firm's small reception area and took her to the conference room. Ever the professional, he explained everything and answered any questions before she needed to ask.

Sitting alone with her in the historic building's small conference room, he twirled a pen in his hands. "Would it be okay if I stopped by in a few days to check on how you're doing?"

"You might want to text me first in case I'm out running errands. I plan to get right on things." Peter's eyes looked into hers. She wanted to be careful to not give Peter too much room. "I look forward to your visit," she said. And with that, she was out the door and walking down the street.

Bethany's high ponytail bobbed behind her. She had dark hair like her mother.

Peter sat in his conference room wondering what to do. Before she died, Marguerite instructed Peter to tell Bethany more, but the timing this afternoon still did not feel right. In a few days, he would come to see her at the house, but before he told her everything, he had to prepare. More time would provide him the right words to share. *A couple more days won't matter,* he told himself. The truth behind her birth had stayed buried for thirty-eight years. What was two more days?

CHAPTER 8

At 8:00 a.m., Bethany checked out of the Jameson Inn. From here on, she would stay at the house to manage projects on-site to speed up the process. Yesterday, right after meeting with Peter, she bought sheets and towels to freshen the place up. She got a coffee maker, too, but still needed to pick up groceries. The lady at the inn directed her to the nearest grocery store, where Bethany filled her trunk with all the fixings to make a salad.

Turning out of the grocery store parking lot, with a few additional turns here and there, and she was on the road to the house. Her car's supercharged engine reluctantly maintained the designated speed limit as it passed through history. A newly-built home interrupted her trip back through time. *City people like me*, she thought. They had found their way to Jameson and built retirement homes or second homes like Peter mentioned.

When she crossed the metal bridge over the creek, she paid close attention this time, turning left on the gravel lane and rounding the bend. Seeing the tall grass caused her to think of what lurked inside the untamed weeds.

Robins perched on an electric wire, staring at her and the empty bird feeders swaying in the breeze. She ignored their eyes and walked up the wide front steps. Her steps. Her biological mother's steps. Her ancestor's steps. *How many Knowles walked here?* Taking the metal key from her purse, she turned it inside the lock and walked into her once-unbeknownst ancestral home.

After putting groceries away, she put new sheets on one of the beds upstairs. The bedroom closest to the blue bathroom with the walk-in shower was the one she chose to use. It had a view to the backyard and the woods behind. She liked its fireplace mantel carved with flowers. It, too, was painted blue but a shade lighter than the bedroom walls. Bethany wondered what the wood looked like underneath the paint. An oval mirror with brass edges hung on the wall above an antique dresser.

Both upstairs bathrooms required extensive remodeling. The other bathroom with pink-tiled walls had a dulled bathtub with worn-off enamel. She imagined a claw-foot tub once stood here, but this one had no charm. The fixtures in both bathrooms were 1980's gold. Adding fresh new towels and soap to all, including the one downstairs, helped a bit, but it also looked dated. Maroon and green flowered wallpaper covered every wall of the downstairs half bathroom, all the way up to the high ceilings. It was too much for the eyes, and the dark color closed in the small room.

After her chores, she needed coffee and chose a single-serve one named "Tall, Dark and Handsome" because it reminded her of Peter. Sitting at the kitchen table, she looked out the back window at the birdbath, its basin dry. *So much to do here, including taking care of the outdoors.*

The doorbell rang and, being alone in the home, she hesitated to open the door. Looking out through a side window, she saw a man in his late fifties wearing glasses and holding a toolbox. He waved and spoke when she peered at him.

"Peter Jameson sent me, ma'am. I'm Walter Fitzsimmons. I service the Timekeeper. Need to rewind the clock and teach you how. Can I come inside, Miss Miller?"

Bethany unlocked the door. "Hello, pleased to meet you. Call me Bethany," she said as she moved aside to let Walter in.

"Wouldn't be proper, Miss Miller." Walter walked straight to the Timekeeper. "Can I show you how to wind it?"

"Uh, okay," she agreed.

Walter opened the grandfather clock's tall, middle cabinet door to show her the inner workings, including the weights and the pendulum. Inside the main cabinet, he picked up a crank before opening the separate glass case by the clock's hands. Putting the crank in one of the holes by the clock face, he turned it until one of the weights reached the top. He began to do the same in the second hole and turned to see if she was watching and learning.

"Now, try it yourself," he said.

Bethany practiced while Walter observed.

"It's an eight-day clock, but I recommend you wind it a minimum every seven days," he said.

"I'd better put a reminder on my calendar."

"Miss Miller, I don't know if Peter told you, but I did a lot of projects for your mother. If you need any help, I can do a little of everything—except electrical."

"I probably will sell it, but there's a slight possibility I might want to keep the place. Regardless, I first want to take note of what's broken or not working. How soon are you available to do a walk-through with me?"

"How about now?" Walter started to close the pendulum cabinet, but Bethany interrupted.

"Wait, what's this key for?" She picked up a small key lying on top of a piece of blue velvet.

Walter shrugged. "Might be for the lower cabinet. Never opened it."

Bethany bent down and turned the key in the lower cabinet's lock. Inside, she found and picked up an old leather-bound notebook. Her fingers moved across flowers embossed on the front, and as she opened it, seeds fell onto the floor. She looked down but did not pick them up.

Being careful to not drop more seeds, she leafed through the notebook. The formal cursive writings and thicker black ink on the opening pages were not of today. The handwriting changed throughout. *Multiple people wrote in this journal.*

"What is this?" Bethany asked.

Walter shrugged his shoulders as he stood there with his toolbox, waiting to get to work.

"I'll look at this later. Just a second." Bethany left him and put the journal on a living room shelf on top of a small stack of books. When she returned, Walter was waiting for her in the hall.

"I charge a fair price, Miss Miller. You can ask any of my customers. Houses like this are not something you want to let just anybody work on.

I'm knowledgeable about the house. Took care of some things for Miss Marguerite the last few years."

"Peter told me, and he gave you his highest recommendation," Bethany said.

Walter's shoulders pushed back, and he stood taller.

At the end of their cursory inspection tour, they composed a list two pages long of house repairs before the internet company technician's knock on the door interrupted their work. As Bethany darted toward the door, Walter called out, saying, "I'd like to go through the house one more time on my own to take measurements and write a list of materials." His words evaporated into the air as she was already at the door and on to her next task.

She showed the technician where she wanted the router and modem connected in the first-floor bedroom. Once his work was underway, she walked through each room of the house and wondered what to do. If she kept the house, she would need to remodel it. Would she use this as a second home and getaway on weekends? It might be a giant waste of money and time. For now, it was best to focus on getting the place in order for no matter what she decided.

Walter finished his second pass and walked Bethany through a plan of what he suggested he take care of first. "Can you give me an estimate?" she asked him.

"Hard to do, being such an old home. You never know what to expect."

She pushed him to give a number, and he summed up a loose total. Bethany thought the dollar amount was fair enough, given the long list.

"When can you start?" she asked.

Walter put his pen on the kitchen table. "I'm waiting on word from another customer when they want to start their remodel. I'll be booked for six weeks on that project. Right now, I have the next two workdays free." Bethany booked him.

"Miss Miller," Walter said as he picked up his toolbox from the kitchen floor. "I'm happy to be here again. Your mother was a fine woman. Real sorry you didn't get to meet her. You look like her, same hair and eyes."

Bethany nodded and stared out the window at the oak trees. For a moment she wondered about a mother she never knew, but she shook off the sentimental longing and pushed forward.

Equipped with internet, she could supervise house projects while she kept in touch with her office. Scott had taken charge, but Baxter expected her to keep a close watch on him. Thinking of Baxter, she remembered she forgot to call Michael Alexander before she had left town. That jarring experience in Costa Rica still bothered her. She intended to ask Michael to check into labor laws and wanted to share her concerns about the plant manager and all those young female workers, including the one with those eyes. That girl used those dark, harkening eyes to tell Bethany something, but exactly *what* Bethany might never know.

CHAPTER 9

"I've been dying to hear from you," Mitzi's high-pitched voice gently scolded on the video call. "You haven't checked in since you arrived in town."

"Sorry. I'm at the house," Bethany said from the kitchen table. "Got internet, food, and a contractor ready to go. I'm going to use one of the bedrooms upstairs and start staying here tonight to keep things moving."

"Did you find out more about your mother?" Mitzi plopped into the chair in her hotel room.

"Peter told me she went to college in Chicago."

"Wait. How were you born in California if your mother went to school in Chicago and she was from Virginia?"

"I don't know. I didn't ask him," Bethany responded.

"Don't you want to know?" Mitzi sat up in her chair.

"I didn't think about it at the moment. I have so many things on my mind, including work. I've been checking in with Scott and Holly. So far, the place is still running without me."

Mitzi kicked off her shoes and pulled one leg up on to the chair. "You know you have a great team."

"But I'm craving my work and feel so far away."

"That's a good thing." Mitzi's face came closer to the phone. "You *need* space," she said.

While on the video call, Bethany walked down the hall. With her phone in one hand, she used the other to reach for the carved finial at the bottom of the steps and turned around, showing the full staircase view to Mitzi. "I've got to figure out how much money I want to sink into this place. It could be a bottomless pit. I've heard of people spending a fortune on historical places."

"But this is *your* historical place. Look at that staircase," Mitzi said, her eyes glowing at the sight. "It's been in your family since the 1850s. This is your legacy."

"I'm still trying to get my mind around that," Bethany said. "Can't believe all that's happened. Time is moving faster than I am."

"That's impossible," Mitzi said. Nothing moves faster than you." Mitzi looked down at her phone. "Oh, my boss is calling. Keep me posted."

As the Timekeeper began its melody and chimes, Bethany wondered if the sound would awaken her in the night. She hoped the bedroom door was thick enough to muffle the sound. Always scurrying when she was awake, she watched the clock to make the most of every second. Looking toward the hall where the Timekeeper stood, she shuddered thinking about when she closed her eyes tonight and tried to sleep. Would she also have to "hear" time slipping away?

Between bites of food, she answered emails, though they were fewer than usual. Her out-of-office message seemed to be working better than expected. She wasn't accustomed to having empty space to fill in as she pleased.

Besides internet, the house now had TV service, but Bethany didn't feel like watching anything. She gave reading a thought but admitted to herself that she was not a casual reader. There was never a moment to read except for business books on airplanes, when she was trapped thirty thousand feet in the air with no way to accomplish anything else. Not being one to bring a book with her on road trips, she remembered the leather journal she found inside the Timekeeper. She would read that after dark, but first she wanted to go outside and check out her property. Besides this old home, she had 167 acres to explore.

CHAPTER 10

It was 7:30 in the evening, and there was still plenty of light outside as Bethany walked down the gravel driveway, surveying the front yard and backyard without need of stepping into the tall grass. She thought to call Peter for a recommendation on who could take care of the yard. *Peter would know who to call.* Bethany liked Peter. He was smart and professional. And like her, he didn't waste time.

She went back inside, and by the time she wrote a shopping list, which included cleaning supplies, the Timekeeper alerted her it was 8:30 p.m. It was early, but she was tired and went upstairs to ready for bed. After washing off her makeup, she pulled out her ponytail and reached for a hairbrush. Looking in the mirror, she startled for a moment. A set of eyes were looking back at her—the eyes of the factory girl. They looked as if she wished death. Her death or Bethany's? Bethany failed to leave the memory of that disturbing encounter behind. It traveled with her to Alexandria and now to Jameson too.

She looked away from the mirror. Everyone told her she needed a break. Mitzi said she needed space. Too much stress for too many years sat like a weight on Bethany's shoulders. She put toothpaste on her electric toothbrush and kept her eyes away from the mirror.

Pulling back the blue-and-white flowered bedcovers, she realized the journal was downstairs on the living room shelf. A few stairs squeaked as she descended barefoot, and she made a mental note to tell Walter.

The Timekeeper's melody and nine chimes echoed through the quiet home.

This clock with its consistent, trusted rhythm reset an occupant's internal one, but would it do the same for her? She picked up the journal, rubbed her hands over the thick, brown leather, and took time to admire the embossing on the front. *Machines today do not make these one-of-a-kind marks.*

A few seeds fell to the floor again. This time, she bent down to pick them up and placed them back inside. And to not lose more as she walked up the stairs, she held the book flat in front of her. *Why did someone put seeds inside?* When she got to her room, she shook the book and collected the seeds on a decorative dish on the dresser.

Settling in beneath the crisp, new blue sheets, she opened the journal, its pages yellowed from age. She didn't know how old it was, but the writing in thick ink looked very old. Bethany read the first entry.

CHAPTER 11

Katherine Knowles Davis
Born 1835
Jameson, Virginia

My beloved William Davis built this home for us in 1858. We were engaged but a week when he said he wanted to give me a home to fill up with children. He chose this very spot on land my grandfather, Samuel Knowles, gifted us. It was the highest point and offered protection from an often-swelling creek. Selecting which trees to fell, William created a clearing, keeping enough trees on each side to provide us shade from the hot summer sun; but not too much that in the winter there was no light. The home faced north to remind us to always seek divine guidance.

In 1859, on the anniversary of our first year of marriage, William graced me with another gift of the heart, a grandfather clock. Its black walnut cabinet was made from trees planted by my ancestors. William said its chimes shall be our constant reminder that the passing of time moves us closer to the One who created all.

Though I know my ultimate goal is abundant life with our Lord, I must not rush this earthly walk. I am reminded of this each day at twelve o'clock when the Timekeeper's hands come together and point upward. As I join my own hands, I give thanks for every hour and blessing I enjoy on this earth. For each moment I spend here is to be treasured, albeit not every experience merry.

Our country withstood hardships, including bloodied battles of brother against brother, freeman and slave fighting for their liberty. War ravaged our beloved Virginia and scarred its natural beauty. The battle raged near Jameson, and though our town was spared from direct attacks, desperate soldiers from both sides raided homes and took what they found. Sometimes, it was another man's wife for the night.

While William fought against the invading Northern armies, I kept our business, "The Jameson Gazette", running as long as possible. But paper shortages from the North's blockade forced our temporary closure. People contributed their rag bags for us to use the cloths to make paper, but it was not enough to keep us printing. Scarce newspapers and books passed from person to person. The North choked us from every necessity, and blockade runners supplied us as best they could.

The war challenged us all until April 9, 1865, when on the other side of Richmond, the two generals from the South and North met at Appomattox Courthouse. Guns and cannonballs went silent, and a Southern general's sword was allowed to remain. Surrounding armies one by one surrendered to the peace. For the South, the war was lost, but bird songs once again floated through Jameson's air.

The Timekeeper's chimes resound in these halls as we continue the healing, bandaging our wounds—physical and all. As children of God, we will someday forget and forgive the atrocities of the past. For the One who knows the hairs on our heads directs our way.

I know because He guided me one evening. Before the war, William's father passed, and he went to England to escort his mother to live with us. For a woman alone, ocean travel was not safe.

One of those nights when I was home by myself, a desperate plea at the door forced me to choose between closing my eyes or helping the most desperate of souls. Fear shook my body, but the good Lord directed me in what to do. And after I helped that stranger at my door, both her life and mine forever changed.

We are each called to a unique purpose. I risked much but gained in joy by helping one poor soul and then others in need. I pray more of God's children answer the beckoning cry of our sisters and brothers in need.

Dearest daughter, as I write this on your first birthday, my wish is for this journal to pass through time's earthly boundaries. May it one day reach your outstretched hands and the hearts of many more Knowles *daughters to come. In earnest, I pray for each to answer the Timekeeper's beseeching call and share grace forward.*

Your loving mother,
Katherine Knowles Davis
Daughter, Wife, Mother, & Soul Rescuer

CHAPTER 12

Arriving right on time as he had promised, Walter Fitzsimmons gave Bethany the bill for materials and tackled loose boards in the living room. She went to ask him about the stair treads and as she approached him, he pulled out a square nail from the wide floorboard. "Made when the house was built," he said as he presented the nail to her. "You might like to keep it as a souvenir. I'll replace it with a new one."

Bethany's fingers rubbed the uneven edges before she turned to look at the stairs. "Some of the steps are squeaking. Maybe they need to be replaced?" She walked to the stairwell and stood, looking at the middle of each step worn from over one hundred years of use. *My ancestors walked these steps. If I replace them, I'll lose the path where they walked.* "I'll think about it later," Bethany said over her shoulder to Walter, who was still on his knees in the living room. "But I wanted to mention it to you."

Walter acknowledged her with a wave of his hand.

"Going to head to the hardware store now to buy cleaning supplies," she said as she picked up her purse and went out the door.

Once there, a clerk directed her to the aisles containing each item on her list, and she quickly filled a cart. Bethany knew she was buying more than was necessary, but the house had not been cleaned in a while. Not knowing if Marguerite's old vacuum worked, she bought a new battery-operated one. She hated messing with cords anyway. They got in her way and slowed her down.

As she looked at the cart, Bethany thought of her cleaning lady, Nancy, back in Alexandria. She imagined her smile at seeing her about to tackle this house by herself. Hiring a cleaning service may have been the better option, and she thought to ask Peter for a recommendation. But for now, she would make a first pass herself. The house needed a good cleaning, and she needed exercise since she hadn't been to the gym in over a week.

Unloading her car in the parking lot, she pulled a mop from her cart. She was about to place it inside her trunk when the sound of squealing tires startled her. She hit the handle on the side of the car. Known for her quick reactions, she turned toward the sound. A pickup truck had run into a shopping cart—her shopping cart! The driver shot her an irritated look as she looked beside her and then back toward the driver as he opened his door and got out.

"I'm so sorry," she said as she pulled her cart from his bumper. "I didn't see it get away from me. Is your truck alright?" Bethany bent down to take a closer look. There were scratch marks across the man's shiny, white pickup truck. Licking her fingers, she tried to wipe the scratches with her hand, but the marks remained. "I'd be happy to pay to get that taken care of," she said, looking at the man towering over her.

He bent down to look closer at his scratched bumper and then shifted his eyes up at Bethany. "Brand-new truck," he said with an accent. "Picked it up from the dealer two days ago. Knew sooner or later something was going to get it . . . It just happened to be *you*." He stood up straight and shook his head side to side at Bethany.

Her eyes opened wide as she looked from him to the bumper and back at him again. "I'm *so* sorry," she repeated as she reached into her purse. "Let me give you my name and number. I'll take care of whatever it costs. You can see my driver's license too."

Putting his hand out to stop her, he said, "That won't be necessary, *senorita*. Give me your name and number, and I'll put it in my phone."

"Bethany Miller. Seven, zero, three, five, five, five, seventy-four, forty-six.

"I think I can use buffing compound to get the scratches out, but I'll let you know if not," he said. "You be careful the rest of the day."

When he pulled away, Bethany noticed a company name on his door, "God's Green Acres Landscaping." She needed a landscaper, and this guy drove a new truck. She hoped that meant he worked for a quality company.

Driving to the house, she spoke into her phone, "Call God's Green Acres Landscaping."

"Nick DeLeon," a man answered.

"Hi, this is Bethany Miller. I saw one of your worker's trucks today and wondered if someone could give me an estimate on landscape projects."

"*Senorita*, that would be my truck your cart ran into."

Bethany's face flushed as her mouth turned out and down. "Oh . . . Sorry, I thought I called an office number."

"This *is* my office. What can I do for you?"

"Uh . . . I need grass cut. Just got to town. The house hasn't been lived in for months. The weeds are almost as high as my knees in some places, and I might want some other projects done around the yard too. I've got several landscape beds that need serious tending."

"It's busy season. Everyone wants things *rapido*. My crews are booked and so is everybody else in town."

"Oh, pleeeeease." Bethany used her damsel in distress voice she applied with contractors when she was out of options. Although there was nothing helpless about her, when she needed something urgently, she knew what "tools" got a job done.

The other end of the phone was silent, so she implored him again. "I've got to get the grass cut and have no way of doing it myself. I just inherited the home. The yard has not been attended to in months. I'm concerned about animals making nests out there. Plus, it's a total mess. The landscape beds are all overgrown, and I'm thinking about fixing the place up to sell it."

"What's the address, *senorita*?"

"Knowles Lane, five minutes from town," she told him as she pulled into her gravel driveway.

"Street number?"

"Just Knowles Lane. It's the only house."

I have to make a quick stop first," he said. "Will you be there in thirty minutes? Can't promise you anything, but I'll come take a look."

⊰◈⊱

Still disturbed by the scratch marks on his brand-new vehicle, Nick DeLeon drove to his prescheduled appointment. In his line of work, he was used to not keeping a perfect truck, but he'd hope to have at least a month with his shiny new vehicle. It was the first one he'd bought in four years—since his world had turned upside down.

The woman who scratched his new truck had long brown hair like Mariana did. He'd checked her out in his rearview mirror when he pulled away. He saw her long legs in those tight jeans and high-heeled sandals. She was hard not to notice, even if his heart was not on the market.

Might be worth a stop, he thought. *This city woman won't be here long, and they tend to spend money fast. Best take every job I can while it's here.*

God's Green Acres was a full-service business and offered landscape design, hardscape, pond and waterfall construction, in addition to general lawn maintenance. The company had three landscape and lawn maintenance crews, and all of their schedules were booked. He would have to push a regular customer back if he decided to fit this one in. Time was of the essence with city people. They were long in dollars but short in patience.

Bethany came through the door with arms full of supplies, ready to drop everything with one misstep. Once Walter saw her plight, he helped her bring in the rest of the bags. She was caught off guard by his offer to help. Most men she worked with understood she wanted to be treated as an equal, displaying her strength as much as theirs when possible. But she let Walter help her with the bags because she was short on time.

In the few days of knowing him, Walter had a way of taking charge without making her feel like he did. Bethany liked Walter. He was quiet, focused, and moved fast when he could, but he also took the time to do things right. He had a fatherly air about him and slowed down to explain things to her while not belittling her for her lack of knowledge about home improvements.

The doorbell rang. Nick DeLeon, landscape architect and owner of God's Green Acres Landscaping, handed Bethany his card.

"Please, come in," she said as she stood aside for him to enter.

"*Senorita*, best we stay outdoors and walk the yard." He looked down at her high-heeled sandals. "You got any proper shoes?"

"These *are* my shoes." Bethany's painted red toes stuck out of her four-inch-high suede taupe sandals. "Suit yourself, *senorita*." He shrugged his shoulders and turned toward the front steps.

She motioned him to go first.

As he walked into the tall grass, Bethany followed right behind him like a baby goose following its mother. She kept close and her open-toed shoes stepped where he did after he cleared a way through the weeds. Not wanting to step on something lurking in the tall grass, she kept her eyes down and watched where she placed her feet. Which is why when Nick stopped abruptly and turned around, Bethany almost ran into him.

A startled Nick pulled his head back and shot her a look after the near-collision. "*Senorita*, I suppose you want the grass cut in front and back? You've got about three acres to cut. Anything else you want done?"

"I'd like to clear things out," she said, heading to a landscape bed to the left of the porch. And with both hands, she pulled out a bunch of tall weeds.

"Stop, *senorita*," he shouted as he rushed toward her. "There are native Virginian flowers mixed in there." But before Nick finished his sentence, Bethany had pulled out two handfuls of plants. The opened-up space gave view to a large rock with the words LILY FIELDS 1858 carved into it.

"Who was Lily Fields?" she asked. "My family members' names were Knowles, Davis, and Marchand.

Nick looked between the native flowers and, with a careful touch, pulled out weeds to expose more of the rock. "Many families back then gave their homes names," he said. "Lily Fields—that's the name of *your* house. And there in your hands, *senorita*, right there along with those weeds you pulled, those are Turk's cap lilies, native to Virginia. Good attractor of butterflies and hummingbirds. The beds are full of them. I checked them out before I rang the bell." He pulled the cap up on his forehead and looked her in the eyes. "Wanted to see what I might be getting into first."

"Oh . . ." Bethany said. She looked at the plants in her hands and saw a bud on one. "Sorry. I pulled them out so fast I didn't see flowers."

"Sweet flowers are slow, and weeds make haste," he said.

"Pardon me?"

"Shakespeare," he answered.

"Love Shakespeare," Bethany said. "But I never heard that one. She turned her head and lips to one side. "You sure it's Shakespeare?"

"*Richard III*. Seemed appropriate for the moment."

"Can you help me?" she asked, using the damsel in distress voice but not as strong this time.

"You need help, alright," he said, taking the plants from her. And when she slapped her dirty hands together, he looked at her feet as dirt landed on her painted red toes.

Raising his head he said, "I'll get one of my crews out here tomorrow. They can cut the grass and get you on the schedule every week. After that, if you want a quote on other things, let me know. But it's going to be a while. We're backed up for weeks."

"Got it. I appreciate you tending to the grass." Bethany stepped up onto the first porch step to get out of the grass and put herself at eye level with the landscaper.

"Hope you are a morning person," he stated. "I'll have to get the crew here right after sunup so they can stay on schedule."

"I'll be up. Thank you," she said, folding her hands together in a yoga-like gesture.

As Bethany entered the house foyer, she noticed her sandals covered in dirt. Turning her shoe to the side, she saw the heels, too, had marks from the rocks in the driveway. *They might be ruined*, she thought. She brought a couple of other pairs of shoes with her, but none of them seemed "proper" as the landscape guy referred to them. Remembering the boutique shop in town, she wondered if maybe they sold shoes.

"Walter, if I go out for an hour, will you still be here when I get back?"

"I plan to be here until six o'clock tonight. Does that work for you, Miss Miller? There's a lot to get done."

"Please, please call me Bethany."

"Wouldn't be proper, Miss Bethany," Walter said, throwing a playful glance at her.

Upstairs, she changed into another pair of heeled sandals, and when she got to the gravel drive, she walked with care before she got into her car.

Passing a farm on the right, cows were eating grass by a fence near the road. A red barn sat to the left of a white farmhouse, and a tall silo sat atop a stone foundation. She hadn't noticed it before, but being away from the hustle was allowing her to spot things she used to pass without noticing.

The quiet road into town contrasted with her usual commute in heavy traffic from her townhouse in Alexandria to her office near Old Town. In Jameson, there was only one stoplight between her "new" home and the edge of town. Like her first day here, she again saw only a few cars along the way.

Hopeful they sold shoes, Bethany went into Molly's Boutique and was relieved to see shelves full of shoes on the left wall. *Could use a pair of sneakers too*, she thought as she picked up a pair. She found the shoes and sneakers she wanted in size eight, slipped them on to make sure they fit, and took them to the counter.

Browsing a display of jewelry, she saw the woman she met in the café her first night in town, the same one she saw cutting hair in the beauty parlor. The woman was looking at long beaded necklaces fitted at the ends with clear beads in a chunky cross-like shape.

"Nice to see you again," Bethany said, trying to get her attention.

The woman turned to look at who spoke to her. "My goodness. You're still here," she said with her hands full of jewelry selections.

"The home I inherited needs a lot of work."

"Where's your home?

"About four miles out of town. Seems most people know it when I say the original Knowles property."

The woman nodded her chin. "Ah, that one's a gem. Poor Marguerite. I used to do her hair. You're her family?"

"She was my biological mother, but we never got to meet before she died."

The woman's hand flew up to cover her mouth from the unexpected revelation. "I'm so sorry," she told Bethany and touched her on the arm. "Remarkable lady. Marguerite told me about her travels and showed me magazines her work appeared in. We shared a common cause to help others." The woman held Bethany's full attention as she talked about her mother. "So caring . . . and she contributed to the Black Women's Scholarship I founded at the local high school. I didn't realize Marguerite had a child."

Bethany winced, but by the woman's cordial expression, she had no idea she misspoke.

"I'm Samantha Lancaster. My friends call me Sam."

"Bethany Miller. Pleasure to officially meet you."

"This is a great boutique. I own the beauty shop next door." Sam pointed her finger to the right. "I pop over whenever I get a cancellation. Let me know if I can ever be of service to you."

Sam surveyed Bethany's lack of hairstyle except for the ponytail pulled up high behind her head. "Maybe some highlights?" she asked.

"My best friend told me to add highlights. I've avoided it because I'm busy and travel a lot. I know you have to keep that up."

Pointing at the top of Bethany's hair, Sam said, "You'd look great with a few highlights to break up the brown. It would give you some dimension. Think about it. I'm right next door at Monarchy. Open five days a week. Closed on Sundays and Mondays."

"I'll keep it in mind," Bethany said, smiling in appreciation for the free consultation. Sam bought the long beaded necklace and headed next door to work.

Besides shoes, Bethany bought a pair of blue jeans and a few casual cotton tops and T-shirts. The tops she brought with her were not appropriate for cleaning floors, and now she had *proper* shoes, as the landscape guy referred to them.

On her drive back to Lily Fields, she thought how little she knew about her biological mother. *How did Sam do my mother's hair?* Bethany had only seen an old photo of Marguerite she found online, and in it, she had long, straight dark hair like hers.

She looked forward to asking Peter more about Marguerite, and maybe he knew about other friends her mother had in town. She would start with Peter. Besides, she wanted to see him again. There was something about him that held her attention and the feeling was unusual for Bethany. She seldom slowed down for men, but Peter Jameson captivated her as few others did.

Returning to the house, she found Walter packing up his tools. A neat worker, he laid drop cloths wherever he worked to not damage the original heart pine floors.

It was late after she finished dinner, but she still had work to do. Scott sent an updated report and included bulleted highlights for each project. Once done with that, it didn't take her long to read and reply to emails. To Bethany's surprise, the number of daily emails slowed more each day she was away. Her calls to clients and meetings with associates before she left town were more effective than she anticipated.

She hadn't watched TV since she got to town and decided to turn on an episode of a home remodeling show. A decorative fringed pillow on the couch supported her head as she lay across the floral design. The home's décor was nothing of her style, and she decided if she kept the house for a getaway, she would redecorate and fill it with new furniture.

Asleep before the show's first commercial break, the Timekeeper's ten chimes awakened her. Following its prompt, she went upstairs to bed.

Tomorrow, she would call Peter to ask about her mother and also the family who built and lived in this home. Katherine Knowles Davis mentioned she wanted to pass the journal to her daughter. Bethany would read further to find out if Katherine's daughter shared about her own life and passed forward her wisdom as well. But her eyes were too tired to read more tonight. The landscaper said to be ready early. Reading the journal needed to wait for another day. So she got into bed and turned off the light.

In Costa Rica, another factory girl disappeared.

CHAPTER 13

The sound of engines awakened Bethany, and her mind raced to make sense of what she heard. She reached for her phone. It was 7:15 a.m. Because she always woke up at dawn, she hadn't bothered to set her alarm. But the silence of the countryside afforded her a deeper sleep than usual, keeping her sound asleep through the Timekeeper's chimes and the sunrise.

Outside the window, a guy on a tractor with a mowing attachment was cutting the tall grass. Other crew members waited to fire up their trimmers and blowers. Bethany scurried to get ready. *No time for a shower.* She threw on a pair of jeans, a cotton shirt, and gym shoes.

Giving the landscape crew a welcoming wave from the front porch, she returned inside to finish getting ready. Afterward, she placed a video call from her makeshift home office in the kitchen.

Holly was in the conference room when the link connected. "All good here," Holly said. "I'm enjoying working on new projects for Scott."

"Where is he?" As soon as Bethany asked, Scott walked into the conference room.

"How's homeownership in Jameson?" Scott asked while taking a seat at the long conference table.

"I've got contractors working on the inside and outside," she said. "The list is long, but after a couple of days, I'm seeing progress. Have you all finished the McArthur project overview for me?"

"We'll send it by end of the day. In the meantime, take time to stop and enjoy yourself a little. We've got this."

Bethany hated people telling her to slow her fast speed, but she knew Scott meant well. "I'm trying to do what you've been telling me to—slow down and smell the roses. I've got so much to do here. I haven't even begun to get to know who my mother was or start the search for my father."

Scott waved his hand in the air. "Bethany, the expression is *stop* . . . stop and smell the roses, not merely *slow down*."

"Oh, well," she said as her free hand hit the side of her jeans. "Slowing is the best I can do. I've got to keep moving. Days are ticking away. Every second counts, you know." She looked at her watch to check the time.

"That's why we are staying late to keep things moving here," Scott said. "So while you are there, try and come to a stop. You might see something you would have otherwise missed."

Looking at the kitchen ceiling while he talked, she didn't want to hear what he preached. "I've still got to find my father," she said and picked up her laptop to carry it to the living room. Walking down the hall she thought, *A family home should bring back memories.* But Bethany never got the opportunity to make any.

"Hate to tell you bad news," Scott said. Bethany stopped her steps. "The French perfume account last minute decided to stay with their current agency."

"Ugh," she said, hunching over as if punched in the gut. "Counted on that one."

"Ya, that's why I had Michael on the contract already. Thought it was a done deal," Scott said.

"Speaking of Michael . . . I need to speak to him about something else. I've got to call him as soon as we hang up." The doorbell rang and interrupted her.

Nick DeLeon stood on the front porch. "Morning, *senorita*. Came by to show you a landscaping plan I put together for you."

"It's not a good time," she said. "I'm really busy. Uh . . . I didn't ask you for a plan," she stated as her eyes pinched together.

"Figured you'd ask me for one," he said, standing on her front porch with a large, folded-over white sheet of paper in his hand.

"I was just about to make a phone call," she said.

Not taking her hint, Nick stayed at her door.

"Okay, a few minutes is all I have," she agreed, closing the door behind her. She smirked upon seeing him smile at her new sneakers and followed him down the steps.

He pointed to the landscape beds. "We'll pull out the weeds and leave the flowers. You've got several varieties of lilies, and there's room to add more lilies or other flowers too. What do you like?"

"Like?" she asked.

"Flowers. What kinds of flowers do you like? We can add whatever you like," he said.

She remembered her conversation with Scott about stopping. "Um . . . roses? Yes, give me some roses."

"Varieties and colors?" he asked.

"No idea. Whatever you think." She threw one hand in the air. "Got bigger things on my mind today."

"Most rose varieties take a lot of time and attention. I suggest we plant a couple of specimen roses by the porch and put shrub roses in all the other spots. Shrub roses require little attention. Those should work best for *you*."

"Sounds fine," Bethany said abruptly as her mind focused forward on the call she needed to make to her attorney. She thought she made it clear she was finished with the consult. But at the top step, she turned to see he had followed her. "Thought we were done," she said. "And I didn't ask you for a landscape plan because you said your schedule was full."

"I know my customers," he said, pulling his cap up on his forehead. "Knew you'd ask for a plan as soon as you saw the cleaned-up yard."

Looking at the plan held out before her, she smelled the fresh-cut grass. And before she got to respond, workers pulled the cords on their handheld trimmers and blowers. She struggled to talk over the loud noise, so she leaned down toward him with one hand cupped beside her mouth. "How long before you can start?"

He leaned in so she could hear him respond. "Couple days. I pushed another job back. It's commercial, and the building owner already gave me the okay." He tipped his cap to Bethany and headed to his truck. He made no mention of the bumper.

Distracted and thus forgetting to make her needed phone call, she pulled out cleaning supplies and the new vacuum. The doorbell rang again. Mr. Bridgewell, the older man she met her first night in town, stood on her front porch.

"Good morning, ma'am. Oliver Bridgewell. Just passing by and thought I'd say hello. How are you getting along in our special little town?"

"Doing just fine," Bethany said as she wondered why he felt he could just pop by.

"Would you have a moment to chat outside? It's a beautiful day."

"I was about to do house cleaning," she responded, staring at the older gentleman in front of her. *If he drove out here once, he would come again.* She chose to join him on the front porch and get him on his way.

Oliver clasped his hands in front of him. "I wanted to check and see if you're interested in selling the place," Oliver said.

"I'm not making any decision yet," Bethany answered, with nothing more to share with this virtual stranger.

"I understand. Here's my card in case you happen to come to that decision soon. I'd be honored to be the first to know."

From his pants pocket, Oliver pulled out his gold pocket watch with two birds etched on the front. Opening it, he said, "It's 9:30 already. The day escapes me. Good day, Miss Miller. Let me know if I can be of service, and good luck with your projects."

Oliver Bridgewell had a knack for appearing out of nowhere. His card, with a drawing of Jameson's Main Street business district, said he was a developer and property owner. *Did he want to turn Lily Fields into a development?* Bethany shook her head at the thought of this home being torn down for new imposters like those she saw on her drive from town. She watched from the porch as Oliver drove down the driveway, around the bend, and out of sight.

Before she started to clean, Peter texted to ask if he could stop by for a visit after lunch today. *Why not. I'm not getting anything done,* she thought.

With all the interruptions, Bethany forgot about phoning her attorney and started cleaning before her next visitor arrived. At least this visit was planned. Peter Jameson had checked in with her first and asked permission to visit.

She vacuumed the living room, but the sight of burnt ash and half-used logs bothered her. Holding a contractor's garbage bag she found in Walter's supplies, she picked up a log that instantly crumbled into pieces and dirtied the floor more.

"Walter!" she called out. "Do you have an industrial sweeper?"

Walter came across the hall from the dining room. "Got one on my truck. Be right back, Miss Bethany."

The sweeper sucked up a thick layer of dust and small shards of wood lining the bottom of the fireplace. Once cleaned out, she saw a piece of metal across the bottom of the fireplace. A slightly raised handle protruded from the top. *Was it a door to sweep ashes underneath?* Reaching her hand for the metal door, she realized it was not attached with a hinge, as she thought; instead, it was heavy and required both hands to pull it aside. It creaked as she pulled it across the bricks. She looked inside the dark, musty-smelling hole.

"What's that?" Walter asked, startling her from behind.

"I don't know," she said, staring into the pitch-dark hole.

Leaning in to get a closer look, Walter declared, "Never seen a hidden room under a fireplace before." He went to retrieve his flashlight, and when he came back, he got on his knees and shined the light into the three-foot-wide hole.

"Some kind of room. About five feet deep. Let me check it out," he said.

Holding on to the brick sides, Walter slid his legs in the hole and lowered himself. Bethany handed him the flashlight. "Come down and see this!" he called to her. "Slide your legs over, and I'll help you down, Miss Bethany."

Bethany hesitated. "Are there spider webs down there?"

"There were, but I think I've got them all cleared out. You have to see this."

Bethany slid her legs inside the hole. She held on to the brick above until her feet touched the ground and Walter told her to let go. Crouching down inside the hole was necessary, and because of the five-foot ceiling height, neither of them could stand erect. Walter shined his flashlight around the six-foot-by-eight-foot room, illuminating straw lining parts of the floor. He reached for Bethany's hand and guided her to the back corner where a spider web hit across her face.

"Ew." She let go of Walter and slapped away the webs from her face and head. They stuck to her hands, and she slapped them against her newly bought jeans.

"Sorry about that, Miss Bethany. Thought I got them all." Walter's flashlight lit up an item in the corner of the dirt floor.

"What are those chains for?" Bethany asked.

"Those are slave shackles, Miss Bethany."

Her hand flew to her mouth. Walter picked up the chains, and they clinked against the attached dark-metal braces. "Hadn't told you," Walter said. "But I found two other sets in the carriage house. Didn't want to alarm you."

Bethany's stomach rushed a sickening bile up into her throat.

"Let's go back up into the light, Miss Bethany. It's damp and stinks down here. I've got allergies." Walter put his hands together to give her a boost, and she pushed off his hands with her foot. Pulling her body the rest of the way through the fireplace, she was careful not to knock her head against the bricks on top. After she slid her stomach and then legs out onto the floor above, Walter handed up the shackles. She pulled her hand back and hesitated to take the burnt metal in her hands. Laying the clinking chains on the living room floor, she turned to see Walter pull himself up and through the fireplace opening. Their hands were blackened, as well as their shirts, pants, and shoes. Putting her hands in the bucket of water she planned to use to wash the floors, she looked down and slid off her muddied sneakers. Walter followed her lead and took off his boots.

"Might have been some kind of hideaway," he said. "I'll hose my boots off outside."

Bethany's eyes riveted on the shackles—an ugly reminder of America's past. "This is why I didn't want to start this journey. Someone was held captive down there?" she asked.

"Don't think so. Looks like a safehouse," he said. Walter left her alone in the living room with the horrific find. And when he came back inside wearing clean boots, behind him walked Peter.

"I was about to say good day, but are you alright?" Peter looked at Bethany in her sock feet and dirty clothes.

"We found these in a hidden basement there." Bethany pointed to the exposed hole inside the fireplace.

Peter picked the chains up from the floor. The clinking sound made Bethany hug both of her arms. Her neck and shoulders tensed, and she pulled them up toward her ears.

Clink. Clink. Bethany turned away from the objects in Peter's hands. "Seen some just like these in the town's museum," Peter said as he laid the chains back on the floor. The metal braces clinked against a chain.

"I looked forward to your visit today," Bethany said, "because I wanted to know more about my mother and the Knowles family. Now, I'm not sure what I might find out."

"Bethany, let's not jump to conclusions." Peter touched her elbow. "Since these were underground, your family must have hidden someone to protect them. Virginia was the largest slave-owning state."

"Ugh," Bethany gasped.

"Walter found two more sets in the carriage house," she said.

Peter turned to look at Walter, who nodded his head yes.

"And my first day here I also found a journal inside the Timekeeper. I already read an entry by Katherine Knowles Davis, the first owner of the home." Peter's eyes opened wide in surprise. "She seemed so sweet and godly." Bethany stood in the living room, shaking her head side to side.

"The person you need to talk to is Agnes Adams," Peter said. "She's the unofficial town historian."

"Where can I find her?"

"She runs the museum and specializes in genealogy too. Looks for things to do. Though she's eighty-six, she's spry as a seventy-year-old. But her husband is ninety-two and not in good health." Peter reached into his jacket pocket and pulled out a notecard. He wrote Agnes's name and phone number and gave it to Bethany. "Give her a call and go meet with her. She's the best person to tell you about your ancestors. If she doesn't know your family's history, no one will."

Peter drove back to town, thinking once again he didn't accomplish the conversation Marguerite asked him to deliver. But seeing Bethany's face when she looked at those chains told him she'd had enough shock for one day. The dark secret about her birth would need to remain hidden for now.

. . . and the Timekeeper chimed two.

CHAPTER 14

On Maple Street, one block north of Harbor Street, Agnes Adam's Cape Cod home had two upper front windows and a low, white wooden fence and gate in front. Holding a small box of cookies Peter suggested she bring to repay Agnes, Bethany rang the doorbell.

"Welcome, child." Agnes offered Bethany a place on the couch while she took a seat in a wing-back chair next to her. Her tabby cat, Penelope, scurried out of the room as they entered. As an eighty-six-year-old, Agnes looked a good ten years younger. After initial pleasantries, Bethany got to the point of her visit.

"Do you know about my family and any slaves?" Bethany flinched as she said the words.

"Oh, my child. I see it on your face." Agnes reached out and patted Bethany's hand. "Your family did not own slaves. Your great-great-great-grandfather employed workers. He owned the gristmill and the town newspaper, the *Jameson Gazette*." Bethany sank back into the couch filled with more pillows than space to sit.

"The gristmill closed many years ago," Agnes said. "The newspaper still exists but is under new ownership now. Several generations of your family members wrote stories for it. Besides your biological mother, you come from a long line of writers. Child, writing is in your blood."

"But we found shackles in a hidden basement under the fireplace."

Agnes's eyes looked upward. "Don't recall knowing the exact location of a hidden room, but I knew about its existence. Your great-great-great-grandmother, Katherine Knowles Davis, was part of the Underground Railroad."

Bethany sat up on the edge of the couch as Agnes continued.

"At much peril to her and the family's wellbeing, Katherine helped enslaved people escape north."

Katherine, the rescuer not the imprisoner. This better fit the journal entry, Bethany thought.

"Let me tell you a story as best I remember it. I know it because Katherine's granddaughter wrote a story about her grandmother, Katherine, for a celebratory newspaper edition. I believe her name was Elizabeth . . . or was it Anna? I'm not sure. It featured prominent townspeople and their accomplishments. Katherine hadn't shared her story earlier because it took many years after the Civil War before townsfolk felt comfortable telling things outside their family."

Bethany sat in silence on the couch and waited intently for Agnes to continue. "In 1859 before the Civil War broke out, Katherine's husband, William, traveled to England to escort his mother. It wasn't safe for women to travel alone on ships back then. Food was scarce and bad things happened to women on ships without a male companion." Agnes's chin went toward her chest as she looked over the top of her eyeglasses at Bethany, who nodded in acknowledgment. Agnes needed not explain more.

"While William was away, Katherine, along with a crew of workers, oversaw the family's gristmill and town newspaper. She drove the wagon herself, at times, to ship milled flour and newspapers on the Rappahannock River and up the Chesapeake. On one particular evening, she hid a runaway slave inside her wagon."

Bethany leaned forward, hanging on Agnes's every word like a young child at story hour being read to by the town librarian. "It was a moonless night. If possible, the conductors—that was the term for Underground Railroad guides—waited for moonless nights to move the slaves to the boats at the mouth of the river by the Chesapeake Bay. Along the way, Katherine's wagon got stopped by slave hunters."

In her mind, Bethany could see the wagon and Katherine holding the horse's reins.

"'You happena see a runaway slave on your way tonight?'" Agnes yelled, impersonating a man's voice.

Bethany jumped, and her hand knocked the box of cookies to the floor. She retrieved the unopened box and sat it on the coffee table.

"She was not the only slave Katherine helped, but she's the one I know about because of the newspaper story her granddaughter wrote many years later. I've got it at the museum. Would you like a copy?"

"I'd love that," she said before getting to the purpose of her visit. "Do you know who my father is?"

"Child," Agnes said, looking at her, "some secrets can't be told. They must be discovered."

A bell rang upstairs. "Oh, my. That's Arthur. I must have startled him when I got carried away with the story. Sorry to end our visit, but I need to help him to the bathroom. Would you mind showing yourself out?"

Bethany walked out through the white gate and down the sidewalk to her car. Although learning more about her ancestor, Katherine, and feeling lighter than when she arrived, she still had unanswered questions and did not learn anything about her father. Peter said Agnes was friends with Bethany's grandmother, so she planned to schedule another visit soon.

Since arriving in town, Bethany had met many people and learned many things, but the further she got into her story, the more confused she became. Here in Jameson, the self-assured Bethany did not feel in control. She wondered how she had left the Bethany she knew behind. For once, she wanted to reverse course and go back in time to retrieve that confident woman. Because in Jameson, as she uncovered more clues to her past, she uncharacteristically found herself wanting help.

Tonight, she would read another entry in the journal and learn more about this Knowles family—her family. She hoped Katherine's daughter continued the journal as requested and might shed light on the latest discovery, the hidden basement and slave shackles. But it wasn't Katherine's daughter who wrote the newspaper story. It was her granddaughter. Bethany wondered if Katherine may have shared the story years earlier with her daughter. If so, maybe this journal entry would provide more details.

CHAPTER 15

Abigail Knowles Davis Johnson
Born 1865
Jameson, Virginia

Mother said I was born on Emancipation Day. Virginia's Emancipation Day, that is, April 3, 1865. President Lincoln issued the Emancipation Proclamation on January 1, 1863. But not until Union troops entered Richmond, the capital of the Confederacy, on April 3, 1865, did all Virginians experience freedom.

My mother told me about this Virginian celebration day. I also read old stories in our family newspaper about how enslaved people hugged Union troops that day and thanked them for their freedom.

Since a very young age, I always felt my birthday a particularly unique celebration time for my family. As I got older and my mother shared stories with me, I realized my family celebrated not just my birth on April 3. They and others celebrated the rebirth of thousands of souls held captive by their fellow man.

Mother and father rejoiced over all our birthdays, but mine seemed to be the one when their hearts lifted the most. I knew I was not more special than my younger brothers. The day itself marked a special date to my parents and an extra special day to my mother. She told me my April 3 birthdate marked the fact I was called to set people free. As an adult, I took on this badge of honor to care for those less fortunate.

Years after the Civil War, in spite of the government's best efforts, the South still struggled to rebuild. Southern resentment from the War's loss long lingered. I grew up in this era after the Civil War. All in Vir-

ginia suffered, and some much more than others. Disparities abounded long after the cannons silenced.

With several lady friends in town, we formed the Jameson Aid Society. As our largest money raisers, our bake sales allowed us to bring supplies to those most in need, and we did what we could to help. The needs being so large, we could not take care of all but still, we pressed forward. We rejoiced in small victories, like seeing beaming smiles on children's faces and hearing gleeful giggles when we brought them a pair of already well-worn shoes.

It was on one of these mornings after I brought essentials to children in need that something spooked my horses and sent them off the road. In the commotion, my arm struck against a tree and got injured. I could not hold the reins with two hands and reorient the horses to free the wagon wheels from the mud. A kind man and young boy came walking along and got me back on the road. He showed great concern and insisted he drive the wagon and me home. To repay his kindness, I fed him and his son lunch. Afterward, he asked if there were any odd jobs he could perform at the barn or on the property. I could tell by the way he and the boy gulped the lunch, he was in need. Of course, we always had things to do at Lily Fields, and I gave him a list with the promise to pay him at the end of the day. When all the tasks were finished right before supper, I paid him gladly.

Days later, I learned from church lady friends that this same man was arrested and accused of assaulting a woman at lunchtime, the same day he helped me with my wagon. I knew it could not be him because he was with me that morning and into the late afternoon. I testified to this fact, and in the end, the man was freed, but my relationships in town numbered fewer. In some people's eyes, I crossed the line and should have left things alone, but in my heart, I knew the good Lord did not give us eyes to see and mouths to speak only for those like us. We are called to a greater purpose.

Though there remains much more still to do, it's time for others to take on this new challenge. The Great Depression has no regard for state boundaries or economic stature. We are all God's children and are in this current fight together.

Though my bones are stiff and my body fails, I rejoice for my years spent here. With gratitude, I celebrate that my birthdate still harkens others to speak for those without a voice.

My prayer, dearest daughter, is for you, and more daughters to come, to answer the silent call.

With love and a celebratory heart,
Abigail Knowles Davis Johnson
Daughter, Wife, Mother, & Devoted Sister to All in Need

CHAPTER 16

"I'm taking my boat out. Are you free this evening for a short sunset cruise?" Peter texted. "I need some stress relief, and you can tell me about your visit with Agnes."

Since she was only five minutes from the marina in town, Peter picked Bethany up at her house. Clouds formed in the distance, but the sky was blue over Jameson. To Bethany, the skies looked different here. There were no tall buildings to break up the expansive view that reached for miles.

"I checked the weather report," Peter said as he drove them to the marina. "We're good well into the evening before any rain comes. We won't be out late. I have to work tomorrow, and know you do too."

Despite Peter telling her not to bring anything, Bethany brought a bottle of wine and was relieved to hear Peter liked red because it was the only kind she drank. She never developed a taste for white wine; she preferred her wines dark and dry.

Following Peter down the wooden dock to his sailboat named *The Waymaker*, she said, "Nice boat. How big is it?"

"Thirty feet," he answered, holding out his hand for her to join him on the boat. She stepped aboard wearing her new sneakers.

"I should have asked. Have you sailed before?"

"I've been on Baxter's boat. He's my client. And I've been on his dad's yacht, too, but they're not sailboats.

He motioned for her to take a seat. "You're in for a treat. Nothing like letting the wind be your guide."

Bethany didn't know anything about the wind. She was used to motors and getting places when she wanted. It was her first time on a sailboat—and her first time depending upon the wind.

"As the captain here . . . hu-hum," he started, clearing his throat, "let me go over a few sailing terms to get you acquainted." He pointed to the horizontal center pole wrapped in canvas. "This is the boom. You'll want to watch out as it could take you overboard if you're not watching."

Bethany threw her head back. She was not looking for that much adventure. "Don't worry. I'm here to look out for you." Peter pointed to the left side of the boat. "This is port side. If you need help remembering it, think of *port* and *left*. They both have four letters. The right side is called starboard," he informed. "And the front of the boat is called—"

"I know that one. It's the bow!" Bethany jumped in, excited by her tiny bit of knowledge in this sport.

"You got it. And the back is—"

"The stern," she finished. "Being around Baxter all these years at least taught me something about boating," she said with pride.

"I'm going to motor out and then put up the sails," Peter said. "You're my guest so enjoy yourself. I often handle this by myself."

She had only seen the Rappahannock the morning after she arrived in town, but that was from the shore. Tonight, she looked forward to an evening on the water where her great-great-great-grandmother shipped her goods and once helped a slave to freedom.

Watching Peter untie the lines from the dock, Bethany was captivated by his good looks. *How did he manage to stay single after his divorce?* He was easy to be with and outgoing without being overbearing.

After they exited Carter's Creek and reached the Rappahannock River, Peter left the helm and said, "I've put it on autopilot while I put up the sails."

As the boat pointed into the wind, she saw the mainsail unfurl and the wind catch hold. Looking up at the white cloth against the backdrop of a deep blue sky, Bethany marveled at the sight. Then Peter put up the jib sail.

"Would you like some of your wine?" he asked when he finished his work. "I won't drink any since I'm sailing and also driving later."

"Oh, I didn't think of that." She frowned. "Water will be fine for me," she said.

Peter stood at the helm. They sailed the Rappahannock River toward the Robert Norris Bridge and the Chesapeake Bay. Here, the river was about two miles wide and gave them an expansive view. Peter's sailboat had plenty of clearance to pass under the bridge's 110-foot center span.

"Great place to find fossils," Peter said, pointing to the shoreline. But Bethany didn't show interest in stopping to search for signs of dead things inside of rocks.

In the summer, there wasn't generally a lot of wind, but there was enough to keep them going at a good pace. The boat glided through the water, and she heard not a sound other than an occasional clink of something attached to a sail. She was not accustomed to silence. And without a motor driving them, she was surprised they were getting somewhere. And it seemed effortless as the wind passed through the channel between the mainsail and jib sail. Depending on the wind did not seem strange after all. She sat back in her seat and her breath and heartbeat slowed.

As they passed houses along the way, they saw docks with oyster floats tied alongside. She smiled as she spotted an otter use one as a table for his picnic lunch. Once moving steadily on the water, their conversation flowed from one subject to the next.

"Tell me about your work," Peter asked. With one hand on the helm, he took a drink of his bottled water with the other.

"I started my agency a couple of years out of college," Bethany said as she turned the ice-cold bottle in her hands. "We represent major brands, mostly in the beauty industry. My good friend, Baxter, asked for my help. He used money his father gave him to buy a cosmetics company and needed a good advertising agency. Although I worked for one, Baxter wanted my time exclusively."

Of Bethany's major clients, Peter recognized a shampoo brand and a successful line of skin lotions sold in drug stores and supermarkets.

"We're best known within the beauty industry, but we do other products too. My VP, Scott, and I are working to add more clients, but it's not easy to balance out millions of dollars overnight. Baxter's brands represent fifty percent of our revenues."

"More clients and a balanced book of business is a smart thing. You know how the saying goes . . . too many eggs in one basket." The sailboat glided through the water past a ski boat, pulling someone behind. As the other boat rushed past their slower-moving vessel, the other captain waved hello.

"Look, a bald eagle." Peter pointed toward the sky.

"Oh, wow. That's cool," she said.

"We see them all the time here, but it never gets old for me."

Bethany watched for a few moments before continuing with her explanation. "I know we have to diversify more, but we're safe with Baxter. I've known him forever. He's like a brother to me. It takes months to get new clients, and once onboard, they take up more of my time. Every second counts, you know," she said as Peter's eyes held her gaze.

She recognized that look because she had seen it before from men. Just talking about business, she hadn't said anything to lead him on, but the look she saw on Peter's face, on any man's face, usually led to heartache—for the man, not her. *Time to get the attention off me and onto him*, she thought.

"How can you keep a good law practice going in Jameson?" Bethany asked.

Peter stood at the helm and watched ahead at another approaching boat. "We're a little over an hour from the edge of Richmond. Close enough to attract wealthy Richmond families who want someone outside the city to handle their confidential matters. Plus, more and more wealthy families in D.C., Baltimore, and Richmond are buying properties in Jameson as second homes or for retirement."

Bethany nodded her head in agreement. She remembered her drives to town with brand-new homes disguised to look old, interspersed between historic homes and barns.

"You've got a nice website," she told him with a smile as she recalled checking out his photograph online. One of the best local advertising tools is a great sign. You've got that too."

A few blocks from the café and across from the town's central park and gazebo, Peter's office had cars and pedestrians passing it every day. "Your office building is very distinctive, taller roofline than the rest and carvings over the windows," she remarked.

Peter got them each another bottle of water out of the cooler and offered her a selection of finger foods from a tray he had wrapped inside. Bethany took cheese, salami, and olives and grabbed a handful of crackers from a box he handed to her.

As the sun lowered in the sky, the clouds swirled beside it like strokes from a painter's brush. The heat of the day released its hold on the air, and the height of the rays above the trees on shore alerted Bethany that only a half hour of sunlight remained. She turned the conversation to the subject Peter called about, her visit with Agnes, and he delighted in hearing about her family being part of the Underground Railroad.

"It was very brave of them to risk their business and their safety as well," he said. "Back in those days, they not only risked their reputations but a good sum of money too. Helping a slave brought a thousand dollar fine—about thirty thousand dollars in today's money. Plus, a person who helped a slave was put in jail for six months," Peter informed.

Bethany gasped. "I had no idea. I don't recall learning that in school."

"Not a surprise your thrice great-grandmother kept her work with the Underground Railroad secret for so long. No telling how other townsfolk would treat her and the family knowing what she did, even years later. Lines were clearly drawn back then." Peter's insights gave Bethany even more reason to feel proud of Katherine Knowles Davis.

He took a seat beside her to watch in silence as the sun fell below the horizon. After what appeared to be its final act, nature continued putting on a display. Even after the sun disappeared below the horizon, the show was not finished. The sky took on an array of colors, including several shades of orange and later swirls of pink.

Bethany watched the sky for a few more moments and got back to her story. "I hoped Agnes could also tell me about my father, but Arthur woke up. I've got another way to possibly find answers because I sent in a DNA kit before I left Alexandria, but the results take weeks."

"We best get back," Peter said.

Bethany noticed an unease about him all of a sudden. She knew he had to work tomorrow, and maybe legal matters were on his mind.

For a quicker ride back, Peter took down the sails and used the motor to return to the marina. He seemed in a rush for something. Back at the dock, he secured the lines to the cleats at his boat's slip before placing the cooler on the dock and helping her out.

When they arrived at Lily Fields, he parked his car in her driveway by the front walkway. "I know it's late for a weeknight, but I hoped to talk to you about something. Any chance we could chat on your front porch?"

Bethany was wide awake and did not have to wake up early tomorrow. "Sure. Let me go inside and turn on the porch light." She returned with her bottle of wine along with a corkscrew and two glasses in her hands. We can open this if you're okay with having a glass?"

Peter opened the wine and poured them each a glass, making his only half full.

Holding hers up to his, she offered a toast with a smile. "To Jameson sunsets," she said.

They clinked glasses together. He sat his down without taking a drink. "Bethany," Peter said with a strange tone she had not heard from him before. His face fell and his eyes saddened.

"What? What's wrong, Peter?" Bethany reached out and touched his hand.

"There's something important I have to share with you. I planned to tell you on the boat, but it was such a nice evening with you out there."

"What is it?" Her voice sweetened to coax him to share.

With his free hand, Peter twirled the stem of his wine glass. "That DNA test you mentioned . . . well, that might be your best chance to find your father. Because although friends with your grandmother, Agnes knows nothing." He moved his eyes up from the porch table and on to hers. "Marguerite did not return to Jameson while pregnant."

Bethany's chin lowered toward her chest, and she squinted for clarity.

"She hid the pregnancy from her parents," Peter said.

Crimping her face in disbelief, she asked, "What?"

Peter looked down at the table before reconnecting with her eyes. "She told her parents she needed to stay at school in Chicago over the summer to work on a project with one of her professors. Weeks later, she called and told them she changed her mind about graduate school in Chicago. She was moving to California for the possibility of a job instead."

Peter took a drink of his wine before he continued. Bethany's remained on the table.

"Her favorite professor was relocating there and said her moving there too would be most beneficial. His connections near Los Angeles could help propel her career."

Bethany understood how much connections mattered. Her friendship with Baxter proved a case in point. *Why was Peter struggling to tell me about this?*

"Your mother asked me to share something with you." He paused, which only made Bethany's heart rate quicken more. "I haven't told you yet because I knew you needed space to absorb the initial news about Marguerite and get settled in Jameson."

"What?" She flipped her hand over in the air, giving permission and urging him to get it out. Peter's speed was slower than Bethany's. He didn't know her well enough to understand she preferred people get to the point.

"As soon as you arrived, you were occupied with house projects, and then when I came by to talk to you, you found the hidden basement. The timing wasn't appropriate." Peter looked down at his wine glass clenched between his hand. And tonight, on the boat . . . it seemed out of place to tell you in the splendor of that sunset."

The slow build drove Bethany nuts. She wanted him to get it out. And taking her hand off his, she twirled her fingers in the air, signaling him to finish. She sat straighter in her chair and waited to hear the message from her mother.

Peter cleared his throat. "As I said, your mother got pregnant in Chicago, and your father was from a prominent family there. Marguerite's boyfriend got nervous about the pregnancy, and he told his father." Peter looked down. He grabbed the edge of the metal porch table and pinched it between his fingers. "Her boyfriend's father made it clear to his son that the situation, uncorrected, meant a wrecked future." Peter's sad puppy eyes met Bethany's and pleaded for relief, but she provided him none because she didn't know where he was headed.

"Marguerite's boyfriend told her he didn't love her," Peter said. "And that news crushed her." Peter paused and took a drink of his wine, emptying his glass. "The boyfriend told Marguerite his father said to handle the matter with haste."

Bethany stared at him as if in a trance and didn't move.

Peter cleared his throat and hesitated once again. He looked down at the patio floorboards before he looked up at Bethany. "Marguerite's boyfriend drove her to a clinic near the college. He wanted her to get an abortion."

Bethany's head fell as if it had been chopped off.

Peter's eyes begged her for forgiveness. He reached across the table for her hand. "I'm so sorry to be the bearer of this awful story. Marguerite wanted you to know this and more." Bethany pulled her hand away and looked out onto the dark front yard. Peter waited for the news to settle and for her to speak.

"Go on," she said with deadness in her eyes.

"Marguerite went inside the clinic alone and stayed a few hours before meeting her boyfriend afterward. When she got in his car, she said she cried uncontrollably and never told him she didn't go through with the abortion. He drove her back to her dorm and dropped her off. They never spoke again—ever."

Bethany slouched in the patio chair and shook her head side to side. Her innards felt empty, carved out by the revelation. "How awful for her."

Peter nodded in agreement. "Your mother wanted you to know what happened."

The word *mother* hung in the air. Bethany heard Peter refer to Marguerite many times as "your mother," but Bethany always referenced her by her first name. Now, she knew Marguerite, as she called her, had held firm against incredible pressure. And although Bethany never met her, she now knew her mother exuded strength.

Bethany's mind caught up with her emotions. "Wait. If she chose to deliver me, why did she give me up for adoption? Was I too much a burden for her career?"

"Last thing on her mind. She said she gave you up in a private adoption to keep your birth hidden."

"Hidden?" Bethany's eyes pinched together, not understanding him.

"Hidden from her boyfriend and from his family. Your mother said she left Chicago and never returned. Peter moved his head to reengage Bethany's downturned face and eyes. "Even once there, she knew it would be impossible to keep your existence concealed long-term. Only Marguerite knew you had been born. Once her pregnancy was showing, her parents didn't see her until after your birth because she didn't want to crush them. Marguerite said they expected better of her."

Bethany's lip quivered and Peter reached across the table. Placing his hand on hers, he said, "I hope you forgive me for not telling you sooner. Along with the news of the inheritance and knowing your biological mother passed, I thought it enough for anyone to absorb."

Bethany shook her head in agreement. Sounds of thunder rolled in from a distance. "I need time to think. I left work to come here to learn about my family and find my father." She removed her hand from his to take a drink of wine.

Looking at her with heartfelt care, Peter reached out his hand again and placed it on top of hers. Though she let him keep it there, she gave him no sign of openness to more comfort than that.

"Anything else?" she asked. "His name?"

"That's all I know. Marguerite never shared the name. I'm sorry I can't help you more."

Bethany's body sat on the porch, but her mind was elsewhere. After a while of her sitting across from him in silence, Peter rose from his chair. He leaned over and gave Bethany a soft, distanced hug while her arms remained flat against her sides.

"It's late. Best you get going," she said, staring out at the darkness. Peter obliged and left her alone on the porch.

After Peter's car left the driveway, she readied for bed and washed off her makeup. But her war paint had done her no good tonight; it provided no protection from learning about the long-ago battle formed against her.

Once she was in bed, it started to rain. "Perfect timing!" she yelled to the ceiling and pounded her fists on the sheets. She hated rain. It stole her adoptive father and robbed her and him of precious time together.

Like she did that night when she was eleven, Bethany brought her legs up to her chest and as her eyes swelled, they released like the clouds that could hold no more. As the booms of thunder continued, she wondered if she dared meet her father.

. . . and the Timekeeper chimed three.

CHAPTER 17

Steaming hot water from the shower washed away dry, crusted tears from her cheeks. She thought about two men in her life who left her for different reasons. One who loved her and got taken away too soon, and the other who, from the start, didn't want her to be born.

A mix of water and fresh salty tears streaked down her face. The bar of soap fell out of her hand, and she struggled to reach it in the small, narrow space. *I need to talk to Walter about remodeling both bathrooms. That will help the house sell faster.*

With the purpose of reclaiming the cherished spot, Bethany made a cup of coffee and took it to the front porch. She wanted to think of something good, but a robin's stare reminded her she forgot to buy birdseed. Nature provided plenty for the birds, but from its perch, the robin's eyes seemed to implore Bethany to feed it. *Marguerite must have kept the feeders full. They're used to it.* Coming back outside may not have been such a good idea after all. She needed consoling, so she video called Mitzi.

After she heard the story, Mitzi's visage went from sadness to a "cheer up your best friend face" in zero to sixty seconds. "Oh, girlfriend. Sorry about your father. Love your awesome biological mother though. So strong to do that all alone."

"Mitzi," Bethany said as she pulled the cell phone closer for emphasis. "Remember, Marguerite *knew* how to find me all these years."

Mitzi shook her head. "I can't imagine how she kept from reaching out to you as an adult."

"When I was young, she committed not to, and when I was older, Peter told me she didn't want to interfere in my life. She wanted me to find *her*. I feel so guilty." Bethany's hands flew out and almost knocked over her coffee. "Can you imagine my mom worrying about Marguerite showing up at our house?"

As soon as the words came out of Bethany's mouth, she remembered the carved wooden butterfly necklace. She had brought the silver box with her to Jameson. *Why did my mother give me up but wanted me to have that butterfly?*

In Costa Rica, another factory girl disappeared.

CHAPTER 18

Nick DeLeon had texted her yesterday. As promised, his crew arrived at 9:00 a.m., right on time. From her perch on the front porch, she watched his crew unload their truck and begin the landscape bed clean up. By 10:30, they had made significant progress and set out pots of roses and lilies beside their truck, ready to be planted.

A vehicle's tires crunched on the gravel as it pulled into the driveway. Bethany looked up from her computer and saw Nick pulling a trailer with a green utility vehicle. *He must be here to supervise.* She put her head down and continued typing. *Click. Click. Click.*

"Nice office, *senorita*," Nick said after walking up her stairs uninvited. "Keeping an eye on my crew too?"

"I got tired of sitting inside. Looks like they will plant the flowers today," Bethany said, without looking up from her keyboard.

"How do you like the roses? Did I pick good ones for you?"

Click. Click. Click. Her fast clicks on the keyboard echoed against the high porch ceiling, and despite the intrusion, her eyes and mind stayed focused on her work. "Didn't notice," she said, still not looking up.

Bethany always lived in a condo or townhouse with an HOA and never bothered with plants. She liked it that way. Less details and decisions for her to make outside of work.

Nick walked down the steps. Although her face pointed at the keyboard, her eyes shifted to see what he was up to. With a careful look to avoid the thorns, he picked a velvety rose bud from a plant inside a black plastic container. "You're going to have your own roses now," he said with a smile and presented a rose to her. "Plenty to fill up a vase each week."

The flower, pressed inches beneath her nose and blocking the screen, gave her no choice but to glance up from her keyboard. The rose was scarlet crimson in color.

Nick pointed to a landscaped bed in the middle of the yard. "You want to keep those bird feeders?"

"I keep meaning to pick up seed," she said.

"Want me to take care of that for you?"

"I'll do it. Just need to make a note." Bethany focused on her keyboard. She didn't want to owe the landscaper any favors.

"Have you toured your property yet?"

"Too busy." *Click, click, click, click . . .*

Nick remained standing next to her as she typed away. "I looked up your property boundaries in county records. 167 acres. Long walk to see the whole thing. I've got a utility vehicle on my trailer. Want to take a ride and check out your land?"

Nick seemed determined to not let Bethany get work done. She had tried to check in with Scott this morning but didn't reach him and needed to call him back, plus emails remained in her in box. "I'm super busy right now," she said, remaining tuned in to her keyboard.

"Want to walk those 167 wooded acres all by yourself?"

Nick's six-two frame towered over her as she sat on the porch. His offer presented an opportunity to save her time. She stopped typing and thought for a second before answering. "Let me check in with Walter."

Getting up from her chair, she waited for him to step out of her way. At the front door, she turned around. "I'll be right back," she said.

Nick shifted his eyes away, but she caught him looking. She knew her toned backside and long legs looked good in skinny jeans, and she'd just provided him the best view.

"I'll unload the vehicle and meet you in the backyard." Nick jumped down the front steps, missing the bottom one.

When she climbed into the utility vehicle, a smile filled Nick's face as he looked down at her feet on the floorboard next to him. She had changed into her new sneakers.

At the back edge of the yard, they entered a partially overgrown trail. Bethany wondered where it led. This guy, Nick, seemed to have a plan, or at least, she hoped he did.

Driving along the potholed trail, Nick slowed down for him or her to push back a bush or tree branch that encroached on the once wider trail. He sped up when he could and didn't say much as he drove. Bethany's ponytail jostled, and she placed her hand on the dash for support as they went in and out of ruts along the trail, driving deeper into the acreage. When the tree-lined path cleared up ahead, he stopped the vehicle and turned off the engine.

"Check out your creek," Nick said, sprinting toward the water. "It's a beauty." With a wave of his hands, he coaxed her to exit the vehicle and join him by the water. Boulders protruded from the banks, and small stones lined the bottom, which spanned twenty-five feet wide.

"He leads me beside quiet waters. He refreshes my soul," Nick said.

Bethany turned her head toward him. "Your Shakespeare stumps me again."

"Not Shakespeare," he said with a surprised look on his face. "It's Psalm 23."

"Oh," she said.

Bethany went to church as a young child with her mother and father, but after her dad's accident, her mother didn't set foot in a church again. She never attended Sunday school and didn't know much about Bible sayings.

"He leads me in paths of righteousness for his name's sake." Nick circled his head and placed his eyes on all the beauty around him. "Did you know you owned a creek?" he asked as he bent down to pick up something.

"I crossed a creek coming from town and wondered if it went inside my property line."

He pointed to a small waterfall about five feet high, formed by alternating layers of stair-stepped boulders and flat rocks. Water flowed over the little falls. It didn't compare in grandeur to others she visited. *Doesn't matter*, she thought. *This waterfall is mine.*

"I knew you owned a creek," he said, looking at her with surprise. "Saw it on the property records. *Que linda es aqui*," he said in his native Spanish.

Bethany took a few years of high school and college Spanish. She understood he said this was a pretty spot.

"It sure is," she replied.

"You know Spanish?" Nick smiled.

"Enough to get by when I go to a Spanish-speaking country on business trips."

"We can practice if you want," he offered.

Bethany turned her head away and let the luring comment go unanswered.

The outdoor scene was quiet except for the slow movement of water and the faint sound of the waterfall.

"Ah . . ." Bethany took in a long, deep breath and released it. After watching the water for a few minutes, she saw it moved toward the south. *Does it connect to the Rappahannock River and then the Chesapeake Bay?* she wondered.

With a quick flick of his wrist, Nick skipped one rock on the water and then another.

"Here," he said as he held out a couple. "These are good, flat ones."

Bethany hadn't skipped rocks since she was eight. Back then, it took several tries to get the rocks to skip, but her dad's grin spurred her on. She hadn't recalled that childhood moment until now because thoughts of her dad were too painful. Therefore, she avoided looking back on memories, even happy ones.

"Here, take them," Nick said, reaching for her hand.

"She took the stones and gave one a flick with her wrist, but it fell flat into the water.

"Do it again. You almost had it," he said with encouragement.

Bethany threw another rock, and this one skipped twice on top of the water. She put her fist in the air to celebrate and then flicked the next one. It skipped three times.

"Yes!" she squealed like a young girl. Nick smiled at her glee before pointing up ahead.

"Let's walk to the waterfall." He motioned for her to go ahead of him.

That Southern gentleman thing again, she thought. She didn't like walking in front of men. She knew it gave them the best view, and she didn't want to give him another chance to watch her from behind.

"No, you go first," she said.

Bethany walked behind Nick and stayed back from the edge of the bank, keeping an eye on the uneven ground lined with boulders. A flock of birds on a tree above abruptly flew out and startled her. She tripped and fell backward, and the thud on the ground prompted Nick to turn around and look for her.

"*Dios, mio.* You alright?" he asked.

Before she could answer, she felt Nick's muscular arms pull her up off the dirt.

"Are you hurt anywhere?"

"The birds startled me," she said.

"No matter the birds. Keep an eye out for snakes. Careful to watch your step by water. It attracts them."

"I was watching," Bethany said, perturbed by his comment. The birds startled me. That's all." Facing him, she defiantly patted dirt off the back of her jeans, careful to keep his eyes on her face and not on her backside.

When they reached the waterfall, Bethany took her phone from her front pocket and made a video of water spilling over boulders into the creek.

Buzzing from Nick's phone interrupted the serene moment, and his face fell. "My crews need their paychecks, and they're locked inside my truck."

When they exited the wooded trail by the carriage house, a silver convertible was parked in her driveway. *What's Amy doing here?*

"Stop! Stop!" she yelled. And as soon as the utility vehicle slowed enough, she swung her legs and jumped out, waving goodbye to her ride.

Sprinting toward the car, she looked in a window, but no one was inside. Amy, and maybe Baxter, must be in the house. *Why did they come without calling?*

CHAPTER 19

While Walter worked on a sticking window, Amy chatted with him from a living room chair. "Hi. Hope you don't mind me popping in," Amy said, spotting her in the doorway. "I went for a ride, and next thing I knew I was heading to Jameson."

Bethany came to hug her. "Always happy to see you, Amy."

"Can't stay long. Left the dogs at home with the cleaning lady. Wanted to come see you and the house."

"I'm glad you did," Bethany said. "Nice surprise. I needed it."

"The whole place is exquisite. Walter told me everything he's fixed. My little hummingbird friend is hard at work down here too. I see the possibilities in this house, and the grounds are beautiful. Love the roses at the front porch."

"Haven't had a chance to notice. They just got planted this morning."

"This will be a great getaway for you," Amy said. "Took me two and a half hours from our condo in Arlington, and the drive cleared my head."

The girls left Walter to work in peace and took their conversation outside to the front porch. When they were midconversation about Amy's tennis team results, Walter opened the door. "Excuse me, Miss Bethany. My other customer called and postponed their work. I can start right away on those bathroom remodel projects."

Bethany clapped her hands in the air. Her four-week plan was in full gear. She was accustomed to getting her way, and sometimes, she just had to wait for it.

The two close friends caught up on life while sitting at the porch table where the night before she had enjoyed a bottle of wine with Peter. Enjoyed, that is, before Peter told her about her father. Now, Amy was here with her carefree outlook on life and wanted to chat, but Bethany didn't have time for chitchat. She needed to finish reading project updates but obliged her friend, who had driven over two hours to see her. And so, she told her what was new.

"Met a lot of people already," Bethany said. "Of course, you've heard about Peter."

"Is he single?"

"Divorced, no kids," Bethany replied. Amy's eyebrows raised.

"I also met a town historian, Agnes Adams. Very helpful. I went to see her after I made discoveries about the house. Oh! And I also found a journal inside the Timekeeper. That's the name of the grandfather clock."

"Who was that man who took you on a ride in the woods?"

"The landscape company owner . . . Nick. He's also a landscape architect. Saved me time from walking the hundred-something acres alone." Bethany pulled her phone out of her pocket and showed Amy the video of the waterfall.

"It looks so serene," Amy said.

"We heard no sounds except nature." Bethany breathed in deeply.

"What color are you going to paint the bathrooms?" Amy asked, changing the subject to one she loved to talk about.

Bethany knew Amy loved to decorate. For her part, she kept things simple. She didn't have time to decide between too many choices. She needed to pick out materials so Walter could get started. She looked at her watch and asked, "How's Baxter?"

"I'm sure he's working." Amy turned her head toward Walter inside the living room window, who was testing the operation he thought he'd fixed. It closed with a hard thud, but at least it now went up and down. Walter left from their view.

"You okay?" Bethany sensed something was off and reached her hand to touch Amy's.

"He's changed," Amy confessed, suddenly spilling personal information. You know I want to adopt, but Baxter told me he didn't want to raise another person's child." The words stung Bethany, but Amy showed no realization the effect her words had on her. Amy never had ill will, but she didn't always think before she spoke.

"His mind is always on business, more than ever before. This new company acquisition has made things worse." Amy's brow tightened.

Bethany took a drink from her cup. She did not want to be in the middle of her friends' relationship.

"Also, Baxter and I fight a lot. Do you think he's having an affair?" Amy asked.

The sip missed Bethany's mouth and coffee spilled on the table. "No way," she told Amy as she sat her cup down and dabbed the table with a napkin.

"Baxter's mind is focused on that Costa Rican factory. That's all," Bethany said assuredly. "It's his crown jewel. Saw it for myself. And speaking of Costa Rica, I've had something on my mind ever since I got back. There's another building at that factory, and I wandered into it. Strange goings on over there. I don't trust the plant manager."

"Why?" Amy asked.

"Too many young people working in there. I asked Baxter about child labor laws. He said the plant manager checks those things."

"He better. Baxter pays his people well," Amy said with an air of contempt.

"I know he keeps a close watch on the plant himself," Bethany said.

Amy mumbled something.

"I'm sorry. What did you say?" Bethany lowered her head to meet Amy's downturned face and eyes.

"That's not the only place he travels," Amy said. "It's like he doesn't want to be at home with me."

Bethany didn't want to get between her girlfriend and Baxter so she changed the subject. "What are you doing to stay busy?"

"The rummage sale and my charity foundation."

Bethany thought about the poor kids she saw outside the factory in Costa Rica. And then she recalled those eyes that locked on hers like a heat-seeking missile to a fighter jet's engine. "Amy, I saw a girl in that Costa Rican factory. Not only was she young, but I've never experienced anything like looking into that girl's eyes. They penetrated right though me. It's like she wanted to tell me something. More like scream it to me through her eyes."

"Scream what?"

"Don't know. There's poverty in that small town. She seemed angry or wanted to warn me, something like that." Bethany shook her head. "I don't know. Left me really shaken. Sad to see teenagers work in a factory to put food on the table." Across from her, Amy sat dressed for a country drive in her four-hundred-dollar workout outfit.

After retelling her Costa Rican experience, Bethany was more concerned than ever. She worried Baxter might get caught in a child labor issue and a PR nightmare. *The girls in that building looked too young.*

Amy began to tell Bethany about a tennis brunch last week, but Bethany held up her hand. "Sorry, Amy. Just a second." Bethany spoke into her phone, "Take a note: Call Michael Alexander. Have him check into Costa Rican labor laws." Bethany needed to look out for Baxter, her cherished friend and number-one client. His business was on the line, and with it, Amy's wellbeing too.

Taking Bethany's disinterested cue, Amy did not talk more about the tennis brunch. Instead, she got back to the point of her visit. "I don't know what to do about Baxter. His mind is always so far away."

"Give him time," Bethany reassured her. "This new company purchase will double his size. It's sucking up his energy. I know how hard Baxter works for his dad's approval."

Amy shook her head. "We both know that seems impossible to achieve."

Bethany agreed. She'd known Baxter's dad for years. He was a hard charger and tough on everyone around him, especially his son. It was Baxter's dream to be a billionaire like his father. And although his dad had a much bigger head start, she knew Baxter's quest to achieve his first billion dollars was a major milestone toward pleasing his much more successful father.

"Want to take a walk?" Bethany asked Amy. I haven't checked out my new flowers." She agreed and the girls walked down the porch steps and into the front yard.

"Jameson is like another world to me, Amy. I have time to think here. I'm still reading reports and giving ideas back to the team, but I feel I have a renewed focus."

An alarm went off on Amy's phone. "Sorry," she said, reaching down to turn it off. "I need to get on the road to feed my doggies."

Bethany watched as Amy put the top down on her convertible. *Baxter was about to double his company size. Perhaps he needed more help with the details so he could pay more attention to Amy.* Bethany intended to check into the Costa Rican factory. She owed it to Baxter. He was always there for her.

Sitting back on the porch, she called her attorney. "Michael, I need you to discreetly check on something for me."

"Of course, what can I do for you?" he asked.

"When I was in Costa Rica, I saw young workers in one of Baxter's factory buildings. It really troubled me, so I asked Baxter about it. He said the plant manager checked the ages to conform with the Costa Rican legal age of sixteen."

Michael agreed with Bethany that one bad news story was all that was needed to damage a brand and a company's sales and profits, but he reassured her.

"I'm sure Baxter's people are looking out for him," Michael said encouragingly.

Bethany was not satisfied. Those girls were too young. "I'd still like you to check out the labor laws for me. Discretely, of course."

"I'll reach out to a Costa Rican legal contact and let you know what I find out."

"The bigger Baxter's business gets, the bigger the target he becomes," Bethany said. "The media loves a good story—a bad one especially. I've got to help keep an eye out for him."

She hung up with Michael and checked in with Scott. This unexpected inheritance forced Bethany to let him take the helm. Being pulled away to Jameson caused her to do what she would not have done otherwise. It was the rare time Scott got a chance to show what he could do by himself. Bethany always mapped, navigated, and piloted the company's course. Everyone else followed her lead. Soon, she would take back control. For now, she kept a careful watch on her business from afar. And being ever the multitasker, she checked into that Costa Rican factory too.

CHAPTER 20

One week had passed since Bethany first walked inside the door at Lily Fields. That day, she had no inkling Peter held a secret regarding the circumstances around her birth and adoption. But she didn't hold it against Marguerite for giving her up. She'd placed her with a loving couple, and for that, she was grateful.

Having never looked for her birth mother, Bethany felt guilty. She had wondered, at times, where she came from, but she didn't feel she needed more family. Her adoptive mother's illness required every spare moment of her time. And after her mother died, she focused even more on her work. It's what fueled her engine; her eyes fixed on growing and winning more business.

Taking a break from reading a project update, she glanced up from the kitchen table to spot a cardinal dunking its body and shaking the water off its wings. She smiled at the bird's bath routine. It reminded her she still needed seed, so she spoke a reminder into her phone. Perhaps it would have been better if she let Nick take care of it, but she didn't want any favors and have him think she owed him something in return.

Walter rang the bell before he used the key she'd provided him to let himself inside.

"Miss Bethany?" Walter called out from the hall.

"I'm in the kitchen," she answered as she read a report.

"These old houses are filled with old wiring and are an accident waiting to happen. I'm certain I'm going to need to call an electrician as soon as I open up a wall.

Bethany nodded her head without looking up from her reading.

"Remember to get the tile and bathroom fixtures if you want to stay on that schedule of yours," Walter said. "The plumbing showroom will have all you need." With no verbal acknowledgment from her, Walter shrugged his shoulders and left her in the kitchen to her work.

She assumed the plumbing store opened at ten o'clock, if not earlier. Envisioning that tiny shower ripped out of the blue bathroom, along with getting rid of the nasty 1960's bathtub in the pink one, she thought staying here for long weekends might be bearable.

Because it's the one she used, she asked Walter to remodel the blue bathroom first. While he worked there, she would use the pink one with the handheld shower.

Driving to town, she looked forward to choosing more modern fixtures but ones that complemented the historic house. Her simple plan included buying white tiles. It provided a blank canvas on which to add a touch of any color. In her bathroom, she would add accents of blue because her bedroom and fireplace were already that color. Being in advertising, she also knew the color blue represented water, sky, intuition, imagination, and freedom. And the expansive Jameson sky was a bluer blue than she'd ever seen.

At Finnigan's Plumbing Supply & Showroom, a nice woman named Yvonne helped her find all she needed: sinks, toilets, tiles, plumbing fixtures, and lighting. And before heading back to Lily Fields, she stopped at the hardware store for birdseed. *Crossed that one off my to-do list.*

On her way back to the house, her phone rang. "How are things with handsome Peter?" Mitzi gushed. "I checked out his picture on his website. If you don't want him, let me have him. That guy is hot."

"He's even better in person," Bethany answered. She liked Peter. He was easy to talk to and a pleasure to look at. He was educated, smart, and confident in a quiet way.

"You should see all the roses and lilies in my yard. The grass looks much better, and the landscape crews cleaned up all the garden beds."

"I thought that landscape dude told you he was too busy?"

"Landscape architect," Bethany corrected her. "He did, but next thing I knew, his crew showed up and started to work. He picked out the most beautiful roses for each side of the front porch steps. Oh, and I'm sending you a video of my creek and waterfall. Nick took me back there yesterday to see it on his landscape utility vehicle."

"Whoa, wait a minute," Mitzi said. "The same landscape company owner who was so busy but comes back a few days later, plants roses, and shows up with a utility vehicle so he could take you to see *your* creek?"

"Yep," Bethany answered with the confident tone of achieving the time savings she needed to check out her property without even having to ask for help.

"Earth to Bethany. I think this landscape guy likes you."

"Nah, he thinks I'm a hot mess. I move way faster than he does."

"What's he like?"

"Speaks Spanish. Nice looking. Great body. Really strong arms."

"What?"

"Birds startled me, and I tripped on a boulder. Fell right on my rear. He helped me up, and that's when I felt his arms."

"A so-called impromptu ride into the woods to see a waterfall. Well, that seals it! He likes you. Done. Over and out," Mitzi said with a chop at the end.

On the other end of the phone, Bethany smirked. Mitzi always had one thing on her mind and was wrong about this guy. He wasn't interested in her, and she wasn't interested in him. Bethany didn't date much and had no love interest to speak about for the past two years. Life was simpler that way. Whenever a man she didn't like showed her too much attention, she made sure she didn't reciprocate. Nick was simply completing her projects and making money while she was in town. He knew she might sell the house soon.

The rearview mirror reflected Bethany's bare face. Every morning she put on makeup but not today. Sitting at the kitchen table since dawn, she didn't realize she hadn't finished getting ready. And because Walter interrupted her work, she never looked in a mirror before leaving the house. "Oh, I'm so embarrassed," she told Mitzi. "I forgot to put my makeup on before I left the house."

"Give me a break. I'll take your makeup-less face over my painted one any day," Mitzi said.

"I could use some kind of a makeover. I haven't changed my hairstyle in forever, and I met a hairdresser in town. Her name is Sam, short for Samantha."

"I told you for years to get highlights."

"Sam said the same thing. I think she's good. Got a 'hip' style."

"Hey, did you find out anything about that heirloom necklace you found in the silver box, the one your mom kept hidden from you?"

"I don't know who to ask about it. Maybe it will come up in the journal. I read the first two entries so far. Along with her husband, William, a Katherine Knowles built the home. Her first daughter was named Abigail, and I think more first daughters are going to be sharing things as I read more. At least I think so. That's what Katherine asked. She wanted it passed forward to the next daughter and onward." Bethany turned the car onto Knowles Lane. "I'm hoping the next entry talks about the Underground Railroad."

"What? You've got to tell me about this," Mitzi exclaimed.

A call came in from Bethany's office. She had ignored an earlier interruption, but now Scott's number was calling in again. *It must be important.* "Got to get this other call. Call you later," she said. But by the time she got switched over, Scott was no longer on the line.

CHAPTER 21

When Bethany arrived home, Walter was in the living room fiddling with a window again. No doubt Amy's unexpected visit and conversation distracted him while he worked, and he tried a new approach to fix the centuries-old window. She went outside to call Scott.

Picking up her call on the first ring, he blurted out, "We lost Baxter's new company projects to another agency."

"What are you talking about, another agency?" Bethany sat up straight.

"Smith, Donnoly, Newsome Communications," Scott said.

"Agency gossip," Bethany said, dismissing him with a swat of her hand in the air. "Baxter promised us that work. Besides, his deal isn't public yet."

"The press release just came out on the business wire."

Bethany lunged forward and stood up. "We do Baxter's PR. We wrote that release." But she was shouting what Scott already knew. "I need to talk to Baxter. I'll clear this up." She clicked the phone off before Scott had a chance to speak.

As Bethany paced the porch floorboards, Baxter didn't pick up, so she left a message. After an hour, she called, and again, there was no answer. Irritated, she texted him to call her.

When she was about to drive to Alexandria to confront him in person, her phone rang. She didn't waste time on social pleasantries. "Baxter, Scott told me something crazy. There's this gossip going around that you're working with Smith, Donnoly, Newsome."

"It's true," he said. "I decided to try them out."

Air stopped entering Bethany's lungs. "What? Why?"

"Time to get fresh insights. I signed a contract, giving all the work on the new company's brand to them."

The words *all* and *contract* struck Bethany like a speeding car she didn't see coming. Her B.R. Miller Advertising business plan included a doubling in revenue. She even went to the bank to get her credit line increased. And after giving Scott the okay, he had hired four new people to get them up to speed for when the projects started coming in.

Veins popped in Bethany's makeup-less forehead. "Baxter, you promised us that work and commissions for millions of dollars of ad placements. We are counting on it."

"Chill out, Bethany. There's plenty of other work for you and Scott. He's doing a great job, by the way. We're working well together."

Bethany's best friend of twenty years had stabbed her in the back, and the whole industry saw him thrust the knife. "This can't be happening," Bethany said.

"Don't worry, Bethany. My other brands are growing, and you and Scott will get plenty of work. We've got a contract on that. By the way, Amy told me all about her visit and chat. Sounds like the house and property are coming along. Got to go. Make every second count." With that quip, using her own expression, he hung up the phone.

Bethany's cell phone dropped from her hand onto the porch table. Her eyes stared ahead, but she saw nothing—no trees, no bird feeders, and no flowers. Her head fell over toward her waist. As she raised it, words came up from her gut, and she screamed, "How could you?" Inseparable in life and business, she, Baxter, and Amy made up the three musketeers. All for one and one for all. That is, *until now.*

Walter flew out the front door. "You alright, Miss Bethany?" he asked with utter concern.

She motioned for him to go back inside. "Just some bad business news." Sitting on the porch chair, the shock from Baxter's reversal set in. She took a moment before she called Scott.

"Makes no sense," Scott said. I met with Baxter at his office two days ago and everything seemed fine. He told me our contracts for the new projects were coming any day now. So I put Michael on alert to be ready to turn them around fast."

Bethany's palm stroked the sides of her face. "What are we going to do about the new hires?"

"We've got to win other new business," Scott said. As always, he was Bethany's calming aid. "I met with two prospective clients last week. One looks promising," he said. Since Scott knew about the other agency sooner than Bethany, he had more time to let the news sink in and regain his footing.

Remembering Baxter's words to her, Scott's positivity did little to assuage her upset. The initial shock wore off, and now, she was angry. Her fist flew in the air and landed on the table, popping her computer onto the porch floor. When she picked it up, dents and scratches marked the laptop's cover.

The rest of the day, she watched Walter rip out bathroom walls. *Why is it men love to demo?* she wondered, then asked him to let her have a swing. Although the sledgehammer was heavy in her hands, after the feeling she got from the first swing, she swung it again and again. Bethany now understood why men loved putting sledgehammers through walls. After her call with Baxter, driving a sledgehammer through a wall felt good to her too.

CHAPTER 22

A glass of wine before bed last night had helped her sleep through all of the Timekeeper's chimes. She checked her phone. Michael Alexander planned to video conference her at eight o'clock with an update on her Costa Rican inquiry. She quicky showered and dressed.

"Baxter is correct," Michael told her. "The legal working age is indeed sixteen years of age, and these younger employees can work up to thirty-six hours a week. And from what I learned from my contact, looks like the factory is within the law. I'm told it has a good reputation."

"Thanks for checking into it for me. Oh, and for Baxter," she said, looking from the kitchen out into the backyard. Although still angry and hurt from Baxter's double-cross, he was still her number-one client. Bethany was skilled at balancing conflicts and knew Baxter expected her to take good care of the other business he gave her. She had to move on, or at least make him think she did.

Seeing Michael's face on the screen in front of her made it hard not to be distracted by the scar in the corner of his upper lip. He held the phone too close, and she fixated on the scar as it moved up and down when he spoke. She wondered why he never had plastic surgery to fix it. He had plenty of money to get that taken care of by the best doctor.

"Don't spend any time worrying about Costa Rica," Michael reassured. "I am sure Baxter's people are looking out for him."

Bethany was grateful that he had looked into it, but she wished she could stop being troubled about what that girl tried to tell her. Even with Michael's reassurance, she couldn't shake the intuitive and unsettling feeling she got in that adjoining building.

Sitting at the kitchen table, she went back to work and lost herself as best she could in projects. An incoming text distracted her usual concentration.

"Free for dinner tomorrow? Pick you up at 6:30?" She read the text from Nick and wondered, *Is this a date?* Bethany didn't think she had given the landscaper any reason to think she liked him. She knew not to use her "power eyes" on him. They were the secret weapon she used when situations merited.

Who asks a girl on a date via text? That's a first, she thought. She didn't respond. *The guy could quote Shakespeare but didn't know how to extend a proper invitation. Do I even want to go? Maybe I do.* She had liked the feel of his muscles when he helped her up after she fell by the creek. Even so, she let him stew a bit.

Like a cat with a captured mouse, Bethany played with him. She was in charge, and he needed to know it. *Let's see if he's man enough to handle me.* Not many were. Bethany left several suitors stranded, watching her from a distance as she moved forward, forgetting they even existed.

Looking inside her closet, nothing seemed appropriate for a dinner date—even in Jameson. *What restaurant?* She only knew about the café. There must be other, nicer restaurants nearby. A casual black dress seemed the best option. She had so many at home in Alexandria but none here.

Her reflection in the dresser mirror caught her attention. She leaned in to look at her hair. Mitzi wanted her to try highlights, and Sam at Monarchy thought the same. She called the beauty shop, and discovered an appointment was open at two o'clock today. That gave her time to look for an outfit at Molly's boutique next door afterward.

She looked at her watch. Nick had texted an hour and a half ago. *Had it been long enough?* She decided to reply.

She texted back, "A lady prefers a phone call or an invitation extended in person."

Ten seconds after she hit Send, her phone rang. On the other end of the line, Nick said, "If it be a sin to covet honor, I am the most offending soul. A fool thinks himself to be wise, but a wise man knows himself to be a fool."

The Shakespeare quote from *Henry V* worked, and Bethany accepted Nick's apology. They made a date for 6:30 the next night, and Nick would pick her up at Lily Fields.

In the beauty shop's waiting area, Bethany waited for Sam to finish with her client. By the way she held the brush and styled hair, Bethany could tell she was very good at her craft.

"Ready to get some highlights?" Sam asked.

Bethany stood up but did not step forward. "Only a few to make sure I like it."

"I understand," Sam said, waving her over to her chair. "You're in good hands. Done hair for twenty years."

Sam's comment put Bethany more at ease. She snapped a bright-blue smock around Bethany to protect her clothes from the hair treatment.

"Want me to trim it a little too?"

"Maybe just the ends," Bethany said reluctantly.

"What made you finally decide on highlights?" Sam asked.

"I'm going on a date," she said surprisingly, sharing a personal detail. Although she knew other people often told hairdressers about their lives, Bethany did not. Well, not until now at least.

"Tonight?"

"Tomorrow," Bethany said.

"Here in Jameson?"

"I think so. He's picking me up at 6:30."

"Can I ask . . . is it Peter Jameson? I saw you walk out of his office the other day. One of the town's most eligible bachelors. Lots of women after that one."

"No, but he's sure good for the eyes. Took me on his sailboat one evening." Bethany smiled before she recalled what he revealed later that night. Not wanting to go down a dark path in her mind, she put that thought aside. "It's Nick DeLeon. He owns a landscaping company, God's Green Acres. He did work for me at the house."

Sam poured highlighting chemicals in a dish. "I've seen his truck driving through town. Nice ride. Looks classy, not some junky old truck like a lot of landscapers in town drive," Sam remarked.

"A nice new truck until my shopping cart ran into it."

Sam twirled the chair around to look at Bethany.

"He got out of his truck and told me it was two days old. He said he knew something would get it sooner or later, and it just happened to be *me*."

Sam slapped her free hand on her side and laughed as she stirred the hair solution with the other. "Oh, this is right out of a romance movie. And he asked you on a date then and there?"

"No. He was by the house a few times giving me landscaping estimates and checking on his crew. The other day he showed up with a utility vehicle on the back of a trailer and asked if I wanted to check out my property. He took me to see a waterfall in my woods."

Reflecting on that moment at the creek, Bethany felt fun, a feeling she thought she forgot how to experience.

"I tripped and Nick helped me up with his muscular arms." Bethany smiled in the mirror, and Sam giggled back at her.

"What are you going to wear?" Sam asked.

"Don't know. I didn't bring anything appropriate from Alexandria. Once we're done here, I'm going next door to look for a casual black dress."

"I went over there yesterday. She received some new dresses, but they weren't out yet."

Bethany handed her foils to fold around strands of hair as Sam brushed on highlights.

"Sam, you have such a great sense of style," she said connecting with Sam's eyes in the mirror.

"Well, thanks. Clothes, jewelry, and hairstyles are my three favorite things, besides men, of course." Sam laughed and prompted Bethany to hand her another foil.

"What about you? Are you single?" Bethany asked.

"Divorced. No kids." Sam finished the highlights and set the timer on her cell phone. Bethany remained in the chair while her hair processed, and the two women chatted at an ease usually found only between long-term friends. The buzzing of Sam's phone from a text interrupted their momentum. "My four o'clock canceled," Sam said aloud and put the phone down on her workstation counter.

The girls chatted about Bethany's work. Sam was fascinated to hear Bethany met a few famous actors who filmed commercials for her clients' brands.

When the alarm went off, Sam took her to the carved-out sink. She sprayed warm water on her head and massaged a sweet-smelling shampoo and conditioner into her long, straight locks. The scalp massage not only tingled her head, but Bethany's whole body began to relax from her head to her toes. *This is why women love going to the salon*, she thought. Because of her busy schedule, Bethany often got dry trims only. Her stylist made good money for ten minutes of work.

Sam wrapped Bethany's hair in a towel and guided her back into the chair. When she removed the towel, it unveiled lighter streaks in her hair mixed between dark-brown strands.

"Hope you like it," Sam said. "I wanted to put more highlights in, but I know you wanted to go easy." Sam gave her a quick trim before turning on the hair dryer and brushing Bethany's hair straight. "My goodness. It looks so good. Do you like it?"

"I'm surprised I do." Bethany smiled in the mirror. "You're really good at this."

"Can I put a few loose curls in for you?"

"I never curl my hair. If it's not in a ponytail, I always wear it straight. Um, do you have time?"

"Last customer just canceled. Let's have a little fun." Sam used a wide barreled curling iron to add loose curls.

"What do you think?" she asked, handing Bethany a mirror and twirling the chair around. The curls softened Bethany's face.

Bethany smiled in approval. "I like it."

As Sam unsnapped the smock, bits of trimmed hair fell to the floor. "Want any company?" she asked. "I'm always looking for an excuse to shop. I can be there in five minutes, but if you want to be alone, I understand."

Relief filled Bethany's face. "That would be great. I could use help. Haven't been on a date in almost a year, and I knew that guy for several years. Did business with him."

Bethany left Sam to close up shop and went next door. Roaming from rack to rack, she was uncertain what to choose. Molly, the owner, assisted another customer. Not wanting it to appear she was trying too hard, Bethany needed to find something that looked good but didn't broadcast the date meant too much. She needed it to appear as though she did this all the time. *At least, let him think that.* Dating presented a careful balance for Bethany, and that's why she didn't take time to do much of it.

Sam arrived and headed straight for a black dress hanging on the back wall. She guessed Bethany's size was medium. With four-inch heels, she was five-ten and thin.

"A simple, sleeveless cotton, plain black dress, formfitted to your curves with a zip up the back," Sam described as she held it up in front of Bethany for approval.

"What's your shoe size?"

"Eight," Bethany said.

"My goodness. Same as mine." She held up a pair of nude-colored wedge sandals. "What do you think? Want to try them on?"

"Sure," Bethany agreed. She shopped out of necessity for work and had a decent eye, but since she met Sam, she realized this lady was much more versed in fashion than she was.

Sam looked through the long strands of necklaces and chose one for Bethany made of beige shiny beads and a chunky crystal cross at the end. "This okay for you?"

"Whatever you think looks good." Bethany said, remembering Sam buying herself a similar necklace the other day.

Using one of the two dressing rooms in the back, Bethany put on the outfit and freshened her BXB2 Cosmetics red lipstick, named Heart's Desire, before coming out to show Sam and Molly.

"My goodness!" Sam shouted as Bethany walked toward them. "You're going to give him heat stroke."

"I want to make sure it doesn't look like I'm trying too hard."

"You don't. This is simple and yet ravishing. I love it." Sam clapped her hands.

Molly gave her thoughts. "I don't know what you girls are up to, but Bethany, you look great in that dress, and the necklace adds just the right touch with a bit of sparkle against the black. It accents your new high-lights."

Walking out of the store with bags in her arms, Bethany asked Sam, "Want to get a glass of wine? My treat for helping me."

Sam stopped on the sidewalk. "Always up for a glass of wine. There's a restaurant I like near the bridge with a great view of the water. If you're hungry, we can also grab a bite to eat." Bethany was hungry because rushing to complete her work before her hair appointment, she ate only a hard-boiled egg for lunch with some crackers.

Getting to know each other over a glass of wine, Sam coaxed Bethany to try one of her chargrilled oysters. Bethany was surprised she liked the smooth, buttery taste. Outside the window, the Rappahannock River moved south toward the Chesapeake Bay.

"The Northern Neck has been famous for its oysters since the nineteenth century," Sam said. "The sea delights in providing work for watermen in this area for hundreds of years. Oyster shells were also used for several purposes more than a century ago." Bethany knew this firsthand; her historic front steps and walkway at Lily Fields contained the shells.

At 6:00 p.m., a duo with guitars entertained in front of a backdrop made of handmade quilts hanging from the ceiling. The two women enjoyed the music while continuing their "get to know each other" conversation.

Driving home feeling like a sophomore about to go out on a date with the senior quarterback, Bethany didn't remember a time when she was this spontaneous. Jameson continued to display its surprises, and once again Bethany was feeling fun.

Readying for bed, she knew tomorrow would come soon, but now she needed to rest. As she crawled into bed and thought about the date, she questioned her judgment. After coming down from the initial high of accepting Nick's invitation, getting her hair done, and shopping for a dress, her mind righted itself back on work. She was here to get things done, not go on dinner dates. A distraction was not in her plans, and her schedule must remain on time. One dinner with Nick might be the only one she had time for in Jameson, but then there was Peter to think about too. Bethany liked Peter. *Stay focused*, she reminded herself. After just a short time away, Bethany had, uncharacteristically, let herself get distracted.

The Timekeeper's chimes signaled it late, and she closed her eyes to her temporary play world in Jameson. But her mind snapped alert when she remembered her talk with Baxter. She raced between options of what to do. As her mind calculated, she was re-energized, which prevented her from relaxing. She needed sleep but the preoccupied mind runs away from rest. Worry has a track of its own, and Bethany's mind knew all about that racecourse. Her thoughts sped around it many a night. And tonight, her mind would not let go of her upset with Baxter and let her play in the make-believe world of Jameson. The two realms wrestled for control, but it was exhaustion that finally won.

CHAPTER 23

Begrudgingly, Bethany put her feet in the nasty bathtub, pulled the curtain closed, and reached for the handheld shower. While the hot water sprayed on her head, she wished for time to move quickly. She awaited this evening with nervous anticipation.

Her casual black dress hung behind her bedroom door with the crystal necklace wrapped around the hanger like in a retail store display, and her new beige wedge sandals sat on the floor beneath them. Everything looked at the ready except for Bethany. Her stomach fluttered, and her eyes didn't want to focus on a computer screen.

She talked to Walter a few days ago about removing paint from the living room fireplace, and he bought supplies to work on it. Since he was busy in the upstairs bathroom, she decided to take the fireplace project on herself today.

While she laid out the supplies to get started, Peter texted. "Can I stop by today at one?" Bethany hadn't seen him since the other night on the porch when he told her the disturbing news about her biological father.

"Works for me," she texted back. She estimated she should be done with stripping the paint off the fireplace mantel well before Peter arrived. She liked Peter's company and wanted to fill time until she got ready for her date with Nick. *Maybe Peter might ask me to dinner some time too—even if just to talk business.*

Kneeling on the drop cloths Walter had put on the floor for her, she read the directions, which said she needed to leave the chemicals on the wood until the paint began to bubble up. After scraping off wet paint for three hours from every nook inside the carved mantel, she realized this more than taxed her limited patience. With each chime of the Timekeeper, she heard time escape, so she didn't stop for lunch.

The doorbell rang. With wet paint and chemical processing solution covering the drop cloths and her yellow rubber gloves, she shouted toward the door, "Come in!" Bethany remained at the fireplace, working on her knees.

"Hi! Sorry about the mess," she said to Peter. "Didn't realize how long this would take. The internet video made it look easy, but these layers of different colored paints are stuck between all these carved flowers." Peter surveyed her and the half-completed project.

"And sorry for the noise." She pointed upstairs. "Walter's breaking up the tile floors. He's almost finished!" she shouted so Peter could hear her.

Peter stared at the fireplace.

"What? You think I can't handle this?" she asked, holding the metal can in one yellow rubber gloved hand and a stained cloth in the other.

Peter leaned in to answer her over the loud noise upstairs, "I'm sure you can handle just about anything you put your mind to. It just takes patience."

"Well, that's one thing besides time that I'm in short supply of. I've worked on this fireplace on and off for more than three hours already. I found three different paint colors so far, and there's still more to go." She puffed a loose strand of hair out of her eyes. "I had no idea how difficult a job it is to remove paint from all the corners and indentations. I should have let Walter do it."

The upstairs noise quieted, and they each sighed at the sudden peace.

"Patience, Bethany. Patience," Peter said. He sat on the sofa to watch while she worked. "That's why they call it home improvement projects. Projects take time. The struggle in the middle is what makes it all worthwhile in the end."

"Taking action is my virtue. And patience is the opposite of action, am I right?" Bethany said, without stopping her work.

"Patience is a form of action," Peter said.

Bethany turned to look at him as if he spoke another language she did not understand.

"It's a quote from Auguste Rodin," Peter explained. "'Patience is a form of action.' My guess is Rodin said it while sculpting." Bethany was puzzled. "Step back and look at your project from a distance," he tried to explain. "Wake up tomorrow with fresh eyes and new energy."

That made sense to her. Besides, she was tired of this project. She took off the plastic yellow gloves and went to the downstairs bathroom to wash up while he waited for her in the living room. Over the sound of the running sink in the bathroom, she shouted out, "Want a cup of coffee or a glass of water?"

"Both would be great."

Bethany went into the kitchen and chose two single-serve coffee containers from the carousel. *Tall, dark, and handsome.* It would be her little secret.

With Peter's help, she opened the living room windows even higher than she had before he arrived. She needed more air circulation for safety reasons and to combat the chemical smell. One window still stuck as she tried to push it up. Another project for Walter to tend to again. *Good thing he had patience.*

The warm June breeze filled the room. Bethany took a seat on the couch next to Peter.

"I hated to leave you the other night after I told you about your father," Peter confessed with a look of heartfelt concern.

Her head shook side to side. "Don't think I want to look for him now. Mitzi tried to get me to consider his young age. Doesn't matter. He didn't want me, and I don't want him either." She looked out the front window to her yard filled with lilies and roses.

"Since I was eleven years old, I had to take control of my life and learn to do things alone. It's worked just fine for me this far."

Peter lowered his face before looking back up at her. "I'm sorry. I grew up with two loving parents." He tried to look into Bethany's eyes, but she focused on the birds filling themselves at the feeders.

Peter shifted the conversation to business. "What makes you work so hard?" he asked.

"I want to grow my business to one of the largest agencies in the Mid-Atlantic."

"Any other purpose?"

"As the business has grown, we're getting recognized for our work. We've won lots of awards."

"Won any hearts?" As soon as he asked, his eyes closed and his face squinched. Too late for him to take back the probing question.

"For my attorney, now you're getting too personal." Bethany smiled to let him know she was joking. "I was engaged to a guy for a year and a half. He waited for me to set a date, but I never did. Not enough time for a relationship. I learned the other Rs: Reading, Riting, and Rithmetic. I just missed the Relationship course." Bethany smiled in jest, but Peter didn't smile back.

"How about you?" she asked, shifting the attention from her to him.

"My career started out as an obligation. My father expected me to go to law school."

"Did you like it?"

Peter took a drink of his water and placed his glass on a coaster on the living room coffee table. "To my surprise, I did. I chose not to work for the family firm right out of college. I wanted to prove myself first. Once my dad passed away, duty called me home to Jameson. The town needed a lawyer."

Bethany put her cup and saucer on the table. "Speaking of legacy," she started, "I read a few entries in the journal, the one I told you I found inside the Timekeeper. The other night, I read a contribution by Katherine Knowles's first daughter, Abigail. She inherited the home from her mother, Katherine, and Katherine mentioned she hoped the Knowles women would continue the journal."

"Quite remarkable women. It's unusual, I might add, how Katherine willed the home to her daughter. I studied Virginia law history, of course. Wasn't until the 1870s when married women could make property decisions without their husband's involvement. I think the Virginian law passed in 1877. Somewhere around there."

"I had no idea we could not fully make our own property decisions until then."

"I think I oversimplified it, but that's about right. Nevertheless, remarkable women in your family and quite remarkable and unusual for a family home to pass down from daughter to daughter." Peter looked into Bethany's eyes, and she held his gaze.

"Remarkable indeed," Bethany said, moving her eyes away from him and onto the teacup in her hand. "So far, I read about Katherine and her daughter, Abigail. Abigail was born on Emancipation Day."

"January 1, 1863," Peter said.

"No, her birthday was later. Abigail's journal entry mentioned Virginians once celebrated emancipation on April 3, 1865, the day the Union Army marched into Richmond."

"You got me on that one," Peter said. "Guess I don't know Virginia history as well as I thought." He stroked his finger in the air, conceding her the one point.

"Your ancestors all sound like remarkable women. It's all throughout the family's DNA, from what I can tell." Peter's eyes sparked.

Bethany blushed at the compliment. "I wish I knew all the first daughters' names and when each lived. They must have had other daughters and sons too."

"The family Bible . . . did you find it?" he asked.

Bethany shrugged her shoulders. "Haven't looked."

Peter got up from the couch and walked to the living room shelves. "May I?" he asked as he pointed to the books.

Bethany nodded for him to go ahead, and within a minute, Peter put his hands on a Bible he found on an upper shelf. He opened the cover and showed Bethany a family tree. Katherine's and William's names were written at the top along with each of their children. Before Abigail's birthdate, it listed a son, Samuel. He died at three days old. Abigail's family consisted of three children, two daughters, and one son.

The family tree continued all the way to the present, including Bethany's mother, Marguerite. Bethany saw Marguerite's birthdate and no date of death. *That would be my job to update the Bible.*

There were blanks on the page under Marguerite. Bethany didn't exist, as far as her family knew. Marguerite hid Bethany's existence even from them.

Turning the page, she found a folded, yellowed paper written with faded ink and cursive writing.

"Look at this." Bethany showed Peter the find, and she read it aloud:

never thot livin in a hole wuld feel good. safe. a place to rest this darknes givs me peece. hidin undergrownd is like a cacun. i is rappd up hidin watin fer the rit time to brak free. soon i use my new wings to fly. fly north to freedum wer we can liv an love as we wer made. to freley feel to freley be. to expurins life with no shackls tyin me to a plas of werk and jus existens with no joy. i rest in darknes noin that soon the lite il shine upon me gidin me alung a uncerten path leeding to a gloreus new beginin.

When Bethany finished, she looked down at the inside of the fireplace covered up again with the metal grate and logs piled on top. "Was this written by the woman from the story Agnes mentioned? One of the slaves Katherine hid below the house?"

"It would be unusual for a slave to read or write. Possible, but not likely," Peter informed.

"Agnes has a copy of a story about my great-great-great-grandmother Katherine helping a slave escape to the North."

"That's incredible. You come from very strong stock indeed."

"Her name was Selah," Bethany said, looking at the last word on the page.

Peter looked over her shoulder at the paper again. "Beautiful name. *Selah* is a biblical term. The word *Selah* appears in the Bible over seventy times." He pulled his head back from the Bible to look at her. "Most notations of it are found in the Book of Psalms, but there are a few in other places too. Here, look." Peter leafed through Psalms and pointed to the notation "Selah" at the end of one. "It is thought *Selah* is a term to tell the musicians or singers to pause and reflect on what was said, sung, or played. *Selah,* by many accounts, is thought to mean 'pause and reflect.'"

"Interesting," Bethany said. "Learn something new every day."

"My parents sent me to an all-boys Christian school. Learned a lot about the Bible," he said. "I thought back then I might go into ministry." Peter stopped as she looked at her watch.

126

"Oh, I'd better get going," Peter announced, taking the hint. "I've taken up enough of your day."

Bethany didn't tell Peter she had a date. Maybe he, too, might ask her out for dinner some time. And even if it was just to discuss legal matters, she would like that. She walked with Peter to the door.

"It's good to see you settling in. Remember, patience is a form of action," he reminded her, pointing back to the unfinished fireplace mantel.

She smiled as she opened the door for him. "I'll take patience into consideration. Can't promise you anything. Thanks for the help finding the family tree and all."

Peter drove back to town feeling better about his chances. The other night after he left, he was concerned the story he shared with Bethany about her birth would make her run back to Alexandria. She'd now started remodeling the bathrooms. It appeared she might choose to stay, and that gave him hope.

. . . and the Timekeeper chimed four.

CHAPTER 24

Bethany finished all she could endure on the fireplace, folded up the drop cloth filled with paint and chemicals, and took it upstairs to the pink bathroom where she put it out of the way in the corner. After breaking up floor tile and doing other projects, Walter had a hard day and left earlier than usual.

As she was about to step into the makeshift bathtub shower, she reached for her ringing phone.

"I want to come do your hair for your big date, no charge," Sam said to Bethany.

"Sweet, but that's too much to ask."

"Nonnegotiable offer. I can be there at a little before five."

Bethany got in the shower and washed her hair. She looked forward to seeing curls in it again.

Dressed in a bathrobe, she opened the door and gave Sam a quick tour of the downstairs before they stopped to marvel at the Timekeeper.

"Isn't it amazing to think so many of your ancestors walked past this same clock and heard its chimes every day?" Sam declared, noting the significance of the antique before continuing with her musing. "The Timekeeper's chimes serve to remind all that time moves forward, but we should slow down to enjoy the moments."

Don't know anything about that, Bethany thought to herself. Bethany viewed the use of time differently, but she didn't want to interrupt Sam's philosophical mood and let her new friend be in her own foreign world alone.

Since only one bathroom upstairs remained untouched by Walter's demolition efforts, Bethany took Sam to set up her stylist's tools in the pink bathroom. The ugly bathtub with a shower curtain around it posed an embarrassing eyesore. "I can't wait until Walter hauls this tub to the dump!" Bethany exclaimed. "I can't bear standing in it to take a shower—and a handheld one at that."

Although small, the bathroom worked fine as a makeshift beauty salon. Bethany sat on the closed toilet lid while Sam put waves into her hair. It was 5:15, and she was getting nervous anticipating what this date might entail.

"Where do you think he might take me?" Bethany asked Sam as her eyes glanced upward into the mirror in front of her.

"Only a couple of nice restaurants around here, including one in The Tides Inn in Irvington. Maybe he's taking you there." Sam finished Bethany's hair and stood back to admire her work.

"My goodness. If he doesn't fall for this, he is not alive."

Bethany stood up to check out her hair in the mirror. She loved it and hugged Sam in thanks.

"Call me tomorrow," Sam said. "I haven't gone on a date for a while. Look forward to hearing about it." She packed up her curling iron before letting herself out the front door.

Bethany's face was a natural base of beauty. Her eyes were her key feature, and she knew how to accentuate them thanks to professional makeup lessons, part of the research to get to know her clients' products. Tonight, she used a combination of brown and champagne to accentuate her brown eyes.

After taking the sleeveless black dress off the hanger, she held it to the ground and slid it on. Wriggling around until her fingers reached the zipper, she pulled it up little by little, first from the bottom, then she reached her arm over her shoulder to pull it up the rest of the way. *I should have had Sam help me with this*, she thought.

The long beaded necklace with its thick, clear-jeweled cross pendant added contrast to the sleeveless, black cotton sheath. Bethany slipped on the nude-colored, three-inch-high wedge sandals Sam picked out. Looking at herself in the bedroom dresser mirror, she looked stunning, yet casual. Just what she wanted to achieve. The waves in her hair added a softness she rarely displayed.

On one wrist, she sprayed her best French perfume, bought months ago while on a trip to New York City. It smelled of a blend of irises and French daffodils, the label boasted. She rubbed her wrists together and then touched each side of her neck. *Only one spray. Got to keep him at bay.*

The Timekeeper chimed once for the half hour. Immediately afterward, the doorbell rang.

It must be him.

CHAPTER 25

He was right on time; it was 6:30 p.m. exactly. She used the second hand on her watch and waited sixty seconds. Every second counted when she wanted to show a man who was in charge. Slowly walking down the creaking steps, she placed her feet where both Katherine and Abigail walked before her.

When she opened the door, she found Nick smiling at her on the porch. His jet-black hair was wavy. His eyes were the darkest of browns and completely focused on her.

After locking the door with her antique steel key, Bethany followed Nick down the walkway to his vehicle. He wanted her to go in front, but she refused.

"Sorry I don't own a car," he said. "My truck is my only transportation."

He opened her door and, despite the high-ride truck and her wedge shoes, she got inside without effort, but her dress rode up her leg a little as she did. When she put it on tonight, it was two inches above her knee.

As Nick pulled out of the driveway and headed toward town, Bethany asked where they were going.

"I'm taking you to my favorite restaurant. It's about fifteen minutes from your home, just on the other side of town."

Bethany was uneasy not knowing precisely where she was going at any given time. "What's the name?"

"Well, that's part of the surprise," he said.

She shook her head. Bethany was used to being the one who made the plans. She didn't like surprises. They usually ended up in disappointment.

They crossed the bridge over the creek. Her creek. *What was that quote he said to her that day? Something about quiet waters and the soul.* Nick was talking about his work, and Bethany didn't want to interrupt him to ask.

They drove into an area with a mixture of homes and retail spaces constructed in the mid-twentieth century. Nick pulled the truck over at a wooded area with a lit pathway. Another hour and a half until sunset, but the pathway lights already lit the way.

"Here we are. Best restaurant in town. Hope you like it. I reserved a special table."

Bethany picked up the wrap she brought in case the air conditioning was too cool.

Nick smiled at her. "I don't think you'll need that."

"Oh, I always bring one in case." She opened her door as he came around to help her out of the high truck. And because he parked near the curb, she let him take her hand. She needed the balance to exit in her new shoes. As she swung her legs out, she tried to hold her dress with her free hand. She didn't want it to ride up her leg too much as she got out of the high seat. Her effort mostly worked.

They walked together down the dense tree-lined path with the undergrowth carefully cleared out between. *Very well-manicured,* she thought.

"This restaurant certainly knows how to create ambiance leading up to it. Love when businesses get it and think about the details." Bethany knew what kept people coming back for more.

The path ended at a beautiful garden area with a multicolored beige stone patio. A creek with a waterfall sat at the far end of the outdoor dining area. It was manmade but almost natural in appearance.

"I know that's got to take a lot of skill to make a waterfall appear that real," she said. "Did your crews do the work here?"

Nick smiled and nodded as he pointed her to a table for two to the right. It was covered in a white tablecloth with two white china place settings on top.

"Where's everyone else? Did you rent the whole place?" she said in jest.

"It's mine," he answered.

Bethany turned on her wedged heels. "You own a restaurant too?"

"I built this garden. My house is right there." He pointed to the backside of a one-and-a-half story, red brick home just beyond the tree line. "If you need it, there's an outside bathroom at the end of the sidewalk there."

Nick left Bethany standing with her mouth open as he walked toward an outdoor gas grill, refrigerator, and icemaker all built in and part of the patio design.

"I work out here a lot in my garden. It's my stress relief. Hope you like Mahi. If not, I have a piece of chicken just in case."

"I love Mahi," she said as she turned toward him at the grill.

"Want wine while I cook?" he asked.

Bethany nodded. She tried to grasp this moment and each moment since they exited his truck and walked down the lighted wooded path to the garden paradise. Nick DeLeon surprised her.

When he removed the wine from the outdoor built-in cabinet next to the mini fridge, she spotted the label. It was a Malbec from Argentina. "That's one of my favorites," she admitted.

"Figured that. Saw the name on a bottle in your recycle bin the other day," he said with a smile.

Bethany shared that bottle with Peter the night he told her about her father not wanting her to be born. Using her ability to compartmentalize, she put that bad memory where it belonged.

"Have a seat while I cook," he said, pointing her to the table.

Bethany chose the chair facing him and sipped her red wine while he prepared their meal. "I don't cook much," she confessed. "Living alone and working late hours makes it easier for me to buy prepared meals or pick up takeout."

The third quarter moon appeared in the still-sunlit sky. The warm air and no breeze made Bethany glad she wore a sleeveless dress.

Nick placed a piece of fish and some asparagus on each plate. This surprise chef with a secret garden wooed Bethany with advance preparation and much thoughtfulness.

A white vase with a single pink rose sat between their plates. Around the patio, automatic landscape lighting came on, illuminating the waterfall and trees like lighting on stage actors. There was no music. None was needed. The moving water set a rhythm, and nature sang its own melody.

He took his seat and lifted his wine glass to make a toast. "To runaway shopping carts."

Bethany laughed, and Nick's eyes stayed on her as he put his glass in the air. His deep-brown eyes smiled in unison with hers. They clicked wine glasses, and each took a drink.

Noticing he didn't remove his gaze, she knew to be careful how she used her best asset. Her eyes had an even brighter sparkle tonight, so she looked away from him to her plate.

Bethany had let her hair down, literally. The waves softened her outward hardened nature. As a strong woman, not many knew a soft heart existed beyond the outer thick wall because she let very few get close enough to find out.

Nick waited for her to take a bite of fish. "How is it?"

"It's incredible. Melts in my mouth." The fish tasted especially good to her. She was extra hungry from having missed eating lunch while working on the fireplace.

"So tell me," she said as she cut another bite of fish. "How did you get into landscaping?"

"My parents owned a nursery in Central America. I grew up around the nursery and came to the Richmond area for college. My family now lives here and owns a nursery outside of Richmond. That's where your roses came from."

"Ah," she said and took another bite of food.

"I picked each rose with a purpose. The ones at your porch are called General Jack, or Jack Rose. They've existed since the house was built. I wanted to give you a time period rose."

"Amazing. Still the same kind of roses. Learn something new every day," she said and took a drink of wine.

"How did you start your agency?" he asked before cutting a piece of mahi.

"My good friend in college wanted me to create advertising and PR campaigns for his company brands."

Bethany's eyes drifted from the table. Her mind went to Baxter and how he had given the new business to a competitive agency, but she needed to put that anger aside tonight. She noticed Nick catch the change in her face when she thought about it. She wanted to enjoy the evening. No point in bringing up what Baxter did to her.

"Have you ever been married?" Nick asked.

"Had a fiancé once, but he tired of waiting on me to set a date," Bethany answered, taking a drink of wine. "He realized my work came first."

Nick's smile went flat.

"How about you?" she asked.

"Her name was Mariana," he said. We married in our late twenties. When she was thirty-two, she discovered breast cancer. I took her to Houston to a cancer hospital after other efforts in Richmond failed. We enjoyed every good moment we had, and there were some in between the hard days." Nick stared off at his waterfall then turned back toward Bethany.

"Mariana's hair looked like yours before she got sick. 'Hair was overrated,' she told people. 'There are many more important things in life.'" Nick had tears in his eyes.

"I'm so sorry." The somber revelation choked up Bethany too. She reached to pat the top of his hand.

Nick took her hand in his and held on to it. "It's been four years now." He took a sip of wine with one hand while still holding hers with the other.

"Time moves slowly when you are grieving and speeds up in joy," Nick said, looking at the waterfall as it flowed into the natural-looking creek. He regained control of his emotions and turned his attention back to Bethany, "If you had all the time in the world, what would you do?"

She gave no answer but with her shoulders said, *I don't know.* Time was a scarce resource for Bethany. To her, it was a ridiculous question. She never had enough time.

He prodded to get an answer out of her. "What's your favorite thing to do when you have time to do it," he asked, attempting to help her respond.

"I don't have time to do the things I need to do, let alone do what I would like to," she responded hastily.

"Think about it."

She thought for a moment, took a breath, and then answered. "I used to like to write. When I was a kid, I made up stories. I had quite the imagination. Characters talked to me in my head, and I wrote down what they said, creating all sorts of tales. I also wrote for my high school newspaper."

"Why didn't you become a writer?"

"Didn't think I could make a good living. Had to be focused. My mom had severe rheumatoid arthritis and other ailments. I cleaned, cooked basic meals, and wrote out the bills for her to sign the checks. Took care of her by myself until I went to college. After that, we hired people to help her."

"You're a hard worker," Nick said before offering her more wine.

Bethany took a drink from her second glass. "I worked for an agency in Los Angeles right out of college. Two years later, my best friend, Baxter, opened his cosmetics company and asked me to start my own agency in Alexandria where we both grew up. I miss Southern California though. Rarely rains. I don't like rain. Hated it since the night an officer knocked on our door." The air inside Bethany left her lungs. "He told us my father had been in a car accident. Unfortunately, I know all about loss too."

It was Bethany's turn to hold back emotion. Her eyes pleaded for him to change the subject, and he obliged.

"So if you had all the time in the world, you would write?" he asked.

"Time waits for no one. Every second counts. Got to keep moving." Bethany walked her fingers on the table. "What would you do if you had all the time in the world?" she asked.

"I'd spend more time in this garden," Nick answered without hesitation. "I love working with my hands and seeing things grow." He looked at his assortment of plants and flowers near the manmade creek and waterfall. "Not enough time right now. A damsel in distress required my immediate attention." He smiled at her and leaned forward. On top of the table, he reached again for her hand.

She almost didn't notice. Her mind was distracted by his wavy black hair. Since the day she met him in the hardware store parking lot, he always wore a ball cap until now. *He is more handsome without the cap.*

"When we met, you said you couldn't help me for weeks, except you could cut my grass. Next thing I knew, there you were with a bunch of other Latino guys running around my yard, pulling weeds and planting roses." She smiled, knowing she'd cornered him.

"Couldn't let opportunity pass by. Something told me to open up space for you," he said.

Nick's words hung in the air for them both to ponder until he asked the next question. "What would you do if you had limited time left?"

Did his wife's death cause him to think about these things? she wondered. *Death made anybody reconsider their priorities, but this is a bit heavy for a first date dinner conversation.* "Hmm . . ." Bethany thought hard about his question. She always made plans with a long list of items. What if she knew her time was limited? She knew he meant in the sense of little time left alive.

She looked into the nighttime sky. Stars were coming out. Bringing her head back in line with his, she said, "I'd move to Lily Fields." Her free hand flew to her mouth. She heard herself speak, but it was as if the words came from another who had taken control inside her.

"And do what?" he asked, ignoring her surprise.

"Ah . . . write maybe," she said, now playing along like she was participating in a strategic vision exercise with one of her clients. "Perhaps run my agency from here. My VP, Scott, is great. Been with me since the first year after I started my agency. I check in every day and have video calls with a few new clients, but he's keeping it running—at least so far. But I do need to get back soon."

"Can't you stay?"

"We lost a big business deal. Counted on it and mapped out plans. Will be really hard to replace all that."

"Maybe it's not meant to be." Nick soothed the top of her hand with his thumb and, after a nod from her, refilled her empty glass with his other but did not refill his own.

"It was supposed to be," she said after taking a sip from her third glass of wine. "Baxter promised us. He's changed. His wife, Amy, came to visit me a few days ago at Lily Fields.

"Why?"

"She's worried about him. Said he stopped paying attention to her. I told her he's just super focused on business. I know him almost as well as I know myself. We're similar in how we tick. Baxter is all business and little pleasure. Always been that way. A grown man on his own, but his dad expects a lot out of him."

Bethany instantly regretted telling Nick intimate details of her friends' lives because of too much wine. She never drank more than two glasses, and today she'd missed eating lunch. The rest of her wine needed to remain in the glass. Turning her attention back on to him, she asked, "And you, what would you do if you knew you had limited time?"

Without a second's hesitation, he answered, "I'd spend it here in my garden with someone special."

Nick looked into Bethany's eyes as if he could find a pathway inside. He took both her hands into his and raised one to his lips. He kissed her hand softly, and she reached for the table with her other hand, steadying herself from a slight feeling of butterflies.

"We should get you back home. I have to meet my crew tomorrow morning at 6:30. A job I pushed back because of someone special can't wait any longer. We've got to make up time."

Nick held on to her hand and helped her rise from the table. He took the pink long-stemmed rose from the vase and presented it to her.

"I chose this one for you. It grows beautiful with no need for thorns.

. . . and the Timekeeper chimed five.

138

CHAPTER 26

When she woke up and opened her eyes, she remembered how Nick walked her up Lily Field's porch steps. She took out her key and unlocked the door, and when she turned around, he caressed her face between his hands, kissing her softly.

"Goodnight, Bethany. Sweet dreams," he said. "I'll call you tomorrow." He walked down the steps and turned back to watch until she got inside.

Bethany wanted to go back to sleep and continue this dream, but it was real. She recalled the smell of his cologne.

"Oh, no," she said, remembering the goodnight kiss at the door. "I know better than to fall for some guy here." She sat up and slapped both palms into the bedspread.

There was a reason Bethany always stopped at two glasses of wine. She liked to keep control of her mind and feelings. Last night, she'd let her heart open. Her work in Alexandria and projects on the house needed her full attention. She had no time for a relationship and half regretted she let herself enjoy the evening.

It was time for her to get out of bed, but she dreaded stepping into the grungy tub and using the handheld shower. Plus, the curtain didn't keep the heat inside.

While in the shower, she received two messages on her phone. The first one was from Nick. He wanted her to know how much he enjoyed dinner last night and said he would try to call her later. Bethany liked the sound of his voice and was disappointed she didn't hear the phone ring.

The second message was from Agnes, asking her to stop by to pick up the newspaper story about the night Katherine rescued the woman. She would do that, but first, she video called Holly to check in.

"Wait, you're refinishing a fireplace . . . like, doing it yourself?" Holly asked.

"Bad move on my part. How are things at the office?" Bethany propped the phone on the dresser and put on a pair of silver earrings.

"Scott is in constant meetings. Everyone is focused on pitching new business."

Bethany knew they needed to win business to supply the four new associates with work. She was accustomed to taking charge, but Scott was not. She must figure out what more to do for him from Jameson. Scott insisted he deserved to take the reins, but no one knows all that the boss handles until she is no longer there to drive the team of horses.

Another number lit up on Bethany's phone. "Got to take a call. Went on a date last night. Talk to you later."

On the other end of the phone, Holly sat at her desk with her mouth hanging open. She had no chance to ask Bethany a question. Her boss's time was up.

CHAPTER 27

As a thank you for styling her hair, Bethany invited Sam to Lily Fields for dinner. Before they ate, the women took a walk to see the flower gardens that Nick's crew transformed inside the long-neglected beds. With the lilies and roses in full bloom, Sam marveled at the varieties and colors, a full palette of whites, pinks, and crimson along with the native Turk's cap lilies.

"Do you know the names?" Sam asked.

"This is the Jack rose." Bethany pointed to the crimson and velvety rose at the bottom of the porch steps. "Nick DeLeon knows the names of all the rest." Bethany liked pronouncing it like *Day Lay Own*. She didn't say it with a Spanish accent as good as his, but the name flowed from her lips.

A butterfly landed on a lily and sucked pollen to fuel its wings. "My goodness. A monarch," Sam exclaimed as she clapped her hands. "My favorite."

"I guess that explains the name of your shop," Bethany said, acknowledging Sam's delight.

"Do you know about the flight monarchs take each year?"

"Don't know much about butterflies," Bethany said, walking toward another landscaped bed with Sam.

"The monarchs winter in Mexico," Sam began. "In the early spring, it takes three to four generations to make it from Mexico to the US or Southern Canada. Once fall approaches, one single generation called the Super Generation flies all the way back to Mexico, up to three thousand miles. I learned about it in a movie."

Bethany stayed attentive and Sam continued. "It's critical to plant milkweed in your garden. Monarchs lay their eggs on or near milkweed because it's the only food source for monarch caterpillars. No milkweed, no transformation into butterflies."

"Maybe I should ask Nick to plant some milkweed?"

"My goodness, you must. Now, tell me about your date," Sam said.

"The favorite restaurant was his house. Well, his garden behind his house where he grilled fish."

"Whoa, that's bold, taking you to his house on the first date." Sam's head cocked to one side, and her eyes opened wide.

"We never went inside. Entered the backyard from a path through trees on a street behind his house. The scenery was incredible, and it was lovely to hear the waterfall. He made the whole garden himself."

"How did you two get along?" Sam asked.

"The conversation was easy. Well, until he asked deep questions."

"Deep?" Sam looked at Bethany in surprise.

"He asked . . . Well . . . if I had all the time in the world, unlimited time, what would I choose to do? I had to think a while. I'm always short on time."

"What did you say?"

"Crazy thing. I told him I would write. Crazier still, when he asked what I would do if I had limited time, I said I would choose to stay at Lily Fields. I couldn't believe I said it. Don't know where that came from."

"Might be what is true, coming from your soul." Sam pointed toward Bethany's heart.

"I don't know about that."

"Have you heard from him yet?" Sam asked.

"He called me first thing this morning. Said he would call again soon."

"Good sign. You always want them calling you right away the next day," Sam said as the women walked up the porch steps.

Bethany poured Sam and herself a glass of sparkling water, and they sat down at the outdoor table. "So much has happened to me here in Jameson. I've made a lot of discoveries. Found a journal written by multiple generations of women in my family, and Walter and I found shackles." Bethany's face winced.

"Horrible part of our history," Sam said.

Bethany nodded in agreement.

"Like many Black Americans, my ancestors were slaves." Sam paused a moment before changing the subject. "You mentioned you also found a journal."

Bethany retrieved the leather-bound book and presented it to her friend, who took it in her hands. Sam rubbed her fingers across the embossed flowers on the front. "Lilies," Sam said, mesmerized.

"Lilies?"

Sam looked up at Bethany. "That woman, Katherine, loved lilies. They're painted on the Timekeeper too."

"I didn't make the connection those both had lilies." *How did I miss that?*

Bringing her mind back to her guest, she asked, "Tell me about your beauty shop. How long have you owned it?"

"Six years. Moved here from a small town called Westfield in upstate New York."

"How did you get to Jameson from there?"

"Got divorced and needed a new start. That's part of why I chose the name, Monarchy. I wanted to map my own destiny, leave the old behind and begin somewhere new. Heard about Jameson from a family member. I came to check out the town and saw a "for rent" sign in the shop window. Called the number and next thing I knew, I was a business owner in Jameson."

"Did you get to know Marguerite when she was your client? Can you tell me about her?" Bethany hoped to learn about the woman she never got to call mother.

"Marguerite was a very interesting woman. She was tall, like you, and had dark hair before she lost it. It grew back, but so did the cancer."

"Can you tell me anything more about her?" Bethany's eyes implored Sam for any piece of information she could offer.

"Very talkative when I did her hair. She told me about the countries she visited. She said she traveled to every single continent and was pretty proud of that."

"Do you know what she liked to do?"

"Mmm . . . She loved chocolate. Brought me a box for Christmas. Made it herself."

"I have no baking abilities," Bethany said.

"Of course, she loved to write and was a very generous person. She helped me with a speech I had to give at the vocational school. I started a foundation for Black girls to go to beauty college. Besides writing my speech for me, Marguerite also donated to the fund. Beautiful woman she was, in every way." Sam's lips folded into each other, and she shook her head side to side. "She seemed too young to retire to me, but I think she was ready to begin a new chapter in her life . . . that is before she started getting sick. She spent weeks at doctor visits before he ordered the right tests." Sam took a drink and Bethany did too.

"How did you get into advertising?" Sam asked, changing the subject to a lighter one. Bethany appreciated the new direction for their conversation. Work was what she loved to talk about.

She told her about how she founded her company, and now her clients' products are sold in almost fifty countries. Sam's eyes widened upon hearing the impressive statement.

"All that really means is I travel a lot," Bethany said, tamping down any sense of greatness.

"Must be fun."

"Not when you have to travel all the time and it's for work. My last trip was to Costa Rica. Filmed one of my client's new factory lines. I saw a young girl working there. Couldn't be more than a teenager. So sad for them to have to work in a factory at a young age."

"I know what you mean. I've done some mission work in other countries," Sam said.

"The strangest thing happened," Bethany said, recalling the moment. "That young girl's eyes burnt right through me. She told me something with her eyes."

"What?"

"I don't know, but it stunned me. I couldn't think right afterward and felt wobbly. When I got back to the States, I asked Baxter, my friend who's CEO of BXB2 Cosmetics, about the legal working age. It's sixteen. I'm telling ya, Sam, I couldn't shake the feeling I had down there. I even followed

144

up with my corporate attorney to check on labor laws in Costa Rica. He found out all seemed to be on the up and up by Costa Rican standards, but I can't forget it. I know Costa Rica is in much better economic shape than some of its neighbors, but there's still poverty in that little town. Broke my heart to see kids without shoes."

Sam nodded in agreement. "I volunteer with my church. Closed my shop a few years ago and went on a mission trip to Belize. Stayed a week but didn't feel we even made a dent. So much need."

"My team is helping some by sponsoring international kids, one per employee and in every country where our products are sold. The whole office has photos of kids all over—including one on my door."

"My goodness. You must have a caring team."

Bethany nodded with a proudful smile.

The sun began to set, and Sam checked her watch. "My first appointment is at eight. I've got to get going soon."

By the time Sam left Lily Fields, the girls were much closer friends. Bethany felt comfortable talking with Sam. Besides what she told her lawyer, Bethany had not fully shared her Costa Rican experience with anyone other than Amy, and she'd known her for years.

Settling into bed, she opened the journal. Reading an entry from another place and time she hoped might help her forget those eyes.

CHAPTER 28

Anna Knowles Johnson Hancock
Born 1884
Jameson, Virginia

My mother and grandmother insisted my middle name be Knowles in order to carry on the family name. My father protested at first but gave in to the two determined women. He didn't stand a chance against them. I was named Anna Knowles Johnson.

My grandmother Katherine's family, the Knowles, gave her this land our home is built on, but in 1858, as a married woman, she could not fully own the home in her name and make her own decisions concerning it.

After the Virginia women's property rights law passed in 1877, my grandmother convinced my grandfather to put the house and land in her name. Grandmother Katherine shared her earthly means equally with all her children but set aside the home and land for her daughter, my mother, Abigail. It was my Grandmother Katherine's wish that I, too, inherit the home and one day save it for my daughter.

Samuel Hancock and I married when we were both eighteen years of age in 1902. I'm Anna Knowles Hancock now. The turn of the century brought such excitement. We left the former century of Civil War, but the fight for other causes was just beginning.

Women had more rights but were not allowed to vote. The political party heads gave little attention to our desire to cast a ballot. At first, this included my beloved husband, Samuel, and we spent many a night in whispered debates while the children slept.

To Samuel's dismay, I marched for the female cause. The Equal Suffrage League of Virginia had three unsuccessful attempts in 1912, 1914, and 1916 to add a women's voting rights amendment to our Virginia Constitution.

In June 1919, the United States Congress debated the Nineteenth Amendment to the US Constitution, and we lobbied our federal representatives from Virginia to join various states to ratify it, but Virginia did not. Thirty-six other states cast the needed votes for the Constitutional Amendment.

Its passage in August 1920 granted women throughout the country, including Virginian women, the right to vote. We were grateful for our fellow sisters' efforts across the country, yet saddened that Virginia missed the chance to be part of changing history.

My friends and I made history ourselves when we cast our first ballots. Afterward, we celebrated with a parade filled with ladies dressed in white dresses marching through the streets of Jameson.

As for me, I think we chose the color white because white is the color of peace. We did not want war over this issue, not inside or outside our families. What we wanted was equal rights without a fight.

Signifying openness to new things, white paper is an empty canvas on which to write. It stands bare before us, allowing our minds to open for God to pour His thoughts, His ways, into us. A white dove of peace and a white flag of surrender we wave to Him, signifying our defenses are down.

As we remain still and listen, we are like sheep who know our Shepherd's voice. We call upon the Lord to fill us with His glory.

It is with Him by our side that we find peace in the present, knowing that He holds our future. It is our choice to accept His hand and, one day, receive our divine inheritance in Heaven.

I'm confident I will see Him soon.

With an open heart filled with peace,
Anna Knowles Hancock
Daughter, Wife, Mother, & Suffragette for Women's Rights

CHAPTER 29

Rising with the sun, Bethany took her coffee and computer to her office on the front porch. In Alexandria, she never got the chance to enjoy mornings outdoors. Instead, she rushed to work or to run an errand. Mornings at Lily Fields were different. They provided her time to sit and reflect before envisioning what lie ahead.

The sun had not yet heated the front of the home, but her black coffee warmed her insides as a light breeze blew. She wasn't the only one awake early at Lily Fields. The birds flocked three at a time to the feeder, reminding her she needed to buy more seed soon. The two bags she bought at Neil's Hardware were going fast.

After a few hours of her checking emails and reading project updates, Peter Jameson's car turned onto Lily Field's gravel driveway. He smiled to her as he walked up the porch steps. "Good day. Was out taking a ride. You doing okay?"

"About to get to work on securing a new client. Have to get this one," she said. With Peter standing near her at the table, politely waiting for an invitation to take a seat, Bethany forced hospitality. It was obvious he specifically drove out to see her.

"Want a cup of coffee?" she offered. She needed another one anyway.

They went inside and Peter waited for her on the living room couch. "I must confess," he started. "I wanted to make sure you were still here and that this old house needing so much work didn't scare you away." He reached for the cup Bethany held out to him.

"I don't scare easily," she said confidently.

Sitting with Peter on the flowered burgundy couch made Bethany cringe. Lily Fields was officially hers, and she was embarrassed to have company visit with all the outdated furniture. She envisioned a much softer designed space with a light-colored plain couch. The large flowers and burgundy color clashed with her modern style and preferred choice in colors.

"Ugh. This furniture. This place needs a refresh . . . maybe transitional furniture and accessories."

"What's transitional?" Peter asked.

"It's a blend of past and present styles . . ."

Walter stood at the doorway, and the distraction interrupted her explanation. Walter looked at Bethany and then at Peter sitting next to her. "Sorry, Miss Bethany, but I need you to show me how large you want the walk-in shower."

When she came downstairs, she picked back up on her conversation. Peter was a gentleman's gentleman. He listened with interest as Bethany talked about the house.

The doorbell rang. "I should get going," Peter said. "Looks like you are busy. I need to get to town for an appointment with a new client from Richmond."

Bethany reached for the coffee cup in his hand, and he held hers a moment before letting go. She walked with him to the hall, and when she opened the door, a giant fistful of roses and lilies met her face. Hidden behind the bouquet of blossoms was Nick, dressed in his landscape uniform and ball cap.

The boyish smile on Nick's face disappeared as soon as he lowered the flowers and saw Peter in his suit and tie standing beside Bethany. Nick still held the flowers, but they were at his waist now, hanging toward the porch floorboards.

"Uh . . . Peter," Bethany said awkwardly, "this is Nick DeLeon. He's a landscape architect, and his crew from God's Green Acres Landscaping did the transformation on my gardens. Nick, this is my attorney, Peter Jameson."

Peter's white SUV was in the driveway, but by the deflated look on his face, Nick did not expect to see another man visiting Bethany.

Peter touched Bethany's arm. "I'll call you soon," he said and walked through the doorway.

Nick looked down at Peter's Italian leather shoes. Work boots were part of Nick's attire today.

"The flowers are beautiful," Bethany said, cutting into the awkward air. She reached for the flowers in Nick's hands.

"I picked them from my garden and yours. It's a blended combination." Nick's eyes held hers as he walked across the door's threshold.

Passing close to her, the feeling of butterflies overwhelmed the usual in-control Bethany. "I never thought of picking flowers from my yard," she said, motioning him to follow her to the kitchen.

Rummaging through the cabinets overstuffed with multiple lifetimes of this and that, she found an etched crystal vase that looked like it belonged to her grandmother or an even older relative. She placed the oversized arrangement in the vase and set it on the small, round kitchen table. "I'll move it later to the living room coffee table," she said. It was an exquisite array of pink roses and white roses mixed with pink and white lilies. She noticed the roses had no thorns.

"Have plans for today?" Nick asked.

"I'm meeting with the town historian, Agnes Adams. She wants to tell me more about my family and has a story that appeared in the town's newspaper about my great-great-great-grandmother Katherine." Bethany had not shared the story with Nick and started to tell him when his phone rang. He looked at the number but let it go to voice mail.

"Sorry I can't stay long. Have to get back to my crew. I'm pitching in to supervise a job. Got a couple guys out sick."

When she opened the front door and turned to tell him goodbye, Nick put his hands on each of her shoulders. He looked at her for a moment, then drew her in to him. This time his kiss lasted long.

Nick drove out the gravel drive and looked in his side mirror at the historic home, but Bethany was already back inside. Meeting the lawyer this morning and seeing him touch Bethany's arm made him realize he had competition. Nick was used to going after what he dreamed about. As an immigrant, he'd started his own company from nothing.

Feeling deep inside something he had not felt in four years, he thought about Bethany being the one for him. If he had competition, so be it. He saw the way she looked into his eyes that night on his patio. His mind thought of little else since, and he needed to think of a way to make her want to stay. She was too lovely and unique for him to let her be won over by that Peter guy. Not that Nick was aggressive; he was simply a man who knew the gift of feeling connected and attracted to someone. And he'd not felt that since Mariana. He at least wanted to be in the running, so it was time to wear his heart on his sleeve a little more obviously.

But besides making his desires known to win Bethany's affection, Nick needed more time. And he was running out of it.

CHAPTER 30

Agnes met Bethany at the door before she knocked. "So sorry, child. Can't talk long. Arthur is having a bad day." Without letting her inside, Agnes handed her a folder with the article Katherine's granddaughter wrote. "I'll be back in touch soon. Have more to tell you, but now is not the time. My apologies, child." Agnes closed the door and left Bethany standing alone on the porch with a folder in her hands.

Although anxious to read the article, Bethany drove home feeling empty. She had hoped to talk to Agnes and get information about her family.

Opening Lily Field's door, she was met by the strong scent of lilies prevailing over the roses. A note from Walter on the kitchen table stated he would return tomorrow morning at eight.

Other than the occasional chimes from the Timekeeper, she had the quiet sanctuary to herself. Taking a seat on the sofa, she opened Agnes's folder to read the story written by Anna Knowles Hancock, the granddaughter of Katherine Knowles Davis. *Will it tell me more about Katherine and the Underground Railroad?*

CHAPTER 31

Jameson Gazette
Anniversary Section
One of Our Town's Heroes
A Story by Anna Knowles Hancock

The names of numerous heroes appear on the plaque at the Jameson townhall, but two names are missing, and one of those is Katherine Knowles Davis.

Katherine was not a known hero. She was a silent rescuer who hid her heroism and only recently shared her story with me. Katherine, my grandmother, did not want it lost to history. She wished the next generations would know the sins of the past and vow to be better to one another.

The story of Katherine's heroism originated with a decision her husband William made. As their home, Lily Fields, was being built in 1858, William asked a trusted local craftsman to construct several secret hiding places for valuables. There was talk of possible conflict between states, and William had the foresight to know that during war, both sides scavenged for silver, gold, and other precious commodities, including food. These hideaways proved to be providential.

In the fall of 1860, William's father passed away in England. After Katherine's insistence that she knew how to use the rifle and hired hands would help with chores, William left her in Jameson to accompany his mother from England to Virginia. Katherine's parents lived on the other side of Richmond, and she promised William she would stay with them part of the time.

But the second week William was away changed Katherine's life for-ever. In the middle of the night, she awakened to the Timekeeper's twelve chimes sounding between desperate pounds on the door. Concerned at first whether to open it, she got a feeling the answer was yes. Holding a candle in her hand, she turned the lock to open her door. When she did, she saw an enslaved woman shackled on both arms and one leg. "Please, have mercy," she begged Katherine. "Hide me."

The woman needed to get North to freedom—back to freedom. Although she was born free in Ohio, when she was nineteen, slave traders kidnapped her. Because of the Fugitive Slave Act, all states, including the Northern States, were required by law to assist in the return of escaped slaves. Unable to prove her free birth in time and disprove the affidavit the slave hunters presented to the judge, stating she was an escaped slave, the hunters bound and brought her to Virginia. And knowing she'd tasted freedom since birth, her new owners kept her shackled since the day they got her nine years ago. She was twenty-eight the night she knocked on Katherine's door.

Once safely inside, Katherine quickly placed a large stone under the woman's foot and then her hands, then pounded a heavy hammer over the metal until the shackles unleashed their grip. Sickened by the smell permeating from the woman's skin and scant clothing, she brought a large tub into the kitchen. Smelling worse than an outhouse, the woman's hair was matted with mud like a pig stye. One bath was not enough, but a bar of soap helped cut the pungent odor along with a clean pair of William's pants, one of his shirts, and a pair of oversized shoes. As for the woman's clothes, Katherine burned those rags in the fire.

Callouses on her feet helped her make the long walk to Lily Fields, but one foot bled and needed attention. Katherine wrapped it in strips of cloth she tore from William's old cotton work shirt.

"Hunters been on my trail since yesterday. I heard the dogs," she told Katherine. Needing a place to hide her, she thought about the hidden room under the stairs, but too many homes had those. It would be the first place they looked. *The basement*, she thought. It was not ideal, but as far as Katherine knew, it was unique to their home.

Before he left for Europe, William placed their wedding silver, china, his gold pocket watch, and Katherine's jewels inside a box and put it in that underground room. The entrance was hidden under the fireplace floor by a metal covering. A grate with logs placed on top and dusted with ashes concealed the metal edges.

Katherine gathered two wool blankets and a jug of water for the woman, but before she lowered herself into the dark hole, she asked Katherine for a knife. Katherine hesitated but retrieved one and handed it to her inside the earthen cavern.

Oxygen needed to get inside, so Katherine didn't put the metal plate back in place. Instead, she placed a few logs on the open grate and stacked other logs around the front and sides to conceal the hole. The woman's hideaway was cold, dark, and damp, but it was better than being hung as an example to others.

Before sleeping in her room upstairs, Katherine prayed and asked God for wisdom. When the Timekeeper's five chimes awakened her, she had had little sleep. To not raise suspicion, she readied to go to the newspaper office as planned. But before leaving home, she lowered fresh baked bread into the hole along with another jug of water. No one was due at the house that day. A hired hand who assisted Katherine with the animals came two days a week, and he had been there the previous morning.

As she did every day while William was away, Katherine went to the newspaper office in town. She did her best to act normal and not like she was harboring a runaway slave in her hidden basement. Already having flour from the family's gristmill, she picked up other ingredients for making bread, telling the general store clerk she expected lady friends for tea that weekend.

After checking on the woman that evening, Katherine made her plan. Ever since William had gone away, she rode along with her helper, Jonathan, to take the newspapers and flour from the gristmill to the river boat on Thursdays for transport upriver. She knew from overhearing ladies in church that there were boats willing to transport escaped slaves to the North for a price, but what price she did not know. Katherine didn't have much cash, and what valuables she had were in the basement with the woman.

The next day before leaving for work, she lowered more bread and water into the hole. At the newspaper office, Katherine told Jonathan that instead of leaving from town with him that evening, she needed to take the wagon home and make the delivery herself. She forgot a box she wanted to ship to her aunt in New York. As she instructed, Jonathan piled sacks of flour in the center of the wagon and newspapers around the sides.

When Katherine arrived back at Lily Fields late that afternoon, she called down to the woman and asked her to hand up a box of valuables in the corner. She selected two gold rings, one with a ruby and one with a pearl and a pair of gold earrings with teardrop pearls. The earrings were a gift from her grandmother. She also took William's gold pocket watch etched with two love birds holding a vine in their mouths between them. Handing the box back down to the woman, Katherine asked her to return it to the corner. Afterward, Katherine pulled the woman up and out of the secret hole and covered the opening with the metal plate and log grate on top.

Tying a long string to a pouch, she attached it to William's belt loop. "Put the pouch inside your pants and put the shirt over it to hide the string. The money inside is for when you get to the North," Katherine instructed the woman. "You will need to buy supplies when you arrive."

Katherine needed the woman's help to ready the wagon, but she feared taking her outside too soon. "Best you stay inside and eat some food while I tend to the horses." The woman asked Katherine for paper and a writing instrument. She said she hadn't been allowed to write since she was captured.

Inside the barn, Katherine removed several sacks of flour from the center of the wagon, just enough for the woman to squeeze into. She brought the horses up to the side of the house and went to retrieve the woman. Once inside the hollowed out hiding spot in the wagon, Katherine handed her three loaves of bread and a jug of water before putting folded blankets and sacks of flour on top of her head. Pulling the tarp over the wagon, she tied it on all sides. In the midst of darkness and little moonlight, she snapped the horse's reins and headed toward the Rappahannock River.

About a mile from Lily Fields, lanterns waved ahead. Two men stood in the center of the road with dogs on leashes. She stopped the wagon.

"Evening ma'am. Surprised to see a woman out here alone," one of the men said.

Shaking mightily on the inside but with a controlled voice, Katherine replied, "My husband is away in Europe, and I'm getting our newspapers and flour to the river for shipment."

"We got a runaway slave around here," a man said. "Best if we check your wagon and make sure there's none hiding inside." Their dogs were going crazy as he spoke. They smelled something.

"By all means. I appreciate you kind gentlemen looking out for my safety." Seeing the dogs pulling at their leashes and lunging for the wagon, she said, "The dogs must be smelling the salt pork I'm carrying."

The men pulled back the tarp and saw the piles of newspapers and flour sacks. When one of them climbed onto the wagon, Katherine flipped open William's gold pocket watch. "Oh, my. Look at the time. I'm going to miss the boat." She thanked them for their concern and asked them to retie the tarp. Katherine snapped the reins and continued toward the river.

She guessed her best option to find a willing boat captain would be one separated from the dock man's watch, and she was right. An unsavory looking gentleman who had two free Black men working on his boat was open to a conversation.

"What do you have to offer?" he asked her.

Reaching into her right dress pocket, Katherine took one of her rings, the pearl one, and presented it to him.

"Not enough," the boat captain told her. "Too much risk."

Fortunately, Katherine put each piece of jewelry in a separate place. The second ring with a ruby was in her left pocket. The two rings met the boat captain's price. She didn't need William's pocket watch or the pearl earrings, each separately hidden inside her laced-up shoes.

"Put her inside here." The boat captain held out a large potato sack. Once Katherine helped get the woman inside, he crawled on top of the wagon and hoisted the bag over his shoulder. He walked to the boat, carrying his human cargo inside that sack, and it was the last Katherine saw of the woman.

Still in need of her real delivery to complete, she drove the wagon to another boat waiting for her. She motioned for the boat captain to help her unload, but since she was late and did not have Jonathan with her, the captain made her pay one of his hired hands to keep him on schedule. Hidden inside another pocket, she had money enough to pay him.

The wagon ride home was uneventful, and she used the time to pray for safe passage for the woman who had lived beneath her home for two days. Katherine did not believe in coincidence. She knew God sent this woman to her, and when the Timekeeper's chimes awakened her that night, she chose to answer and help the stranger at her door.

The next morning, when she came downstairs to the kitchen, there on the table was a piece of paper with garbled writing that said:

> *never thot livin in a hole wuld feel good. safe. a place to rest this darknes givs me peece. hidin undergrownd is like a cacun. i is rappd up hidin watin fer the rit time to brak free. soon i use my new wings to fly. fly north to freedum wer we can liv an love as we wer made. to freley feel to freley be. to expurins life with no shackls tyin me to a plas of werk and jus existens with no joy. i rest in darknes noin that soon the lite il shine upon me gidin me alung a uncerten path leeding to a gloreus new beginin.*

The note was signed *Selah*. Beneath the paper was a small, wooden butterfly Selah had carved when she was in the hole. The butterfly has been a treasured family heirloom ever since that day and passes like our home per Katherine's wishes, from first daughter to first daughter.

CHAPTER 32

On the kitchen table, perhaps in a similar spot where Katherine found Selah's note and gift, Bethany checked her email, as always, first thing in the morning with a cup of black coffee in her hand. A note from Holly said to expect an overnight envelope today with several items inside.

Bethany reflected on the story she had read yesterday. She was grateful Anna wrote the account of Katherine's bravery. Still wanting to know more about her family, she went into the living room and opened the family Bible to look at the list of names.

With all the awards on her Alexandria office wall, Bethany felt insignificant next to these women. Each had a purpose, a higher calling for their lives. She thought about Peter's questions to her. *What was the purpose of all her striving? What true significance did it produce?* Bethany thought of the jobs she provided. The work she hired people for helped put food on many families' tables. *All true, but do I sound like Baxter? What will become of that girl and the other young workers in that other building? What will their futures be like?* Their childhoods were cut short like hers, but she continued in school and helped at home instead of working in a factory.

Bethany picked up Selah's note from inside the family Bible. And thinking of that carved butterfly led her upstairs to retrieve the silver box. She removed the contents from the royal-blue velvet lining. Rubbing the carved wood between her fingers, she thought how this gift passed through three centuries from daughter to daughter, generation to generation. And even though another woman raised her, Marguerite wanted Bethany to have this treasure. It was her birthright, and she almost missed finding it.

If Amy had not asked Bethany to gather clothes for her charity sale, and if Mitzi had not badgered her to go through her mother's boxes, Bethany might not have discovered the butterfly for years, if ever. *What if I gave the contents away without going through the box?* Instead, a series of coincidences occurred for her to find it. Coincidences, as Anna Knowles Hancock noted in her story, were not something Katherine believed in. *Was I meant to find it when I did?* She wondered about the timing.

Nick's number buzzed on her phone. "Sorry for not checking in last night," he said. "I've been working nonstop and fell asleep on my couch."

"I understand," Bethany answered.

"It's busy season," he said. "Been my best year ever. Hard to find workers, so I have to pitch in with my crews. But enough about work. So good to hear your voice."

"Good to hear yours too," she said with the sweet sound of a schoolgirl infatuated with a new boy.

"Can I stop at your house this afternoon? My arborist crew is doing tree work a couple of miles down the road. When we rode into the woods, I noticed a dead tree at the edge of your backyard. I'm concerned it could fall on the carriage house. I can stop by with my crew and take care of it for you."

With Nick coming to visit, Bethany wondered if she should change her clothes. She thought yes and put on a tight pair of jeans and a flowy, hot-pink blouse with tiny white flowers. Because it was see-through, she put a flesh-colored camisole underneath. Pulling her hair out of the high ponytail, she brushed it and reached inside the bathroom cabinet for the curling iron she bought online after Sam showed her the benefits of adding soft waves.

Doing her best, she styled her hair. Sam made it look effortless and easy, but it was not. The hands of a professional with a tool made all the difference. She slid on the wedge shoes she wore on the date night in Nick's garden. With added height, her long legs looked even longer. After squirting her French perfume on each side of her neck, she added another squirt on her wrist and rubbed them together. This man was getting three puffs of perfume. If he only knew how lucky he was.

The doorbell rang and interrupted her finishing touches. Holly's delivery arrived, and Bethany took the envelope to the kitchen while she made her second cup of coffee. Inside the manila file folder were copies of team reports for each project. At the back she found a heart printed with a photo of her nine-year-old sponsored child, Carmen, from Honduras. Attached to the paper was a handwritten note from Holly.

> *I thought you might like some company. Carmen looked lonely on your office door. I've included a letter she sent you.*

Bethany unfolded a child's drawing of a flower along with a note written in a red-colored pencil.

> *Querida Bethany, Muchas gracias por los libros. Me gusto mucho.*

Beneath the handwriting was a written translation by the sponsorship organization:

> *Dear Bethany, Thank you very much for the books. I like them a lot.*

In the photo, Carmen wore a dirty blue skirt, flowered top, and flip-flops. Standing on muddy ground near a shanty house, she was smiling. Even while living in poverty, Carmen's face showed joy. Bethany went back to reading the rest of Holly's note:

> *Everyone is engaged with the child they are sponsoring. Letters are being passed around the office. It's always a happy day when an associate receives a letter from their child. We have a connected purpose for what we do now. Thanks for making us reach outside our geographic boundaries to touch hearts and bring beauty around the world. We miss you. ~Love, Holly*

Bethany called Holly to thank her for the package and more. Besides being the best executive assistant ever, Holly did lots of things for Bethany, like managing repairs at her townhouse, arranging deliveries, and picking up dry cleaning when she was out of town. She was as close to Bethany and knew more about her life than most, except for Amy and, of course, Mitzi, who knew her better and longer than anyone.

The women caught up on work and their personal lives. "I've been on a few more dates," Holly said. "It's going well. We'll see." Holly had started dating a new guy before Bethany left town. She was married once for two years when she was right out of high school, but she had not yet found true love. "How about your date?" she asked. "How are things going in Jameson?"

Bethany didn't share how much she looked forward to seeing Nick again. She wasn't ready to admit it out loud. Romantic relationships were something she was not good at. The best she ever had was with her former fiancé, but even he couldn't compete against Bethany's incessant drive and focus on her business. She chose to only answer Holly's second question.

"I expect to finish the projects here in a few more weeks. Walter is a single-handed machine. Except for the electrical work we still need to do, he's made real progress. I'm thinking of asking my landscaper, Nick, what other ideas he has for the front yard. Maybe plant a few new trees."

The doorbell rang and cut the phone visit short. They agreed to talk again soon. When Bethany opened the door, she found Nick standing behind another handful of flowers, and she recognized them.

"I picked you a variety," he said. "Nothing like having cuttings all from your own garden this time." Nick had the biggest of grins on his face as he handed the bouquet to her.

"They're beautiful, but I still have the other ones from your garden and mine."

"I wanted to give you more." His eyes flowed into hers and mixed with the strong emotion they both held inside. After she accepted the bouquet from his hand, he followed her into the kitchen to find another vase.

Walking ahead of him in her wedge shoes, she felt his eyes staring at her long legs. She heard him breathe in deeply and absorb the perfume that no doubt lingered behind her.

Acting on instinct, she added a sway to her step as she led the way. She had the man's attention and knew it. She was proud of her shape.

Years of private Pilate's workouts had elongated her muscles. *Good thing I'm not in a bikini*, she thought. *Or maybe I wish I were?*

Bethany opened cupboard after cupboard but did not find another vase. "I've got to do some shopping." She apologized to Nick as she put the flowers in a plastic pitcher and set them in the middle of the table next to the envelope from Holly. They each took a seat.

On top of the table was Carmen's photo and her handwritten note. She showed them both to Nick. "This is the child I'm sponsoring in Honduras. Each one of our ninety-seven employees is sponsoring a child, at least one in all forty-four countries where our clients' products are sold."

"Honduras is not far from my country," Nick said.

"You never told me where you were born. You only told me you immigrated here from Central America."

"I'm from Costa Rica."

Bethany's eyes widened as surprise filled her face. "I've been to your country once, recently actually. Baxter, the one I told you about who owns the cosmetic company—my main client and old friend—he has a factory in Costa Rica. I was there a week before coming to Jameson. We were filming a video of his new factory lines."

"How did you like my home country? It's beautiful, isn't it?" Nick beamed with pride.

"I didn't get to see much of it except through my hotel or car window. Like most of my travels, it was all business. So much to do and not enough time to do it. Every second counts when you are building a business."

Nick sat next to her at the kitchen table and listened as she described her hurried life. He stood up, took her two hands in his, and looked into her eyes. "No profit grows where no pleasure is taken." He stood close to her beating chest.

Bethany didn't speak. She waited for him to do something, but he remained still and silent, just staring. Finally, she asked him, "From *Julius Caesar*?"

"No, *Taming of the Shrew*."

The sound of chain saws drew their attention out back as a large, rotted oak tree fell to the ground. They walked outside to inspect it. Its wood was dry and cracked, and bugs had eaten the center of the dead tree.

"What a pity to see such a large tree taken down," Bethany said. "No telling how many years it stood here with my ancestors."

"*Querida mia*. No saving it. Either we take it now or the next storm would have. It's dangerous to keep such a large, dead tree. It could fall on someone or hit the carriage house."

Nick's workmen used chain saws to cut through the large tree trunk on the ground, and he yelled something in Spanish to one of them. A worker cut a three-inch slice of wood from the trunk and brought it to Nick.

"See these rings here?" he said to her. "Each one represents a year. Without counting them, I'd say your tree was one hundred fifty years old."

Bethany remembered Katherine had mentioned the trees on the property. Her husband, William, had selected which ones to remove for the placement of the home. This tree was alive when many in her family lived here. Bethany wanted to keep the piece of wood, but Nick took it from her hands.

"Best not to bring it inside. Let me take it to the shop first. We will seal it, and then you can bring it into the house as a keepsake." He rubbed the side of her arm with one hand as he held the wood slice in his other.

Nick's workers sawed the rest of the tree in pieces and loaded it into the truck. One of them shouted something to Nick in Spanish and flashed a wide, toothy smile at him. Bethany didn't understand, but it was obvious the worker was teasing Nick, and it was about her. Feeling exposed, Nick motioned for Bethany to go inside with him to end the male razzing.

Back inside the kitchen and protected from the leering eyes and open ears of his workers outside, Nick took her hand in his. As he walked down the hall to leave through the front door, he asked, "Are you free this evening or tomorrow for dinner?"

"Either works for me," she said.

As they reached the front door, he turned to look at her and asked, "How about both?"

Nick was pursuing her, that was clear. She started to think she might like spending more time with him, but she was leaving soon. The house was almost finished, and her work awaited her in Alexandria. Soon, she needed to return to her old life. But this new one here in Jameson had slowed her down enough to wonder if there might be something she was missing.

Maybe Scott was right about slowing down, but moving fast was all Bethany knew. Work fulfilled her and never disappointed. Well, not until she lost those big projects from Baxter. Something wasn't right with him. Was he still mad about her questioning him about his factory?

CHAPTER 33

Bethany and Nick spent the next two days sharing dinner and conversation. The first night they ate at a restaurant inside an old home in the nearby town of Gloucester. After dinner, they strolled through Gloucester's well preserved historic district and marveled at the 1766 courthouse and surrounding buildings.

The second night Nick finished work late, which forced him to push back their dinner time. Bethany suggested she meet him at the café in Jameson. Afterward, they took a walk while streetlamps illuminated the meticulous historic buildings. Children ran around the center park's grass and caught fireflies as parents observed the summertime fun.

Nick and Bethany stopped for ice cream cones. He got chocolate and she got strawberry. "My dad always got chocolate. My mom got strawberry," she said before taking a lick of her strawberry ice cream. "They seemed in love, at least to me as a kid. Friday nights were ice cream nights, whether at a restaurant or at home. I loved Fridays mostly because they were right before Saturday mornings when my dad did something with me, just the two of us. He always slowed down for me."

"I can see why," Nick said, using his arm to pull her closer to his side.

If she were back in Alexandria, she would be at home at her computer working. Here, she took the time to be with someone other than herself.

They walked with their ice cream cones and stopped to sit in the gazebo where the band had played the first night she arrived in town. Even though the sun was down, it was still hot outside, melting the ice cream at record speed. Without her noticing, Bethany's dripped down her chin, and Nick wiped it clean with his napkin. And then he kissed her. Opening her eyes, she looked at him for a moment. And then she leaned in and kissed him back. Her lips met his, and the soft embrace enveloped her inside a feeling she had never known before. Whatever this was, it felt good. She didn't want this night to end but knew he had another early day tomorrow. As he put her inside her car, he leaned inside to stroke her cheek before saying goodnight. He waited to make sure she was safely on her way.

On her drive home alone to Lily Fields, Bethany thought about how much had changed. Her structured life full of business meetings and travels no longer seemed to be her life. It seemed like someone else's. The problem was that other life was still her life. Employees and customers needed her and counted on her. Soon, she would need to return to Alexandria, but during this summer break, she felt things other than her competitive drive. She felt fun and in love. She was living in the moment and enjoying being Bethany, the Bethany she left behind all those years ago.

In Costa Rica, another factory girl disappeared.

CHAPTER 34

P eter stopped by Lily Fields with a document the paralegal had missed when they filed the paperwork. "We won't worry about the notary," he said, holding it out for Bethany's signature. "My assistant will take care of that back at the office." His phone rang and Peter apologized for taking the call in front of her. "I'm here with her now," he informed.

"Serendipitous!" Agnes exclaimed through the phone, loud enough for Bethany to hear. "I have some items from the museum for each of you. Are you both free today at two o'clock?"

Peter took the phone away from his ear and addressed Bethany, "I think you can hear it's Agnes," he said. "She wants to see us both. Are you free today at two?" Bethany nodded. She would meet Peter there.

Inviting her into the living room, Agnes motioned for Bethany to sit on the couch next to Peter. The cookies he brought her were on the coffee table. "We waited for you to arrive, child, before having one." Agnes's cat, Penelope, was nowhere in sight. *Peter must have scared her away when he arrived.*

"I was just going over Peter's family tree with him, child."

Bethany sat on the couch next to Peter and listened as Agnes told him about various relatives in the eighteenth and nineteenth centuries. *I wonder how long it will take before Agnes gets to me,* she thought as she looked at Peter's thick report, no telling how many pages it held.

When Agnes took a break from her painstakingly detailed report, Bethany interjected. "I'm curious, did you find out any more about my family's involvement in the Underground Railroad?"

"No, not yet, but I do have other information for you, child. Your grandmother, Elizabeth, she was my friend, you know." Bethany nodded. "She gave me a newspaper article for our museum, and I just found it there in a box."

"I already have it," Bethany said.

"No, a different one from a newspaper in Chicago. Your grandmother gave me a copy." Agnes picked up a folder on the end table beside her and handed Bethany a newspaper article with the headline: "Boat Capsizes on Lake Michigan." Agnes motioned for Bethany to read the article out loud to them. "Your mother is in that story."

The newspaper article chronicled an early summer night when a boat with eight passengers capsized on Lake Michigan. The story shared details of the lake being 118 miles wide and 307 miles long. And it said it averaged 279 feet in depth and was 925 feet at its deepest point.

Bethany read aloud, "It was after midnight when large waves from the storm capsized the boat, and the passengers clung to the hull. After the weather cleared, one of the passengers, who was a triathlete, swam to shore for help. Two hours later, the Coast Guard rescued all the others."

"Was this my mother who swam to shore for help?"

"No, child. Keep reading. The story is from the year you were born. Look at the names of the boat passengers under the photograph. Read them out loud."

Bethany began, "John Schmidt from Chicago, IL; Sally Rhodes from Columbus, OH; Mary Jo Burgess from St. Louis, MO; Michael McDermott from Champagne, IL; Brenda Lipscomb from Miami, FL; Marguerite Marchand from Jameson, VA." Bethany raised her head. "My mother was on this boat."

This revelation was one more piece of her mother's puzzled life becoming known, including what she liked to do, who her friends were, her love of writing and her willingness to help others. Bethany's mother was strong, like her. And now she envisioned her clinging to that boat, holding on for her life—maybe Bethany's life inside her too. That thought shook Bethany. She visualized Marguerite in the dark of night, trying to save them both.

"Continue, child," Agnes said with a pat on Bethany's arm.

"Larry Churchill from Indianapolis, IN; Peter Jameson II from Jameson, VA."

Peter lunged forward and reached for the article in Bethany's hands.

"He never told me about this accident," Peter said in shock.

Peter looked at Agnes, but she was looking at Bethany.

"Your grandmother, Elizabeth, gave me the article years ago, child. She thought since it mentioned two prominent townspeople in a big city newspaper, it should be saved in the museum."

Bethany turned toward Peter. "I didn't know your father attended college with Marguerite in Chicago."

"He didn't," Peter said. "My father attended Georgetown, just like his father."

Agnes cut in on the conversation to explain. "Your parents had been friends since high school. Evidently, Peter visited Marguerite in Chicago. It was Marguerite's last year in college."

"I knew my parents and Marguerite were all friends, "Peter said. "But I didn't know about this boating accident with my dad and Marguerite. It sounds like a traumatic scene, but he never shared the story." Peter sat on the couch, rubbing his forehead.

"Thank you for this," Bethany said. "Agnes, may I keep it or make a copy?"

"I've already made one for you, child, and have it in a folder for you along with some other items. I made a copy for you, too, Peter."

"I need to ask my mother about this," Peter said. "Strange my father never shared this story. He loved boating. Maybe that's why he preached safety so much to my sister and me." Peter's eyes squinted as if he was searching to remember a conversation long ago.

"Back to the report I've been working on for you, Peter," Agnes said to regain his attention. Thanks for letting me have your login and password so I could work directly with your online DNA report to complete your family tree. As you know, your family came to America in 1731. They went first to Baltimore and then settled on land now known as Jameson."

Peter nodded his head. He knew all this, and Bethany listened politely until Agnes stopped and said, "Bethany, I'd be happy to do a report for you, too, someday. Have you ever taken a DNA test?"

"I sent one in right before I came to Jameson. Don't think the results are back yet."

"Did you set up an account?" Agnes asked.

"Yes, but I haven't checked it because it's connected to a personal email account I rarely use."

"Did you think to use a pseudonym for your protection? You can't be too careful these days, child."

"I used my favorite expression, *Every Second Counts.*"

Agnes smiled at the reference. "I remember hearing you say that expression when we first met." She turned back to Peter, who waited silently on the couch while the ladies talked. "Peter, can you turn to the final page of the report I made you? I wanted to mention one other item. Read the bottom row, please," Agnes instructed Peter with a point of her finger.

Peter flipped to the back page. "It says close family match . . . *Every Second Counts.*"

His eyes shot up at Agnes and then to Bethany beside him on the couch. Bethany's hand was across her mouth.

"You are half brother and half sister," Agnes announced. "I suspected it but needed proof. I knew your parents dated when they were young."

"I can't believe this," Bethany said with her mouth remaining open.

"Bethany, I had no idea, believe me." Peter caressed her arm and promptly removed his hand. He sat back on the couch. His face filled with the competing emotions of surprise and horror, but Bethany was in shock. The pair had grown to like each other, and now the knowledge they were half brother and sister changed their dynamic drastically.

Bethany's mind kicked in and replayed Peter saying Marguerite told him how important it was he tell her the story surrounding her birth. Marguerite wanted Bethany to know that she saved her and moved to California to hide the fact she was born and given up for adoption. His father was Marguerite's boyfriend, the one who drove her to the clinic and insisted she have an abortion. Those memories and the result of the past generation's actions collided on Agnes's present-day couch.

Peter's bewilderment reigned across his face. Before coming to Jameson, Bethany read on his website that his grandfather was a US senator, and his father served in the Virginia State House. In the family's law practice, wealthy families entrusted their secrets to the Jameson's.

Peter's was the prominent family Marguerite referenced. His grandfather, a senator, was the one who pressured Peter's dad to take care of "this thing," as he called it, that threatened to ruin Peter's father's future and political career. The family name was at stake back then. And today, the whole family's guilt showed across Peter's face.

"I am so sorry," Peter said with sincerity and sadness in his voice. "I didn't know my father was your father. Marguerite didn't tell me."

Bethany turned her shoulders and looked at Peter. "Marguerite wanted us to find out. She set this all up."

Agnes watched the natural interaction between the two half siblings. A bell rang upstairs. "So very sorry," Agnes said and stood up from her chair. "I must attend to Arthur."

When they got beside Peter's white SUV, he said, "I don't know what to say, Bethany. I only knew my father as the utmost gentleman. As a twenty-one-year-old, he must have been put under so much pressure. He and my mother were both pro-life advocates. I wonder if my father ever told her?"

"Well, at least your mother is still alive so you can ask her," Bethany remarked with a tinge of attitude.

Her reactive words hurled across the sidewalk at Peter and struck a blow. But she wasn't mad at *him*, she was mad at herself for not sending in that DNA test sooner. The timing of Mitzi's Christmas gift may have been soon enough for her to find clues and meet her mother, if only she had sent it in. But work had gotten in the way, as usual, and she didn't want to bother looking for someone who had nothing to do with her life, or so she thought.

"I am so very sorry," Peter said. "As a Jameson, I take responsibility for my father's actions." He held his hands to his heart before holding them out to her.

Bethany did not respond until the heat inside her cooled from a big breath she took in and then exhaled. She regretted snapping at him. This news shocked her, but it crushed him. "Peter, that was your dad, not you. You are not to blame. All you've done is try to help me through all this."

Peter looked around the neighborhood as if searching for an answer. "What if we never found out?"

"Marguerite at least made sure we were brought together. Let's take it from here. Every second counts," Bethany said.

"I have to admit," Peter said, "I had a moment of horror back inside Agnes's house. He looked down at the sidewalk before bringing his head back up to face her. "If not for being interrupted and seeing the landscaper at your door that day, I planned to ask you to dinner."

Bethany's face blushed. "Saved by the bell," she said. "I thought you were pretty handsome yourself. Ew!" Her face scrunched. "That could have ended up really bad."

"I've got to tell my sister," Peter said. "She's got two kids—a boy and a girl. That makes you Aunt Bethany."

"An aunt? I've never been one. How do you think your sister will take the news?"

"I'm not sure, but she should be glad to hear she has a half sister. She's had to put up with just me all these years." Peter laughed as he stood beside Bethany at his car.

Bethany could not believe what just occurred. Less than an hour ago, she had walked into Agnes's house, searching for more information about her grandmother and the Underground Railroad. She came out with her half brother, who told her to get ready to meet her half sister, niece, and nephew.

Two of her key discoveries were crossed off her list, but there were still more women in her family to get to know. More of the Timekeeper's journal entries waited to be read—she'd completed only the first three out of six. What more did each of these women have to share?

⊰◇⊱

At Lily Fields, the Timekeeper's melody and chimes rang throughout the house as if in joyful celebration. Choices people freely made were unveiled in Agnes's living room, and earlier discoveries unearthed in the home showed human triumph over evil. A journal filled with each of the six women's gift to the next generation was being read page by page.

Operating within the scarcity of time, Bethany still busied herself to make every second count. There was much more for her to learn. But for Bethany, a time-rich melody was not yet ready to be understood.

CHAPTER 35

Before she drove away from Agnes's house, Bethany left a message for Mitzi telling her the news, and now Mitzi was calling her back on video. Mitzi clapped her hands into the phone. "I told you to send in that DNA test!"

Bethany passed the red barn next to a historic white farmhouse. "Peter couldn't bear it was his dad who drove my mother to get an abortion. He took the family burden all on himself."

"Poor guy. Such a sweetie," Mitzi said. "Hey . . . here's some good news. Now that's he's your half brother, that opens him up for me, right?"

"Oh, Mitzi. You're always on one track. Wait 'til Peter gets a load of you. I'd better prepare him. He's going to have to love you like I do because we are best friends forever."

"You got that right. You're both stuck with me," Mitzi said.

"Oh, I'm an aunt too," Bethany added. "Peter's sister, who is my half sister, has two kids, a boy and a girl. Peter is going to tell her, and I hope she wants to meet me." Bethany crossed the bridge over the creek as she neared Lily Fields.

"Be prepared, Bethany. You never know how someone might react. A lot of people don't like digging up the past. She might need time," Mitzi warned.

"More time? Time is slipping by every minute. It's been thirty-eight years already."

"You can wait. Consider her side of things," Mitzi said.

Bethany turned on Knowles Lane. "Consider *my* side of things. I'm exhausted from all this. My hot lawyer, whom I was really starting to like, is my half brother. It's all so crazy. Good thing we didn't go down that path. Things almost got really weird." Pulling her car back by the carriage house, she put it in park and turned off the engine.

"Yep, that would have been weird for sure," Mitzi affirmed. "But look at you now. I see such a difference in your eyes."

In the rearview mirror, a brighter light shined out from Bethany's brown eyes. The burden of not knowing who her father was had been lifted, and this knowledge brought enormous relief. Relief that is, right before the mirror's reflection changed. Now, she saw the brown eyes of that young girl in Costa Rica.

The past was not finished with Bethany yet. It still had more secrets to share.

CHAPTER 36

A rediscovered newspaper article caused the past to divulge long-forgotten events. And if no one ever knew Bethany existed, that article would have been simply viewed as two high school friends in a boating accident. But in death, Marguerite got Bethany out into the light for all to see. Inheriting Lily Fields brought Bethany to Jameson, the place where her half brother lived. And with anxious anticipation, she looked forward to meeting her half sister, niece, and nephew soon too.

Peter wanted to share the Jameson family tree with her, and she arranged for him to visit her tomorrow. His family, her father's family, founded this town. Jameson was her town now too.

She spread all her discoveries on the kitchen table. The Timekeeper's journal was there, the newspaper account of her heroic great-great-great-grandmother Katherine, the Chicago boating accident article with her biological mother and father's names, the note from Selah, the carved butterfly, and the family Bible. She also had photographs she and Walter took of the hidden basement, the shackles, and other items they found underground and in the carriage house too.

This is what movies are made of, she thought. But sitting on her kitchen table were not movie props. These items represented her family's lives, and she looked forward to reading even more about her maternal side.

The family Bible was a big help to her so far to keep names straight, but she might still take Agnes up on her offer to create a family tree—a tree that included her father's side as well. Bethany's mother was Marguerite Knowles Marchand, and her father was Peter Jameson II. Bethany now knew where she came from, but she didn't know why she was supposed to be here. What was she born to do? Peter called it her "purpose in life."

Her phone buzzed on the table next to the artifacts, and Baxter's number appeared on the screen. She hadn't spoken to him for two weeks, ever since he gave the new company's projects to another agency. Good thing he hadn't called her earlier. She needed the time to cool off and waited until the third ring to pick up the phone.

"How's the house coming along?" Baxter asked.

"Getting lots done," Bethany said, looking at the artifacts. "Found out more about my mother and learned who my father was. He passed away too."

"I'm sorry, Bethany. Was hoping you would find some living relatives," Baxter said.

"Oh, I did. Just not my parents." She snapped the lid closed on the single-serve coffee maker and placed a cup under it.

"All is going well here," Baxter reassured. "Thought you'd want to know Scott and I are working together just fine. Miss talking to you though."

"Amy said you've been traveling a lot. How's the factory in Costa Rica doing?"

The dark, steaming coffee filled the cup.

"Going well. I'm traveling down there a lot."

"I heard." Her curt tone was obvious, and it gave away part of what Amy shared with her.

Baxter didn't acknowledge the pointed remark, but Bethany was certain he'd made the connection. The coffee heated her insides, and she opened the kitchen window to let in a breeze.

"Just called to let you know Scott is doing a good job. We miss you but want you to take all the time you need before coming back home."

Home. That word never sounded more confusing to Bethany. Alexandria was her home. That was clear before she came to Lily Fields, but now she knew she was also a Jameson. She could now officially call this place her home, too, possibly more so than Alexandria. Her family had lived in this home since 1858. They rescued people here and got them on boats to freedom. One of her relatives testified for another and one marched for women's voting rights. This town was growing on her. It was her legacy.

She thought about B.R. Miller Advertising and her office wall lined with advertising awards. It all seemed trivial to Bethany now. What was significant about her life? She remembered the conversation with Nick. What would she do if she had all the time in the world?

"Hello?" Baxter asked. "Bethany, how long do you plan to stay in Jameson? Are you there?"

"Yes, sorry. What did you say?" She reached for her brewed coffee, noticing the steam had already worn off.

"When are you coming back to work?" Baxter's tone changed from his caring voice to a direct, business-like one.

"It will be a few more weeks before the remodeling projects are done. I plan to come back to Alexandria as soon as I'm finished. But I'm also thinking about going back and forth while the projects get completed. I know I need to help Scott." She sipped her coffee and took a seat at the kitchen table.

"What all are you remodeling?" Baxter asked.

"Two upstairs bathrooms. I'm leaving the downstairs as is for now. Several more fix-it items still to do, like the nagging windows. They're original and keep sticking no matter how much time Walter spends on them. He's a gem. Never gives up trying to find a solution."

"My recommendation is you stay there," Baxter said. "If there's one piece of advice I can give you, it's to do it all at once. Remodel all the bathrooms while you are there, and get the kitchen done too. Trust me. You'll thank me for this."

Baxter often gave Bethany direction. He overstepped his bounds sometimes, but she forgave him for it because Baxter always meant well.

"During your remodeling, you can keep in touch with the business. It's the Digital Age, you know. We miss you but want you to focus on the house right now."

Baxter's voice was sweeter than usual. Bethany knew how busy he was, but he took time to check on her. *Stop being so greedy*, she thought, but she could not forget what he did and how he did it. It was not the Baxter she knew.

She tried to focus her mind on the good. The breakdown with Baxter caused B.R. Miller Advertising to diversify their account base even more.

In the long run, she knew it would be best for her business, but right now, she had ninety-seven people plus four new ones to keep fed—and their families too. Keeping the business Baxter currently gave her and new accounts happy was critical to making sure her company stayed on track. Could she keep her business in Alexandria running well while she was here supervising the remodeling in Jameson?

She would think about that later. Now, she had a new family to get to know, and that included the women in the journal. Tonight, she would read the next journal entry. Glancing ahead, she saw it was written by her great-grandmother Victoria. In the family Bible, she learned Victoria was born in 1909, married in 1932, and died in December 1982.

Like the other messages she had read so far, Bethany looked forward to what her great-grandmother Victoria had to share. Though all the women were born in different eras and much before Bethany's time, she had an innate connection with each of them, and it was not just because they shared her same blood. Their messages were reaching her in a deep space no one had accessed before. Words purposely placed on the page from centuries ago were opening the way into her soul.

. . . and the Timekeeper chimed six.

CHAPTER 37

Victoria Knowles Hancock McKinley
Born 1909
Jameson, Virginia

Lily Fields's oak leaves are as golden as sunsets over the Rappahannock. Change comes soon. The heavenly-painted leaves won't remain long. Might we enjoy them so much if they did? Fall pauses us after summer chores and harvesting no longer consume our time.

I sit on Lily Fields's porch and watch in wonder as trees cast away the old, automatically releasing their past. With perfect timing their discarded foliage provides nutrients for the coming season.

But not all change brings spring growth. Try as some might, indelible scars remain etched into lives. Fighting for all mankind, youths were forever taken by guns and bombs. Many of those who returned from World War II remain haunted by memories. Although oceans away, the past traveled home with them.

Three years before that fateful seventh day of December 1941, Joshua and I married. In honor of fallen countrymen, he enlisted on December 8, and his Marine unit saw the deadliest of horrors.

Busying myself with writing, the "Jameson Gazette" became a lifeline as I prayed for Joshua's safe return, but only half of him did. His war-tortured mind after time as a prisoner could not handle the stress of our family business, and to honor this brave man I drove him to the office with me each day. He greeted guests in the lobby and, when able, handled new subscriptions. While I managed the staff, my mother, Anna Knowles

Hancock, kept my daughter. She is grown now with two offspring of her own.

Years have passed since the Second World War took the mind of the Joshua I knew. Lives forever changed, but I held steadfast, knowing the Timekeeper watches over us through seasons of hope and despair. His careful glance remains upon us as we travel this rocky road of life. Turning this way and that way, our journey appears random. We make choices, and sometimes unwanted choices make us. We feel in control and out of control, and both are right depending on whose perspective we are looking from.

Through it all, the Timekeeper's eye never wavers. For He is present even when we are not. Waiting patiently for us to reach out to Him, the hands of time embrace us in an all-encompassing way. The old is gone and the new is born. The Timekeeper rejoices.

I hear time calling me from this earthly life, which I filled with written words. Soon, I will reach into the heavens and meet the Giver of my gifts face-to-face. I look forward to the future He planned for me and will enter joyously free of cares into the realm of glory.

Victoria Knowles McKinley
Daughter, Mother, Reporter, Business Owner, & Time Honorer

CHAPTER 38

A ride into town to shop for flower vases and other items at Home Again Décor refreshed her. While in town, she wanted to share her family news with Sam.

"What have you been up to?" Sam asked as she processed her customer's credit card.

"Shopping." Bethany held back the rest of her news until Sam's customer paid and left the shop.

"I found out Peter Jameson is my half brother," Bethany finally blurted out.

"My goodness! That's incredible." Sam stopped sweeping up the hair on the floor around her chair. "The single girls in town will be glad you're out of Peter's picture, darlin'."

Bethany laughed along with Sam. How funny it was to think back when she and Peter first spent time together. She thought of him as rather handsome, and at the time, she had a feeling he liked her too.

"Have you read any more journal entries?" Sam asked.

"I have. It's fascinating to learn about each of these women. I feel insignificant next to them."

"No way. Look who you are," Sam boasted.

Bethany was used to people acknowledging her success because she was a success. She owned a multimillion-dollar advertising company that made TV commercials for well-known global brands. Why did she not feel the excitement of the advertising world anymore? She wondered about possible burnout. She heard others in her CEO group talk about it, and once a leader got away for a while, they rebounded from it. But would *she*?

"Hi, Oliver," Sam said as Mr. Bridgewell walked into the shop. She went to the counter and reached for an envelope. "I've got the rent check all ready for you."

"Well, hello, Miss Miller," Oliver said. "Very good to see you again. I hope you are enjoying yourself in our special little town." Oliver put the envelope in the inside pocket of his sport coat.

"Very much so," Bethany answered from the waiting area chair.

"Have you decided to stay in Jameson?"

"I need to get back to my business, but first, I'm doing a few more projects, including remodeling the two upstairs bathrooms."

"Sounds like you are keeping the house?" Oliver asked.

"I'm liking spending time there. It's such a beautiful place. I might keep it for getaways, but not sure I have the time to use it."

"There's always time for things you want." Oliver gave an innocent wink to Sam and reached into his pants pocket for his gold pocket watch. Bethany saw it up close this time and noticed the etching. A pair of birds held a vine between their two beaks. It reminded her of William's watch, the one Katherine used to interrupt the slave hunters from searching her wagon. *Could there be two alike?* The story's description matched what Oliver held in his hands.

"Time is slipping from me," Oliver said. He snapped the pocket watch closed and returned it to his pocket. "I bid you ladies *adieu.*"

Out the window, Bethany watched Oliver walk down the sidewalk toward the river. "Have you known Oliver long?" she asked Sam.

"Ever since I came to Jameson. I called him when I saw the "for rent" sign on the building." A woman walked inside, and Sam twirled her chair around to greet her next client. Bethany waved goodbye.

From her parked car in front of the beauty shop, she called Agnes and asked if she could stop by her house to see her, but Agnes wasn't home.

"Meet me at the museum, child," Agnes said. "I've got a caretaker at the house today for Arthur."

It was the first time Bethany visited the museum. She had passed it several times but never when it was open. Besides, she didn't have much interest in old things.

Bethany wanted to get right to asking Agnes questions, but Agnes insisted she take a tour first. "The museum is my lifeline, child. It's my purpose to preserve the old and share it with the young." She pulled Bethany to a glass case.

"There are so many things to share about the town," Agnes said. "It was founded in 1757. Peter's family, your family, was among the first settlers. Inside the glass case, Agnes showed her relics. "And you are a Daughter of the American Revolution." Bethany knew women who touted this lineage, and now she could as well.

Walking her by the hand to the next exhibit, Agnes pointed to a list of townsmen who died in the Civil War. Bethany searched for relatives but found none. Katherine's husband, William, was not listed because she knew he returned to Lily Fields at the war's end.

Next, Agnes took her to a glass-encased exhibit that housed front pages from the *Jameson Gazette*, founded by her great-great-great-grandfather William. "Katherine did her best to keep it open during the Civil War, but paper shortages caused its temporary closure," Agnes informed her. "Many newspapers in the South went out of business during the war." She pointed her finger to an advertisement that asked townspeople to bring in their rag bags. "In those days, recycled linen and rags were used to make paper, a scarce resource in the South. Everything was scarce. The Union blockade made Southern life hard." Agnes shook her head.

As Agnes continued teaching her unexpected pupil, she explained that large scale production of paper was not made from wood in the US until a machine invented in Germany came to America. Some of the newspapers she showed Bethany were printed on half sheets during the war. "Rationing was necessary. People wanted news about the war effort, but with the North blocking supply lines, commodities were hard to acquire. Sometimes, books were bound on the outside with wallpaper. Businesses had to get creative," Agnes said.

"I had no idea they used wallpaper for book coverings." This museum gave her a new sense of wonder about this town and her ancestors.

"Youngins today with all their talk of being *green* have nothing on people of that era. They repurposed anything and everything." Agnes returned to her main lecture on Jameson history.

"Jameson avoided being a battlefield, but that didn't stop Union and Confederate soldiers alike to take whatever they needed or wanted when they passed through by land or docked their boats nearby. Homes in and out of town were ransacked. Soldiers were hungry and not just for food. Many women endured atrocities off the battlefields." Agnes gave Bethany the look women use when they need no words. "Folks in Jameson did their best to protect what little they had."

Bethany thought about all the stories she read in the journal and Anna's newspaper article, including details of the dugout space below the fireplace, the one William made for the family's valuables. With keen foresight, the secret space not only saved the family's jewels, but most importantly, it saved a woman's life.

Another journal entry detailed how after the Civil War, Abigail stood up for what was right and saved a man from jail for a crime he did not commit. Anna organized marches to fight peacefully for women's right to vote. It was Victoria who kept the newspaper in operation when her husband, Joshua, after being imprisoned during World War II, did not have the mental capacity to drive a car—let alone operate a business.

Bethany admired these women. They weathered brutal wars and fought for people and causes they believed in. Agnes showed Bethany a 1916 photograph of the women's march in the Jameson town square. It was black-and-white, but Bethany saw the women wore white as they demanded the right to vote. Anna was not named in the photo, but Bethany knew she must have been out front, leading the way years before the passage of the constitutional amendment.

The Jameson's were not the only royalty in this town, Bethany thought. The women from her maternal side deserved crowns. Both sides of Bethany's family made their marks in history here.

Agnes completed her loop around the room, pointing out each saved piece of history she knew so well. They stopped their walk near the front counter where Bethany said, "I called because I wanted to ask you something. It's about Oliver Bridgewell. I noticed him a few times checking a pocket watch. It looked familiar to me."

Agnes moved closer to Bethany.

"It has the very same markings described in the story written by Anna Knowles Hancock about her grandfather William's pocket watch, the one Katherine had with her that night on the wagon."

"That's because it *is* William's watch," Agnes said with a smile.

Bethany's neck darted forward like a turtle leaving its shell. "How did Oliver Bridgewell get William's watch?"

"After he returned from the Civil War, William gave it to Oliver's great-grandfather, Harold Bridgewell, who was a craftsman. He helped William build Lily Fields and also the secret room. After you asked me about it at the house, I checked into it. As they were constructing the home in 1858, William grew concerned that trouble was coming to the fledgling America. Since one war was already fought to found the country, he feared another might break out in years to come." Agnes looked back at the Civil War exhibit.

Before William left to fight for the South, he asked Harold Bridgewell, Oliver's great-grandfather, to help look after Katherine. Harold was much older than William and not eligible for Confederate Army service. When William returned home after the War, he asked Katherine's permission to give Harold his anniversary gift from her, the pocket watch, as appreciation. She said she didn't need a reminder of her true love. She had him back home with her."

"So Oliver inherited the pocket watch from his great-grandfather?"

Agnes patted Bethany's hand on the front counter. "Yes, child. The Knowles, Davis, and Bridgewell families share a very special bond."

"But he keeps popping up and asking me if I intend to sell the house. Is he wanting to divide the land for a development?"

"Oh, no, child. Oliver loves history. He wants to preserve it."

Bethany wondered how she got Oliver so wrong.

"Child, Oliver feared you would be like most others who inherited a home here. When he learned you owned a big agency in Alexandria, he thought you would sell the place to a housing developer. Oliver wants to preserve Lily Fields just like he did with many of the town's buildings. He appreciates the workmanship here." Agnes pointed out the window to the town's restored buildings. "That skill and attention to detail cannot be found again. By saving these buildings, he is preserving the town and his own personal heritage."

Bethany nodded her head. She was beginning to understand this man better.

"Since his family worked on Lily Fields, he feels an extra connection to it and wanted it to remain standing for generations to come," Agnes explained.

Bethany felt bad for thinking Oliver a conniving businessman, snooping around, trying to scoop up her family's property. Instead, he wanted to ensure his great-grandfather's craftsmanship endured.

Agnes's smile grew larger. "His great-grandfather also built the Timekeeper," she said.

"The Timekeeper?" Bethany questioned what she heard.

"Yes, made from trees felled right there at Lily Fields.

"Remarkable," she said fully taking in the connection Oliver had to her family.

The museum tour enriched Bethany's knowledge of the town's history, and she now knew why Oliver Bridgewell was so interested in Lily Fields. He didn't want to tear it down and sell off the land in pieces. Oliver Bridgewell wanted to protect and preserve time.

At Lily Fields, the Timekeeper greeted Bethany's arrival. She heard its chimes many times a day, but this afternoon it sounded like it sang to her. The grandfather clock did not chime nor play its music nonstop throughout the day. With restful retreats in between, the Timekeeper orchestrated perfect timing.

Reflective pauses . . . She thought about Peter telling her about the word *Selah* and how it was used in the Psalms. The Psalms were thought to have been sung, and the word *Selah* may have been a note to tell singers to pause so the audience could reflect on what they just heard. "Pause and reflect" is what Peter said *Selah* meant. Was it really the woman's name or merely a word she added at the end?

CHAPTER 39

While putting away laundry, Bethany chatted on the phone with Nick, who was on his way to meet a new client. He called Bethany every morning and most nights, too, since they'd had dinner at his house.

An urgent text from Scott interrupted their conversation, but Nick understood because he owned a business too. "Before you go," Nick said, "I've got a meeting tonight at the firehouse. All of us volunteers have to be there. It will be late when I'm done, so I'll call you tomorrow." Bethany looked forward to his calls. They provided a respite from her focus on business and projects at Lily Fields, but mostly, she enjoyed hearing his voice. His accent and the way he pronounced certain words transported her into a different world, one where romance existed inside a magical place she was experiencing for the first time.

"Please call me ASAP," the text from Scott read.

Waiting for Scott to pick up, she hung clean shirts on hangers in her bedroom.

"I hate to ask, but I need you in Alexandria for a day," Scott requested. "You can get right back to your house remodeling afterward."

Bethany used her shoulder to hold the phone to her ear as she continued her laundry chore. "Let's just do a video call."

"You need to be here," Scott said. "Before making a decision, the CEO of Essential Hair Products wants to meet us both. He's old-school and expects to meet you in person."

Scott had her full attention. She put down the clothes and took the phone in her hand. This prospective client represented a seven-figure opportunity, and since losing the new business from Baxter, they needed to make up revenue.

"Okay. When?" she asked.

"He's coming to town tomorrow. Sorry for the late notice. I just found out that he expects you to be here."

For the last five years, she dreamed of winning this client's business, so she didn't hesitate to answer. "I don't have plans tomorrow," she said. "I'll drive up tonight and check on my house too. What time is the meeting?"

"Ten o'clock," Scott said. "It will last an hour, maybe two max. You know CEOs. Time is money."

"I already reviewed the slide deck presentation but send me more background info. I want to know all about him before he walks in the room," Bethany said.

She spent the rest of the morning reviewing research Scott sent her about the CEO. Bethany read articles he wrote or that his public relations firm wrote for him. If they did a good job, they wrote in his voice, and the writings accurately described how he thought. The company experienced large sales growth, and the CEO projected even more ambitious gains. After her research, including learning how the CEO grew up on a farm in Wisconsin, Bethany felt she had a good read on him.

Since she would be in town, she asked Holly to schedule time with Baxter for tomorrow afternoon at his office. She wanted to visit with him in person and continue to repair their relationship. The timing of his giving the new business to another agency stuck in her mind. *Is he still mad I asked him about the Costa Rican labor laws?* She never knew Baxter to hold a grudge. Surely, he understood she was looking out for his best interest. If that plant manager was hiring underage workers, Baxter needed to be aware and put a stop to it.

She thought back to that day at the factory. If she hadn't wandered into that other building and that girl's eyes burned into her, she might not be in this mess with Baxter. *Did it cost her the new brand work?* That she didn't know, but Baxter's company still comprised fifty percent of her business, and she was determined to keep it. Visiting with him while she was in town for another client was a good idea.

All she needed to pack was a small overnight bag because most everything was at her townhouse. Tomorrow she would wear something from her closet up there. Not expecting to be home until tomorrow evening, she told Walter to use the key in the morning and carry on without her.

Wanting to beat afternoon rush hour in Alexandria, at 1:30, she pulled out of the drive at Lily Fields and crossed the creek. It hadn't rained in several days, and the water was lower. A strange feeling tugged at her heart when she passed the town. Jameson was growing on her, but she didn't fully understand why. She was a city girl and accustomed to a faster paced life. Small-town life was never her thing. Jameson might be okay for a weekend away once in a while, but that's all.

She didn't take the same route she took to Jameson. Instead, she took I-95. Passing through Fredericksburg, she thought Jameson a perfect distance for a getaway. Not too far from Alexandria, but far enough so she felt away—away from stress. Perhaps it was true that every business leader needed a getaway. She never before took time to consider having a second home and wasn't sure if it was what she wanted or not. But as she drove farther away, something called her back.

The moment she opened the door to her Alexandria townhouse, it was as if she was walking into a model home. Returning after a few weeks away, the home didn't appear lived in to her. Everything was too perfect and too much in order.

Comparing it to Lily Fields with the remodeling and landscape projects going on, her townhouse was eerily quiet. There was no sound, nothing at all. No Timekeeper's chimes declaring the hour and half hour. She got a glass of sparkling water and, to end the silence, she turned the TV on low before deciding to video call Mitzi.

"Hi. How's it going at Lily Fields? Wait, where are you?" Mitzi asked

"I'm at home," Bethany answered.

"Oh, geez. You finally come home, and I'm back in Denver again. "You better go back to Lily Fields and finish that house. Promise me." Mitzi gave Bethany a stern look.

"I'm just here to see a prospective client tomorrow and visit with Baxter. Haven't seen him since I asked him about the Costa Rican factory."

"Think he's still mad?"

"Not sure, but I want to see him in person." Bethany stared at a commercial on TV.

"How's your handsome Latin landscaper—Mister strong arms and soft kisses?" Mitzi's eyebrows raised and lowered.

Bethany gulped the water. She didn't tell Nick she left town. He'd called in the early morning before she had made the decision. *Should I call and tell him I'm in Alexandria?* But Nick wasn't home tonight; he had a meeting at the firehouse. And besides, she planned to be back first thing tomorrow anyway.

"Earth to Bethany?" Mitzi waved her hand in the air.

"I'm here. You got me thinking about Nick."

"Is it still going well?"

"He's making me think about things. Crazy coincidence, running into a landscaper of all people, and he's just what I needed."

"In more ways than one," Mitzi said, getting up from her chair. Walking to her hotel room's closet, she retrieved an outfit and hung a long necklace on the hanger before placing it back inside. "It's time you let someone get close and stay close to you," Mitzi said. "Quit pushing great guys away. You're nearing forty, you know. The best men are almost gone."

She didn't answer Mitzi's comment and instead took a drink.

"Are you keeping the house?" Mitzi asked. "Great place to plan a summer party. Overflow guests could stay at the Tides Inn. Looks like a first-class place on the water . . . and with a spa too.

"I want to make sure I can maintain the house while living in Alexandria."

"You can do anything you put your mind to."

"I learned why Oliver kept asking if I wanted to sell the house. I just texted you a close-up photo of the Timekeeper. Look at the workmanship. Oliver's great-grandfather built it."

As she looked at the photo, Mitzi said, "The woodwork is incredible."

"Oliver is a historic preservationist and was afraid I'd be like most people who sell their inherited homes and land to developers. He owns a bunch of buildings in town, and his attention to detail on preserving buildings is unmatched."

"So his motives were pure and not nefarious after all?" Mitzi kicked off her shoes. Propping up two pillows, she laid down on the hotel bed.

"Exactly," Bethany said. "And that pocket watch he always pulls out of his pocket? Turns out my family gave it to his relative as a thank you for helping Katherine while her husband was fighting in the Civil War."

Mitzi sprang upright from the pillows. "You've got to get it or buy it back from Oliver."

Bethany's face squinched. "What would I do with a man's pocket watch?"

"Duh . . . It belonged to your family," Mitzi said, throwing her hand up in the air.

"If my great-great-great-grandfather gave it to Oliver's great-grand-father, then that's where he wanted it to be." Bethany thought to ask Oliver if she could see it up close. She would like to hold it in her hands as Katherine did that night when she hid the woman in her wagon.

Talking things through with her best friend was all Bethany ever needed, up until now. Now alone in a stagnant home, she missed Nick. *Should I call him and let him know I'm in Alexandria?* She thought it best to wait and tell him when he called tomorrow.

Nick pulled into a Jameson gas station and saw Walter fueling his pickup truck. "How's the house coming?" Nick asked.

"Working on the second bathroom upstairs. Maybe Miss Bethany will find a sink she likes in Alexandria while she's up there."

"Alexandria?"

"Left today for a big client meeting tomorrow," Walter said. Told me to go ahead with what I'm doing. Gave me a key a while back."

The gas pump clicked off, signaling his tank was full, but Nick didn't notice at first. After replacing the handle on the pump, he left without saying goodbye to Walter. *Why didn't she tell me she was leaving town?* Nick almost missed a stop sign and slammed the brakes.

He hoped to not lose her to the city because after that first night's dinner and subsequent ones, he began to envision a life with her in Jameson.

It all was too soon and too fast, but he felt what he felt. It had been a long time, and he didn't want to wait. She was the one. He was sure of it. His parents would like her once they, too, realized her super-charged personality was all a front. Inside, she was sweet, loving, and soft. Her hardened shell cracked open at the creek and even more that night on his patio.

When he gave her the rose from the dinner table, it was because he wanted her to know. And when he kissed her on her front porch, he didn't want to stop. He had sprinted down the steps to avoid further temptation. She was a siren on the shore calling him to her, and he was under her spell. *Did she feel the same? If she did, wouldn't she have called to tell me she left town?*

After his volunteer meeting, Nick surprised Bethany with a phone call.

"How was your day?" she asked him after answering on the first ring.

"Good and yours?" Nick's voice was flat.

"I had to make a quick trip. I'm in Alexandria."

"I heard," Nick said as he cracked an egg in the steaming hot skillet.

"How did you know?" Bethany's voice shuddered.

"I saw Walter at the gas station."

"I didn't know I had to come here until Scott called me later this morning, after you called. A big prospective client is coming in with their CEO, and Scott said I had to be here to meet him in person. It was short notice, but I'm coming back to Jameson tomorrow, right after I meet with him and Baxter too."

"I thought you might not want to come back." The eggs seared in the skillet.

"I want to come back. I miss you."

Nick flipped his burnt over-easy eggs, but it was of no matter to him. Her answer made his shoulders relax, and he turned off the stove. "When I saw Walter, I worried you'd get back to your old world and want to stay."

Bethany reassured him she would come right back and ended the call with a sweet goodnight.

She felt guilty for not telling him she left town. Nick had gotten past her hardened exterior. Even her former fiancé did not feel as comfortable to her, and she had only known Nick for a few weeks. *How can I feel this much for him?* She and Nick were different. She rushed through work and he took his time, focusing on the small details. Yet his magnetism drew her to him like her shopping cart to his truck bumper. She may never have met him if not for that runaway cart.

Nick was making her slow down to smell those roses and lilies he had planted for her. Her old life and work were no longer fulfilling her as they once did.

After reading work papers, she fell peacefully asleep in the recliner before experiencing a nightmare. Jostling abruptly in the chair, she awakened in a sweat, her silk pajamas sticking to her skin. In her dream, fire shot out of a girl's eyes, alighting Bethany's clothes in flames.

CHAPTER 40

Leaving her house at 7:50 a.m. to get to the office in plenty of time before her ten o'clock meeting, she found the morning traffic as bad as she remembered. Due to road construction, she lost time and hit every red light between her townhouse and the office. When she pulled into her reserved parking spot, she checked her watch. It was 8:20. "Every second counts," she said aloud in her car.

Dressing for this particular client, today she wore a conservative business suit and closed toed shoes. As usual, she rushed into the lobby.

While the elevator ascended, her mind focused on her opening line to the CEO. The elevator jolted and stopped. She pushed the third-floor button again and nothing happened, so she rang the call button. A few minutes later, a dispatcher asked what the emergency was.

"I'm stuck between floors."

"Be patient," the female dispatcher told her.

Bethany called Holly's office number but there was no signal. "Ugh. Elevators. I should have taken the stairs."

It was 8:29. Still, plenty of time to make the meeting. She wanted to sit down but didn't want to dirty her pants on the floor. Not one to waste a moment, she shook off her high heels, pulled out a file from her briefcase, and got in the zone to focus like no other.

There were times when working in her office, she didn't hear Holly calling her name multiple times right outside the door. Earth to Bethany called, but she stayed high in the clouds. She spent a lot of time thinking about strategic plans and things to come. The future was where she was most comfortable. The present was only a place she rushed through on the way to her planned-out future.

In Bethany's life, moments were not there to be enjoyed; instead, they were to be used to get something done. The present was foreign land to her, but Nick forced her to stop and meet him in the present. His strong arms were in the present. His kissing lips were in the present. But as much as she was falling for him, she wasn't sure the present is where she could afford time to linger. She had big plans for herself and the agency in the future, and that future she mapped out for herself was in Alexandria.

Hearing technicians' voices meant they were working to get her moving. When they finally did, it was 9:20. She calculated she had fifteen minutes to spend in her office before going to the conference room to meet with Scott and her team.

When the doors opened on the third floor, Holly greeted her with a stack of files in front of her chest, readying for Bethany's upset. "So sorry about the elevator," Holly said. "We got a new service provider, like you asked, but things don't seem to be any different."

"I got some work done while I waited. Patience is a form of action, you know," Bethany kindly educated.

She walked down the hall and looked back as Holly stood frozen with her mouth open. Her boss took off toward her office and because she left so fast, she didn't get a chance to comment on her new hairstyle. Bethany's hair hung around her shoulders and highlights went all throughout it. At first, she had directed Sam to put in a few highlights to see if she liked it. But days after her first date with Nick, she told Sam, "Give me highlights all over!" The added streaks matched a subtle new lightness she carried inside.

She looked at the awards on her wall. This new high-profile client would set her up to receive another one. Smiling at the vision in her mind, she picked up her files and walked down the hall to make it happen.

Entering the conference room behind her, Scott said, "Sorry about the elevator this morning." He took a seat across from her at the head of the table.

"Every second counts. I used the time to study. All set and ready to go?" Bethany asked.

"I'll introduce you like we discussed, and you can take it from there," Scott directed.

Bethany did take it from there. From her research on the CEO, she purposely emphasized certain details. Based on his comments, he liked her, the team, and their presentation, and by the end of the meeting, he promised them a decision within the week.

The B.R. Miller Advertising team walked the CEO and his executives to the elevator, hoping it would get their prospective clients to the ground floor without incident, and it did. Afterward, Bethany regrouped with Scott in her office.

"You seem different, and it's not just your hair," Scott said. "Looks good, by the way."

"I sleep better at Lily Fields." Except for noises Walter produced during the day while he remodeled, the house remained quiet at night. She was surprised the Timekeeper's chimes did not interrupt her sleep. Sleeping through the night was not something she did much in Alexandria or anywhere. Down time in Jameson gave her body a chance to set a new rhythm.

Holly brought in lunch for Bethany and Scott to continue their one-on-one meeting. "Are you going to keep the house? Scott asked before he took a bite of his chicken sandwich.

"It's like two different worlds," she said and added dressing to her salad.

"Every CEO needs a getaway. When do you come home?" Scott asked.

Alexandria was her home, but Jameson called her back. Nick lived there, and her roses and lilies graced her front yard there. Surprisingly, her full speed had slowed after Nick appeared in her life. He and others she met along the way showed her another way to live, an unhurried way that she never knew possible. Could she create a new life outside of work where she paused to get away to Lily Fields? She didn't know.

On her desk, the hummingbird picture Amy gave her with the words BE STILL AND KNOW drew her attention. She knew that a hummingbird's wings beat eighty times per second. Now, she realized even the hummingbird stops at the flowers to refuel and take a drink of nectar.

Other people had lives outside of work. Maybe she could try to enjoy one too? Lily Fields might make a good retreat, a place to slow down from time to time before returning to her fast-paced schedule. But she had a company to run. Sure, Scott was doing well, but it had only been a few weeks. She knew she had to take back full control soon.

"I'm really enjoying leading the team," he revealed. "Losing Baxter's new business was a serious blow but may have been a blessing in a way." She shot him a quizzical look across the table. *Is he talking about the same problem I know about?*

"We've diversified our portfolio and spread out the business risk across more clients," Scott explained. "It's put us in better shape. We still have to generate more revenue to hit the business plan, but I know next year will be great."

"Thanks for leading the charge while I've been away," she said. "Couldn't do it without you." Bethany smiled at Scott but thought about Baxter and what he had done.

Through the years since college, she counted on Baxter to give her advice. He was as good as family to her, and much like him, they were both hard chargers building their businesses as fast as they could. Now, she had a true brother, biologically speaking. She felt an ease with Peter from the beginning. And as she spent time in Jameson, she lost some of her former reliance on and closeness to Baxter. Instead of her, Scott spoke to him every day now. Baxter's reaction to her questioning him about the Costa Rican factory and the jolt of him denying her the new company's business cut into her heart and made her ties to him weaker.

Although office rent in this part of Alexandria close to Old Town was high, for the last several years she leased space a few blocks away from Baxter to be close by. Either he would come to her or she would go to him a couple of times a week. But before today, she always took her car. Since the sun was out, she chose to walk to his office.

Cruising the Potomac, boats were out in plenty. It was a weekday, but motorboats and sailboats alike took advantage of the warm summer day.

Baxter's twentysomething blonde assistant in a too-tight dress greeted her. "Baxter is tied up in a meeting, but he said to let you into his office to wait." His grand corner office with a view of the Potomac River made a statement. He liked to show off, but deep inside, Baxter was a good guy who was like the brother she never had—until now, of course. Now, she had Peter.

"Sorry for being late." Baxter rushed in and hugged her. "Love your hair." He pointed to one of her loose curls. "Amy told me all about the house. Sounds like you are on it as usual and getting things taken care of," Baxter said as he sat in a leather chair across from her. His office included multiple parts: an executive desk, a conference table, and a separate casual seating area with four chairs around a coffee table, which he used with her today.

"How's Amy doing?" Bethany asked.

"She's focusing on her foundation. I'm glad she has something to do while I'm traveling. She's alone a lot. Any chance you could invite her to Jameson soon for a few days? Would really help me out."

"Sure. Let me finish the bathrooms." Bethany knew it a good idea to see Baxter in person. She always looked up to him and idolized his business prowess. Making him mad when she questioned him about his factory troubled her since that day in her conference room. She was looking out for him because he always looked out for her. And despite him giving the new business to another agency, their relationship seemed to be back on track.

. . . and the Timekeeper chimed seven.

CHAPTER 41

Waiting until she finished errands and was through the heaviest traffic, Bethany phoned Nick to let him know she was on her way back to Lily Fields.

"Since you'll be back too late tonight, how about I stop by and see you tomorrow? he asked.

Bethany looked forward to seeing him. She was gone only twenty-four hours, but she missed him. And driving gave her time to think. Being in Alexandria, she questioned where she truly belonged. Her world order reshuffled, and she didn't know in which world she belonged anymore. She had only known one and now didn't feel it energized her the way it used to. Since that night she found the butterfly necklace, Bethany's life seemed more and more driven by someone or something outside herself.

The sun lowered in the sky. Passing barns she never noticed before, she wondered, *What is it about barns that call to my soul?* She found them captivating her attention, but she'd never liked barns before. *Maybe it's because Lily Fields had a barn once?* She knew it did because the newspaper article mentioned it, and Walter showed her an old stone foundation he found in the woods.

Rumbling over the bridge, she thought about her waterfall. She hadn't seen it up close since that day with Nick. Its movement and sound soothed her and drowned out her typical incessant worry and inner chatter about what was to come. Before that day, she could never enjoy the moment because she was never in it. But at the creek with Nick, she slowed down and felt fun.

She parked her car in the back by the carriage house, and as she walked up to the back door, a bluebird paused between drinks from the birdbath. Her approach startled him, and he flew away. Walter was gone, so she checked on the progress he'd made upstairs. He'd exposed all the walls in the pink bathroom and, after a full day of work and clean up, his shop vac sat in the middle of the floor. He hadn't put it away like he usually did.

Since neither upstairs bathroom had a sink, Bethany would use the downstairs bathroom to ready herself for bed. She made a note to phone the plumbing supply store tomorrow to check on the status of her two sinks.

Hyped up from the coffee she had enjoyed on her drive, she thought, *A walk through the yard will do me good.* She stopped to smell the crimson roses, the Jack roses, at the front porch steps. Nick had done a masterful job with the yard and filled in the existing beds by adding more roses and lilies in just the right places. The Turk's cap lilies, native to Virginia and the ones she had mistakenly pulled, grew taller. Some plants had twenty to thirty bright-orange blooms on them. A blue-and-black butterfly passed her. It wasn't a monarch, but she studied the markings on its wings. *Nature never missed a detail. No wonder Turk's cap lilies attract both hummingbirds and butterflies,* she thought. *These intense flowers stand out among the rest.*

She took a seat at the front porch table where Peter had told her about her father and his father too. For some reason, Marguerite wanted Peter to tell her the story, but Bethany would never know why. *Did Marguerite want me to feel bad about my father?* Perhaps instead, Marguerite wanted Bethany to feel good about *her* as her birth mother. After all, she gave her life.

Bethany didn't know Marguerite's complete feelings toward Peter's father. The two people involved in the decision about Bethany's birth were both deceased. If only she would have looked for her birth parents sooner. She let out a deep sigh. "Move forward," she told herself. "Look to the future." The past had nothing good in it except heartache. She'd had enough of pain that night the patrolman knocked on her door. The father she idolized would never again call her his rising star.

Peter had filled in some of the blanks about their father, Peter Jameson II, but the biological father she never knew didn't feel real to her. No affection dwelled inside her for a man who preferred she not exist. How could she care about him when he didn't care about her? A parent is supposed to love a child, but he hadn't given her a chance. He dropped off Marguerite outside that clinic and expected the inconvenience would go away and keep him on the road to his future, a future without her in it.

Mitzi tried to persuade her to consider her father's age and the pressure from Peter's grandfather, but she didn't want to give him the honor of trying to understand. Her adoptive father was the man she called Dad. He had made it clear he loved her, and her adoptive mother had too. She always felt special and the father she knew never wished her dead.

After she brushed her teeth in the downstairs bathroom, she retrieved the journal from the living room table. For now, she wanted to forget about the man Marguerite once loved.

Her grandmother, Elizabeth, had not yet shared her story. Tonight, Bethany would read about Elizabeth and think about the other Knowles women she'd gotten to know through these journal pages. Writing from a depth of heart and soul unknown to her, they lived and loved from a place Bethany struggled to comprehend.

CHAPTER 42

Elizabeth Knowles McKinley Marchand
Born 1933
Jameson, Virginia

My mother named me Elizabeth and gave me the middle name Knowles. She taught me many things, but the most important one was to focus on the light. Ever since I was young, my father experienced many dark times. And so, when his light was on, Mother and I enjoyed that often singular moment.

When I was nineteen, I met a bright light in town. His name was Philippe, and he owned a fishing boat on the Chesapeake Bay. We met at lunch one day when he came to town for supplies and courted me for over a year until we married. I continued my newspaper writing, although my contributions grew smaller as we added to our family a son, Jean Pierre, and a daughter, Marguerite.

Though Philippe was a waterman, we spent a lot of free time next to the sea. One evening as the sun went down over the barrier island, we witnessed an event to which no ticket was needed. While walking along the beach, we stopped to see people pushing sand with their hands to create a roadway in the sand. They hoped newly hatched loggerhead turtles would use it to make their way to the ocean. Farther up from the water's edge, three-inch-sized baby turtles pushed their way out of a sandy nest. I cried as we witnessed this natural birth.

What a glorious experience to see these tiny creatures emerge from darkness. All of them instinctively knew the plan. Once out of their nest, they headed toward the light, the moon hanging brightly over the ocean.

Desire, a strong effort, and perhaps a divine hand played a part in their making their way to water before a bird or other prey found them on dry land.

My reporter instinct knew this to be a story to share, so I researched turtles and learned more. A sea turtle nest can house one hundred eggs, but many hatchlings become misguided and turn away from the ocean. This not only takes them off course but costs them their very survival. Every moment counts for a sea turtle out of water.

And so in the mornings, volunteers walk beaches, looking for nests made overnight. One woman I met showed me turtles left behind after their siblings made their way to the ocean the night before. She provided aid by placing them in a bucket of sand. Confined inside, they pushed with their front and back legs. After a while, she released them close to the ocean's edge where they scooted the rest of the way to the sea on their own. She never put them directly in the water, she said, because sea turtles need this time of struggle. Breaking out of their shell, digging out of the hole, and pushing their arms and legs on the sand was part of the natural process. The struggle was purposely designed to strengthen their muscles, fill their lungs, and make them capable to live on their own. What a pity to hear some never make it to the water because of man-made lights disorienting them.

We humans are also taken off course when distractions abound. Scarcity of time permeates our minds. In my desire to know God more deeply, I've learned that life on earth is only a practice session for our real home in Heaven. Our time on earth may indeed be finite, but when we look toward our heavenly home, we see an abundance of time. Eternity is our rightful inheritance.

My life has been filled with struggles, but I stayed focused on the light. Nature taught me a thing or two. As a mother watching a son battle alcoholism, I experienced a tearing out of the heart. Heartache can challenge even the strongest spiritual muscles.

Demons took reign of my son, Jean Pierre's life. And though Philippe and I pointed him toward the light, we knew he must make it the rest of the way by himself. My beloved son's war with alcohol lasted more than twenty years before he conquered it. We celebrated that new beginning, and for four short years, he enjoyed newfound peace before his body could endure no more. I take comfort in knowing without a doubt he found his heavenly home.

When our defenses are down, the way forward is opened to us. As we become still and listen, we hear the Shepherd's voice. It is with Him by our side that we find peace in the present, knowing He has our future already laid out.

Life's journey is not smooth. We must push forward. When I find myself in the midst of a challenge, I look upward and focus on the light. It guides me to an ocean full of His glory.

Elizabeth Knowles Marchand
Daughter, Mother, Writer, & Light Seeker

CHAPTER 43

With the morning light filtering through the elongated living room windows, Bethany arranged an eight-by-ten rug and a picture of a garden scene she brought from her townhouse. She thought they looked better at Lily Fields and helped add her own touch to the home. New furniture was on her list, but not for now. More remodeling projects took up her mind, and the walls needed new paint. She thought about painting them all a creamy white to brighten the space. The fireplaces in each bedroom needed refinishing, and she'd tackled only the living room one so far. Next time, she planned to pay someone to do the painstaking work of stripping the paint off the other mantels.

The doorbell rang and Bethany opened the door to find Agnes Adams on Lily Fields's front porch with an envelope in her hands. She was dressed up today in a pink church dress, low-heeled shoes, and a set of pearls.

Bethany made them both a cup of tea to enjoy on the living room couch.

"Good to be here again, child. I used to often visit your grandmother at Lily Fields. By the way, have you found the original barn's foundation? Been meaning to ask you about that."

"Yes, Walter found it and showed me. It's just inside the woods out back."

Agnes sat down her teacup and picked up the large manila envelope from the coffee table. Inside were copies of century-old articles Knowles women wrote for the *Jameson Gazette*.

"I thought you might like to have these, child. Have you read the Jameson paper since you came to town?"

"I have not," Bethany said. She saw it for sale in stands outside of stores but never purchased one.

Agnes pulled her lips in atop one another. "I suggest you subscribe to it."

Bethany nodded her head yes. "Whatever happened to my family owning the newspaper?"

"When your grandfather died, your grandmother, Elizabeth, didn't have the desire to keep it going. Your uncle, Jean Philippe, died from—" Agnes stopped short and looked at Bethany. "Well, he died from a long illness. Did I tell you that?" Bethany knew Marguerite had a brother. She saw his name in the Bible. It also listed his date of death, but she didn't know how he died until she read it last night in her grandmother Elizabeth's journal entry.

"Elizabeth wished Marguerite would come home to run the newspaper and keep it in the family, but Marguerite traveled all the time and did not return except for quick trips for major holidays. I recall Elizabeth saying when Marguerite visited, she never wanted to go into town with them." Agnes looked up at the ceiling before bringing her eyes back to Bethany. "I now suppose Marguerite didn't want to run into Peter's father."

Both women reached for their cups and took a sip of tea.

"Even after her mother died, other than attending the funeral, Marguerite didn't return to Lily Fields to live right away. She hired a caretaker for the house until she retired from her work. Waited to return, I suppose, until after Peter's father died." Agnes brushed her lap and smoothed out her dress.

Bethany thought about the struggle Marguerite must have endured. Her birth father moved on with his life not knowing she existed. It was Marguerite who carried the joy of birthing her but also endured the sorrow in giving her up.

Agnes patted the folder on the living room table. "I put a few of your mother's magazine articles inside there for you as well. Elizabeth was so proud of Marguerite. Her stories appeared in major travel and national news magazines too."

The mention of Marguerite made Bethany's eyes water. She regretted not meeting her biological mother. Before she died, she was too busy and didn't care enough to search. Guilt caught hold of her. She needed to stop the feeling, and so she said to Agnes, "Do you know anything about my grandmother Elizabeth's mother, Victoria? I read she ran the newspaper during and after World War II."

"Strong woman, much like you, child. During World War II, the Japanese took Joshua, Victoria's husband, let's see . . . your great-grandfather, prisoner on an island in the Pacific. For months, Victoria heard nothing about him. Once the Marines told her about his imprisonment, she worked even more to keep busy. Victoria dreaded stopping to sleep because she often dreamed she heard her husband's screams from afar. After the war, he returned home but never returned to his old self." Agnes glanced out the window, and Bethany waited for her to continue. "Victoria ran the home and the newspaper business. Joshua had some good days, but in between, his mind filled with demons." Agnes shook her head. "I recall my friend Elizabeth sharing stories about her father with me. No telling what that man endured. There were no visible scars, but nightmares raged inside him."

Bethany and Agnes exchanged a look that needed no words. Her mind created pictures of the World War II atrocities, and the silence between them held on until Agnes reached for her cup and took another drink.

Bethany continued with her questions. "Since the newspaper was so important to my great-grandmother Victoria and also to her daughter, my grandmother Elizabeth, I'm surprised Marguerite didn't want to keep the newspaper going," Bethany said, determined to sort it out.

"Marguerite got involved in a global cause, and it captured all her attention. She advised her mother to sell the paper."

"Who owns it now?" Bethany asked.

"Oliver Bridgewell."

Bethany sat back on the couch and drips of her coffee spilled on the new rug. There was Oliver again, connected to her family's history.

"Why Oliver?" Bethany asked.

"He wanted to preserve the paper," Agnes said matter-of-factly, putting her teacup and saucer on the coffee table. "The *Jameson Gazette* existed since 1855 and, as I told you, it only stopped printing for a short time during the Civil War. Oliver makes little money from the paper. The advertisements barely cover the expenses, but in its heyday, it was sold not only in Jameson but in several other towns along the river."

"I didn't know," Bethany said.

"Lots to learn, child." Agnes smiled.

"It's sweet of you to visit and bring me these." Bethany picked up the envelope from the table.

"I wanted to see you and the house. Today is my museum day, but I kept the "closed" sign on the door. How are you getting along with that handsome man whose truck you ran into outside of Neil's Hardware?

Bethany did not ever recall telling Agnes about Nick and certainly not about how she met him. *Who needs a newspaper when small town news travels fast on its own?* "I like him, and it seems he likes me too," Bethany shyly responded.

Agnes smiled. "About time you settled down and had a baby, don't you think?" Agnes's eyes opened wide.

"Oh, no. I'm not ready for babies," Bethany said as she shook her finger.

Agnes pointed at Bethany's stomach. "Wait any longer, child, and those eggs of yours won't work."

Bethany grimaced at Agnes's mention of her reproductive organs. Changing the subject, she asked, "Have you heard from Peter?"

"Stopped by to see me yesterday. He's still struggling with the news about his father and grandfather. He wanted to talk to me about them." Agnes turned her attention toward the hall.

"Excuse me, Miss Bethany," Walter said. "Hello, Miss Agnes. Sorry to interrupt, ladies. Miss Bethany, I need to show you something upstairs."

Agnes took the cue to end her visit and said goodbye.

When Bethany met Walter upstairs in the pink bathroom, she saw its walls exposed.

"Seeing inside these walls, it's a miracle nothing has happened," Walter stated. "Stay out of here. I've scheduled an electrician to come tomorrow."

Bethany didn't know anything about electricity, but if Walter said it was a problem, she believed him. She wanted to take care of whatever was necessary.

"I'm going to keep the house," she surprisingly informed him. "I'll use it for weekend getaways."

"That's great news, Miss Bethany." Walter started to reach and hug her but stopped himself. "Hated thinking all this work would benefit someone else. Now that you are staying, my wife's been asking to invite you to a ladies' luncheon. All her friends want to meet you too. She checked you out on your company's website and saw all the awards you've won and the TV commercials you've made for famous brands."

Bethany smiled as he mentioned her accomplishments.

"They think you are Superwoman, Miss Bethany."

Bethany swatted her hand downward. These were normal things she did in the course of her career. A knock at the front door caused her to leave Walter to do his work. When she opened the door, Nick DeLeon put his arms around her and pressed his lips against hers.

Still holding her in his arms, he said, "When Walter told me you went back to Alexandria, I thought I lost you."

Bethany assured Nick she intended to return often to Jameson. Although her agency ran well so far without her, she needed to get back there. "My name is on it. Not to mention almost one hundred people and their families who count on me."

"I know all about people depending on you, but I worry once you reengage up there, you might want to stay," Nick admitted, holding on to her hand.

"I plan to be in Jameson for the next several weeks."

A broad smile filled Nick's tanned face. "Then I intend to make use of that time. Every second counts, as you say. Dinner tomorrow at my place at 6:30?"

"Sounds great," Bethany confirmed. After all, it was the best restaurant in town.

Bethany hadn't recalled a time she felt happiness like this. Experiences from her past trained her to keep her mind firmly engaged on work and in the future. Because whenever she let a good time creep in without notice, she began to fear something bad was about to happen.

CHAPTER 44

After a long day that included a couple of visitors and a trip into town for a quick lunch at the café with Sam, she grew tired. The fireflies lit up the front yard, and she thought it time to retreat upstairs to review the items Agnes brought her earlier in the day. The summer heat made it hard for the air conditioner to keep up, so she folded the blue-and-white flowered bedspread across the bottom of the bed and propped up two pillows behind her head.

Putting her hand inside the envelope, she pulled out copies of newspaper articles. She would read the oldest ones first. One from the late nineteenth century noted the winners of the blue-ribbon pie contest that took place at the town's center park. Good thing she was born in another century. By old standards, Bethany's lack of baking abilities might have kept her from catching a good man.

Agnes had told her right. She needed to read the papers to discover the town. The price of a newspaper when Victoria ran it in 1944 was two cents. And in one of the obituary sections, she read about her Uncle Jean Pierre, who died at too young an age from alcoholism.

Amongst the Jameson newspapers, she found a copy of the Chicago article about the boating accident. Emotional after learning her biological father's name that day with Peter, she'd left the copy behind at Agnes's house. The news shocked Bethany and Peter even more because he knew his father, and she did not. Peter's family pride took a giant blow that day in Agnes's living room. He gained a half sister but lost a dose of regard for his father and grandfather.

Still wanting to know more about her lineage, Bethany set the envelope on top of newspaper articles strewn across the sheets. Sitting up in bed, she reached for her laptop to check her DNA account for the first time. Seeing "Georgetown III" was a half-sibling match, she remembered Peter was third in his family to attend Georgetown Law.

A parental match said, "Lily Fields." Bethany fell back against the pillows and threw her arms out from the laptop, hitting a plastic glass on her nightstand. The water dripped onto the heart pine wood floor. *How long before she died did Marguerite send this in?*

Bethany reviewed what she knew. Peter said Marguerite never reached out because she wanted Bethany to initiate the search for her. She didn't want to interfere in Bethany's life if she didn't want to know her. And Mitzi gave Bethany the DNA kit months before Marguerite died. *If I sent the test in at Christmas, could I have met my mother? Why didn't I take Mitzi's advice sooner?* Back then, Bethany thought she needed no one else in her already-full life—full of work, that is.

Getting out of bed, she retrieved a towel from her nearly complete blue bathroom to finish wiping up the spilled water. Down the hall, she smelled something fishy and walked toward the pink bathroom where Walter worked today. The smell came from inside there. *Hmm*, she thought. *Walter must have eaten fish for lunch upstairs today while I was out.*

Settling back into bed, she read a few articles from Marguerite's earliest work in travel magazines. The more serious news magazine stories she would save to read when she had more energy.

As if signaling it time for her to sleep, an owl hooted outside her window. Pushing the articles and envelope to the side of the bed, she turned off the light and closed her eyes, but her mind stayed alert. The heavy guilt of not searching for her mother weighed on her. Now, she could only learn about Marguerite through articles she wrote and accounts from others.

With papers still spread out across one side of her bed, Bethany fell asleep next to stories written by and about the family she never knew. And while she slept, a destructive force lurked inside the walls.

CHAPTER 45

Awakening to the sounds of the Timekeeper's chimes, Bethany's nostrils breathed in strange air. Her brain battled to decipher the smell. *Smoke*, her mind informed her. She reached for the light beside her bed, but it didn't turn on. In the darkness, her hand patted for the phone. With help from the flashlight app, she looked out the bedroom door and saw no fire, but the smell grew stronger. Now coughing, she knew she needed to get downstairs, if possible.

She descended the stairs step by step and several treads squeaked. Throwing open the front door, she dashed out on to the lawn and into the moonlight.

The cool grass slapped her mind to attention, and she dialed 911. With few stars lighting the sky, she waited in horror wondering about the destruction inside. But outside there was silence.

She shook in anxious fear at the plight of her ancestral home. At first she saw nothing, but within moments, white smoke began exiting through window cracks.

Finally, the sound of sirens cut through the still air as help approached from town. A blaring firetruck charged onto Knowles Lane. Fireman jumped out and gathered their equipment before rushing to the house. Running to the front steps, she met them. "I've got to go inside," she pleaded.

A man who introduced himself as the captain blocked her way. "Stay back, ma'am. No telling how much spread there is, and smoke alone can be toxic."

In full gear and breathing apparatus, firemen went in the front door, leaving it hanging open. Bethany saw only darkness inside, but fire appeared on the roof. Two firemen rushed to extinguish the outside fires as others worked inside.

Sounds from the gravel driveway announced a vehicle's fast approach. Leaving his lights on and engine running, Nick raced toward her, scooping her into his arms.

"*Gracias a Dios,* you are okay. I heard the address on the scanner and got here as fast as I could. I'm not on call this week."

"Nick, I left the Timekeeper's journal inside. I haven't read my mother's message."

Exiting the front door, a fireman pulled off his breathing apparatus. Smoke appeared to push him from behind and down the porch steps. Before Nick could catch her, Bethany ran toward the fireman. She screamed through tears. "I have to get inside and get the journal!" When she tried to aggressively push past the fireman, Nick took her arm. He was strong, but Bethany was, too, and with adrenaline flashing through her veins, she made Nick use much of his strength to keep her away from the house.

The fellow volunteer fireman acknowledged Nick with a nod.

Bethany pulled on Nick's white T-shirt. "I have to get the journal."

Nick looked at the fireman for help.

"Where can I find that book you're wanting, miss?" the fireman asked.

"It's on the nightstand in my bedroom upstairs, the blue room at the back of the house."

"Wait outside." He put his gear back on and reentered the home.

When Bethany saw him exit empty-handed, she fell to the wet ground. Her family's heritage was lost. Messages from every first daughter since the mid-1800s were gone. She never thought to make a copy of the journal.

With her head down, she didn't see the fireman reach inside his jacket. "Is this what you were looking for, ma'am?"

Still on her knees, Bethany took the journal and pulled it to her chest, breaking into convulsive tears of relief. "Thank you! Thank you!"

Smoke still seeped from window cracks, and from her knees, she begged for the house to be spared. Lily Fields survived the Civil War and every decade since. Guttural cries came out as she looked toward the home.

"I didn't protect it. I'm supposed to protect it," she wailed.

With her screams using up her strength and attention, Nick pulled her up off the grass and back into his arms. She cried into his shoulder, guarding the Timekeeper's journal between her body and his. Greyish smoke came from the roof, and now, it was turning blacker.

Two other firemen spoke to the captain before he came to talk to Bethany and Nick.

"We've got it under control," the captain said. "Good thing you were awake when you smelled smoke, ma'am. It was toxic, and you could have died in your sleep."

With widened eyes, Bethany pulled back to look at Nick. "I was already asleep. The Timekeeper woke me with its chimes. Nick, the Timekeeper saved me." She tugged with both hands at his white T-shirt between her fingers. Nick's arm went around her shoulders, holding her tight.

"Most of the damage is to the front bathroom and roof," the captain said. "These old houses were built with balloon framing. That framing let the fire find a void, then the fire went straight up through the roof." Nick nodded his head with a look of understanding, but Bethany didn't know anything about balloon framing. "Rest of the house looks okay except for those areas. Lots of smoke damage everywhere else though. Going to need a good airing out. You can't stay here tonight, miss. Do you have family or a friend you can stay with for the night?" the captain asked.

Nick looked at Bethany. "Sam," she said. "I can call Sam."

Bethany called her friend, who answered after a few rings.

"I'll turn on the porch light and wait for you," Sam said protectively.

Nick helped Bethany into his truck, and as he drove toward town, he looked over at her dressed in her pink pajamas. Because she wore no shoes, he offered to carry her, but she refused. She opened the truck door and walked beside him barefoot up Sam's front steps, all the while keeping the Timekeeper's journal close to her chest. As Nick reached for the doorbell, Sam opened the door and gasped at Bethany in the porch light. Black soot surrounded Bethany's mouth and nostrils. Before she had awakened and got outside, she'd breathed in that toxic smoke.

"Nick, please come inside too," Sam said. This was Sam's first time meeting him. Wearing grey sweatpants and a white T-shirt with untied gym shoes, his wavy black hair was disheveled from sleeping before he awakened to the fire alarm.

"I'd better get home," he said as he stood on the porch. "Thank you for taking care of Bethany for me." He looked at Bethany's dried tear-streaked face and stroked her cheek. "I'll call you in the morning. I can drive you to the house." He kissed Bethany on her forehead and hugged her goodnight.

Taking Bethany by the arm, Sam helped her shocked friend across the front door threshold. "Want to take a shower? You can use my master bath."

Bethany shook her head no, so Sam brought her a pair of workout pants and a T-shirt and showed her the half bath where she cleaned up with a bar of soap.

"You take my bed, and I'll sleep on the couch," Sam said to an obstinate Bethany who would have none of it. Realizing she'd not win, Sam patted the couch for Bethany to come settle in, but Bethany remained standing.

"I fell asleep sometime before ten, after I read old stories in the *Jameson Gazette* and magazine articles my mother wrote. Sam, I only awakened because of the Timekeeper's chimes. I smelled smoke and ran out of the house. The Timekeeper saved me."

Listening to her friend emote, Sam patted the couch again and got her to sit beside her.

"The fireman went back inside and found the journal for me. I thought I'd lost it." Bethany held out the journal. Sam touched the embossed leather cover and opened the pages. She picked up a small seed inside and held it between two fingertips.

"I must have missed one," Bethany said. "Seeds fell out the day I found the journal inside the Timekeeper. I saved them on a dish in my bedroom. I hope they survived."

Sam pinched the small seed between her fingers. "Do you know what these are?"

"No, but Nick will know," Bethany said.

"I'm sure he will," Sam said, placing the seed inside the journal.

Bethany shot both her hands in the air and stood upright, startling Sam.

"The Timekeeper saved me!" Bethany cried out. "The fire captain said no one survives that toxic smoke. I was sound asleep. The Timekeeper saved me."

Sam rose from the couch and put her arms around her friend. "I'm sure it did. Thank God for keeping you safe," she said, rocking her side to side. But Bethany pulled her head away from Sam's shoulder.

"I almost died tonight, and I almost lost the one connection to my mother and her family. She entrusted Lily Fields to me. She saved me, Sam. My mother saved me when my father wanted her to get rid of me. She wanted me to have Lily Fields and know my family by reading the Timekeeper's journal. I almost lost it all tonight." Bethany sobbed while Sam pulled her back in to her.

"I'm not worthy of these women. They had a strength I don't know. I'm nothing. These women had something, Sam. They knew something. Something I don't know. They said their strength came to them from above."

Sam nodded her head as she patted Bethany's back. "I know, sweetie. Their lives were built on a solid foundation. When storms came, they weren't blown away by them."

Bethany pulled away to look at Sam. "I want what they had. You have that strength. I see it in you. Where do I get it?" Bethany begged her friend.

"I was waiting for you to ask," Sam said as she invited Bethany to sit on the couch beside her. Picking up a Bible from the table she shared, "It's all in this good book and the relationship I have because of who's inside my heart."

"But how is it you always look joyful?" Bethany asked in between gulps and tears. "I noticed it when I met you at the café and saw you working in your beauty shop."

"That's because I've been set free," Sam said. "When you know God, peace transcends all understanding. This peace lets you know good can come from evil. And our time here on earth takes on new meaning. Although where we are is temporary and time is limited, we know love and enjoy peace by living in the now, knowing our future is planned for us. For where we are going . . . well, that's Heaven. With our Father, time is eternal.

Father. There was that word that caused Bethany so much pain. She lost one in a rainstorm and learned about another who tried to prevent her from being born. Tears poured from her eyes, and Sam handed her a tissue from a box on the coffee table. But it was of little use against the exponential flow.

Sam waited a moment before continuing. She opened the Bible to the book of John and explained to her, "For God so loved the world He sent his only son, Jesus, to be with us. And because of our sins, He died for us on the cross."

Bethany took Sam's hand and asked between sobs, "Sam, what do I have to do to have what you have and what the Knowles women had? Tell me what I have to do," she implored.

"There's nothing to do, sweet friend. It's not about doing. It's about asking," Sam said lovingly. "The shackles of sin are removed when we ask Him to forgive us and come into our hearts." She lifted Bethany's chin with her hand. "Our past hurts and burdens are lifted. He fills us with His peace and love. God is love."

More tears came from deep inside Bethany, stored since that rainy night. Every bit of that eleven-year-old's grief released tonight from this now thirty-eight-year-old woman.

"You've been through a lot. Time to get some rest," Sam said. "I'll leave this here in case you want to read more in the morning. And if you want, we'll talk more then."

. . . and the Timekeeper chimed eight.

CHAPTER 46

The morning sunlight entered the home, signaling a new day. Sam called out for Bethany in the living room, but she was not there—and neither was the Bible. Bethany was in the kitchen, writing in a notebook she had found on the kitchen sink.

Bethany finished writing and read aloud, "Most everything serves a purpose if we seek to understand what good can come after bad. As smoke from Lily Fields billowed in the night, my heart tore apart. Six strong women penned guidance to reach the light, and in my rush, I deserted it inside. Succumbing to anguish and acknowledging my power alone useless, I fell to my knees. In surrender, I asked Him to come into my heart. He leads me now and refreshes my soul."

Sam hugged Bethany. "You've been given a gift more significant than you know," she said, looking at her. "And time will reveal more."

"I don't know how I can ever thank you, Sam."

"No thanks required. It's why I'm here."

"Can you drive me to Lily Fields?"

Surveying Bethany's puffy eyes and messy hair, Sam said, "You'll need some clothes first . . . and some shoes."

While Bethany cleaned up in the bathroom, Sam found her a sundress and size eight flip-flops.

Along their way to Lily Fields, Nick called. Bethany breathed easier knowing he was checking on her, and his sweet tone reassured her. "You're going to make Lily Fields better than ever. The most important thing is you are alright. I thanked God for that last night," he said.

The girls pulled into Lily Fields's driveway as the fire restoration company Nick had called during the night removed fans from the windows. Walter's truck was in the drive, and as soon as Bethany saw it, she realized she forgot to call or text him last night.

"Miss Bethany, I'm so glad you are alright. They told me what happened," Walter said as he rushed up to them.

Bethany stroked his arm. "I'm so sorry I didn't think to call and tell you."

"The fire captain is inside completing a report. He's a friend of mine, and he said the fire started in the front bathroom," Walter said. "A spark from bad wiring ignited drop cloths on the floor. They must have had paint and chemicals on them and caused a toxic smoke."

Bethany remembered folding the paint and chemical-stained drop cloths after her work on the living room mantel. She put them out of the way in the corner of that bathroom.

Walter looked at the house and then back at Bethany. "The fire captain said the smoke was lethal. Toxic particles were smaller than the dust you see flying in the air."

Still holding on to his arm, she said, "Walter, the Timekeeper awakened me. I was fast asleep when the fire started. The Timekeeper saved me." As tears filled Bethany's eyes, Walter's face wilted at the sight of the strong woman he'd gotten to know. For the first time, she was showing vulnerability.

"Ah, Miss Bethany," Walter said. "It's going to be alright. I knew as soon as I opened up that wall there was a big problem. That's why I asked the electrician to come right away. Almost a day too late. I'm so sorry, Miss Bethany." Walter faced the ground. "You could have died in that house."

Bethany squeezed his hand "Walter, you are not to blame. I knew what I was getting into in this old house. Without you opening those walls, who knows what more might have happened later. How's the house?"

Walter lifted his head. "Miss Bethany, they wouldn't let me inside, but it looks like there's substantial damage to the front side of the roof. We need to get the house protected as soon as possible. I know a good roofer. I can also ask the fire restoration company for an estimate to clean the inside of the house. I know from other jobs that black soot goes everywhere."

The fire captain walked out the front door and, seeing Bethany, he motioned for her. "It appears the electrical fire started in the front bathroom, the former pink one as Walter called it. Did you happen to smell anything fishy yesterday?" he asked.

She nodded and remembered last night thinking Walter ate fish for lunch. "That smell is the sign of a possible electrical fire," the captain said.

Bethany would remember that fact from now on and not dismiss an odd smell off-handedly.

"You need to get the roof covered up." He pointed to the charred shingles and hole in the roof, exposing the home to the weather.

"I'm taking care of it," Walter answered.

"Can I go inside now?" Bethany asked.

"You can, but keep away from that front part of the upstairs and get an electrician to check out the whole house today, if possible," the fire captain said.

"He's on his way," Walter said.

Bethany admired Walter for taking charge in a fatherly manner on her behalf. She hugged him in thanks, but he did not return the gesture. Bethany didn't take offense. She knew as a married man, he didn't feel comfortable showing affection for women outside his family.

Nick arrived and hugged Bethany, but after a moment of enjoying the comfort of his strong arms, she pulled away. She had to get inside.

Rushing up the steps, she sprinted inside the open door. The fishy smell was gone, but the smell of smoke lingered. Putting her hand over her nose and mouth, she walked straight toward the Timekeeper. The time was 8:35 a.m. Despite the commotion last night, the Timekeeper bore no sign of it.

"That's your lucky charm right there, ma'am," the fire captain observed.

Bethany knew it was more than luck or coincidence that saved her. She was meant for something more in this life. Her life was spared twice for a reason. First by her mother and then by the Timekeeper's chimes. She was certain of this but didn't know why.

Before he left, the fire captain told her one more thing, "Be sure to get smoke alarms in all the bedrooms. Saw one downstairs in the kitchen, and one in your room, but each bedroom needs one. And check the batteries in the ones you've already got. My bet is the batteries are old." Nodding to the captain, Walter put smoke detectors and batteries on his list to pick up at the hardware store.

Peter found her in the downstairs hallway. "So glad you are alright," he said as he reached out to hug her. "I called the insurance company, and they're on their way."

Walking toward the stairs in her borrowed sundress and flip-flops, Nick, Peter, and Sam followed her. She touched the one-of-a-kind carved finial and looked at the indents in each stair tread. Once again, she placed her feet where other Knowles women walked.

When she got to the top, she headed to her bedroom to gather the newspapers along with news magazines she had not yet read, the articles written by her mother. The Timekeeper's journal was still in Sam's car. "Remind me to get the journal from your car," Bethany said. She wanted to make a copy of it as soon as possible.

Finding the seeds on the glass dish, she asked, "Nick, do you know what kind of seeds these are?"

"Looks like Turk's cap lilies. You've got them out front. These seeds take a year or more to make a bulb and then more time to bloom," he said, putting the seeds back in the dish.

Bethany pulled open the dresser drawer. Inside the silver box, unfazed by last night's destructive forces down the hall, the carved wooden butterfly sat on the blue velvet lining. She picked it up and stroked it.

Speaking on the phone below, Walter's voice traveled up the stairs. "Plan to bring extra hands with you today," he said to the electrician.

When Bethany arrived in Jameson just weeks ago, she first focused Walter on minor projects, but ones she felt were necessary, like the windows and fixing broken things in the house. When the electrician arrived today, she planned to talk to him about rewiring the whole house. She wanted it safe. Lily Fields was her responsibility to preserve. The Knowles women saved it for her, and she needed to save it for the next generation and the next.

Ever thinking toward the future, Bethany's mind began to formulate a plan. But this time, her plan for the future included the present, and she needed time alone to be in the moment.

CHAPTER 47

With an electrician and multiple crew members descending on her house, her company left so she could focus on directing repairs and cleanup. "I'm comfortable now with the safety of the blue bathroom," the electrician told her when they finished their inspections and work for the day. "We can talk later about what more needs to be done in the house, but you are alright to stay here."

After all the contractors left, Bethany changed clothes and retreated to the front porch with her computer. But before starting her work, she went down the steps to smell the flowers. Activating her senses helped dull the memory of the smoke inhalation the night before. She breathed in the fragrance of the lilies and then the crimson roses. *Nick never misses a detail*, she thought. He made sure to choose rose varieties that existed when the house was built.

After a few moments of breathing in the floral delights, she went back up the porch steps. Opening a new document on her laptop, she focused on the blank page and began to design her future. She understood this was not about what she did before. The empty white space encouraged her to create who she wanted to become.

By releasing the shackles of her past, she could embrace something brand new. A white flag of peace beckoned her to a life where scarcity of time no longer rushed her; instead, time waited with an abundance of moments to be experienced in joy. Discarding the pain of the past and envisioning what could be, the openness on the page called her to begin anew.

And so, she thought, *What would I do if I had all the time in the world?*

Her mind looked toward a place where she lived in the present and time advanced without her worrying that it would run out.

She looked at her agency. Scott ran it well in her absence as she checked in daily from afar. She believed he could continue to grow it with new accounts while still keeping Baxter happy. Scott acted in the role of president of the B.R. Miller Advertising these past weeks, and she planned to give him the official title while she kept the CEO role. Since a president is responsible for executing the CEO's vision, she made an organizational chart with almost all of the executives reporting to him. Besides Scott, the chief financial officer would report to Bethany so she could continue to keep an eye on cash flow. And with her plan to offer Scott the opportunity to own twenty percent of the company, she made a note to ask Peter to draw up a contract.

Turning her attention to Lily Fields, Bethany would put the money her mother left her to good use. She envisioned a white barn she would build on the original stone foundation Walter found at the wood's edge. It would house a women's business training center and include speakers from across the country who would educate women in business and leadership skills.

Inside the woods near the path leading to the creek, she imagined three white guest cabins with four bedrooms, four baths, and a communal living room in each. Catered lunches and dinners would take place in the barn. Twice a year she intended to invite B.R. Miller Advertising's top clients to a women's executive forum. At other times, she would invite women entrepreneurs to learn business skills and pitch their ideas to investors.

In her future vision, Bethany's agency continued to focus on beauty brands. The women's forum and conference center created a perfect match with the B.R. Miller Agency's brand. Its purpose aligned with her agency.

Another vital piece of her new plan was in town, but first, she needed to use the copier in Peter's office. She made two copies of the Timekeeper's journal pages and gave one set to him to keep in his office safe. And she asked him to put the other copy in a safe deposit box at the First Federal Bank of Jameson. The original journal remained with her.

"Where can I find Oliver Bridgewell?" she asked.

Peter pointed across the street. "His office is two blocks down."

Sitting across from Oliver at his antique desk, its carvings reminded her of the desk in the White House. He offered her a glass of water, but she wanted to get right to business.

"I know your great-grandfather did work at Lily Fields," she said.

Oliver smiled with pride.

"Do you know about Katherine Knowles Davis helping a woman escape North to freedom?"

Oliver scooted his chair closer to his desk. "Knew about the hidden room my great-grandfather built, and Agnes showed me a story written about it years ago."

"I read about the gold pocket watch, the one you have that belonged to my family," Bethany said.

Oliver's hands tightened on the sides of his chair.

Bethany recounted the story's details that pertained to Oliver. "Katherine took out her husband's pocket watch to check the time and throw off the slave hunters. That pocket watch saved the woman and her. Do you have the watch with you?" she asked.

Oliver's eyes and face flashed a look of fear.

"I remembered reading about the etching of two doves holding a vine, and I want to have a look," Bethany said.

Oliver hesitated before he removed the watch from his pocket. With his fist clenched around it, he handed it across his desk to Bethany for inspection. "The workmanship is exceptional," he remarked. "It still keeps perfect time like the Timekeeper."

Bethany stroked the love birds and opened the watch to see the hands inside. She studied the movement for a moment. "It's in the right hands," she said, snapping it closed and handing it across the desk. "It's the least my family could do for your family helping mine during the Civil War."

A look of relief came over Oliver's face. He inherited the gold watch and owned it fair and square, but of course, it was original to her family.

"How long have you owned the *Gazette*?" Bethany asked.

"Bought it fifteen years ago. Operates just above break-even with a small salary for me as publisher. Couldn't ever bring myself to shut it down." He looked out the window. "The townspeople look forward to it every week. Jameson kids enjoy seeing their names in print when they make the principal's list or the baseball, soccer, and football teams."

Bethany remembered her name being in her own town's paper and her father beaming. "I'd like to make you an offer," she said with a serious tone.

"An offer for what?"

"For the newspaper." Bethany sat upright with perfect posture.

Oliver looked at her quizzically. Sitting across from him, a big city advertising CEO saw value in this small town's newspaper.

Bethany felt the need to answer the question on his face. "It's part of my family's heritage, and I want to preserve it."

"I like how you said that," Oliver said. "When you first came to town, I thought you would be like many others who inherited homes and land. Their interest lies in money from a quick sale. They tear down irreplaceable homes and divide hundreds of acres into smaller lots. I vowed to not let that happen to Lily Fields. I had to preserve it."

Oliver looked out the window again at the town's buildings before turning his attention back to her. "After Marguerite died, I phoned a friend at the county records office. She alerted me as soon as Peter recorded the will. Since it was a public document, I read it. A real estate friend placed the call to your office and sent the certified letter on my behalf."

"It was *you*. Peter said he was surprised how information about the house was known so fast."

Oliver grinned like a Cheshire cat, and Bethany's head tilted to the side. "But how was it the first night I came to town you were on that bench?" she asked.

"Coincidence," he said. "I went with a friend to the gazebo concert but became bored with the music. I sat on a bench by the jewelry shop and waited for the concert to end. That's when I saw you looking in the shop window. I could tell by your clothes and the speed in which you walked, you weren't from here."

"I mentioned I was meeting with an attorney."

"Yes, the only one in town." Again, the grin filled Oliver's face.

"When you continued to ask me if I wanted to sell, I thought you wanted to develop my property."

"Too much history in that house," Oliver said. "I couldn't let it fall into the wrong hands."

Bethany confirmed her new opinion of Oliver Bridgewell. He valued history and wanted the next generations to honor the old by preserving what came before them.

Oliver shared more with the city woman who now took time to listen. He owned most of the downtown buildings. And he researched and hired the best craftsmen across the United States to save and refinish original floors, windows, doors, and tin ceilings. The building's bricks also looked new. Signs outside businesses conformed to a uniform design. As a brand expert, Bethany applauded Oliver for his attention to detail. "Impeccable restorations inside and out."

Getting back to the reason she came to meet with him, she said, "About the newspaper. Would you be open to entertaining an offer for it?"

"What were you thinking to do with it?"

"Operate it and write stories for it."

"Are you a writer?" he asked.

"I've never been published, if that's what you mean. I've won lots of awards for things I've written, though—TV commercials, radio spots, things like that."

"Anything I might recognize?" Oliver asked.

Bethany thought of one she worked on and wrote herself. "Hmm . . . A recent commercial has gotten a lot of national play. You might have seen it. It's where a girl reluctantly lets her good-for-nothing ex-boyfriend sleep on her couch for one night. In the morning, he comes out of the shower wrapped in a towel and tells her, 'I opened your new shampoo. The one in the blue bottle.' Her dogs jump all over him on the couch and lick him. She turns to him and says, 'That's the dogs' shampoo.'"

Oliver threw his head over the back of his chair and laughed. "I recall the last line is, 'Good for all the dogs in your life.' My daughter loves that one. She's got two dogs and bought two bottles of it right after she saw that commercial. Very clever."

"Had a great director on that spot. Client loved it. The product sales are off the charts, and we also won multiple awards."

"I'd say you are quite a writer. Your mother won lots of awards too. Other types of writing, of course," he added.

"I read a few of her travel magazine articles last night before I fell asleep—before the fire. That smoke was toxic." Her eyes pinched together as if she were in deep thought. "The Timekeeper's chimes awakened me and saved me."

Oliver looked across the desk. "You remind me of your grandmother, Elizabeth," he said. "I've heard many stories about the Timekeeper. The family regarded it as more than a clock," Oliver said, prodding her for a reaction, but she said nothing in response. "Getting back to that offer you want to make me on the *Gazette*. You're a businesswoman, and I'm a businessman. I have to tell you straight up the profits are slim."

"Yes, you're keeping it running for nostalgic purposes," Bethany said but didn't mean it. She knew Oliver made a salary from the paper. She was willing to pay anything for it within reason. The paper was a big part of her plan. Reading the writings of her ancestors and knowing many of them wrote for the paper, she now felt called to it too. She had to bring it back into the family. The thought of owning the paper, building a barn, and operating the women's forum excited her. It reminded her of the energy she felt years ago when she started her advertising company. That limitless drive fueled her then, and now, it would be put to a new purpose.

"It's more than nostalgia," Oliver said. "A town like Jameson needs a newspaper for its future. It brings people together. Sure, there are cell phones, email, and internet today, but reading stories each week and seeing photos about people in the town knits people together in a way social media alone cannot. Sharing and seeing stories makes a community. There's something special about people seeing their stories in print."

Bethany understood his point about stories. Brands are a type of story. The job of a great marketer is to tell that story. Uncrossing her legs, she asked. "Tell me what you'd take for it."

"First, I need assurance you will keep it running at least as long as I am alive," Oliver requested. "If you ever stopped publication, I want ownership back for one dollar."

She stared straight at his eyes without blinking. "Got it, but what do you want for it?"

"One dollar," he answered. His hands unclasped and rested on the sides of his chair.

Bethany grew tired of the cat-and-mouse routine. She wanted the newspaper in her hands, back in the hands of a Knowles daughter. "I know. You want to buy it back for one dollar if I stop publishing. How much do you want for it on the front end?"

"One dollar," Oliver said, smiling. He folded his arms across his chest and sat back comfortably in his chair.

"Deal," she said, slapping her hand on his desk and shaking him to attention. "I'll ask Peter to draw up a contract for us to review." She stood up and went to his office door. Turning around she said, "Pleasure doing business with you, Oliver."

Bethany walked out of the *Jameson Gazette* as its soon-to-be new publisher. She looked up at the blue sky above the office signage. She was a Knowles, and the *Jameson Gazette* was about to be owned by one again soon.

Driving back to Lily Fields, she passed the red barn. She envisioned the white one she would build on the grounds of Lily Fields. She imagined women gathering inside to learn and grow. She only needed to think of a name for it.

When she pulled in the driveway, Walter was standing outside, supervising the roofers. She smiled hearing him talk to them like the man of the house. He cared about Lily Fields like it was his own, and he cared about Bethany too. His fatherly manner was apparent to her now. Appreciating his help and also his concern for her, she looked forward to inviting his wife and a few of her lady friends to tour Lily Fields once the repairs to the roof and upstairs bathrooms were completed.

After Walter and the workers left, Bethany made dinner and sat at the kitchen table alone. She looked out the window where Nick's crew cut down the old dead oak. He had his crew plant a new one in its place, and she vowed to watch it grow.

With the house quiet and all to herself, she picked up the Timekeeper's journal and went outside to sit. The fireflies were not out yet, but the sun had lowered in the sky. She opened the journal to Marguerite's entry. Bethany hoped reading it would make her mother come alive. She wanted to know the woman who saved her life thirty-eight years ago.

CHAPTER 48

Marguerite Knowles Marchand
Born 1963
Jameson, Virginia

For thirty years I traveled and wrote stories about breathtaking places, beckoning visitors to take far-away journeys. Awards filled my walls and desk, but they didn't fill the hole in my heart. As a student, I made a difficult choice to give away a life formed inside of me. Afterward, not much remained to share with another.

I never let roots take hold. I thought if I kept moving, the past would never catch me. When I was running to avoid what was behind and seeking instead to catch what was ahead, passersby saw only a spinning top that blurred the here and now.

In my travels, I saw monuments and palaces, jungles and formal gardens, but nothing gave me joy. When I stopped fighting the darkness and looked where I could shed light, I truly started to succeed.

From the world's most iconic cities, I passionately wrote about a subject more critical than the beauty before one's eyes. Shameful stories hidden in plain sight are what my pen captured. I discovered slavery did not end in 1865. It expanded and took on different forms and included all colors and nationalities. Modern slavery's masters used new highways and airways. My grand hopes of ending this dark, secret business did not triumph, but my efforts did help some souls find their way to freedom.

I spent my last working years living my purpose, the why for my existence. Discovering and living this purpose is what created meaning and gave me direction.

Friendships formed along the way. One special friend named Achara in Thailand taught me that unforgiveness and running away from life would not get me ahead of the pain. I helped Achara escape her tormentors, and this wise woman helped me escape mine.

Although free to travel anywhere I pleased, inwardly, I had lived life in bondage. Choosing to forgive the one who abandoned me and forgiving myself for long-ago decisions set me free from shackles of regret and bitterness.

It was in confronting pain that I came to know joy. Burying hurt let weeds control the surface, and seeds of hope stood no chance. Avoiding my heartache did not offer protection. It made my vulnerability more so.

I stopped running and came home to Lily Fields. Working in the gardens, I found that roots are good. They provide anchors in storms and establish secure foundations from where one can flourish.

Despite a raging illness, I pushed aside worry of what might come and instead found pleasure in the artful display of the lilies. Starting from small seeds shed by others before it, they share their splendor for all who stop to see. In watching them grow, I innately understood why they toil not. Though their bloom is limited, they make no rushed appearance. In nature's perfect timing, they activate talents placed inside their seeds. From darkness under the soil, they grow toward the light, unleashing beauty from the deep.

As I sit at the hearth and a small fire burns, winter departs, and spring is near. My heart lifts knowing the wildflowers will soon fill the fields. And here in this special place, you, too, will come. And when you do, I pray you find happiness in fleeting seconds. Before you know it, after sixty of them, you will have a single moment. And at that moment, may you feel the presence of so great a love.

My dearest daughter, forgive me for missing your moments. Though I watched you secretly from afar, I was not part of your known world. But my regret cannot change the past. Today, with guiding faith, I press on with hope in a place where all things renew. For I know a time for tomorrow is in Heaven's realm and there, by the grace of God, my arms will finally know what it is to hold my baby girl. Until then, my sweet

Bethany, as you fully experience life in the present, be sure to make every second count.

With a heart full of love,
Marguerite Knowles Marchand
Daughter, Mother, Writer, & Champion for the Forgotten

. . . *and the* **Timekeeper** *chimed nine.*

CHAPTER 49

Bethany cried on the front porch. As she read her mother's writing and absorbed the beauty and fragrance of the lilies, she longed for the woman she never knew. Marguerite protected Bethany and gave her life. She put her up for adoption to hide her existence from men whose political futures wanted no interruption.

Nick called and wanted to come over. She wanted to see him, too but had no energy left tonight for more conversation. The last twenty-four hours exhausted her, and with what strength she had left, she wanted to finish reading her mother's other writings and focus on the new plan she had created. Although wanting desperately to share it with Nick, she thought it best to wait until after she put it in motion.

"Can I see you when I get back? she asked. "I need to go to Alexandria tomorrow morning." She stood up from her chair and walked down the porch steps.

"How long?" he asked.

"I need to talk to Baxter and Scott. Let me do that, and then I'm all yours. Dinner soon?"

Bethany knew Nick worried about the lure of her work in Alexandria. She worried too. *Can I really do this?* She was concerned about getting sucked back into the whirlpool of work that nearly drowned her before but also fretted about getting Baxter's buy-in. He was critical to her plan. She would tell Nick the good news after she put things in motion. No use getting him excited until it all could be worked out.

She saw Nick in her future and hoped he saw her in his too. She was pretty sure he felt the same way she did. The look on his face during the fire and when he left her at Sam's door told her she was more than a new girlfriend. From what she knew about his life, Nick DeLeon played for keeps.

"Come back, *mi amor*," Nick spoke lovingly. His tone also offered freedom. Freedom for her to be who she needed to be and fulfill her personal destiny. He wasn't threatened by her calling or her drive.

"I will. I promise," she said.

Nick hung up and scrolled to her picture on his phone, the one of her standing next to the waterfall. He snapped it that day without her looking. *She went back to Alexandria once and came right back. Surely she will come right back again,* he thought. After almost losing her in the fire, he didn't want to wait on starting a life together. He wanted to drive over there and tell her how deeply he felt for her, but she hadn't given him the chance. Of course, he knew she had gone through a lot and needed rest, but he needed to hold her in his arms. They ached for her. He lost one love and couldn't afford to lose Bethany too.

CHAPTER 50

Early in the morning, Bethany pulled out of the driveway at Lily Fields. Her mind still held the memory of smoke, so she pushed her window button to breathe in Jameson air. The GPS pointed her north, but first, she drove through town. It read 7:30 a.m. on the town hall's clock. She should arrive at Baxter's by ten. Turning right onto Harbor Street, the "closed" sign on Sam's shop reminded her it was Sunday. She tuned the radio to the station Sam played in her beauty shop. The praise music uplifted her, and she tapped her fingers on the steering wheel, following the rhythmic beat.

Receiving no answer when she called Baxter earlier that morning, she pulled off at a Fredericksburg exit and sent him a text, asking him to call her. And when she arrived in Arlington, she phoned him. Again, she got no answer. *Amy always has her phone by her side*, she thought.

"I'm in California visiting my mother," Amy said after answering her call.

"Oh, sorry if I woke you up."

"I don't know why Baxter didn't answer. I talked with him minutes ago. Maggie threw up on the rug, and I made an appointment for Baxter to take her to the on-call veterinarian this morning. Go ahead and stop by, but make sure he isn't late for the vet." Baxter and Amy had no children. Besides Baxter, the dogs meant the world to Amy.

In the heart of Arlington, Virginia, Bethany pulled onto Baxter and Amy's street along the Potomac River. She called Baxter once more. He texted her back. "Busy. Can't meet." But she had to see him, so she called him again. "Give me five minutes before you come up," he texted. "And then I don't have much time to spend." It was typical Baxter. He was always in a rush.

She sat in her parked car and waited four minutes before entering the lobby. Using the elevator pass key Amy had given her long ago, she pushed the penthouse floor button. Bethany sweated through her cotton blouse. When the elevator doors opened across from the apartment, she fanned herself to cool down and knocked on the door. It took a minute before Baxter answered.

"Must be something important. Good to see you." Baxter kissed her cheek and turned, leaving her at the door. She followed him into the living room where a smooth jazz song played through the speakers.

Sweeping floor-to-ceiling windows gave view to the Potomac River below. On the walls, bright abstract paintings complemented the modern furniture. Amy loved to decorate, and it showed.

Baxter motioned her to follow him down the hall toward Amy's office at the far end of the apartment. Sitting himself in a chair, he offered her a seat on the couch across from him. It was apparent she had caught him off guard. His sandy-blond hair was disheveled; his sweatpants and wrinkled BXB2 T-shirt looked like he had pulled them out of a corner on the floor.

Baxter looked at his watch, and she got the not-so-subtle message she also often used.

"Are things going well with Scott?" Bethany asked.

"Yes, but I'd still like to have some video calls with you."

"Sure thing," she said. "We can schedule that." Bethany knew Baxter enjoyed bouncing ideas off her, even ones that did not include advertising. She was a confidante and one whose input he sought, just like when he acquired the new company. Though she was still upset with him about losing that work, she had to keep it out of her mind for now. Bethany owed a lot to Baxter for all the other business he continued to give her.

She owned B.R. Miller Advertising outright, but Baxter kept a keen eye on her business. He enjoyed keeping his hands in things that were not his. Baxter Buchanan II liked ownership, as did his even more mega-successful father.

Bethany always kept him abreast of her business health and understood his now one-billion-dollar global business was tied to hers. Scott thought Baxter meddled too much in their agency business, but Bethany knew how to push Baxter back when needed. She let him think he had more influence over her and her business than he did.

Twisting her French handbag handles in her hand, she said, "My other side of the business is going very well. We got another new client recently, a new skin lotion."

"Good for you," he said and looked down at his watch again.

"How's Costa Rica doing? Have you moved more lines down there yet?" she asked.

"We're up and running," he said curtly.

"Amy told me you're still traveling a lot there. Makes sense since so much business is riding on that place even more now."

Baxter's lips twisted to one side. Bethany caught his reaction. They both knew Amy talked too much, and Baxter didn't like it. The women were close friends who shared many things. "When is Amy coming home?"

"Next Saturday." He looked at his watch again. "Sorry. I've got just ten minutes. Maggie threw up twice, and I've got her in a crate until I leave for the vet—in just a few minutes."

Bethany knew it was time to use her prepared line. She put her purse aside and sat up as best she could on the sinking couch. "Like you taught me from the start, I've always operated from a plan. I've far exceeded my last three-year strategic plan. Next year looks to be one of our biggest years yet. We've added new accounts, and Scott stepped up by running your projects."

"You being out of the office gave Scott a chance. Poor guy needed that," Baxter said.

Bethany nodded in acknowledgment.

"I always thought Scott was a good guy, but he lived in your shadow. Since you left town, he's shown real leadership. He's an excellent operator."

Bethany was glad to know she and Baxter still thought in synch. "We had a fire at Lily Fields."

Concern filled Baxter's face.

"Not too much damage," she said.

"What happened?"

"Electrical fire. I've already got a crew rewiring because I've decided to keep the house."

Baxter leaned over and high-fived her. "You made the right decision. It will be a perfect getaway for you. Amy and I can go there too. How often do you think you'll use it?" he asked in anticipation.

"That's what I wanted to talk to you about. I made another decision." She paused before continuing. "I'm going to make Scott president of B.R. Miller Advertising, and I'll remain CEO.

"Scott deserves the title," Baxter said nodding in approval. "He's earned it."

Bethany's heart beat stronger. "My plan is to let Scott take on even more. I'm going to stay in constant touch and come into the office but less often." She watched his face for a reaction, but it showed no difference. "My home base will be in Jameson. I'm buying the town newspaper," she said, grabbing the side of the couch.

"What? You've lost it," he said, throwing his hands in the air.

No, I've found it, she said to herself as Baxter's tone grew louder.

"I know you, Bethany," he said as he pointed at her face. "You won't last long living in a small town with nothing going on. You need work like I do—and lots of it. A small-town newspaper is a waste of your talent and energy. The smoke from that fire must have clouded your brain."

Bethany feared Baxter wouldn't understand at first. He was as addicted to the hustle of work as she had been. Inside the swirl of busyness, the rest of the world looked foreign. A spinning top is home to those who live in it. It's chaos and stress, but it's the only way they both knew how to live . . . until now, at least for her.

Since coming to Jameson, she'd formed a new understanding, and from a distance, she gained perspective. Bethany was in a new world she wanted to call home. A world with less rush and filled with purpose-driven actions. And there was a man in this new world with whom she wanted to explore having a future. With Nick, she stopped to enjoy the moment. He not only unleashed her playful nature, he also made her feel loved.

Once Baxter finished raging at her, Bethany put her eyes in line with his. "There is more to my plan," she told him. She shared her idea to build a barn on Lily Fields's property and make it into a women's business conference center, but Baxter turned his head away.

"I'm going to build guest cabins for the women's forums we will host for clients, and multiple times a year, we will have conferences for women entrepreneurs. It's in perfect alignment with the B.R. Miller Agency brand and with BXB2 Cosmetics too."

With the mention of his business, Baxter's eyes reengaged hers.

She continued. "We can plan conferences together and tie them into your beauty brands. Women are your sole target market, and this is a fresh way to reach them. The public relations benefit will be enormous."

"I see the possibilities," Baxter said with a reanimated face. "Once again, Bethany, you are ahead of the rest. You haven't lost it after all. In fact, you are on it. I love it. How fast do you think you can build it and get the conferences underway?"

"I'd need architectural plans and permits. The rough timelines are mapped out. I've already talked about any town issues with Peter Jameson, my attorney there. Uh . . . did I tell you he's my half brother?"

"What? No."

"It's a long story. I'll tell you and Amy all about it. But back to the woman's conference center. Peter was confident the town council would vote to approve it since it would bring business to Jameson. Women will want to shop and eat in town when they are not in meetings. It will be a big win for Jameson."

Baxter's face lit up with excitement. "This is a big win for my company's brand," he said. She knew he would come around once he knew her idea benefited him too.

In time, Baxter would pressure her to get more involved in the agency again, but she planned to resist. She would run the newspaper, even if he thought it a crazy waste of her time. It was her heritage and was important to the town. Thinking about the women's conference center and having a new venture to build and run invigorated her. It was as if she'd graduated again but this time, to a new way of life.

Baxter checked his watch. With her mission now complete, she jumped up from the couch, grabbed her purse, and hugged him. "I knew I could count on you."

"I'll be leaving right behind you," he said. "I've got to get Amy's baby to the vet, or she'll kill me. I'm taking the other dog with me for a checkup, just in case."

"Every second counts," Bethany said as she kissed his cheek and waved goodbye.

Sitting in her car, she reviewed what just happened. She was on a new course, and the road led to Jameson. She would bring women entrepreneurs and women executives there. They would learn leadership and business skills, and she would help launch women leaders and business owners. The Knowles women would be proud. Their strength and words had guided Bethany to this point.

She looked forward to sharing her plan with Nick and asking him to draw up landscaping designs for the conference center, the new barn, executive cabins, and surrounding grounds.

The sound of squealing tires from Baxter's bright red sports car as he exited the underground parking garage snapped her to attention. He was late for the vet. She reached inside her purse for her phone. She needed to call Scott who was next on her appointment list. But her phone was not in her purse. *I must have dropped it along the way.*

She retraced her steps outside but didn't see it. *It must be in the building.* After checking inside the elevator and not knowing how long Baxter would be at the vet, or if he would even return home right away, she remembered the other key inside her purse, the one to his and Amy's condo. Amy had given it to her last year when her dog sitter was out of town. Besides the sitter, she trusted no one other than Bethany with her beloved animals.

Bethany didn't like the thought of letting herself into someone else's home without them knowing, but she knew Amy wouldn't mind and hoped Baxter wouldn't either. She needed her phone, so she turned the key and entered.

CHAPTER 51

The smell of a too-sweet candle crimped her nose, but she didn't see one burning and hadn't smelled it when she walked in before. Off to the right of the living room, toward the hall leading to the master bedroom, the sound from a TV game show caught her attention. *Baxter must have left it on in his rush.* She walked down the opposite hall to Amy's office.

Not seeing her phone on the couch, she reached into a cushion. Relief filled her face as she pulled out her phone. It was her lifeline, and she had more to accomplish today, including meeting with Scott. She looked forward to telling him about his promotion and scurried to get on with that and out of someone else's house—someone who didn't know she had let herself in with their extra key.

Dashing through the living room, a whimper stopped her quick steps. *Was it the other dog?* Baxter said he was taking them both with him. No, it was muffled crying, and it was coming from the master bedroom down the other hall.

Amy was out of town, or so she thought, and she saw Baxter leave. *Was Amy really here?* She heard the sound again. "Amy!" she called out. The sound grew louder, and she walked toward it. "It's Bethany. Are you alright?" Gasping sounds came from the master suite.

If Amy was home, and she and Baxter had a fight, she shouldn't meddle. *Stay out of it,* Bethany thought. Amy was her friend. Baxter was her friend. Suddenly, she was in the middle.

Crash! Bethany jumped. Something hit the wood floor in the bedroom.

"Amy?" Bethany called out again, inching closer toward the sound. The master bedroom door was ajar, and she called, "Amy?" The answer was a whimpered cry.

She took another step. Through the cracked door, Bethany saw those piercing eyes.

CHAPTER 52

The eyes of the Costa Rican factory girl desperately pleaded for help. She was handcuffed to the metal headboard, and a woman's scarf was tied around her head and over her mouth. Tears streamed down the girl's face, and her eyes implored Bethany. Wearing only a man's white T-shirt, her tanned, thin legs were strung over the side of the bed.

With shaking hands, Bethany reached for the scarf tied tight around the girl's head, but she could not loosen the knot. "I'll be right back," she told the girl, who couldn't answer. Her dark, Latin eyes screamed, *Don't leave me!* Bethany held up one finger. "One moment," she said to the bound and gagged girl.

She pulled out kitchen drawers, leaving them hanging open after her hurried rummaging through each. Silverware was in one, stationery in the next, cooking utensils in another, and then in the catch-all drawer, she saw a pair of scissors. She rushed back to the bedroom. Cutting the top knot gave her room to reach the second knot tied tighter on her head. But when the scarf released, the girl still could not talk. Reaching into her mouth, Bethany pulled out a man's wadded-up black sock. The girl gasped for air. With her mouth stuffed and her nose clogged from crying, she had been suffocating.

"I'm so sorry. I'm going to help you," Bethany assured, speaking over the incessant beat inside her chest. Still handcuffed to the bed, the girl used her tear-streaked eyes to point toward the dresser and a key on top. Bethany didn't know how to open handcuffs, but she picked up the key. Despite her shaking hands, the shackles released from the girl's arms.

"Oh, thank God!" Bethany shouted in relief as she helped the girl's arms break free from their locked position over her head.

"*No hablo ingles.*" The girl didn't speak English.

Bethany knew Spanish well enough to get by, but raw emotion took over her usually cool head. She reached for her phone and, along with the girl's help, used the translation app to interpret. "Men brought me here from Costa Rica," the translation read. "I want to go home to my family." When Bethany found out she was only fourteen, vomit came up her throat, and she turned her head into Baxter's sheets.

Her mind raced. *No time to call 911*, she thought. *Baxter might return before help arrived.* She had to get both of them out of this condo. A black backpack with a yellow smiley face stitched on front sat on the floor. Bethany reached inside and found a sundress and pair of flip-flops. Throwing the dress over the girl's head, she ran with her out of the apartment, closing the door behind her.

CHAPTER 53

Holding on to the thin girl, Bethany waited for the elevator to reach the twenty-eighth floor. Sunday mornings were busy days in the building. People took their dogs for walks, got groceries, went to breakfast, and attended church.

The elevator dinged and the doors opened. Bethany hesitated. Seeing it was empty inside, she pulled the girl in and pushed the button for the ground floor. Though knowing the girl didn't understand English, Bethany told her, "Everything will be alright." Right now, it was hard enough for Bethany to think and speak in her own language.

The chance of getting from the twenty-eighth to the ground floor without someone stopping the elevator was remote. She wiped the girl's face with her hands and tried to calm her. Recalling a Spanish word, she said to her, "*Tranquila.*" It meant *calm*.

The girl's eyes and nose continued to run. Bethany found a tissue she had long ago stuffed inside her purse. Attempting to freshen the girl's disheveled mess, she put her fingers through her long, brown hair, but what it needed was a good washing.

She had to make her stop crying. If someone saw her, they would ask questions. "Think Bethany, think," she said aloud. In case an explanation was needed, she created a story, and it was that the girl had a bad toothache. They were going to the dentist for an emergency visit. *That should do if anyone asked.*

Twenty-second floor. *Ding.* The elevator doors opened. A mother and her four-year-old son entered. "Please. I want ice cream." He tugged on his mother's purse. "You always make me go with you. I hate the grocery store." When the doors closed, the mother turned around and smiled at

Bethany. The kid kept whining and stood next to Bethany with his face defiantly facing the corner and away from his mother's glance.

Sixteenth floor lit up. *Ding.* The elevator door opened. Pulling the girl closer to her, Bethany put her face against her own body. She was short for fourteen, and her head easily fit under Bethany's arm.

A man in his seventies got on. He looked at the woman and her son and then at Bethany and smiled. "Good morning, all." Bethany nodded and acknowledged his greeting without speaking. Standing in front of her and the girl, he faced the elevator doors.

The little boy next to her kept badgering his mother. "Not today, Johnny," his mother turned back to tell him. Bethany wanted her to say yes and shut him up. The man turned around to see the little boy and caught Bethany's glance. She saw him look at the girl, too, but Bethany said nothing, and the man turned back around.

Ding. Ninth floor. The doors opened. A teenage boy stood in the hall with two big dogs. He heard the whiny kid and saw the crowd. "I'll wait for the next one," he said, and the doors closed.

The elevator continued down. Bethany willed the man to keep looking straight ahead and not turn around. They were almost down and past the third floor.

The second-floor light lit up. *Ding.* The elevator stopped and opened for a cleaning lady with a bucket of rags. The man moved to the side and left the cleaning lady right in front of Bethany and the girl. She wondered if the woman could hear her heart beating against her chest. The pounding echoed in her ears.

Ding. They reached the lobby floor and the doors opened. The cleaning lady exited, and the older gentleman moved aside to let others out first. He soon realized he was blocking those behind him and had to exit. Next, the mother and son stepped out.

Bethany pushed Open so the doors wouldn't close on her. She wanted to let the others go out through the building's front door ahead of her. With her arm around the girl, Bethany walked out of the elevator. And as she exited the building, a man's voice shouted, "Have a nice day." Behind the front desk sat a concierge who wasn't there earlier. The thoughtless greeting made Bethany's quick steps speed up, and she raced toward her parked car.

CHAPTER 54

She didn't know when Baxter would return. He might drop off the dog and come right back home. She had to get the girl out of there. Clicking the key fob twice, she unlocked both doors and helped the limp girl inside, putting the backpack on her lap. When she rounded the front of the car, the embroidered yellow smile peered at her through the windshield.

She looked down the street. There was no sign of Baxter's car. Without putting on her seat belt, she pulled out of the on-street parking place. The safety dings reminded her and the passenger to fasten their belts, but she ignored them, keeping her attention on the road ahead.

Nerves tingled in her extremities, and adrenaline rushed through her veins. Her mind jumbled from the horrific scene upstairs. "Think, Bethany. Think," she said aloud again. The seatbelt dings continued to interrupt her thoughts. Reaching her right arm over her chest, she grabbed her seatbelt and snapped it in place.

The girl stared dead straight through the windshield. "How could Baxter do something like this?" Bethany said aloud to no one who understood. The safety dings continued. She had to stop the dinging so she could think.

She tapped the girl's arm and pointed at the passenger door. Awakening from her dazed look, the girl took the nonverbal cue and pulled her seatbelt from the door, just enough for Bethany to reach and snap it. As she did, her car crossed the center line. Approaching at fast speed, an oncoming delivery truck beeped his horn. She swerved and righted the car in time.

As she turned into her driveway, a neighbor waved. Without acknowledging him, she reached for the programmed garage door button next to her visor. A ding from her phone signaled someone was at her garage door camera. She remembered Baxter and Amy had security cameras, too, and theirs was state-of-the art. *Did Baxter turn his cameras on before he left?* He was in a rush, but she thought he did. He would know it was Bethany who took the girl.

CHAPTER 55

Bethany pulled out of her driveway. The girl said not a word. Holding the smiley-face backpack in her lap, she lifelessly stared out the windshield. *Find somewhere to go, Bethany. Think*, she inwardly scolded herself.

"Call Holly," she said into her phone. Holly answered on the first ring and Bethany cut her off.

"I need help."

"What's wrong?"

"I need a place to stay. I'll explain later."

"I'm house sitting for my mom this week," Holly answered. "You can come here if you want." Bethany counted on Holly for many things in the eight years she worked for her. Now, Bethany knew she could count on Holly for . . . well, anything.

When she got to the next street, out of sight from her townhouse, she punched in Holly's mom's address. Forcing a smile at the frightened and tearful girl, she reached to click open the glove box and retrieved a napkin from a drive-through restaurant. Without the mental means to speak to the girl in her native language, she stroked her arms and tried to reassure her she would be alright.

"Can I pull inside the garage?" Bethany called Holly from the driveway. Holly's mom lived in a small wood-frame house ten minutes from Bethany in Alexandria. As Bethany's car pulled inside, Holly stood at the kitchen doorway. "Shut the garage door," Bethany said as she sprinted to the passenger side. Holly obeyed the frantic command.

Whisking the backpack off the girl's lap, she took her inside.

"Something terrible happened," Bethany said. "She doesn't speak English. Do you know Spanish?"

"A little," Holly said, standing at the kitchen counter confused by the unexpected visitors. "But you know more. All I remember is, *Que es su nombre?*"

"Isabela," the girl answered.

She had a name to go with those eyes. Bethany pointed at herself and said, "Bethany," then introduced Holly.

Bethany hadn't yet explained what was going on and who this girl was, but being a proper hostess, Holly gave them both a glass of water. She took grapes from the refrigerator and opened a box of donuts to put on the table.

"*Donde esta tu baño?*" Isabela asked after she took a drink.

"Bathroom," Bethany said, understanding the words.

Holly showed her the hall bathroom, but first Isabela returned for the backpack. There were more clothes inside. Bethany put on her only what was necessary to get out of Baxter's fast.

"What's with bringing some young girl here?" Holly asked.

"I forgot my phone in Baxter's apartment, and since I saw him leave to go to the vet, I used the key Amy gave me to let myself inside. That's when I found her. She's the same girl I saw at Baxter's Costa Rican factory."

"What are you talking about?"

Bethany recounted to Holly her first experience when she laid eyes on the girl in Costa Rica.

Holly's eyes squinched. It was the first she heard about Bethany's strange experience in Costa Rica.

"I stressed about the possibility of the plant manager getting Baxter caught up in a violation of another country's child labor laws. That day I got back, I talked to Baxter about it, but he reassured me they operated within Costa Rican laws."

Bethany wrung her hands together. "Oh my gosh, Holly. So many young girls worked there. I knew something wasn't right, so I asked Michael Alexander to check into it. I was concerned the plant manager was not telling Baxter right, but Michael confirmed the legal working age was sixteen as long as the teenager had a parental note."

Bethany clenched her hands on top of the table. "From what I shared with him, Michael said he had concerns, too, but his Costa Rican legal contact told him the factory had a good reputation and all was in order. He told me to let it go, but I couldn't forget her eyes." Bethany began to cry. It was the first time she cried since finding the handcuffed girl.

Holly reached for Bethany's hand. "You never told me any of this."

"I didn't want to say a word until I could talk with Baxter. But then the inheritance news came, and I left for Jameson."

Isabela turned off the bathroom sink and came back to the table. "Would you like to watch TV, honey?" Holly asked to no response. "Uh . . . television?" Holly did her best version of saying the word with a Spanish accent. Then she pointed to the TV, and Isabela nodded yes.

In the den off the kitchen, Holly gave Isabela the remote control and showed her the channel up and down buttons.

"What was Baxter doing with this girl in his condo?" Holly said, walking back to the kitchen table. "Did he bring her here to clean for them?"

Bethany's shoulders fell. She hadn't told Holly the worst yet. "I told you I let myself into Baxter's apartment to retrieve my phone. That's when I heard a lamp crash and saw Isabela's eyes through the cracked open master bedroom door. When I entered, I saw her handcuffed to the bed."

"What?" Holly shrieked from disbelief.

"*Esta bien*," It's okay, Bethany said to Isabela, who jumped up from the couch to see what was the matter. Bethany motioned her to return to watch TV.

Turning back to Holly, Bethany explained the details of how she found the girl in Baxter's bedroom.

Holly's hand flew up to her mouth. Her face went white with the look of someone being told a family member died, and her eyes darted from Bethany to Isabela.

"I brought her to my house then remembered Baxter's cameras. He will find it was me who took her. I couldn't go home." Bethany's phone buzzed. When they both saw the name on the screen, the women looked at each other in fright. Baxter would go to Bethany's house looking for her, and when that failed, he'd go to Holly's condo. A stroke of luck had Holly at her mom's.

CHAPTER 56

C an you close all your blinds? Bethany asked Holly as she switched off her phone. "And whatever you do, don't answer your phone."

"But if he calls and I don't answer, he might think something is up."

"Baxter knows you don't like him," Bethany said. "He'll think you're ignoring him on a weekend."

"I know I had to be nice to him, but I never liked how he treated Amy as his prized object. That woman has the sweetest heart there is."

Bethany shook her head in agreement. "I never imagined Baxter would do anything like this. This is a nightmare," she said but knew she could not wake up and erase what she saw. This wasn't a bad dream. Bethany was wide awake.

"We need to talk to her," Holly said, walking into the den to retrieve the girl.

Although Bethany knew enough Spanish to ask Isabela what happened to her, she required the help of the online translating tool to explain Isabela's answer.

Isabela typed her answer in her native language, and the translation app did its work. "The plant manager hired many young girls and a few young boys." Holly looked up from the phone at Bethany.

Isabela retrieved the phone and typed in more. "The manager helped us obtain forged documents. After working for BXB2 cosmetics for a few weeks, a few of us were selected to earn extra money to work a party for Americans. I needed the money because my mom died three years ago, and my father was an alcoholic. My little sister, my brother, and I live with my aunt and uncle. They have four kids of their own. My siblings depend on me."

"How old are they?" Bethany asked.

"My brother is eight, and my little sister is four."

Bethany and Holly braced for the rest of the story, which neither wanted to hear.

"After the plant manager drove us to the party, he gave us special outfits to wear. Since it was my first time, he put a sticker on my uniform. Along with the other girls, I took trays of food to the American men as the plant manager supervised from a doorway. I wanted to do a good job and smiled as a man with salt-and-pepper hair was the first to take a piece of shrimp from my tray." Isabela looked up at Holly and Bethany before she typed in more.

Holly wrapped her arms around her stomach.

"I saw the plant manager nod. He came from his doorway perch and asked me to come with him. As he walked me down a hall, he said I did an excellent job and was selected to earn even more. He handed me money and told me to wait in a back room. I was excited at first. We already got paid upfront after we changed into the server uniforms. Hired for three hours of waitressing work . . . we had already been paid for two full days' of factory work. I waited alone in the room, but I felt like something was wrong. There were chairs and a table in the room . . . and also a bed. The American man entered and closed the door. And that's when I heard it lock from the outside."

When Isabela began to type in what happened next, tears rolled down Holly's face. Bethany got up from her chair and hugged Isabela.

Isabela stopped before sharing more intimate details, but she explained other things. "There were more parties after that first one over a year ago. The plant manager threatened we would lose our jobs if we told anyone or did not agree to go to more parties. I needed a job because my brother and little sister depended on me."

"Did you tell your aunt or uncle?" Holly typed on the phone for Isabela to read in Spanish.

"Not everything. I told them that I didn't like to work the parties, but they knew how much I needed the money. They don't have extra for us." Holly and Bethany exchanged a look of bewilderment.

"How did you get to the United States?" Bethany asked her in Spanish.

"A few of us went to work a party, and when we arrived, no one was there but the manager. He said we were getting a special treat and going to an amusement park in America. We were told our parents and my aunt and uncle approved of the surprise. He gave us backpacks with clothes and took us to Mexico. Then smugglers took us across the US border at night."

"You said *we*. Are there others here?" Holly asked.

"There were six of us girls. We thought we were going to an amusement park because we had been good, and this was our prize."

Holly and Bethany's eyes met in horror. Through the translation tool, Isabela said, "After an hour's walk, a van picked us up on a dirt road. A driver took us to a dark parking lot where that man I met at my first party, the one with greying hair, was waiting for us. Well, for me. He took me away from the other girls and put me in the back of a car. He greeted me like he always did with a long kiss on my lips."

Holly put her head on the table and covered it with her hands. She looked up at Isabela and rose from her chair to hug her. She rocked her side to side before letting her go.

Isabela shared more through the translation app. "He put me on a plane with him and when it landed, he took me off and put me in the backseat of another car, but he didn't get in with me. The factory boss man was inside. The one named Baxter. I knew him a long time, too, from the parties."

Bethany's head fell toward her chest.

"He took me inside his apartment and handcuffed me to the bed before he kissed me and moved his hands all over me. He took my clothes off and then his too."

Bethany and Holly exchanged a horrified glance.

As Isabela cried, she looked at Holly.

"It's going to be alright, sweetie," Holly told Isabela. We are not going to let him or anyone else do this to you ever again." Remembering Isabela didn't understand a word she said, she took the phone and typed it into the translation app and showed Isabela. And then Holly asked, "When was this?"

"Three days ago," Isabela answered. "I want to go home to my brother and little sister. I know they must be crying for me."

Bethany remembered the little boy and sweet face of the little girl without shoes. "We will get you home," she said, without knowing how.

Holly took Isabela back to the TV room, and this time she carried the plate of donuts with her.

"Human trafficking," Holly said when she came back and sat down next to Bethany.

"What?" Bethany asked, wiping her eyes with a napkin.

"That's what this is. Human trafficking. It's modern-day slavery. He brought Isabela here against her wishes. She's well underage, and he not only took her across state lines, but he also brought her here from another country—and for one specific reason." A look of hate and disgust filled her face. "What a pig," Holly said.

"Remember that charity event I went to in your place last year?" Holly recalled. "The guest speaker told us more than we wanted to know about human trafficking and child sex trafficking."

Bethany's mind tried to catch up with her eyes. It seemed too much to believe, but evidence of child sex trafficking sat in the den watching TV love stories. Her stomach churned and warned bile could explode up through her mouth at any moment. She took a drink of water to no avail and dashed into the hall bathroom.

Holly waited for Bethany to return. "You okay," she asked? Bethany nodded. She motioned for Holly to talk because she had no life inside to lead a conversation.

"After I attended that human trafficking fundraiser in your place, I asked you for a company donation. Remember, you wrote a check?" Holly asked.

Bethany nodded and thought about Baxter. They'd known each other since they were eighteen. No one could have convinced her he would do this. She was now in the stage beyond initial shock and adrenaline rush. She was numb. *This can't be real*, she thought. If only it were a nightmare, then she could wake up, but those piercing brown eyes were here now, watching TV in the next room. And Bethany could not forget what horrors Isabela shared about the man she considered a brother.

. . . and the Timekeeper chimed ten.

CHAPTER 57

"Who should we call? The police? The FBI? A hotline? My neighbor is an FBI agent. I think I have a picture of his card on my phone." Holly scrolled through her pictures with speed. "Here it is—Tom. Real nice guy and his wife is sweet too. He can tell us what to do."

"Go ahead and ask him, please," Bethany pleaded. "This situation is more than local police jurisdiction because Baxter arranged to bring her across state lines and across the border."

With Holly at the helm on her laptop, the two women constructed an email to send Tom. Telling him the situation but without naming names, Holly asked if he could direct her to someone in the FBI or recommend another agency to contact. They reviewed the email twice before Holly hit Send.

Since it was a Sunday, Bethany hated the thought of waiting until tomorrow for an answer. *What if Baxter finds me first?*

Bethany didn't have the usual look of nervous impatience on her face. This time her look revealed desperation, a cry for help. "I can call Tom at home," Holly said. "He's in my community's online directory." But Holly didn't have to call because, within minutes, Tom replied. He would arrange for someone to speak with her friend, but for her to meet at his office, he needed the woman's full name, date of birth, and social security number.

Bethany hated for Holly to give Tom her name and info but knew she had to do it. Tom worked in IT, and his office was inside the FBI headquarters building in Washington, D.C. He would meet Bethany in the lobby tomorrow morning at ten o'clock. The girls finally had a plan.

Coming to the kitchen table, Isabela pointed to Holly's phone to type in a message. She asked if she could call her friend in Costa Rica. She could let her aunt and uncle know she was alright. Suspecting the plant manager did not reach out or at a minimum did not tell them the truth, she knew her family must be looking for her. It was her little brother she was most worried about. He would know something was not right because he knew she would never leave him.

"What do you think?" Bethany asked Holly.

"Okay, sweetie," Holly agreed. "Tell her you are alright and coming home soon, but don't tell her who you're with—at all. Not that we are two women, our names, or anything. Okay? Just tell her to let your aunt and uncle know you are in the US, and people are helping you to come back home soon."

Isabela took the phone to the den, but hearing her cry to her friend was too much for Holly and Bethany to bear. Without understanding Isabela's words, tears poured from them both. As women, they instinctively understood the anguished sobs from a fourteen-year-old girl.

Holly took Bethany by the hand and brought her over to the sink. The added distance helped muffle Isabela's voice.

"We all need to eat something," Holly declared.

"I can't think about food right now."

"I'm going to cook." Holly took out a frying pan. She pushed a bottle of red wine and a corkscrew toward Bethany. When she didn't pick either up, Holly opened it herself and poured them each a glass. Removing fish from the freezer, she placed it on the sink to thaw. Bethany sat at the table staring at Isabella who, after finishing her phone call, watched a rerun of a star's dancing competition.

Bethany remembered her promise to Nick. She turned on her phone and texted him, "I miss you. I want to see you as soon as I get back to town. Lots to share. I need to spend the night here and will come back to Jameson tomorrow."

He texted back. "Miss you too. Hurry home to Lily Fields. It's not the same without you here." After reading his sweet message, she quickly turned her phone off. Baxter had texted her more than ten times already.

"Oh, no," Holly said. She brought her phone to Bethany. The text said, "Do you know where Bethany is? I need to talk with her right away." It was from Baxter.

"Text him and say you talked to me late this morning when I was on my way back to Jameson." Holly did as Bethany instructed, and Baxter did not reply.

While Holly cooked fish, Bethany sat at the table and looked at the backyard. Finches took turns eating at the bird feeder hanging from Holly's mother's maple tree. *Nature had an order to it, but people (some men, that is) were more beastly.*

Holly's phone buzzed. "Let it go to voice mail!" Bethany yelled out to her.

Scott's voice mail message said, "Have you seen Bethany since she came to town? Baxter is looking for her. He said he met with her this morning and needs to talk to her again. Call me if you hear from her."

"Text him the same thing you told Baxter," Bethany instructed.

During dinner, with broken Spanish and help from the translation app, the women did their best to converse with Isabela. Keeping the subject lighter this time, they asked her about school. She told them she quit when she was thirteen to work. Holly and Bethany exchanged a quick look, and the sickening feeling they had grew worse.

Holly scrolled through the guide on the TV remote and found a Spanish language TV station to occupy Isabela. While Holly washed the frying pan, Bethany robotically loaded the plates in the dishwasher. Her mind was not with her body.

"I'm sorry I got you into this. I didn't know where else to go," Bethany said.

"Never thought when I went to a fundraising event in your place last year, I'd help uncover modern slavery," Holly said. "That's what it is, you know. It's slavery in our time."

Bethany's eyes glanced up, "My great-great-great-grandmother Katherine battled against slavery, and here it is in my lifetime too."

"We think human trafficking is mostly an international problem, but it's an American problem too," she said as she scrubbed a crusty piece of fish from the pan. "The internet makes it too easy for men to find these young women—American or otherwise, like Isabela." Holly looked at the young girl in her mother's den, a mere four-eleven in stature. "Too easy to find *children* and exploit them. Human trafficking is a multi-billion-dollar industry, and most of it is sex trafficking," Holly said. "Every state in the US has cases. Men prey on girls. Some are runaways, and others don't realize who they are getting caught up with before it's too late."

"I had no idea it was that big," Bethany said.

"Most people don't want to talk about it. I can tell you that was not a fun evening you sent me to in your place, but now I'm really glad I went," Holly said.

"I keep thinking about Amy," Bethany said. "She visited me in Jameson. I knew it was strange when she said Baxter traveled so much to Costa Rica. There are plenty of other people to watch over his factory. But now I know those trips weren't about work for him. That was his getaway place."

Holly nodded while drying a utensil.

"Amy worried about Baxter having an affair, and I told her I never saw Baxter look at another woman. I was right. It wasn't another *woman*. How could Baxter turn into this monster?" Bethany pushed a plate into the dishwasher, banging it beside another.

Retreating to the den, they all watched a Spanish-language TV show that only one of them understood. Bethany picked up Isabela's feet on the couch and put them on her lap. With her heightened emotions finally crashed, Bethany's eyelids struggled to stay open.

"Best we all get some rest," Holly said. "I'll keep Isabella here while you meet with Tom tomorrow. In the morning, I'll text Scott to tell him I'll be in late because of a doctor's appointment."

Upstairs, Holly's mom had two small guest rooms. *"Buenas noches,"* Bethany said to Isabela after she tucked her under the covers and turned off the light.

Poking her head in Holly's room, Bethany told her, "Forgot to tell you one more thing. Remember that pretty heart bracelet you gave me for my birthday? I believe I gave it to Isabela's little sister when I was in Costa Rica."

CHAPTER 58

"**S**ee you downstairs," Holly said to Bethany in the sunlit hall. "I'll take a quick shower, too, and then make us coffee." Bethany pulled her wet hair into a high ponytail. She folded the T-shirt Holly gave her to sleep in and put on her same casual clothes from the day before. Out of necessity, she lifelessly put on her makeup, but there was no hope for her eyes. No amount of professional training could fix them today.

Seeing Bethany dressed the same as yesterday, Holly said, "Oh, you need clothes. Help yourself to coffee downstairs. I don't have anything that will fit you, but my mom at least has a shirt that might do."

Sitting at the kitchen table, Bethany turned on her phone. Three more texts from Baxter popped up on the screen. "I need to talk to you and explain," one text said. She shook her head. "Not even the world's best salesman can explain this away," she said aloud. Seeing his name on her phone sickened her, so she turned her phone off and flipped it upside down. She wanted to "unknow" him.

When Holly came downstairs with a shirt for Bethany, she brought Isabela with her. While Bethany changed in the downstairs bathroom, Holly made eggs and pancakes. Bethany came out of the bathroom wearing a slightly oversized shirt. If they could forget yesterday, this would be like a fun morning after a slumber party. Bethany wished she could forget yesterday, but she couldn't leave it behind. She brought yesterday with her to Holly's house, and now, that girl from yesterday waited to taste Holly's all-American pancakes.

"What's Tom's address?" Bethany asked Holly. "I want to get going to the metro."

As Isabela tasted a pancake for the first time, Bethany typed a note in the translation tool. She told her she was going to meet someone who could arrange to get her back home soon. Holly would take good care of her while Bethany went to the appointment.

Isabela got up from the table and hugged the woman who was so different than the day she saw her in the factory. That day Bethany initially walked in like a woman, confident and secure. *"Tranquila,"* Isabela told her.

Bethany smiled and kissed Isabela's head. And as she rocked her in her arms, Holly came to hug Bethany too.

As instructed, Holly closed the garage door as soon as Bethany's car pulled out. Grabbing the steering wheel tightly, Bethany shifted into drive. She accelerated, but no amount of speed could leave this nightmare behind. Isabela was one of many girls exploited at Baxter's factory and those weekend parties. *Where are the others?*

Her mind raced forward to her meeting with the FBI, and she missed the turn to the metro station. When she got to the next street, she hit a red light. It seemed like forever before it changed green, and after reorienting herself, she pulled into the metro station's parking lot. Putting her head into the steering wheel, she released the pent-up anguish. "Why God?" she cried out.

On the metro, she found two open seats where she could be by herself. The rush of the train pulled her closer to the reckoning. She wanted it to speed up but also to slow down.

This day had started differently than most. Bethany couldn't answer emails or speak to anyone who might lead Baxter to her or the girl. She had to protect them both.

Confined in the underground vehicle racing her to a place she never sought to go, her lungs demanded more air, but only short breaths entered and exited. On the inside, she shook, but outwardly, her eyes focused. They fixed on the target like pesticide about to spray upon a growing evil.

As she exited the Triangle metro station, the midsummer sun rose over the US Capitol. American flags lined the FBI headquarters where agents awaited her arrival. Once she entered, there would be no reversing what she set in motion.

Guided by six generations of Knowles women, she stood resolute. The wisdom found inside a centuries-old journal directed her steps.

She reached for her neck, and between her fingers, she stroked the carved wooden butterfly necklace. Drawing strength from wings of freedom earned two centuries prior, she looked toward the sky and took a deep breath. *Every second counts, now more than ever.*

CHAPTER 59

"**B**ethany Rose Miller," she stated to the security guard. And with a quivering hand, she pulled out her ID. Tom greeted her in the lobby and escorted her upstairs to a conference room where two of his colleagues waited for them. The 1960s FBI headquarters building was frozen in time. All of the walls in the building were white, and the whole place needed a refresh.

"I called colleagues who specialize in this area," he said, motioning her inside a small conference room. The room was stark except for the table, chairs, and a clock on the wall. "Miss Miller, this is Agent Fuentes from CAC, that's Crimes Against Children, and this is Agent Rogers," Tom said. Bethany and Tom took seats across from the agents, one a woman and the other a man. "When you're ready," Tom began, "tell us why you are here."

Bethany stuck her clear-coated fingernails into the leather handles on her purse. "A few weeks ago, while I was in Costa Rica filming for my client, BXB2 Cosmetics, I entered an adjoining factory building. That's where I noticed the workers were young girls." She paused to look at each of them and waited for a question. They didn't ask any, so she continued. "My initial worries were about possible underage workers. On the first day back in the US, I brought my concern to my good friend and client, Baxter Buchanan, CEO of BXB2 Cosmetics." As she said his name aloud, memories from college parties, graduation, and building their businesses together flashed before her eyes. But by being here and saying his name, she had just outed her best friend to the FBI.

The two agents sat across from her, scribbling notes. They stopped their pens and waited a moment for her to regroup. Agent Fuentes motioned for Bethany to continue.

"Baxter told me the legal working age was sixteen and that his manager made sure they were doing everything by the book. Something told me it was not right." The two agents took notes again as Bethany spoke. "I saw this one young teenage girl's eyes. They tried to tell me something. The look on her face horrified me." Bethany folded her arms and rubbed them to take away the chill. "Take your time," Tom told her.

"I got preoccupied with the need to handle major personal issues but later, contacted my corporate lawyer, Michael Alexander. He checked with a Costa Rican colleague who said sixteen was the minimum age and that the factory had a good reputation. I still had concerns, but I needed to be careful not to meddle more in my client's business. He was already agitated with me about questioning him. I think it may have cost me new business contracts with him."

Agent Rogers wrote notes on his lined pad while Agent Fuentes looked at Bethany as she continued.

"I met with Baxter at his penthouse yesterday—about other matters. And after I left, I realized I forgot my phone. He had left for the vet, so I used the key that Amy, she's Baxter's wife, gave me to let myself inside." Bethany stopped and looked down at her lap. She pinched the purse handles. "To my horror, I found a young girl, the very same one I saw working in the Costa Rican factory." Agent Fuentes looked at Rogers, who stopped taking notes.

"She was gagged and bound in handcuffs." Both agents looked across the table at Tom. "I got her out of there and brought her to my assistant's house, Holly's. Well, her mom's house actually.

"Holly is the one who reached out to me yesterday," Tom told the agents. He motioned for Bethany to continue.

"Baxter has security cameras. I knew he would look for the girl at my house. That's why I called Holly."

"That was a wise move to not go home," Agent Rogers said. It was the first time he spoke since greeting her. "Is the girl still at Holly's mother's house?" Agent Rogers asked.

"Yes, Isabela is there," Bethany said.

"We'll arrange to come by the house and also have a social worker meet us there to pick up Isabela."

Bethany was sick to her stomach. She knew the agents must have heard her stomach gurgle.

"Thank you for coming forward," Agent Rogers said. "We got a tip weeks ago about a human trafficking ring operating out of Costa Rica. Our Central America liaison office covers Costa Rica, and although US citizens may be involved in the alleged crime, it's Costa Rican jurisdiction and up to them to take the lead. Having Isabela here in the US is the proof we need to bring charges and get a warrant to make an arrest on our soil."

The word *arrest* hung in the air. Bethany thought about the man she called friend for twenty years, and then she thought about Amy. This would destroy her sweet friend.

Just twenty-four hours earlier, she had left Jameson to get Baxter's blessing on her new business plan. And the first time she left his apartment, she was elated. She was on course to a new future, one she had designed herself but with a divine hand guiding her. Now, Baxter's business and hers were about to crash, along with the lives of two people she considered family.

"You're very brave, Miss Miller," Agent Fuentes told her.

But Bethany didn't feel brave. She felt sick. And after finishing her account with the agents, she was glad to get off the metro and back into the security of her car. Alone, with no one expecting her to be strong, she let her emotions collapse.

When she arrived back at the house, Holly pushed the garage door button. Once the door closed behind her car, Bethany got out. The girls hugged inside the kitchen.

Holly's phone rang. It was a neighbor asking if she or her mother knew anyone with a black SUV. The neighbor said she saw one pass the house a few times. A man was at the wheel, and he was staring at the home. After rounding the block and approaching the house a third time, he had made a phone call before he pulled away.

"Maybe it's the FBI?" Holly asked Bethany after she hung up from the snooping neighbor.

"They wouldn't be here that fast. And if it were them, they would have come inside. Keep the doors locked," Bethany said, pacing the kitchen sink area. "Does your mom have a gun?"

Holly shook her head no. There was a knock on the door. Holly looked at the knife rack on the sink.

CHAPTER 60

D on't open it," Bethany said in a whisper. "Find out who it is first." Holly went to the door and called out, "Who is it?" A man responded. "FBI Agent Rogers along with Agent Fuentes. Crimes Against Children and Social Services is here too." Holly looked back at Bethany, who nodded the okay to unlock the door.

Agent Rogers introduced each of them to Holly. Neither of the agents smiled. Staying outside by her car, the woman social worker waited to transport Isabela. Holly led the agents to the kitchen.

"Thank you for alerting us, ma'am," Agent Fuentes said to Bethany. "We will talk to Isabela and get her looked after." Bethany knew what they meant. The next days would not be easy for Isabela. This poor girl would have to go through more trauma. "We employ experts in this field who will take the utmost care," Fuentes said in response to the look on Bethany's face.

"Does Isabela have any belongings?" Agent Rogers asked. Holly gave him Isabela's smiley-face backpack, the one she thought she was taking with her to the amusement park.

Bethany took Agent Fuentes to meet Isabela. They greeted each other in Spanish, and she left the two alone. After a few minutes, Bethany saw Isabela nod yes. Agent Fuentes came to talk to Bethany, who was standing at the kitchen sink with a coffee cup clenched between two hands.

"Isabela hopes we get the other guy too," Fuentes said. "The one who drove her to the plane once she was inside the US border. She said he's a friend of Baxter's."

"A friend of Baxter's?" Bethany asked.

Agent Fuentes explained, "Isabela said he has black-and-grey hair and a scar near his upper lip. His name is Miguel; that's Michael in English."

As the second round of bomb strikes hit her, Bethany's mouth dropped open. She grabbed the sink behind her for support.

"Michael Alexander is Bethany's attorney," Holly jumped in to inform. His indistinguishable scar was hard to forget.

Bethany's legs wobbled under her. Holly held her arm as she pulled her to a kitchen chair. "They're all friends," Holly told the agents. "Baxter and Bethany have known Michael for years."

Seeing the commotion with Bethany, Isabela rushed to the table. She didn't understand English and had no idea what Agent Fuentes told Bethany to make her look sick. But she showed concern for her new friend because Bethany didn't look well.

"*Estoy bien.*" Bethany stroked Isabela's arm and told her she was okay.

"We best get on our way," Agent Rogers said after a few moments.

At the front door, Isabela hugged Bethany goodbye. "*Gracias,*" Isabela said before walking out the door, and then she turned and said, "*Tranquila,*" with a smile.

Bethany tearfully waved to her from the front porch until the social worker's car pulled out of sight. The FBI agents got in their car parked one house down across the street. They didn't pull away but instead sat in their car talking. Bethany closed and locked the door.

Holly gave her a tissue and placed a fresh cup of black coffee on the table in front of her. But Bethany stared into the backyard and didn't acknowledge the steaming cup in front of her. "I should have been smarter."

Holly reached for her boss's hand. "You saved a young girl and God knows how many others too," she consoled.

Bethany shook her head. The last several weeks were a series of shocks, revelations, and what seemed at the time to be random coincidences. But now she understood more about what she once called coincidences. To her, it was no coincidence she lost her phone at Baxter's and still had a key.

"I came home to Alexandria to meet with Baxter to tell him about a new plan I put together." Bethany shook her head wishing to forget what she saw in that bedroom. "And also to give good news to Scott."

"What good news for Scott?"

"I'm going to make Scott President of B.R. Miller Advertising. I'll remain CEO, but Scott will run the day-to-day."

"Whoa, that's big news," Holly said, sitting back in her chair. "He will do great helping you lead the company."

Bethany wondered what would be left of her company after all this.

Holly's phone rang. "It's my mom's neighbor," she said. "Someone's getting arrested outside the house. Quick, look out the window."

Bethany recognized the red sports car and bolted out the door. As Agent Fuentes cuffed his arms behind his back, Agent Rogers read him his Miranda rights, placing Baxter under arrest. A discarded handgun lay on the road. It was not one of the agents' guns. Theirs were both on them.

Bethany ran toward Baxter. Stopping inches from his face, she looked him in the eyes. The painful memory of when she found Isabela swelled inside her. She swung her arm behind her and with all her might, she slapped him hard across his face, knocking his sunglasses onto the pavement.

Yanking Baxter's bound arms, Agent Fuentes tugged him back from Bethany. "We got him, ma'am," she said and put Baxter in the back seat of the agents' car.

"Good thing we hadn't pulled away yet," Agent Rogers said as he carefully collected the gun for evidence. "We saw him drive up, take a gun from his car, and approach the house. You take care now. We'll be in touch." Agent Rogers got in the car and started the engine.

Standing in the middle of the road, with her two feet planted firmly in the present, Bethany watched as her past was driven away.

. . . and the Timekeeper chimed eleven.

CHAPTER 61

By the time Bethany and Holly talked through all that had transpired, it was 1:30 p.m. "I need to call Scott," Bethany said at the table with an untouched cup of coffee in front of her. It was unfortunate she could not meet with him in person, but her emotions were too raw. The joy of sharing her plan with him was gone. All she wanted now was to get to Jameson and back to Nick. Her body shook inside from the two-days-long ordeal. She needed to feel the strength of his arms around her.

Yesterday morning, she was elated thinking about her future life and business plan. Now, she would return to Jameson after seeing her friend, and the one responsible for fifty percent of her business revenues, get arrested. All her employees and their families depended on her. She had to call Scott and tell him what had occurred.

Sitting upstairs in the guest room she had used the night before, its light-yellow walls and white bedspread presented a cheerful scene, a stark contrast to how she felt inside. Holly must have made the bed while Bethany was at the FBI headquarters, and she sat down on the smooth bedspread to call Scott.

"Did Baxter finally reach you?" Scott said without first saying hello.

"Just saw him." Her fingers clenched the white bedspread with her free hand. "First off, I have good news to share with you," she flatly said before pausing a moment. "I'm making you president of B.R. Miller Advertising."

"That's awesome. Wow. I didn't see that coming yet. Thank you," Scott said. She afforded him a few minutes to absorb the good news and then talked through details of how she saw his new role. When they finished that business, she looked around the sunny yellow bedroom. Her eyes darted from the framed seaside print on the wall beside her to a glass angel figurine on the bedside table.

Bethany knew she had to tell Scott the rest. She pivoted the conversation to her visit with Baxter yesterday, finding Isabela and her visit to the FBI. "They arrested him outside Holly's mom's house right in front of me. He was headed toward the house with a gun."

Throughout her story, Scott shouted profanities. He had two daughters. One was six and the other eight. "Sorry for the swearing," he said. "This is unbelievable. An animal right in our midst."

"We've got to be ready for whatever this means for us," Bethany said as she looked at her reflection in the mirror. The usually well-kept Bethany lacked sleep, and her makeup could not correct her puffy eyes. She turned away from her reflection and looked toward the coastal print instead.

"I met with Baxter last week," Scott said. "He introduced me to two new major investors in BXB2 Cosmetics. I'm sure they will put someone else at the helm of the company. We've got multiyear contracts and should be good for a while."

"News like this can destroy a company. We need to prepare."

"I'll get a team on it," Scott said.

Bethany liked hearing Scott take charge. She was about to hang up and remembered one more thing. "Oh, find us a new lawyer. We can no longer use Michael. It needs to be an immediate break. He was in on all this."

"What?" Scott asked.

"Have no more communication with him, and stop the monthly retainer payments immediately," Bethany said.

She gathered her things from the guest room and went downstairs. As her head began to clear, a conversation with Holly was next on her mind. She apologized for getting her in the middle of this.

"I'm glad you asked me to attend that charity event last year. Never thought I'd use that knowledge."

Bethany remembered receiving the invite. As a company owner, it was one of many she received from local and national charities. "I was

273

too busy with work to accept those invitations," she said as she hung her head down and sighed.

Holly reached out for her hand. "Glad I could be of help. Maybe this year we can write them an even bigger check for their work."

After a long, strong hug, Bethany said goodbye to Holly. From inside the open garage, she texted Nick to let him know she was on her way back to Jameson. And for the next two-and-a-half hours, she would drive toward fresher air.

Looking in the rearview mirror, she did her best to leave the nightmare behind. Her new life's dream was ahead; her future was with Nick. She was sure he felt the same way. The night of the fire she saw how concerned he was about losing her, not just to her work in Alexandria but losing her completely. She remembered being barefoot and how he wanted to carry her up Sam's steps. Bethany thought about the creek, skipping rocks, dinner at Nick's, and his hands full of roses and lilies. Nick's heart was good, and the thought of being in a relationship with him felt right. For the first time, Bethany wanted to slow down and experience where a relationship with him might lead. Nick knew how to be present, and he didn't incessantly worry about the future the way Bethany always did. She wanted to pause and feel fun. And most importantly, she wanted to be loved.

As soon as she got into town, she drove straight to Nick's office. His shiny white truck was parked out front, and the marks on his bumper were no longer visible. Anxious to tell him she had decided to stay in Jameson, Bethany would save the horrific story to tell him later.

At the same time she got out of her car, Nick walked out of his office. She smiled when she saw his face. It was the first happy thing she'd seen in two days, but he looked back at her with contempt. *Why was he angry?*

"Hi, missed you," she said, touching his arm as he reached for the door handle of his truck.

He shook her hand away. "How could you ever work with a demon like that?"

"What?" she asked, astonished.

"It's all over the news. They arrested that guy, your friend. How could you do work for that animal? All that money you earned these years. It's blood money. You have my country's blood on your hands!"

Nick's deep Latin roots inflamed, and his words hit Bethany like rapid mortar fire. Passion ran both ways with him, but she had never seen him mad, not even that day when her shopping cart ran into his new truck.

"I didn't know he was anything like that!" she cried out, reaching for him to stop getting inside his truck.

"How could you be best friends and work all these years with him and not know he was a disgusting piece of scum?" Nick's eyes looked at her as if she were a thief who had stolen something from him.

"Please, listen to me." Bethany took a step toward his truck door and begged him, but he got inside and put the truck in reverse. In her hand, she clutched a stack of papers. It was the new plan for her future. She had brought it to surprise him, but he pulled away and left her standing alone.

CHAPTER 62

Nick's truck disappeared in the distance. Her feelings wreaked havoc inside her, making her want to escape into the future. When she planned or strived for what was next, she didn't have to feel. Feeling caused her to run away from the moment and rush into the next.

Like a zombie, limp and needing direction, she drove to Monarchy. The sign read CLOSED. *Ugh. It's Monday.* Laying her head against the steering wheel, she clenched the leather tightly. *I can't take any more.* She needed help to stop the pain.

Answering the doorbell at first with a look of delight on her face, Sam's smile left as soon as she saw Bethany behind a wall of liquid heartache. What Bethany said at Sam's doorstep made no sense. So she gathered up Bethany's limp arms and pulled her inside.

"I lost everything," Bethany said after telling Sam the story.

Sam embraced her friend sitting next to her on her couch. "It's going to be alright. You did the right thing. You saved Isabela and who knows how many others. And Nick will be alright. Give him time. All things work together for good."

As if suddenly awakened from a deep sleep, Bethany's arm flew out and slapped the couch. "He won't listen to me," she cried.

"He will. Don't stop trying," Sam said as she reached for Bethany's hand. "You are so much like your mother. I see it now." She scanned Bethany's face. "Marguerite did a similar thing in her later work too."

"What?" Bethany said through broken breaths between sobs.

"Your mother's later work focused on writing about human trafficking," Sam revealed.

Bethany gulped in breaths as she turned to Sam to tell her more. "She showed me news magazine articles she wrote about young women being lured or captured and then trafficked. It's run like a business, but it is pure evil."

"I didn't get to read all her articles yet," Bethany said, taking a tissue from the box on the coffee table. "After the fire, I wanted to put everything into action so I could relocate to Jameson. And then, I found Isabela at Baxter's. How could he do this?" Her head shook from side to side. "He was my friend. I can't believe what happened, but I saw it with my own eyes."

Sam patted Bethany's arm and pulled her closer to her on the couch.

"When they arrested him, I looked him straight in the eyes and slapped him as hard as I could." Bethany turned to face Sam. "That disgusting pig still had the nerve to look at me." Her momentary dry face enveloped again in tears.

Sam rocked her before letting go and reaching for her phone. "I have a quote that Marguerite, your mother, used in one of her articles. I know it's here somewhere." Sam scrolled through her phone. "Remember I told you Marguerite and I had a shared interest in helping a cause? When I spoke at a fundraising event for human trafficking, Marguerite kindly wrote my speech and included that quote. Here it is. It's by Hiram Powers from over a hundred years ago."

> "The eye is the window of the soul, the mouth the door. The intellect, the will, are seen in the eye, the emotions, sensibilities, and affections, in the mouth. The animals look for man's intentions right into his eyes. Even a rat, when you hunt him and bring him to bay, looks you in the eye."

"Now you know Baxter is a rat," Sam said.

Bethany didn't respond. She was in shock.

"You shouldn't be alone," Sam said, looking at her. "My couch is still here for you."

Sam made dinner and directed their conversation onto a lighter topic. She told Bethany about a date she had on Saturday night. Bethany was happy for her, but all her mind could think about was that she was sick in love with Nick, and he'd rejected her.

When Sam finished eating, Bethany's eyes closed at the table. And although Bethany had eaten three bites of food, it was only because of Sam's insistence. "Let's turn in early," Sam said, getting up from the table and reaching for Bethany's plate. "Tomorrow, you'll have a clearer head. Get some rest. Be still and know . . . everything will be alright. All that's needed is time."

Sam had an early morning client and left Bethany a note telling her to help herself to coffee. But coffee was not on Bethany's mind. When she awakened, all she wanted was to get to Nick and explain.

Cleaning up as best she could in the half bathroom, she put on the summer's top color BXB2 lipstick, a light shade of coral. Immediately feeling sick at the realization of what she had just rolled onto her lips, she tore off a piece of toilet paper. After pushing it hard against her lips and forcing it side-to-side to remove the color, she flushed it down the toilet. Tearing another piece from the toilet roll, she used it to grab the head of the lipstick and pulled it off the base of its shiny container. And between her fingers, she smashed the lipstick. Once she could destroy it no more, she chucked it and the container in the trash.

Bethany pulled into God's Green Acres Landscaping's parking lot. Inside the office, she found Nick sitting behind his desk. Closing his office door, she stood in front of it, cornering him inside. "You're not going anywhere. You're going to listen to me," she said to Nick, who sat at his desk with the expression one has when looking into the eyes of a wild animal. "After the fire, I made a plan," she said, grasping the doorknob behind her back. "I wanted to wait to tell you about it until after I talked to Baxter and Scott." Bethany adjusted the purse on her shoulder. "But after I talked to Baxter and left his condo, I realized I forgot my phone. He had already left for a vet appointment, so I let myself in with a key. That's when I found a young girl handcuffed to his bedpost." Nick stared at her speechless.

"I got her out of the handcuffs and took her to Holly's mom's house because I was afraid Baxter would find us at my house. Holly and I called the FBI, and I met with them yesterday. They came and took the young girl, Isabela, to get help and get her back home to Costa Rica . . . and then I personally saw them arrest Baxter." Bethany stood with her back against the door, blocking it for any possible retreat. Nick leaned forward on his desk and looked as if he might get up, but he did not.

She pinched her fingers into the purse handle on her shoulder and continued. "I went up there to talk to Baxter and Scott about making Scott president of B.R. Miller Advertising. I plan to remain CEO but live in Jameson and check-in from afar. And two days ago, I made a deal to purchase the *Jameson Gazette* from Oliver Bridgewell."

Nick's eyes opened wide as Bethany remained lit from a fire inside. "I want to build an executive women's retreat center at Lily Fields," she said. "I plan to build a barn and guest cabins and want you to design landscape plans. Jameson is going to be my new home."

She took the purse from her shoulder, hung it down from her hand, and moved to the side of the door, opening an escape route. "That's it. I'm finished. You can go now if you want."

Nick rose from his chair and walked to the door. Pulling her tight against him, he embraced her. As he moved his head away to look at her, he saw those eyes. Eyes he first saw in the hardware store's parking lot. Today they were sparked by passion, and he pressed his lips against hers.

"*Querida mia, perdoname. Te amo. Te amo.* My dear. Forgive me. I love you," he said after kissing her and holding her again tightly.

"I love you too," she repeated back.

Nick's phone buzzed, interrupting the romantic interlude. He ignored the first two calls that came in when Bethany had him blocked behind his desk. Releasing her from his tight embrace, he reluctantly explained, "I've got to get this call." His crew waited for him at a job where the owner had questions only he could explain.

"Are you alright to drive home?" he asked. After walking her to the car, he leaned in to kiss her again through the open window. "Let me take care of this, and I'll meet you as soon as I can at Lily Fields. We have much more to talk about. I've been making a plan too," he said.

But Bethany did not head to Lily Fields; instead, she drove toward town. She wanted to thank Sam for taking her in again last night and let her know she talked to Nick. When she walked into Monarchy, Sam waved to her. A customer sat in Sam's chair while she blow-dried the woman's blonde hair.

Bethany sat patiently alone in the customer waiting area. The other stylist's chair was empty. *Did she have the day off?*

Sam hummed along to a praise and worship song playing through overhead speakers. Joy shined from Sam's face as she worked.

After the customer paid and left, Sam assured Bethany they were alone in the shop. "I talked to Nick and told him everything that happened," Bethany said. "He told me he loves me, Sam, and I told him I love him too."

"My goodness, that's wonderful news." Sam reached out to hug Bethany but realized she still wore the smock she put on to dye her client's hair. She unsnapped it and folded it over the chair. When she turned around, Bethany's eyes fixed on Sam's necklace. "Sam, where did you get that necklace?"

"A friend made the glass beads," Sam said as she picked up a broom and started to sweep the floor.

Bethany's eyes never left the distinctive wooden centerpiece. "I'm talking about the butterfly in the center," Bethany said, anxious to hear the reply. *It looks so similar to the one my mother left me.*

"Oh . . . my great-great-great-grandmother made it. Remember, I told you I had ancestors who were slaves? She carved this butterfly. Her story is partly what inspired my shop name, Monarchy. And it's what got me to check out this town. She was once enslaved here but escaped and eventually made her way to New York where she started a business. She sent money back South to help others escape on boats up the Chesapeake like she did. An amazingly strong woman who helped many others."

Bethany struggled to get words out. "Sam, what was her name?"

Sam stopped sweeping and looked at Bethany. "Selah. Her name was Selah."

. . . and the Timekeeper chimed twelve.

EPILOGUE

Bethany stood at the podium in front of the banner announcing the commemoration of the SELAH CENTER FOR ENTREPRENEUR-SHIP and spoke into the microphone. "I'd like to thank everyone for coming out today to celebrate the grand opening of the Selah Center. Next week, our first class of women entrepreneurs arrives in Jameson."

She reached for her neck and touched the heirloom butterfly necklace as she looked out at the audience. Nick sat in the front row next to Holly and Peter. Beside Peter were Mitzi, Sam, Walter, and his wife. Oliver Bridgewell and Agnes Adams sat in the row behind them. Scott was there with his wife and two daughters, along with a large group of townspeople. The Jameson newspaper reporter took notes as a Richmond TV station aimed its camera at Bethany.

"This new barn and event center built on the stone foundation of my family's original barn, I dedicate to the woman it was named after—a strong, smart, determined woman named Selah. Her great-great-great-granddaughter, and my dear friend, Samantha, is with us today. Sam is a board member and will also be working with the foundation teaching entrepreneurship." Bethany motioned to Sam and the audience clapped. "We are fortunate to have her skills and dedication to helping women achieve their dreams of leadership and business ownership."

Bethany turned a page. "I also dedicate this center to the other brave woman, the one who helped Selah and others get to freedom, my great-great-great-grandmother, Katherine Knowles Davis. Like Selah, she is also one of our town's heroes." Bethany smiled with pride as the audience clapped.

Her mind took her off script and she said, "I had hoped another special person in my life could be here. She's another strong, brave young woman I want to honor. If all goes as hoped with the paperwork, soon Isabela—her little brother and sister, too—will be joining our new family." Bethany's eyes met Nick's with a look so deep in love it almost brought her off the stage into his arms.

In the back of the room, someone opened the rear door, distracting Bethany. Taking a seat in the last row, Amy nodded and smiled at her best friend, whom she hadn't seen in months. Bethany smiled back and took in a deep breath before continuing with her speech.

"Selah's great-great-great-granddaughter, Sam, and the Knowles women taught me a lot about life, love, and about a heavenly family we all can choose to become a part of."

Sam cried and wiped her eyes as Bethany continued.

"Since 1859, six Knowles daughters each left behind a journal entry to guide the next generation, the next first daughter. I'm proud to be the seventh, and today, I have here with me the eighth." Bethany touched her growing stomach, and Nick smiled as wide as the front row. He clapped along with the crowd as he held the program in his hand. The front cover had a monarch butterfly sitting on a lily.

Bethany took a moment to compose herself. "As I reflect on the influence my family's journal had on me, my thoughts turn back to Katherine, who started it. I wonder, was it merely for the love of her daughter and one day a granddaughter that she began this compilation? Or did she instinctively know the wisdom and insights many more daughters in the future would need to live purpose-filled lives? Words, I've found, can be roadmaps left behind to point the way forward.

"As I prepared this message to commemorate the Selah Center for Entrepreneurship and make remarks about what this one initiative could produce, for inspiration I was drawn to sit beside Lily Field's waterfall. Though small, and at times a mere trickle, its drops pour into the stream. Encountering others, each drop makes its way to where the river meets the sea. And there, in the open waters where nothing confines, is where dreams are unleashed and true freedom comes to be."

Bethany looked out across the audience.

"I've learned a lot in this special little town. Filled with confidence and rushing toward achievement, we plan our way. But all the while, it is another who directs our steps, often pausing us for reflection. Quieting the noise of our hurried pace, we can hear the cry of a silent voice. And as we obey the gentle tug inside, our once-blind eyes see divine missions sent from above.

All alone, we feel those in need number too many for us to make a difference. Yet an opened heart knows the Helper, the One by our side. Receiving the faith of courage, we take action. And through new eyes, we see hope. Though gains seem small against unsurmountable numbers, we press on. For it is in the peace of silence that we hear Heaven whisper, 'Keep going my child. Your efforts matter . . . to this One.'"

ACKNOWLEDGMENTS

A very special thank you to Peggy who got me going, Jenna who guided along the way, and Cortney who brought the story home. And for their perspectives, input, or location insights, I express heartfelt gratitude to Vern, Nanette, Erin, Michelle, Becky, Linda, Donna, David, Josh, Dee Dee, Taft, and other helpful folks in Alexandria, and Laurie and Wells for a wonderful time spent with them in the Northern Neck.

Thank you to my beta readers: Dave, Donna, Denise, Vern, Sally, Lee-Ann, Michelle, Jan, Wendy, Gracie, Kenna, Emmy, and David.

Thank you also to Morgan James Publishing for making this story reach far and wide.

It takes a village to write a novel, but most of all, it takes a deeply caring and patient husband named Dave. I am blessed indeed!

ABOUT THE AUTHOR

Barbara Zerfoss is a former marketing vice president for a multibillion-dollar global corporation. Now, she serves as an executive coach, working with CEOs and other executives to create purpose-filled visions for the futures they desire. The proud mother of two grown sons, Marco and Mario, she's married to Dave, who welcomed her into his family of four grown children and six grandchildren. Barbara spends most of her time at her home in North Carolina, where her backyard ponds and frequent guests to her bird feeders call upon her daily to pause her hectic life and enjoy the moment. When not in North Carolina, she enjoys her residence in Florida, what she calls her place of retreat and renewal. There, she especially enjoys sea turtle nesting season when new hatchlings make their way to an ocean full of His glory.

To contact Barbara, visit her page, Author Barbara Zerfoss on Facebook, or visit www.BarbaraZerfoss.com to download book club questions and more.

A free ebook edition is available with the purchase of this book.

To claim your free ebook edition:

1. Visit MorganJamesBOGO.com
2. Sign your name CLEARLY in the space
3. Complete the form and submit a photo of the entire copyright page
4. You or your friend can download the ebook to your preferred device

Morgan James BOGO™

A **FREE** ebook edition is available for you or a friend with the purchase of this print book.

CLEARLY SIGN YOUR NAME ABOVE

Instructions to claim your free ebook edition:
1. Visit MorganJamesBOGO.com
2. Sign your name CLEARLY in the space above
3. Complete the form and submit a photo of this entire page
4. You or your friend can download the ebook to your preferred device

Print & Digital Together Forever.

Snap a photo   Free ebook   Read anywhere

CPSIA information can be obtained
at www.ICGtesting.com
Printed in the USA
JSHW042042080422
24760JS00001B/1